CONSTANCE STOOD ON THE SHORE WATCHING HIM.

—*The Three Fates.*

THE COMPLETE WORKS OF
F. MARION CRAWFORD
In Thirty-two Volumes ✒ Authorized Edition

The Three Fates

BY
F. MARION CRAWFORD

WITH FRONTISPIECE

P. F. COLLIER & SON
NEW YORK

THE COMPLETE WORKS OF F. MARION CRAWFORD

—18—

THE THREE FATES

THE THREE FATES.

CHAPTER I.

JONAH WOOD was bitterly disappointed in his son. During five and twenty years he had looked in vain for the development of those qualities in George, which alone, in his opinion, could insure success. But though George could talk intelligently about the great movements of business in New York, it was clear by this time that he did not possess what his father called business instincts. The old man could have forgiven him his defective appreciation in the matter of dollars and cents, however, if he had shown the slightest inclination to adopt one of the regular professions; in other words, if George had ceased to waste his time in the attempt to earn money with his pen, and had submitted to becoming a scribe in a lawyer's office, old Wood would have been satisfied. The boy's progress might have been slow, but it would have been sure.

It was strange to see how this elderly man, who had been ruined by the exercise of his own business faculties, still pinned his faith upon his own views and theories of finance, and regarded it as a real misfortune to be the father of a son who thought differently from himself. It would have satisfied the height of his ambition to see George installed as a clerk on a nominal salary in one of the great banking houses. Possibly, at an earlier period, and before George had finally refused to enter a career of business, there may have been in the bottom of the old man's heart a hope that his son might some day become a financial power, and wreak vengeance for his own and his father's losses upon Thomas Craik or his heirs after him; but if this wish existed Jonah Wood had honestly tried to put it out of the way. He was of a religious disposition, and his moral rectitude was above all doubt. He did not forgive his enemies, but he sincerely meant to do so, and did his best not to entertain any hope of revenge.

The story of his wrongs was a simple one. He had formerly been a very successful man. Of a good New England family, he had come to New York when very young, possessed of a small capital, full of integrity, industry, and determination. At the age of forty he was at the head of a banking firm which had for a time enjoyed a reputation of some importance. Then he had married a young lady of good birth and possessing a little fortune, to whom he had been attached for years and who had waited for him with touching fidelity. Twelve months later, she had died in giving birth to George. Possibly the terrible shock weakened Jonah Wood's nerves and disturbed the balance of his faculties. At all events it was at this time that he began to enter into speculation. At first he was very successful, and his success threw him into closer intimacy with Thomas Craik, a cousin of his dead wife's. For a time everything prospered with the bank, while Wood acquired the habit of following Craik's advice. On an ill-fated day, however, the latter persuaded him to invest largely in a certain railway not yet begun, but which was completed in a marvellously short space of time. In the course of a year or two it was evident that the road, which Craik insisted on running upon the most ruinous principles, must soon become bankrupt. It had of course been built

to compete with an old established line; the usual war
of rates set in, the old road suffered severely, and the
young one was ruined. This was precisely what Craik
had anticipated. So soon as the bankruptcy was declared
and the liquidation terminated, he bought up every bond
and share upon which he could lay his hands. Wood
was ruined, together with a number of other heavy
investors. The road, however, having ceased to pay
interest on its debts continued to run at rates disas-
trous to its more honest competitor, and before long the
latter was obliged in self-defence to buy up its rival.
When that extremity was reached Thomas Craik was in
possession of enough bonds and stock to give him a con-
trolling interest, and he sold the ruined railway at his
own price, realising a large fortune by the transaction.
Wood was not only financially broken; his reputation,
too, had suffered in the catastrophe. At first, people
looked askance at him, believing that he had got a share
of the profits, and that he was only pretending poverty
until the scandal should blow over, though he had in
reality sacrificed almost everything he possessed in the
honourable liquidation of the bank's affairs, and found
himself, at the age of fifty-seven, in possession only of
the small fortune that had been his wife's, and of the
small house which had escaped the general ruin, and in
which he now lived. Thomas Craik had robbed him, as
he had robbed many others, and Jonah Wood knew it,
though there was no possibility of ever recovering a
penny of his losses. His nerve was gone, and by the
time people had discovered that he was the most honest
of men, he was more than half forgotten by those he had
known best. He had neither the energy nor the courage
to begin life again, and although he had cleared his reputation of all blame, he knew that he had made the great
mistake, and that no one would ever again trust to his
judgment. It seemed easiest to live in the little house,
to get what could be got out of life for himself and his
son on an income of scarcely two thousand dollars, and
to shut himself out from his former acquaintance.

And yet, though his own career had ended in such lamentable failure, he would gladly have seen George begin where he had begun. George would have succeeded in doing all those things which he himself had left undone, and he might have lived to see established on a firm basis the great fortune which for a few brief years had been his in a floating state. But George could not be brought to understand this point of view. His youthful recollections were connected with monetary disaster, and his first boyish antipathies had been conceived against everything that bore the name of business. What he felt for the career of the money-maker was more than antipathy; it amounted to a positive horror which he could not overcome. From time to time his father returned to the old story of his wrongs and misfortunes, going over the tale as he sat with George through the long winter evenings, and entering into every detail of the transaction which had ruined him. In justice to the young man it must be admitted that he was patient on those occasions, and listened with outward calm to the long technical explanations, the interminable concatenation of figures and the jarring cadence of phrases that all ended with the word dollars. But the talk was as painful to him as a violin played out of tune is to a musician, and it reacted upon his nerves and produced physical pain of an acute kind. He could set his features in an expression of respectful attention, but he could not help twisting his long smooth fingers together under the edge of the table, where his father could not see them. The very name of money disgusted him, and when the great failure had been talked of in the evening it haunted his dreams throughout the night and destroyed his rest, so that he awoke with a sense of nervousness and distress from which he could not escape until late in the following day.

Jonah Wood saw more of this peculiarity than his son suspected, though he failed to understand it. With him, nervousness took a different form, manifesting itself in an abnormal anxiety concerning George's welfare, combined with an unfortunate disposition to find fault. Of late, indeed, he had not been able to accuse the young man of idleness, since he was evidently working to the utmost of his strength, though his occupations brought him but little return. It seemed a pity to Jonah Wood that so much good time and so much young energy should be wasted over pen, ink, paper, and books which left no record of a daily substantial gain. He, too, slept little, though his iron-grey face betrayed nothing of what passed in his mind.

He loved his son in his own untrusting way. It was his affection, combined with his inability to believe much good of what he loved, that undermined and embittered the few pleasures still left to him. He had never seen any hope except in money, and since George hated the very mention of lucre there could be no hope for him either. A good man, a scrupulously honest man according to his lights, he could only see goodness from one point of view and virtue represented in one dress. Goodness was obedience to parental authority, and virtue the imitation of parental ideas. George believed that obedience should play no part in determining what he should do with his talent, and that imitation, though it be the sincerest flattery, may lay the foundation for the most hopeless of all failures, the failure to do that for which a man is best adapted. George had not deliberately chosen a literary career because he felt himself fitted for it. He was in reality far too modest to look forward from the first to the ultimate satisfaction of his ambitions. His lonely life had driven him to writing as a means of expressing himself without incurring his father's criticism and contradiction. Not understanding in the least the nature of imagination, he believed himself lacking in this respect, but he had at once found an immense satisfaction in writing down his opinions concerning certain new books that had fallen into his hands. Then, being emboldened by that belief in his own judgment which young men acquire very easily when they are not brought into daily contact with their intellectual equals, he had ventured to offer the latest of his attempts to one editor and then to another and another. At last he had found one who chanced to be in a human humour and who glanced at one of the papers.

"It is not worthless," said the autocrat, "but it is quite useless. Everybody has done with the book months ago. Do you want to earn a little money by reviewing?"

George expressed his readiness to do so with alacrity. The editor scribbled half a dozen words on a slip of paper from a block and handed it to George, telling him where to take it. As a first result the young man carried away a couple of volumes of new-born trash upon which to try his hand. A quarter of what he wrote was published in the literary column of the newspaper. He had yet to learn the cynical practice of counting words, upon which so much depends in dealing with the daily press, but the idea of actually earning something, no matter how little, overcame his first feeling of disgust at the nature of the work. In time he acquired the necessary tricks and did very well. By sheer determination he devoted all his best hours of the day to the drudgery of second class criticism, and only allowed himself to write what was agreeable to his own brain when the day's work was done.

The idea of producing a book did not suggest itself to him. In his own opinion he had none of the necessary gifts for original writing, while he fancied that he possessed those of the critic in a rather unusual degree. His highest ambition was to turn out a volume of essays on other people's doings and writings, and he was constantly labouring in his leisure moments at long papers treating of celebrated works, in what he believed to be a spirit of profound analysis. As yet no one had bestowed the slightest attention upon his efforts; no serious article of his had found its way into the press, though a goodly

number of his carefully copied manuscripts had issued
from the offices of various periodicals in the form of
waste paper. Strange to say, he was not discouraged by
these failures. The satisfaction, so far as he had known
any, had consisted in the writing down of his views;
and though he wished it were possible to turn his ink-
stained pages into money, his natural detestation of all
business transactions whatsoever made him extremely
philosophical in repeated failure. Even in regard to
his daily drudgery, which was regularly paid, the least
pleasant moment was the one when he had to begin his
round from one newspaper cashier to another to receive
the little cheques which made him independent of his
father so far as his only luxuries of new books and
tobacco were concerned. Pride, indeed, was now at the
bottom of his resolution to continue in the uninteresting
course that had been opened before him. Having once
succeeded in buying for himself what he wanted or needed
beyond his daily bread he would have been ashamed to
ever go again for pocket-money to his father.

The nature of this occupation, which he would not
relinquish, was beginning to produce its natural effect
upon his character. He felt that he was better than his
work, and the inevitable result ensued. He felt that he
was hampered and tied, and that every hour spent in
such labour was a page stolen from the book of his reputation; that he was giving for a pitiful wage the precious
time in which something important might have been
accomplished, and that his life would turn out a failure
if it continued to run on much longer in the same groove.
And yet he assumed that it would be absolutely impossible for him to abandon his drudgery in order to devote
himself solely to the series of essays on which he had
pinned his hopes of success. His serious work, as he
called it, made little progress when interrupted at every
step by the necessity for writing twaddle about trash.

It may be objected that George Wood should not have
written twaddle, but should have employed his best

energies in the improvement of second class literature by systematically telling the truth about it. Unfortunately the answer to such a stricture is not far to seek. If he had written what he thought, the newspapers would have ceased to employ him; not that it is altogether impossible to write honestly about the great rivers of minor books which flow east and west and north and south from the publishers' gardens, but because the critic who has the age, experience, and talent to bestow faint praise without inflicting damnation commands a high price and cannot be wasted on little authors and their little publications. The beginner often knows that he is writing twaddle and regrets it, and he very likely knows how to write in strains of enthusiastic eulogium or of viciously cruel abuse; but though he have all these things, he has not yet acquired the unaffected charity which covers a multitude of sins, and which is the result of an ancient and wise good feeling entertained between editors, publishers and critics. He cannot really feel mildly well disposed towards a book he despises, and his only chance of expressing gentle sentiments not his own, lies in the plentiful use of unmitigated twaddle. If he remains a critic, he is either lifted out of the sphere of the daily saleable trash to that of serious first class literature, or else he imbibes through the pores of his soul such proportional parts of the editor's and the publisher's wishes as shall combine in his own character and produce the qualities which they both desire to find there and to see expressed in his paragraphs.

It could not be said that George Wood was discontented with what he found to do, so much as with being constantly hindered from doing something better. And that better thing which he would have done, and believed that he could have done, was in reality far from having reached the stage of being clearly defined. He had never felt any strong liking for fiction, and his mind had been nourished upon unusually solid intellectual food, while the outward circumstances of his life had necessarily left much to his imagination, which to most young men of five and twenty is already matter of experience. As a boy he had been too much with older people, and had therefore thought too much to be boyish. Possibly, too, he had seen more than was good for him, for his father had left him but a short time at school in the days of their prosperity, and, being unable to leave New York for any length of time, had more than once sent him abroad with an elderly tutor from whom the lad had acquired all sorts of ideas that were too big for him. He had been wrongly supposed to be of a delicate constitution, too, and had been indulged in all manner of intellectual whims and fancies, whereby he had gained a smattering of many sciences and literatures at an age when he ought to have been following a regular course of instruction. Then, before he was thought old enough to enter a university, the crash had come.

Jonah Wood was far too conscientious a man not to sacrifice whatever he could for the completion of his son's education. For several years he deprived himself of every luxury, in order that George might have the assistance he so greatly needed while making his studies at Columbia College in his native city. Then only did the father realise how he had erred in allowing the boy to receive the desultory and aimless teaching that had seemed so generous in the days of wealth. He knew more or less well a variety of subjects of which his companions were wholly ignorant, but he was utterly unversed in much of their knowledge. And this was not all, for George had acquired from his former tutor a misguided contempt for the accepted manner of dealing with certain branches of learning, without possessing that grasp of the matters in hand which alone justifies a man in thinking differently from the great mass of his fellows. It is not well to ridicule the American method of doing things until one is master of some other.

It was from the time when George entered college that he began to be a constant source of disappointment to his father. The elderly man had received a good, old-fashioned, thoroughly prejudiced education, and though he remembered little Latin and less Greek, he had not forgotten the way in which he had been made to learn both. George's way of talking about his studies disturbed his father's sense of intellectual propriety, which was great, without exciting his curiosity, which was infinitesimally small. With him also prevailed the paternal view which holds that young men must necessarily distinguish themselves above their companions if they really possess any exceptional talent, and his peace of mind was further endangered by his sense of responsibility for George's beginnings. If he had believed that George was stupid, he would have resigned himself to that dispensation of Providence. But he thought otherwise. The boy was not an ordinary boy, and if he failed to prove it by taking prizes in competition, he must be lazy or his preparation must have been defective. No other alternative was to be found, and the fault therefore lay either with himself or with his father.

George never obtained a prize, and barely passed his examinations at all. Jonah Wood made a point of seeing all his examiners as well as the instructors who had known him during his college life. Three-quarters of the number asserted that the young fellow was undeniably clever, and added, expressing themselves with professorial politeness, that his previous studies seemed to have taken a direction other than that of the college "curriculum," as they called it. The professor of Greek presumed that George might have distinguished himself in Latin, the professor of Latin surmised that Greek might have been his strong point; both believed that he had talent for mathematics, while the mathematician remarked that he seemed to have a very good understanding, but that it would be turned to better account in the pursuit of classical studies. Jonah Wood returned to his home very much disturbed in mind, and from that day his anxiety steadily increased. As it became more clear that his son would never accept a business career, but would probably waste his opportunities in literary dabbling, the good man's alarm became extreme. He did not see that George's one true talent lay in his ready power of assimilating unfamiliar knowledge by a process of intuition that escapes methodical learners, any more than he understood that the boy's one solid acquirement was the power of using his own language. He was not to be too much blamed, perhaps, for the young man himself was only dimly conscious of his yet undeveloped power. What made him write was neither the pride of syntax nor the certainty of being right in his observations; he was driven to paper to escape from the torment of the desire to express something, he knew not what, which he could express in no other way. He found no congenial conversation at home and little abroad, and yet he felt that he had something to say and must say it.

It should not be supposed that either Jonah Wood's misfortunes or his poverty, which was after all comparative, though hard to bear, prevented George from mixing in the world with which he was connected by his mother's birth, and to some extent by his father's former position. The old gentleman, indeed, was too proud to renew his acquaintance with people who had thought him dishonourable until he had proved himself spotless; but the very demonstration of his uprightness had been so convincing and clear that it constituted a patent of honour for his son. Many persons who had blamed themselves for their hasty judgment would have been glad to make amends by their cordial reception of the man they had so cruelly mistaken. George, however, was quite as proud as his father, and much more sensitive. He remembered well enough the hard-hearted, boyish stare he had seen in the eyes of some of his companions when he was but just seventeen years old, and later, at college, when his father's self-sacrifice was fully known, and his old associates had held out their hands to his in the hope of making everything right again, George had met them with stony eyes and scornful civility. It was not easy to forgive, and with all his excellent qualities and noble honesty of purpose, Jonah Wood was not altogether displeased to know that his son held his head high and drew back from the renewal of fair weather friendships. Almost against his will he encouraged him in his conduct, while doing his best to appear at least indifferent.

George needed but little encouragement to remain in social obscurity, though he was conscious of a rather contemptible hope that he might one day play a part in society, surrounded by all the advantages of wealth and general respect which belong especially to those few who possess both, by inheritance rather than as a result of their own labours. He was not quite free from that subtle aristocratous taint which has touched so many members of American society. Like the wind, no man can tell whence it comes nor whither it goes; but unlike the ill wind in the proverb it blows no good to any one. It is not the breath of that republican inequality which is caused by two men extracting a different degree of advantage from the same circumstances; it is not the inevitable inequality produced by the inevitable struggle for existence, wealth and power; but it is the fictitious inequality caused by the pretence that the accident of a man's birth should of itself constitute for him a claim to have special opportunities made for him, adapted to his use and protected by law for his particular benefit. It is a fallacy which is in the air, and which threatens to produce evil consequences wherever it becomes localised.

Perhaps, at some future time yet far distant, a man will arise who shall fathom and explain the great problems presented by human vanity. No more interesting study could be found wherewith to occupy the greatest mind, and assuredly none in the pursuit of which a man would be so constantly confronted by new and varied matter for research. One main fact at least we know. Vanity is the boundless, circumambient and all-penetrating ether in which all man's thoughts and actions have being and receive manifestation. All moral and intellectual life is either full of it and in sympathy with it, breathing it as our bodies breathe the air, or is out of balance with it in the matter of quantity and is continually struggling to restore its own lost equilibrium. It is as impossible to conceive of anything being done in the world without also conceiving the element of vanity as the medium for the action, as it is to imagine motion without space, or time without motion. To say that any man who succeeds in the race for superiority of any sort is without vanity, is downright nonsense; to assert that any man can reach success without it, would be to state more than any one has yet been able to prove. Let us accept the fact that we are all vain, whether we be saints or sinners, men of action or men of thought, men who leave our sign manual upon the page of our little day or men who trudge through the furrows of a nameless life ploughing and sowing that others may reap and eat and be merry. After all, does not our conception of heaven suggest to us a life from which all vanity is absent, and does not our idea of hell show us an existence in which vanity reigns supreme and hopeless, without prospect of satisfaction? Let us at least strive that our vanity may neither do injury to our fellow-men, nor recoil and become ridiculous in ourselves.

Enough has been said to define and explain the character and life of the young man whose history this book is to relate. He himself was far from being conscious of all his virtues, faults, and capabilities. He neither knew his own energy nor was aware of the hidden enthusiasm which was only just beginning to make itself felt as a vague, uneasy longing for something that should surpass ordinary things. He did not know that he possessed singular talents as well as unusual defects. He had not even begun to look upon life as a problem offered him for solution, and upon his own heart as an object for his own study. He scarcely felt that he had a heart at all, nor knew where to look for it in others. His life was not happy, and yet he had not tasted the bitter sources of real unhappiness. He was oppressed by his surroundings, but he could not have told what he would have done with the most untrammelled liberty. He despised money, he worked for a pittance, and yet he secretly longed for all that money could buy. He was profoundly attached to his father, and yet he found the good man's company intolerable. He shrank from a society in which he might have been a welcome guest, and yet he dreamed of playing a great part in it some day. He believed himself cynical when he was in reality quixotic, his idols of gold were hidden behind images of clay, and he really cared little for those things which he had schooled himself to admire the most. He fancied himself a critic when he was foredestined by his nature and his circumstances to become an object of criticism to others. He forced his mind to do what it found least congenial, not acting in obedience to any principle or idea of duty, but because he was sure that he knew his own abilities, and that no other path lay open to success. He was in the darkest part of the transition which precedes development, for he was in that period during which a man makes himself imagine that he has laid hold on the thread of the future, while something he will not heed warns him that the chaos is wilder than ever before. In the dark hour before manhood's morning he was journeying resolutely away from the coming dawn.

CHAPTER II.

"It is very sad," observed Mrs. Sherrington Trimm,
thoughtfully. "Their mother died in London last
autumn, and now they are quite alone — nobody with
them but an aunt, or something like that — poor girls!
I am so glad they are rich, at least. You ought to
know them."

"Ought I?" asked the visitor who was drinking his
tea on the other side of the fire-place. "You know I do
not go into society."

"The girls go nowhere, either. They are still in
mourning. You ought to know them. Who knows,
you might marry one or the other."

"I will never marry a fortune."

"Do not be silly, George!"

The relationship between the two speakers was not
very close. George Winton Wood's mother had been a
second cousin of Mrs. Sherrington Trimm's, and the two
ladies had not been on very friendly terms with each
other. Moreover, Mrs. Trimm had nothing to do with
old Jonah Wood, the father of the young man with
whom she was now speaking, and Jonah Wood refused
to have anything to do with her. Nevertheless she
called his son by his first name, and the latter usually
addressed her as "Cousin Totty." An examination of
Mrs. Sherrington Trimm's baptismal certificate would
have revealed the fact that she had been christened
Charlotte, but parental fondness had made itself felt
with its usual severity in such cases, and before she was
a year old she had been labelled with the comic diminutive which had stuck to her ever since, through five and
twenty years of maidenhood, and twenty years more of
married life. On her visiting cards, and in her formal
invitations she appeared as Mrs. Sherrington Trimm;
but the numerous members of New York society who

were related to her by blood or marriage, called her
"Totty" to her face, while those who claimed no connection called her "Totty" behind her back; and though
she may live beyond three score years and ten, and
though her strength come to sorrow and weakness, she
will be "Totty" still, to the verge of the grave, and
beyond, even after she is comfortably laid away in the
family vault at Greenwood.

After all, the name was not inappropriate, so far at
least, as Mrs. Trimm's personal appearance was concerned; for she was very smooth, and round, and judi-
ciously plump, short, fair, and neatly made, with pretty
little hands and feet; active and not ungraceful, sleek
but not sleepy; having small, sharp blue eyes, a very
obliging and permanent smile, a diminutive pointed
nose, salmon-coloured lips, and perfect teeth. Her good
points did not, indeed, conceal her age altogether, but
they obviated all necessity for an apology to the world
for the crime of growing old; and those features which
were less satisfactory to herself were far from being
offensive to others.

She bore in her whole being and presence the stamp
of a comfortable life.   There is nothing more disturbing
to society than the forced companionship of a person
who either is, or looks, uncomfortable, in body, mind,
or fortune, and many people owe their popularity almost
solely to a happy faculty of seeming always at their
ease.   It is certain that neither birth, wealth, nor talent
will of themselves make man or woman popular, not
even when all three are united in the possession of one
individual.   But on the other hand they are not draw-
backs to social success, provided they are merely means
to the attainment of that unobtrusively careless good
humour which the world loves.   Mrs. Sherrington
Trimm knew this.   If not talented, she possessed at all
events a pedigree and a fortune; and as for talent, she
looked upon culture as an hereditary disease peculiar to
Bostonians, and though not contagious, yet full of dan-

ger, inasmuch as its presence in a well-organised society must necessarily be productive of discomfort. All the charm of general conversation must be gone, she thought, when a person appeared who was both able and anxious to set everybody right. She even went so far as to say that if everybody were poor, it would be very disagreeable to be rich. She never wished to do what others could not do; she only aimed at being among the first to do what everybody would do by and by, as a matter of course.

Mrs. Trimm's cousin George did not understand this point of view as yet, though he was beginning to suspect that "Totty and her friends" — as he generally designated society — must act upon some such principle. He was only five and twenty years of age, and could hardly be expected to be in the secrets of a life he had hitherto seen as an outsider; but he differed from Totty and her friends in being exceedingly clever, exceedingly unhappy, and exceedingly full of aspirations, ambitions, fancies, ideas, and thoughts; in being poor instead of rich, and, lastly, in being the son of a man who had failed in the pursuit of wealth, and who could not prove even the most distant relationship to any one of the gentlemen who had signed the Declaration of Independence, fought in the Revolution, or helped to frame the Constitution of the United States. George, indeed, possessed these ancestral advantages through his mother, and in a more serviceable form through his relationship to Totty; but she, on her part, felt that the burden of his cleverness might be too heavy for her to bear, should she attempt to launch him upon her world. Her sight was keen enough, and she saw at a glance the fatal difference between George and other people. He had a habit of asking serious questions, and of saying serious things, which would be intolerable at a dinner-party. He was already too strong to be put down, he was not yet important enough to be shown off. Totty's husband, who was an eminent lawyer, occasionally asked George to dine with him at his club, and usually said when he came home that he could not understand the boy; but, being of an inquiring disposition, Mr. Trimm was impelled to repeat the hospitality at intervals that gradually became more regular.   At first he had feared that the dark, earnest face of the young man, and his grave demeanour, concealed the soul of a promising prig, a social article which Sherrington Trimm despised and loathed.   He soon discovered, however, that these apprehensions were groundless.   From time to time his companion gave utterance to some startling opinion or freezing bit of cynicism which he had evidently been revolving in his thoughts for a long time, and which forced Mr. Trimm's gymnastic intelligence into thinking more seriously than usual.   Doubtless George's remarks were often paradoxical and youthfully wild, but his hearer liked them none the less for that.   Keen and successful in his own profession he scented afar the capacity for success in other callings.   Accustomed by the habits and pursuits of his own exciting life to judge men and things quickly, he recognised in George another mode of the force to which he himself owed his reputation.   To lay down the law and determine the precise manner in which that force should be used, was another matter, and one in which Sherrington Trimm did not propose to meddle.   More than once, indeed, he asked George what he meant to do in the world, and George answered, with a rather inappropriate look of determination that he believed himself good for nothing, and that when there was no more bread and butter at home he should doubtless find his own level by going up long ladders with a hod of bricks on his shoulder.   Mr. Trimm's jovial face usually expressed his disbelief in such theories by a bland smile as he poured out another glass of wine for his young guest.   He felt sure that George would do something, and George, who got little sympathy in his life, understood his encouraging certainty, and was grateful.

Mrs. Trimm, however, shared her cousin's asserted

convictions about himself so far as to believe that unless something was done for him, he might actually be driven to manual labour for support. She assuredly had no faith in general cleverness as a means of subsistence for young men without fortune, and yet she felt that she ought to do something for George Wood. There was a good reason for this beneficent instinct. Her only brother was chiefly responsible for the ruin that had overtaken Jonah Wood, when George was still a boy, and she herself had been one of the winners in the game, or at least had been a sharer with her brother in the winnings. It is true that the facts of the case had never been generally known, and that George's father had been made to suffer unjustly in his reputation after being plundered of his wealth; but Mrs. Trimm was not without a conscience, any more than the majority of her friends. If she loved money and wanted more of it, this was because she wished to be like other people, and not because she was vulgarly avaricious. She was willing to keep what she had, though a part of it should have been George's and was ill-gotten. She wished her brother, Thomas Craik, to keep all he possessed until he should die, and then she wished him to leave it to her, Charlotte Sherrington Trimm. But she also desired that George should have compensation for what his father had lost, and the easiest and least expensive way of providing him with the money he had not, was to help him to a rich marriage. It was not, indeed, fitting that he should marry her only daughter, Mamie, though the girl was nineteen years old and showed a disquieting tendency to like George. Such a marriage would result only in a transfer of wealth without addition or multiplication, which was not the form of magnanimity most agreeable to cousin Totty's principles. There were other rich girls in the market; one of them might be interested in the tall young man with the dark face and the quiet manner, and might bestow herself upon him, and endow him with all her worldly goods. Totty had now been lucky enough to find two such young ladies together, orphans both, and both of age, having full control of the large and equally divided patrimony they had lately inherited. Better still, they were reported to be highly gifted and fond of clever people, and she herself knew that they were both pretty. She had resolved that George should know them without delay, and had sent for him as a preliminary step towards bringing about the acquaintance. George met her at once with the plain statement that he would never marry money, as the phrase goes, but she treated his declaration of independence with appropriate levity.

"Do not be silly, George!" she exclaimed with a little laugh.

"I am not," George answered, in a tone of conviction.

"Oh, I know you are clever enough," retorted his cousin. "But that is quite a different thing. Besides, I was not thinking seriously of your marrying."

"I guessed as much, from the fact of your mentioning it," observed the young man quietly.

Mrs. Trimm stared at him for a moment, and then laughed again.

"Am I never thinking seriously of what I am saying?"

"Tell me about these girls," said George, avoiding an answer. "If they are rich and unmarried, they must be old and hideous —— "

"They are neither."

"Mere children then —— "

"Yes — they are younger than you."

"Poor little things! I see — you want me to play with them, and teach them games and things of that sort. What is the salary? I am open to an engagement in any respectable calling. Or perhaps you would prefer Mrs. Macwhirter, my old nurse. It is true that she is blind of one eye and limps a little, but she would make a reduction in consideration of her infirmities, if money is an object."

"Try and be serious; I want you to know them."

"Do I look like a man who wastes time in laughing?" inquired George, whose imperturbable gravity was one of his chief characteristics.

"No — you have other resources at your command for getting at the same result."

"Thanks. You are always flattering. When am I to begin amusing your little friends?"

"To-day, if you like. We can go to them at once."

George Wood glanced down almost unconsciously at the clothes he wore, with the habit of a man who is very poor and is not always sure of being presentable at a moment's notice. His preoccupation did not escape cousin Totty, whose keen instinct penetrated his thoughts and found there an additional incentive to the execution of her beneficent intentions. It was a shame, she thought, that any relation of hers should need to think of such miserable details as the possession of a decent coat and whole shoes. At the present moment, indeed, George was arrayed with all appropriate correctness, but Totty remembered to have caught sight of him sometimes when he was evidently not expecting to meet any acquaintance, and she had noticed on those occasions that his dress was very shabby indeed. It was many years since she had seen his father, and she wondered whether he, too, went about in old clothes, sure of not meeting anybody he knew. The thought was not altogether pleasant, and she put it from her. It was a part of her method of life not to think disagreeable thoughts, and though her plan to bring about a rich marriage for her cousin was but a scheme for quieting her conscience, she determined to believe that she was putting herself to great inconvenience out of spontaneous generosity, for which George would owe her a debt of lifelong gratitude.

George, having satisfied himself that his appearance would pass muster, and realising that Totty must have noticed his self-inspection, immediately asked her opinion.

"Will I do?" he asked with an odd shade of shyness, and glancing again at the sleeve of his coat, as though to

explain what he meant, well knowing that all explanation was unnecessary.

Totty, who had thoroughly inspected him before pro-
posing that they should go out together, now pretended
to look him over with a critical eye.

"Of course — perfectly," she said, after three or four
seconds.   "Wait for me a moment, and I will get ready,"
she added, as she rose and left the room.

When George was alone, he leaned back in his comfortable chair and looked at the familiar objects about
him with a weary expression which he had not worn
while his cousin had been present. He could not tell
exactly why he came to see cousin Totty, and he generally went home after his visits to her with a vague
sense of disappointment. In the first place, he always
felt that there was a sort of disloyalty in coming at all.
He knew the details of his father's past life, and was
aware that old Tom Craik had been the cause of his ruin,
and he guessed that Totty had profited by the same
catastrophe, since he had always heard that her brother
managed her property. He even fancied that Totty was
not so harmless as she looked, and that she was very
fond of money, though he was astonished at his own
boldness in suspecting the facts to be so much at vari-
ance with the outward appearance. He was very young,
and he feared to trust his own judgment, though he had
an intimate conviction that his instincts were right.
On the whole he was forced to admit to himself that
there were many reasons against his periodical visits to
the Trimms, and he was quite ready to allow that it was
not Totty's personality or conversation that attracted
him to the house. Yet, as he rested in the cushioned
chair he had selected and felt the thick carpet under his
feet, and breathed that indefinable atmosphere which
impregnates every corner of a really luxurious house,
he knew that it would be very hard to give up the habit
of enjoying all these things at regular intervals. He
imagined that his thoughts liquefied and became more

mobile under the genial influence, forgetting the grooves
and moulds so unpleasantly familiar to them. Hosts
of ideas and fancies presented themselves to him, which
he recognised as belonging to a self that only came to
life from time to time; a self full of delicate sensations
and endowed with brilliant powers of expression; a self
of which he did not know whether to be ashamed or
proud; a self as overflowing with ready appreciation, as
his other common, daily self was inclined to depreciate
all that the world admired, and to find fault with everything that was presented to its view. Though conscious
of all this, however, George did not care to analyse his
own motives too closely. It was disagreeable to his pride
to find that he attached so much importance to what he
described collectively as furniture and tea. He was
disappointed with himself, and he did all in his power
not to increase his disappointment. Then an extreme
depression came upon him, and showed itself in his face.
He felt impelled to escape from the house, to renounce
the visit Totty had proposed, to go home, get into his
oldest clothes and work desperately at something, no
matter what. But for his cousin's opportune return, he
might have yielded to the impulse. She re-entered the
room briskly, dressed for walking and smiling as usual.
George's expression changed as he heard the latch move
in the door, and Mrs. Sherrington Trimm must have
been even keener than she was, to guess what had been
passing in his mind. She was not, however, in the
observant mood, but in the subjective, for she felt that
she was now about to appear as her cousin's benefactress,
and, having got rid of her qualms of conscience, she
experienced a certain elation at her own skill in the
management of her soul.

George took his hat and rose with alacrity. There
was nothing essentially distasteful to him in the prospect
of being presented to a pair of pretty sisters, who had
doubtless been warned of his coming, and his foolish
longing for his old clothes and his work disappeared as
suddenly as it had come.

It was still winter, and the low afternoon sun fell across the avenue from the westward streets in broad golden patches. It was still winter, but the promise of spring was already in the air, and a faint mist hung about the vanishing point of the seemingly endless rows of buildings. The trees were yet far from budding, but the leafless branches no longer looked dead, and the small twigs were growing smooth and glossy with the returning circulation of the sap. There were many people on foot in the avenue, and Totty constantly nodded and smiled to her passing acquaintances, who generally looked with some interest at George as they acknowledged or forestalled his companion's salutation. He knew a few of them by sight, but not one passed with whom he had ever spoken, and he felt somewhat foolishly ashamed of not knowing every one. When he was alone the thought did not occur to him, but his cousin's incessant smiles and nods made him realise vividly the difference between her social position and his own. He wondered whether the gulf would ever be bridged over, and whether at any future time those very correct people who now looked at him with inquiring eyes would be as anxious to know him and be recognised by him as they now seemed desirous of knowing Totty and being saluted by her.

"Do you mean to say that you really remember the names of all these friends of yours?" he asked, presently.

"Why not? I have known most of them since I was a baby, and they have known me. You could learn their names fast enough if you would take the trouble."

"Why should I? They do not want me. I should never be a part of their lives."

"Why not? You could if you liked, and I am always telling you so. Society never wants anybody who does not want it. It is founded on the principle of giving and receiving in return. If you show that you like people, they will show that they like you."

"That would depend upon my motives."

Mrs. Sherrington Trimm laughed, lowered her parasol, and turned her head so that she could see George's face.

"Motives!" she exclaimed. "Nobody cares about your motives, provided you have good manners. It is only in business that people talk about motives."

"Then any adventurer who chose might take his place in society," objected George.

"Of course he might — and does. It occurs constantly, and nothing unpleasant happens to him, unless he makes love in the wrong direction or borrows money without returning it. Unfortunately those are just the two things most generally done by adventurers, and then they come to grief. A man is taken at his own valuation in society, until he commits a social crime and is found out."

"You think there would be nothing to prevent my going into society, if I chose to try it?"

"Nothing in the world, if you will follow one or two simple rules."

"And what may they be?" inquired George, becoming interested.

"Let me see — in the first place — dear me! how hard it is to explain such things! I should say that one ought never to ask a question about anybody, unless one knows the answer, and knows that the person to whom one is speaking will be glad to talk about the matter. One may avoid a deal of awkwardness by not asking a man about his wife, for instance, if she has just applied for a divorce. But if his sister is positively engaged to marry an English duke, you should always ask about her. That kind of conversation makes things pleasant."

"I like that view," said George. "Give me some more advice."

"Never say anything disagreeable about any one you know."

"That is charitable, at all events."

"Of course it is; and, now I think of it, charity is

really the foundation of good society," continued Mrs. Trimm very sweetly.

"You mean a charitable silence, I suppose."

"Not always silence. Saying kind words about people you hate is charitable, too."

"I should call it lying," George observed.

Totty was shocked at such bluntness.

"That is far too strong language," she answered, beginning to look as she did in church.

"Gratuitous mendacity," suggested her companion. "Is the word 'lie' in the swearing dictionary?"

"Perhaps not — but after all, George," continued Mrs. Trimm with sudden fervour, "there are often very nice things to be said quite truly about people we do not like, and it is certainly charitable and magnanimous to say them in spite of our personal feelings. One may just as well leave out the disagreeable things."

"Satan is a fallen angel. You hate him of course. If he chanced to be in society you would leave out the detail of the fall and say that Satan is an angel. Is that it?"

"Approximately," laughed Totty, who was less shocked at the mention of the devil than at hearing tact called lying. "I think you would succeed in society. By-the-bye, there is another thing. You must never talk about culture and books and such things, unless some celebrity begins it. That is most important, you know. Of course you would not like to feel that you were talking of things which other people could not understand, would you?"

"What should I talk about, then?"

"Oh — people, of course, and — and horses and things — yachting and fashions and what people generally do."

"But I know so few people," objected George, "and as for horses, I have not ridden since I was a boy, and I never was on board of a yacht, and I do not care a straw for the fashions."

"Well, really, then I hardly know. Perhaps you had

better not talk much until you have learned about things."

"Perhaps not. Perhaps I had better not try society after all."

"Oh, that is ridiculous!" exclaimed Mrs. Trimm, who did not want to discourage her pupil. "Now, George, be a good boy, and do not get such absurd notions into your head. You are going to begin this very day."

"Am I?" inquired the young man in a tone that promised very little.

"Of course you are. And it will be easy, too, for the Fearing girls are clever ——"

"Does that mean that I may talk about something besides horses, fashions, and yachting?"

"How dreadfully literal you are, George! I did not mean precisely those things, only I could think of nothing else just at that moment. I know, yes — you are going to ask if I ever think of anything else. Well, I do sometimes — there, now do be good and behave like a sensible being. Here we are."

They had reached a large, old-fashioned house in Washington Square, which George had often noticed without knowing who lived in it, and which had always attracted him. He liked the quiet neighbourhood, so near the busiest part of the city and yet so completely separated from it, and he often went there alone to sit upon one of the benches under the trees and think of all that might have been even then happening to him if things had not been precisely what they were. He stood upon the door-step and rang the bell, wondering at the unexpected turn his day had taken, and wondering what manner of young women these orphan sisters might be, with whom cousin Totty was so anxious to make him acquainted. His curiosity on this head was soon satisfied. In a few seconds he found himself in a sombrely-furnished drawing-room, bowing before two young girls, while Mrs. Trimm introduced him.

"Mr. Winton Wood — my cousin George, you know.

You got my note? Yes — so sweet of you to be at home. This is Miss Constance Fearing, and this is Miss Grace, George. Thanks, no — we have just been having tea. Yes — we walked. The weather is perfectly lovely, and now tell me all about yourself, Conny dear!"

Thereupon Mrs. Sherrington Trimm took Miss Constance Fearing beside her, held her hand affectionately, and engaged in an animated conversation of smiles and questions, leaving George to amuse the younger sister as best he could.

At first sight there appeared to be a strong resemblance between the two girls, which was much increased by their both being dressed in black and in precisely the same manner. They were very nearly of the same age, Constance being barely twenty-two years old and her sister just twenty, though Mrs. Trimm had said that both had reached their majority. Both were tall, graceful girls, well-proportioned in every way, easy in their bearing, their heads well set upon their shoulders, altogether well grown and well bred. But there was in reality a marked difference between them. Constance was fairer and more delicate than her younger sister, evidently less self-reliant and probably less strong. Her eyes were blue and quiet, and her hair had golden tinges not to be found in Grace's dark-brown locks. Her complexion was more transparent, her even eyebrows less strongly marked, her sensitive lips less firm. Of the two she was evidently the more gentle and feminine. Grace's voice was deep and smooth, whereas Constance spoke in a higher though a softer key. It was easy to see that Constance would be the one more quickly moved by womanly sympathies and passions, and that Grace, on the contrary, would be at once more obstinate and more sure of herself.

George was pleasantly impressed by both from the first, and especially by the odd contrast between them and their surroundings. The house was old-fashioned within as well as without. It was clear that the girls' father and mother had been conservatives of the most severe type. The furniture was dark, massive, and imposing; the velvet carpet displayed in deeper shades of claret, upon a claret-coloured ground, that old familiar pattern formed by four curved scrolls which enclose as in a lozenge an imposing nosegay of almost black roses. Full-length portraits of the family adorned the walls, and the fire-place was innocent of high art tiles, being composed of three slabs of carved white marble, two upright and one horizontal, in the midst of which a black grate supported a coal fire. Moreover, as in all old houses in New York, the front drawing-room communicated with a second at the back of the first by great polished mahogany folding-doors, which, being closed, produce the impression that one-half of the room is a huge press. There were stiff sofas set against the wall, stiff corner bookcases filled with histories expensively bound in dark tree calf, a stiff mahogany table under an even stiffer chandelier of gilded metal; there were two or three heavy easy-chairs, square, dark and polished like everything else, and covered with red velvet of the same colour as the carpet, each having before it a foot-stool of the old style, curved and made of the same materials as the chairs themselves. A few modern books in their fresh, perishable bindings showed the beginning of a new influence, together with half a dozen magazines and papers, and a work-basket containing a quantity of coloured embroidering silks.

George looked about him as he took his place beside Grace Fearing, and noticed the greater part of the details just described.

"Are you fond of horses, yachting, fashions, and things people generally do, Miss Fearing?" he inquired.

"Not in the least," answered Grace, fixing her dark eyes upon him with a look of cold surprise.

CHAPTER III.

The stare of astonishment with which Grace Fearing
met George's singular method of beginning a conversation rather disconcerted him, although he had half expected it.   He had asked the question while still under
the impression of Totty's absurd advice, unable any longer
to refrain from communicating his feelings to some one.

"You seem surprised," he said.   "I will explain.   I
do not care a straw for any of those things myself, but
as we walked here my cousin was giving me a lecture
about conversation in society."

"And she advised you to talk to us about horses?"
inquired Miss Grace, beginning to smile.

"No.   Not to you.   She gave me to understand that
you were both very clever, but she gave me a list of
things about which a man should talk in general society,
and I flatter myself that I have remembered the catalogue pretty accurately."

"Indeed you have!"   This time Grace laughed.

"Yes.   And now that we have eliminated horses,
yachts, and fashions, by mutual consent, shall we talk
about less important things?"

"Certainly.   Where shall we begin?"

"With whatever you prefer.   What do you like best
in the world?"

"My sister," answered Grace promptly.

"That answers the question, 'Whom do you like
best —?'"

"Very well, Mr. Wood, and whom do you like best?"

"Myself, of course.   Everybody does, except people
who have sisters like yours."

"Are you an egotist, then?"

"Not by intention, but by original sin, and by the
fault of fate which has omitted to give me a sister."

"Have you no near relations?" Grace asked.

"I have my father."

"And you are not more fond of him than of yourself?"

"Is one not bound to believe one's father, when he speaks on mature reflection, and is a very good man besides?"

"Yes — I suppose so."

"Very well. My father says that I love myself better than any one else. That is good evidence, for, as you say, he must be right. How do you know that you love your sister more than yourself?"

"I think I would sacrifice more for her than I would for myself."

"Then you must be subject to a natural indolence which only affection for another can overcome."

"I am not lazy," objected Grace.

"Pardon me. What is a sacrifice, in the common meaning of the word? Giving up something one likes. To make a sacrifice for oneself means to give up something one likes for the sake of one's own advantage — for instance, to give up sleeping too much, in order to work more. Not to do so, is to be lazy. Laziness is a vice. Therefore it is a vice not to sacrifice as much as possible to one's own advantage. Virtue is the opposite of vice. Therefore selfishness is a virtue."

"What dreadful sophistry!"

"You cannot escape the conclusion that one ought to love oneself at least quite as much as any one else, since to be unwilling to take as much trouble for one's own advantage as one takes for that of other people is manifestly an acute form of indolence, and is therefore vicious and a cardinal sin."

"Selfishness is certainly a deadly virtue," retorted Grace.

"Can that be called deadly which provides a man with a living?" asked George.

"That is all sophistry — sophistical chaff, and nothing else."

"The original sophists made a very good living,"

objected George. "Is it not better to get a living as a sophist than to starve?"

"Do you make a living by it, Mr. Wood?"

"No. I am not a lawyer, and times have changed since Gorgias."

"I may as well tell you," said Grace, "that Mrs. Trimm has calumniated me. I am not clever, and I do not know who Gorgias was."

"I beg your pardon for mentioning him. I only wanted to show off my culture. He is of no importance —— "

"Yes he is. Since you have spoken of him, tell me who he was."

"A sophist, and one of the first of them. He published a book to prove that Helen of Troy was an angel of virtue, he fattened on the proceeds of his talking and writing, till he was a hundred years old, and then he died. The thing will not do now. Several people have lately defended Lucretia Borgia, without fattening to any great extent. That is the reason I would like to be a lawyer. Lawyers defend living clients and are well paid for it. Look at Sherry Trimm, my cousin's husband. Do you know him?"

"Yes."

"He is fat and well-liking. And Johnny Bond — do you know him too?"

"Of course," answered Grace, with an almost imperceptible frown. "He is to be Mr. Trimm's partner soon."

"Well, when he is forty, he will be as sleek and round as Sherry Trimm himself."

"Will he?" asked the young girl with some coldness.

"Probably, since he will be rich and happy. Moral and physical rotundity is the natural attribute of all rich and happy persons. It would be a pity if Johnny grew very fat, he is such a handsome fellow."

"I suppose it could not be helped," said Grace, indifferently. "What do you mean by moral rotundity, Mr. Wood?"

"Inward and spiritual grace to be always right."

At this point Totty, who had said all she had to say to Constance, and was now only anxious to say it all over again to Grace, made a movement and nodded to her cousin.

"Come, George," she said, "take my place, and I will take yours."

George rose with considerable reluctance and crossed the room. There was something in Grace Fearing's manner which gave him courage in conversation, and he had felt at his ease with her. Now, however, the ice must be broken afresh with the other sister. Unlike Mrs. Trimm, he did not want to repeat himself, and he was somewhat embarrassed as to how he should begin in a new strain. To his surprise, however, his new companion relieved him of any responsibility in this direction. While listening as much as, was necessary to Totty's rambling talk, she had been watching the young man's face from a distance. Her sympathetic nature made her more observant than her sister, and she spent much time in speculating upon other people's thoughts. George interested her from the first. There was something about him, of which he himself was wholly unconscious, which distinguished him from ordinary men, and which it was hard to define. Few people would have called him handsome, though no one could have said that he was ugly. His head was strongly modelled, with prominent brows, and great hollows in the temples. The nose was straight, but rather too long, as is generally the case with melancholy people; and the thin, dark moustache did not conceal the scornful expression of the mouth. The chin would have been the better for a little more weight and prominence, and the whole face might have been more attractive had it been less dark and thin. As for the rest, the man was tall and well built, though somewhat too lean and angular, and he carried himself well, whether in motion or repose. He was evidently melancholic, nervous, and impressionable, as might be seen from his brown and sinewy hands, of which the smooth and pointed fingers contrasted oddly with the strength of the lower part. But the most minute description of George Wood's physical characteristics would convey no such impression as he produced upon those who first saw him. He was discontented with himself as well as with his surroundings, and his temper was clouded by perpetual disappointment. Sometimes dull and apathetic, there were moments when a vicious energy gleamed in his dark eyes, and when he looked like what fighting men call an ugly customer. Mirth was never natural to him, and when he laughed aloud there was scarcely the semblance of a smile upon his features. Yet he had a keen sense of humour, and a facility for exhibiting the ridiculous side of things to others.

"What do you do, Mr. Wood?" asked Constance Fearing, when he was seated beside her.

"Nothing — and not even that gracefully."

Constance did not laugh as she looked at him, for there was something at once earnest and bitter in the way he spoke.

"Why do you do nothing?" she asked. "Everybody works nowadays. You do not look like a professed idler. I suppose you mean that you are studying for a profession."

"Not exactly. I believe my studies are said to be finished. I sometimes write a little."

"Is that all? Do you never publish anything?"

"Oh yes; countless things."

"Really? I am afraid I cannot remember seeing ——"

"My name in print? No. There is but one copy of my published works, and that is in my possession. The pages present an irregular appearance and smell of paste. You do not understand? My valuable performances are occasionally printed in one of the daily papers. I cut them out, when I am not too lazy, and keep them in a scrap-book.

"Then you are a journalist?"

"Not from the journalist's point of view. He calls me a paid contributor; and when I am worse paid than usual, I call him by worse names."

"I do not understand — if you can be what you call a paid contributor, why not be a journalist? What is the difference?"

"The one is a professional, the other is an amateur. I am the other."

"Why not be a professional, then?"

"Because I do not like the profession."

"What would you like to be? Surely you must have some ambition."

"None whatever, I assure you." There was an odd look in George's eyes, not altogether in accordance with his answer. "I should prefer to live a student's life, since I must live a life of some kind. I should like to be always my own master — if you would give me my choice, there are plenty of things I should like. But I cannot have them."

"Most of us are in that condition," said Constance, rather thoughtfully.

"Are we? Is there anything in the world that you want and cannot have ?"

"Yes. Many things."

"No, I mean concrete things," George insisted. "Of course I know that you have the correct number of moral and intellectual aspirations. You would like to be a heroine, a saint, and the managing partner of a great charity; you would like to be a scholar, historian, a novelist, and you would certainly like to be a great poetess. You would probably like to lead the fashion in some particular way, for I must allow you a little vanity with so much virtue, but on Sundays, in church, you would like to forget that there are such things as fashions. Of course you would. But all that is not what I mean. When I speak of wants, I mean wants connected with real life. Have you not everything you desire, or could you not have everything? If you do not like New York, can you not go and live in Siberia? If you do not like your house, can you not turn it inside out and upside down and trim it with green parakeet's wings, if you please? If you have wants, they are moral and intellectual."

"But all the things you speak of merely depend upon money," said Constance a little shyly. "They are merely material wants — or rather, according to your description, caprices."

"I do not call my desire to lead the unmolested life of a student either a caprice or a material want, but the accomplishment of my wish depends largely upon money and very little upon anything else."

Constance looked furtively at her companion, who sat beside her with folded hands, apparently contemplating his shoes. He had spoken very quietly, but his tone was that of the most profound contempt, whether for himself, or for the wealth he was weak enough to desire, it was impossible to say. Constance felt that she was in the presence of a nature she did not understand, though she was to some extent interested and attracted by it. It is very hard for people who possess everything that money can give, and have always possessed it, to comprehend the effect of poverty upon a sensitive person. Constance, indeed, had no exact idea of George Wood's financial position. He might be really poor, for all she knew, or he might be only relatively impecunious. She inclined to the latter theory, partly because he had not the indescribable look which is supposed to belong to a poor man, and partly on account of his readiness to speak of what he wanted. A person of less keen intuitions would probably have been repelled by what might have been taken for vulgar discontent and covetousness. But Constance Fearing's perceptions were more delicate. She felt instinctively that George was not what he represented himself to be, that he was neither weak, selfish, nor idle, and that those who believed him to be so would before long find themselves mistaken. She made no answer to his last words, however, and there was silence for a few moments.

Then George began to speak of her return to New York, and fell into a very commonplace kind of conversation, which he sustained with an effort, and with a certain sensation of awkwardness. Presently Totty, who had finished the second edition of her small talk, rose from her seat and began the long operation of leave-taking, which was performed with all the usual repetitions, effusive phrases, and affectionalities, if such a word may be coined, which are considered appropriate and indispensable. As a canary bird pecks at a cherry, chirps, skips away, hops back, pecks, chirps, and skips again and again many times, so do certain women say good-bye to the dear friends they visit. Meanwhile George stood at hand, holding his hat and ready to go.

"I hope we shall see you again," said Constance as she gave him her hand.

"May I come?" he asked.

"Of course. We are generally at home about this time."

At last Totty tore herself away, and the ponderous front door closed behind her and her cousin as they came out into the purple light that flooded Washington Square.

"Well, George, I hope you were properly impressed," said Mrs. Sherrington Trimm, when they had walked a few steps and were near the corner of the avenue.

"Profoundly."

"In what way? Come, be confidential."

"In what way? Why, I think that the father and mother of those girls must have been very rich, very dull, and very respectable. I never saw anything like the solidity of the furniture."

Totty was never quite sure whether George was in earnest or was laughing at her.

"Did you spend your time in looking at the chairs?" she asked rather petulantly.

"Partly. I could not help seeing them. I believe I talked a little."

"I hope you were sensible. What did you talk about? I do not think the Fearing girls would thoroughly appreciate the style of wit with which you generally favour me."

"You need not be cross, cousin Totty. I believe I was decently agreeable."

"Oh!" ejaculated Mrs. Trimm.

"You think I flatter myself, do you? I daresay. The opinion of the young ladies would be more valuable than my own. At all events my conscience does not reproach me with having been more dull than usual, and as for the furniture, you will admit that it was very impressive."

"Well," sighed Totty, "I suppose that is your way of looking at things." She did not know exactly what she wanted him to say, but she was sure that he had not said it, and that his manner was most unsatisfactory. They walked on in silence.

"I am tired," she said, at last, as they reached the corner of the Brevoort House. "I will go home in a cab. Good-bye."

George opened the door of one of the numerous broughams stationed before the hotel, and helped his cousin to get in. She nodded rather indifferently to him, as she was driven away, and left him somewhat at a loss to account for her sudden ill temper. Under any ordinary circumstances she would assuredly have bid him enter the carriage with her and drive as far as her house, in order to save him a part of the long distance to his own home. The young man stood still for a moment and then turned into Clinton Place, walking rapidly in the direction of the elevated road.

He had spoken quite truly when he had said that the visit he had just made had produced a profound impression on him, and it was in accordance with his character to keep that impression to himself. It was not that he felt himself attracted by either one of the sisters more than by the other. He had not fallen in love at first sight, nor lost his heart to a vision of beatitude that had only just received a name. But as he walked he saw constantly before him the two graceful young girls in their simple black dresses, full of the freshness and beauty of early youth and contrasting so strongly with their old-fashioned surroundings. That was all, but the picture stirred in him that restless, disquieting longing for something undefined, for a logical continuation of the two lives he had thus glanced upon, which belongs to persons of unusual imagination, and which, sooner or later, drives them to the writing of books as to the only possible satisfaction of an intimate and essential want.

There are people who, when they hear any unusual story of real life, exclaim, "What a novel that would make!" They are not the people who write good fiction. Most of them have never tried it, for, if they had, they would know that novels are not made by expanding into a volume or volumes the account of circumstances which have actually occurred. True stories very rarely have a conclusion at all, and the necessity for a conclusion is the first thing felt by the born novelist. He dwells upon the memory of people he has seen, only for the sake of imagining a sequel and end to their lives. Before he has discovered that he must write books to satisfy himself, he does not understand the meaning of the moods to which he is subject. He is in a room full of people, perhaps, and listening to a conversation. Suddenly a word or a passing face arrests his attention. He loses the thread of the talk, and his thoughts fly off at a tangent with intense activity. As before the sight of a drowning man, the panorama of a life is unfolded to him in an instant, full of minute details, all distinct and clear. His lips move, repeating fragments of imaginary conversations. His eyes fix themselves, while he sees in his brain sights other than those around him. His heart beats fast, then slowly, in a strange variety of emotions. Then comes the awakening voice of the persecutor. "A penny for your thoughts, Mr. Tompkins," or, "My dear Tompkins, if you do not care to listen to me," etc. The young man is covered with confusion and apologises for his absence of mind, while still inwardly attempting to fix in his memory the fleeting visions of which he has just enjoyed such a delicious glimpse.

Fortunately for George Wood, there was no one to disturb his meditations as he strode along the quiet street, ascended the iron steps and mechanically paid his fare before passing through the wicket gate. Nor did the vivid recollection of Constance and Grace Fearing abandon him as the snake-like train came puffing up and stopped before his eyes; still less, when he had taken his seat, and was being carried away up-town in the direction of his home.

He lived with his father in the small house which the latter still owned, and in which, by dint of rigid economy the two succeeded in leading a decently comfortable existence, so far as their material lives were concerned. A more complete contrast to the residence in Washington Square, where George had just been spending half an hour, could hardly be imagined. The dwelling of the Woods was one of those conventional little buildings which abound in the great American cities, having a front of about sixteen feet, being three stories high, and having two rooms on each floor, one looking upon the street and one upon a small yard at the back. Within, everything was of the simplest description. There was no attempt at anything in the nature of luxury or embellishment. The well-swept carpets were threadbare, the carefully-dusted furniture was of the plainest kind, the smooth, tinted walls were innocent of decoration and unadorned with pictures. There were few books to be seen, except in George's own room, which presented a contrast to the rest of the house, inasmuch as there reigned in it that sort of disorder which seemed the most real order in the opinion of its occupant. A huge deal table took up fully a quarter of the available space, and deal shelves full of

books both old and new lined the walls, indeed almost
everything was of deal, from the uncarpeted floor to the
chairs. A pile of new volumes in bright bindings stood
on a corner of the table, which was littered with printed
papers, sheets of manuscript, galley proofs, and cuttings
from newspapers. A well-worn penholder lay across a
half-written page, and the red cork of a bottle of stylo-
graphic ink projected out of the confusion.

George entered this sanctum, and before doing anything
else proceeded to divest himself of the clothes he wore, putting on rusty garments that seemed to belong to different
epochs. Then he went to the window with something like
a sigh of relief. The view was not inspiring, but the
familiarity of it doubtless evoked in his mind trains of
thought that were pleasant. There was the narrow brick-
yard with its Chinese puzzle of crossing and recrossing
clothes' lines. Then a brick wall beyond which he could
see at a considerable distance the second and third rows
of windows of a large house. Above, a row of French
roofs and then the winter sky, red with the last rays of
the sun. George did not remain long in contemplation
of this prospect; a glance was apparently enough to restore the disturbed balance of his mind. As he turned
away and busied himself with lighting a green glass kerosene lamp, the vision of Constance and Grace Fearing
dissolved, and gave place to more practical considerations.
He sat down and laid hold of the uppermost volume from
the pile of new books, instinctively feeling for his paper-
cutter with the other hand, among the disorderly litter
beside him.

After cutting a score of pages, he began to look for the
editor's letter. The volumes had been sent him for
review, and were accompanied by the usual note, stating
with appalling cynicism the number of words he was
expected to write as criticism of each production.

"About a hundred words a-piece," wrote the literary
editor, "and please return the books with the notices on
Monday at twelve o'clock, at the latest."

It was Thursday to-day, and there were six volumes to be read, digested, and written about. George made a short calculation. He must do two each day, on Friday, Saturday, and Sunday, in order to leave himself Monday morning as a margin in case of accidents. Six books, six hundred words, or rather more than half a column of the paper for which he wrote. That meant five dollars, for the work was well paid, as being supposed to require some judgment and taste on the part of the writer. There was of course nothing of much importance in the heap of gaily-bound printed matter, nothing to justify a serious article, and nothing which George would care to read twice. Nevertheless the exigencies of the book trade must be satisfied, and notices must appear, and editors must find persons willing and able to write such notices at prices varying from fifty cents to a dollar a-piece. Nor was there any difficulty about this. George knew that the pay was very good as times went, and that there were dozens of starving old maids and hungry boys who would do the work for less, and would perhaps do it as well as he could. Nor was he inclined to quarrel with the conditions which allowed him so short a time for the accomplishment of such a task. He had worked at second class reviewing for some time, and was long past the period of surprises. On the contrary, he looked upon the batch of publications with considerable satisfaction. The regularity with which such parcels had arrived during the last few months was a proof that he was doing well, and it seemed probable that in the course of the coming year he might be entrusted with more important work. Once or twice already, he had been instructed to write a column, and those were white days in his recollections. He felt that with a permanent engagement to produce a column a week he should be doing very well, but he knew how hard that was to obtain. No one who has not earned his bread by this kind of labour can have any idea of the crowd that hangs upon the outskirts of professional journalism, a crowd not seeking to enter the ranks of the regular newspaper men, but hoping to pick up the crumbs that fall from the table which appears to them so abundantly loaded. To be a professional journalist in America a man must in nine cases out of ten begin as a reporter. He must possess other qualifications besides those of the literary man. He must have a good knowledge of shorthand writing and a knack for the popular style. He must have an iron constitution and untiring nerves. He must be able to sit in a crowded room under the glaring gaslight and write out his impressions at an hour when ordinary people are in bed and asleep. He must possess that brazen assurance which sensitive men of taste rarely have, for he will be called upon to interview all sorts and conditions of men when they least expect it and generally when they least like it. He must have a keen instinct for business in order to outwit and outrun his competitors in the pursuit of news. Ever on the alert, he must not dwell upon the recollections of yesterday lest they twine themselves into the reports of to-day. Altogether, the commencing journalist must be a remarkable being, and most remarkable for a set of qualities which are not only useless to the writer of books, but which, if the latter possessed them, would notably hinder his success. There is no such thing as amateur journalism possible within the precincts of a great newspaper's offices, whereas the outer doors are besieged by amateurs of every known and unknown description.

In the critical and literary departments, the dilettante is the cruel enemy of those who are driven to write for bread, but who lack either the taste, the qualifications, or the opportunities which might give them a seat within, among the reporters' desks! Cruellest of all in the eyes of the poor scribbler is the well-to-do man of leisure and culture who is personally acquainted with the chief editor, and writes occasional criticisms, often the most important, for nothing. Then there is the young woman who has been to college, who lacks nothing, but is ever ready to write for money, which she devotes to charitable purposes, thereby depriving some unfortunate youth of the dollar a day which means food to him, for whose support the public is not already taxed. But she knows nothing about him, and it amuses her to be connected with the press, and to have the importance of exchanging a word with the editor if she meets him in the society she frequents. The young man goes on the accustomed day for the new books. "I have nothing for you this week, Mr. Tompkins," says the manager of the literary department as politely as possible. The books are gone to the Vassar girl or to the rich idler, and poor Tompkins must not hope to earn his daily dollar again till seven or eight days have passed. His only consolation is that the dawdling dilettante can never get all the work, because he or she cannot write fast enough to supply the demand. Without the spur of necessity it is impossible to read and review two volumes a day for any length of time. It is hard to combine justice to an author with the necessity for rushing through his book at a hundred pages an hour. It is indeed important to cut every leaf, lest the aforesaid literary manager should accuse poor little Mr. Tompkins of carelessness and superficiality in his judgment; but it is quite impossible that Tompkins should read every word of the children's story-book, of the volume of second class sermons, of the collection of fifth rate poetry, and of the harrowing tale of city life, entitled *The Bucket of Blood, or The Washer-woman's Revenge,* all of which have come at once and are simultaneously submitted to his authoritative criticism.

George Wood cut through thirty pages of the volume he held in his hand, then went to the end and cut backwards, then returned to the place he had reached the first time, and cut through the middle of the book. It was his invariable system, and he found that it succeeded very well.

"It is not well done," he said to himself, quoting Johnson, "but one is surprised to see it done at all. What can you expect for fifty cents?"

CHAPTER IV.

Many days passed before George thought of renewing his visit to Washington Square, and during that time he was not even tempted to go and see Mrs. Trimm. If the truth were to be told it might appear that the vision of the two young girls, which had kept George in company as he returned to his home, did not present itself again for a long time with any especial vividness. Possibly the surroundings and occupations in the midst of which he lived were not of a nature to stir his memories easily; possibly, too, and more probably, the first impression had lacked strength to fascinate his imagination for more than half an hour. The habit of reading a book, writing twenty lines of print about it and throwing it aside, never to be taken up again, may have its consequences in daily life. Though quite unconscious of taking such a superficial view of so serious a matter, George's mind treated the Misses Fearing very much as it would have treated a book that had been sent in for notice, dealt with and seen no more. Now and then, when he was not at work, and was even less interested than usual in his father's snatches of conversation, he was conscious of remembering his introduction to the two young ladies, and strange to say there was something humorous in the recollection. Totty's business-like mode of procedure amused him, and what seemed to him her absurd assumption of a wild improbability. The ludicrous idea of the whole affair entertained his fancy for a few seconds before it slipped away again. He could not tell exactly where the source of his mirth was situated in the chain of ideas, but he almost smiled at the thought of the enormous, stiff easy-chairs, and of the bookcase in the corner, loaded to the highest shelf with histories bound in tree calf and gold. He remembered, too, the look of disappointment in Totty's eyes when he had alluded to

the respectability of the furniture, as they walked up
Fifth Avenue.

Those thoughts did not altogether vanish without suggesting to George's inner sight the outlines of the girls'
faces, and at the same time he had a faint memory of
the sounds of their voices. It would not displease him
to see and hear both again, but, on the other hand, a
visit in the afternoon was an undertaking of some importance, a fact which cannot be realised by people who
have spent their lives in society, and who go to see each
other as a natural pastime, just as the solitary man takes
up a book, or as the sailor who has nothing to do knots
and splices odds and ends of rope. It is not only that
the material preparations are irksome, and that it is
a distinctly troublesome affair for the young literary
drudge to make himself outwardly presentable; there is
also the tiresome necessity of smoothing out the weary
brain so that it may be capable of appreciating a set of
unfamiliar impressions in which it anticipates no relaxation. Add to all this the leaven of shyness which so
often belongs to young and sensitive natures, and the
slight exertion necessary in such a case swells and rises
till it seems to be an insurmountable barrier.

A day came, however, when George had nothing to do.
It would be more accurate to say that on a particular
afternoon, having finished one piece of work to his satisfaction, he did not feel inclined to begin another; for,
among the many consequences of entering upon a literary life is the losing for ever of the feeling that at any
moment there is nothing to be done. Let a writer work
until his brain reels and his fingers can no longer hold
the pen, he will nevertheless find it impossible to rest
without imagining that he is being idle. He cannot
escape from the devil that drives him, because he is
himself the driver and the driven, the fiend and his
victim, the torturer and the tortured. Let physicians
rail at the horrible consequences of drink, of excessive
smoking, of opium, of chloral, and of morphine — the

most terrible of all stimulants is ink, the hardest of taskmasters, the most fascinating of enchanters, the breeder of the sweetest dreams and of the most appalling nightmares, the most insinuating of poisons, the surest of destroyers. One may truly venture to say that of an equal number of opium-eaters and professional writers, the opium-eaters have the best of it in the matter of long life, health, and peace of mind. We all hear of the miserable end of the poor wretch who has subsisted for years upon stimulants or narcotics, and whose death, often at an advanced age, is held up as a warning to youth; but who ever knows or speaks of the countless deaths due solely to the overuse of pen, ink, and paper? Who catalogues the names of those many whose brains give way before their bodies are worn out? Who counts the suicides brought about by failure, the cases of men starving because they would rather write bad English than do good work of any other sort? In proportion to the whole literary profession of the modern world the deaths alone, without counting other accidents, are more numerous than those caused by alcohol among drinkers, by nicotine among smokers, and by morphine and like drugs among those who use them. For one man who succeeds in literature, a thousand fail, and a hundred, who have looked upon the ink when it was black and cannot be warned from it, and whose nostrils have smelled the printer's sacrifice, are ruined for all usefulness and go drifting and struggling down the stream of failure till death or madness puts an end to their sufferings. And yet no one ventures to call writing a destroying vice, nor to condemn poor scribblers as "ink-drunkards.

George walked the whole distance from his house to Washington Square. He had not been in that part of the city since he had come with his cousin to make his first visit, but as he drew near to his destination he began to regret that he had allowed more than a fortnight to pass without making any attempt to see his new acquaintances. On reaching the house he found that Constance Fearing was at home. He was sorry not to see the younger sister, with whom he had found conversation more easy and sympathetic. On the other hand, the atmosphere of the house seemed less stiff and formal than on the first occasion; the disposition of the heavy furniture had been changed, there were flowers in the old-fashioned vases, and there were more books and small objects scattered upon the tables.

"I was afraid you were never coming again!" exclaimed the young girl, holding out her hand.

There was something simple and frank about her manner which put George at his ease.

"You are very kind," he answered, "I was afraid that even to-day might be too soon. But Sherry Trimm says that when he is in doubt he plays trumps — and so I came."

"Not at all too soon," suggested Constance.

"The calculation is very simple. A visit once a fort-night would make twenty-six visits a year with a fraction more in leap year, would it not? Does not that appal you?"

"I have not a mathematical mind, and I do not look so far ahead. Besides, if we are away for six months in the summer, you would not make so many."

"I forgot that everybody does not stay in town the whole year. I suppose you will go abroad again?"

"Not this year," answered Miss Fearing rather sadly.

George glanced at her face and then looked quickly away. He understood her tone, and it seemed natural enough that the fresh recollection of her mother's death should for some time prevent both the sisters from returning to Europe. He could not help wondering how much real sorrow lay behind the young girl's sadness, though he was somewhat astonished to find himself engaged in such an odd psychological calculation. He did not readily believe evil of any one, and yet he found it hard to believe much absolute good. Possibly he may have inherited something of this untrustfulness from his father, and there was a side in his own character which abhorred it. For a few moments there was silence between the two. George sitting in his upright chair and bending forward, gazing stupidly at his own hands clasped upon his knee, while Constance Fearing leaned far back in her deep easy-chair watching his dark profile against the bright light of the window.

"Do you like people, Miss Fearing?" George asked rather suddenly.

"How do you mean?"

"I mean, is your first impulse, about people you meet for the first time, to trust them, or not?"

"That is not an easy question to answer. I do not think I have thought much about it. What is your own impulse?"

"You are distrustful," said George in a tone of conviction.

"Why?"

"Because you answer a question by a question."

"Is that a sign? How careful one should be! No— I will try to answer fairly. I think I am unprejudiced, but I like to look at people's faces before I make up my mind about them."

"And when you have decided, do you change easily? Have you not a decided first impression to which you come back in spite of your judgment, and in spite of yourself?"

"I do not know. I fancy not. I think I would rather not have anything of the kind. Why do you ask?"

"Out of curiosity. I am not ashamed of being curious. Have you ever tried to think what the world would be like if nobody asked questions?"

"It would be a very quiet place."

"We should all be asleep. Curiosity is only the waking state of the mind. We are all asking questions, all the time, either of ourselves, of our friends, or of our books. Nine-tenths of them are never answered, but that does not prevent us from asking more."

"Or from repeating the same ones — to ourselves," said Constance.

"Yes; the most interesting ones."

"What is most interesting?"

"Always that which we hope the most and the least expect to have," George answered. "We are talking psychology or something very like it," he added with a dry laugh.

"Is there any reason why we should not?" asked his companion. "Why do you laugh, Mr. Wood? Your laugh does not sound very heart-felt either." She fixed her clear blue eyes on him for a moment.

"One rarely does well what one has not practised before an audience," he answered. "As you suggest, there is no reason why we should not talk psychology — if we know enough about it — that is to say, if you do, for I am sure I do not. There is no subject on which it is so easy to make smart remarks."

"Excepting our neighbour," observed Constance.

"I have no neighbours. Who is my neighbour?" asked George rather viciously.

"I think there is a biblical answer to that question."

"But I do not live in biblical times; and I suppose my scratches are too insignificant to attract the attention of any passing Samaritan."

"Perhaps you have none at all."

"Perhaps not. I suppose our neighbours are 'them that we love that love us,' so the old toast says. Are they not?"

"And those whom we ought to love, I fancy," suggested Constance.

"But we ought to love our enemies. What a neighbourly world it is, and how full of love it should be!"

"Fortunately, love is a vague word."

"Have you never tried to define it?" asked the young man.

"I am not clever enough for that. Perhaps you could."

George looked quickly at the young girl. He was not

prepared to believe that she made the suggestion out of coquetry, but he was not old enough to understand that such a remark might have escaped from her lips without the slightest intention.

"I rather think that definition ends when love begins," he said, after a moment's pause. "All love is experimental, and definition is generally the result of many experiments."

"Experimental?"

"Yes. Do you not know many cases in which people have tried the experiment and have failed? It is no less an experiment if it happens to succeed. Affection is a matter of fact, but love is a matter of speculation."

"I should not think that experimental love would be worth much," said Constance, with a shade of embarrassment. A very faint colour rose in her cheeks as she spoke.

"One should have tried it before one should judge. Or else, one should begin at the other extremity and work backwards from hate to love, through the circle of one's acquaintances."

"Why are you always alluding to hating people?" asked the young girl, turning her eyes upon him with a look of gentle, surprised protest. "Is it for the sake of seeming cynical, or for the sake of making paradoxes? It is not really possible that you should hate every one, you know."

"With a few brilliant exceptions, you are quite right," George answered. "But I was hoping to discover that you hated some one, for the sake of observing your symptoms. You look so very good."

It would have been hard to say that the expression of his face had changed, but as he made the last remark the lines that naturally gave his mouth a scornful look were unusually apparent. The colour appeared again in Constance's cheeks, a little brighter than before, and her eyes glistened as she looked away from her visitor.

"I think you might find that appearances are deceptive, if you go on," she said.

"Should I?" asked George quietly, his features relaxing in a singularly attractive smile which was rarely seen upon his face. He was conscious of a thrill of intense satisfaction at the manifestation of the young girl's sensitiveness, a satisfaction which he could not then explain, but which was in reality highly artistic. The sensation could only be compared to that produced in an appreciative ear by a new and perfectly harmonious modulation sounded upon a very beautiful instrument.

"I wonder," he resumed presently, "what form the opposite of goodness would take in you. Are you ever very angry? Perhaps it is rude to ask such questions. Is it?"

"I do not know. No one was ever rude to me," Constance answered calmly. "But I have been angry — since you ask — I often am, about little things."

"And are you very fierce and terrible on those occasions?"

"Very terrible indeed," laughed the young girl. "I should frighten you if you were to see me."

"I can well believe that. I am of a timid disposition."

"Are you? You do not look like it. I shall ask Mrs. Trimm if it is true. By-the-bye, have you seen her to-day?"

"Not since we were here together."

"I thought you saw her very often. I had a note from her yesterday. I suppose you know?"

"I know nothing. What is it?"

"Old Mr. Craik is very ill — dying, they say. She wrote to tell me so, explaining why she had not been here."

George's eyes suddenly gleamed with a disagreeable light. The news was as unexpected as it was agreeable. Not, indeed, that George could ever hope to profit in any way by the old man's death; for he was naturally so generous that, if such a prospect had existed, he would have been the last to rejoice in its realisation. He hated Thomas Craik with an honest and disinterested hatred, and the idea the world was to be rid of him at last was inexpressibly delightful.

"He is dying, is he?" he asked in a constrained voice.

"You seem glad to hear it," said Constance, looking at him with some curiosity.

"I? Yes—well, I am not exactly sorry!" His laugh was harsh and unreal. "You could hardly expect me to shed tears—that is, if you know anything of my father's misfortunes."

"Yes, I have heard something. But I am sorry that I was the person to give you the news."

"Why? I am grateful to you."

"I know you are, and that is precisely what I do not like. I do not expect you to be grieved, but I do not like to see one man so elated over the news of another man's danger."

"Why not say, his death!" exclaimed George.

Constance was silent for a moment, and then looked at him as she spoke.

"I hardly know you, Mr. Wood. This is only the second time I have seen you, and I have no right to make remarks about your character. But I cannot help thinking—that——"

She hesitated, not as though from any embarrassment, but as if she could not find the words she wanted. George made no attempt to help her, though he knew perfectly well what she wanted to say. He waited coldly to see whether she could complete her sentence.

"You ought not to think such things," she said suddenly, "and if you do, you ought not to show it."

"In other words, you wish me to reform either my character or my manners, or both? Do you know that old Tom Craik ruined my father? Do you know that after he had done that, he let my father's reputation suffer, though my father was as honest as the daylight, and he himself was the thief? That sounds very dramatic and theatrical, does it not? It is all very true nevertheless. And yet, you expect me to be such a clever actor as not to show my satisfaction at your news. All I can say, Miss Fearing, is that you expect a great deal of human nature, and that I am very sorry to be the particular individual who is fated to disappoint your expectations."

"Of course you feel strongly about it — I did not know all you have just told me, or I would not have spoken. I wish every one could forgive — it is so right to forgive."

"Yes — undoubtedly," assented George. "Begin by forgiving me, please, and then tell me what is the matter with the worthy Mr. Craik."

"Mrs. Trimm seems to think it is nervous prostration — what everybody has nowadays."

"Is she very much cut up?" George asked with an air of concern.

"She writes that she does not leave him."

"Nor will — until ——" George stopped short.

"What were you going to say?"

"I was going to make a remark about the human will in general and about the wills of dying men in particular. It was very ill-natured, and in direct contradiction to your orders."

"I suppose she will have all his fortune in any case," observed Constance, repressing a smile, as though she felt that it would not suit the tone she had taken before.

"Since you make so worldly an inquiry, I presume we may take it for granted that the mantle of Mr. Craik's filthy lucre will descend upon the unwilling shoulders of Mrs. Sherrington Trimm. To be plain, Totty will get the dollars. Well — I wish her joy. She is not acquainted with poverty, as it is, nor was destitution ever her familiar friend."

"Why do you affect that biblical sort of language?"

"It seems to me more forcible than swearing. Besides, you would not let me swear, I am sure, even if I wanted to."

"Certainly not ——"

"Very well, then you must forgive the imperfections

of my style in consideration of my not doing very much worse. I think I will go and ask how Mr. Craik is doing to-day. Would not that show a proper spirit of charity and forgiveness?"

"I hope you will do nothing of the sort!" exclaimed Constance hastily.

"Would it not be a proof that I had profited by your instruction?"

"I think it would be very hypocritical, and not at all nice."

"Do you? It seems to me that it would only look civil——"

"From what you told me, civility can hardly be expected from you in this case."

"I am not obliged to tell the servant at the door the motive of my curiosity when I inquire after the health of a dying relation. That would be asking too much."

"You can inquire just as well at Mrs. Trimm's——"

"Mr. Craik's house is on my way home from here— Totty's is not on the direct line."

"I hope you— how absurd of me, though! It is no business of mine."

George could not say anything in reply to this statement, but an expression of amusement came over his face, which did not escape his companion. Constance laughed a little nervously.

"You are obliged to admit that it is none of my business, you see," she said.

"I am in the position of a man who cannot assent without being rude, nor differ without impugning the known truth."

"That was very well done, Mr. Wood," said Constance. "I have nothing more to say."

"To me? Then I herewith most humbly take my leave." George rose from his seat.

"I did not mean that!" exclaimed the young girl with a smile. "Do not go——"

"It is growing late, and Mr. Craik may be gathered to

his fathers before I can ring at his door and ask how he is."

"Oh, please do not talk any more about that poor man!"

"If I stay here I shall. May I come again some day, Miss Fearing? You bear me no malice for being afflicted with so much original sin?"

"Its originality almost makes it pardonable. Come whenever you please. We shall always be glad to see you, and I hope that my sister will be here the next time."

George vaguely hoped that she would not as he bowed and left the room. He had enjoyed the visit far more than Constance had, for whereas his conversation had somewhat disquieted her sensitive feeling of fitness, hers had afforded him a series of novel and delightful sensations. He was conscious of a new interest, of a new train of thought, and especially of an odd and inexplicable sense of physical comfort that seemed to proceed from the region of the heart, as though his body had been cheered, his blood warmed, and his circulation stimulated by the assimilation of many good things. As he walked up the Avenue, he did not ask himself whether he had produced a good or a bad impression upon Miss Fearing, nor whether he had talked well or ill, still less whether the young girl had liked him, though it is probable that if he had put any of these questions to his inner consciousness that complacent witness would, in his present mood, have answered all his inquiries in the way most satisfactory to his vanity. For some reason or other he was not curious to know what his inner consciousness thought of the matter. For the moment, sensation was enough, and he was surprised to discover that sensation could be so agreeable. He knew that he was holding his head higher than usual, that his glance was more confident than it was wont to be, and his step more elastic, but he did not connect any of these phenomena in a direct way with his visit in

Washington Square. Perhaps there was a vague notion afloat in his brain to the effect that if he once allowed the connection he should be forced into calling himself a fool, and that it was consequently far wiser to enjoy the state in which he found himself than to inquire too closely into its immediate or remote causes.

It is also probable that if George Wood's condition of general satisfaction on that evening had been more clearly dependent upon his recollection of the young lady he had just left, he would have felt an impulse to please her by doing as she wished; in other words, he would have gone home or would have passed by Totty's house to make inquiries, instead of executing his purpose of ringing at Mr. Craik's door. But there was something contradictory in his nature, which drove him to do the very things which most men would have left undone; and moreover there was a grain of grim humour in the idea of asking in person after Tom Craik's health, which made the plan irresistibly attractive. He imagined his own expression when he should tell his father what he had done, and he knew the old gentleman well enough to guess that the satire of the proceeding would inwardly please him in spite of himself, though he would certainly look grave and shake his head when he heard the story.

Constance Fearing's meditations, when she was left alone, were of a very different character. She stood for a long time at the window looking out into the purple haze that hung about the square, and then she turned and went and sat before the fire, and gazed at the glowing coals. George Wood could not but have felt flattered had he known that was the subject of her thoughts during the greater part of an hour after his departure, and he would have been very much surprised at his own ignorance of human nature had he guessed that her mind was disturbed by the remembrance of her own conduct. He would assuredly have called her morbid and have doubted the sincerity of her most sacred convictions, and if he could have looked into her mind, that part of his

history which was destined to be connected with hers
would in all likelihood have remained unenacted. He
could certainly not have understood her mood at that
time, and the attempt to do so would have filled him
with most unreasonable prejudices against her.

To the young girl it seemed indeed a very serious
matter to have criticised George's conduct and to have
thrust her advice upon him. It was the first time she
had ever done such a thing and she wondered at her own
boldness. She repeated to herself that it was none of
her business to consider what George Wood did, and
still less to sit in judgment upon his thoughts, and yet
she was glad that she had spoken as she had. She knew
very little about men, and she was willing to believe
they might all think alike. At all events this particular
man had very good cause for resentment against Thomas
Craik. Nevertheless there was something in his evident
delight at the prospect of the old man's death that was
revolting to her finest feelings. Absolutely ignorant of
the world's real evil, she saw her own path beset with
imaginary sins of the most varied description, to avoid
committing which needed the constant wakefulness of a
delicate sensibility; and as she knew of no greater or
more real evils, she fancied that the lives of others must
be like her own — a labyrinth of transparent cobwebs, to
brush against one of which, even inadvertently, was but
a little removed from crime itself. Her education had
been so strongly influenced by religion and her natural
sensitiveness was so great, that the main object of life
presented itself to her as the necessity for discovering
an absolute right or wrong in the most minute action,
and the least relaxation of this constant watch appeared
to her to be indicative of moral sloth. The fact that,
with such a disposition she was not an intolerable nui-
sance to all who knew her, was due to her innate tact and
good taste, and in some measure to her youth, which
lent its freshness and innocence to all she did and
thought and said. At the present time her conscience

seemed to be more than usually active and dissatisfied.
She assuredly did not believe that it was her mission to
reform George Wood, or to decorate his somewhat peculiar character with religious arabesques of faith, hope,
and charity; but it is equally certain that she felt an
unaccountable interest in his conduct, and a degree of
curiosity in his actions which, considering how slightly
she knew him, was little short of amazing. Had she
been an older woman, less religious and more aware of
her own instincts, she would have asked herself whether
she was not already beginning to care for George Wood
himself rather than for the blameless rectitude of her
own moral feelings. But with her the refinements of a
girlish religiousness had so far got the upper hand of
everything else that she attributed her uneasiness to the
doubt about her own conduct rather than to a secret attraction which was even then beginning to exercise its influence over her.

It was to be foreseen that Constance Fearing would
not fall in love easily, even under the most favourable
circumstances. The most innocent love in the world
often finds a barrier in the species of religious sentimentality by which she was at that time dominated, for
morbid scruples have power to kill spontaneity and all
that is spontaneous, among which things love is first, or
should be. Constance was not like her sister Grace, who
had loved John Bond ever since they had been children,
and who meant to marry him as soon as possible. Her
colder temperament would lose time in calculating for
the future instead of allowing her to be happy in the
present. Deep in her heart, too, there lay a seed of
unhappiness, in the habit of doubting which had grown
out of her mistrust of her own motives. She was very
rich. Should a poor suitor present himself, could she
help fearing lest he loved her money, when she could
hardly find faith in herself for the integrity of her own
most trivial intentions? She never thought of Grace
without admiring her absolute trust in the man she
loved.

CHAPTER V.

Thomas Craik lay ill in his great house, listening for the failing beatings of his heart as the last glow of the February afternoon faded out of the curtains and withdrew its rich colour from the carved panels on the walls. He lay upon his pillows, an emaciated old man with a waxen face and head, sunken eyes that seemed to have no sight in them. Short locks of yellowish grey hair strayed about his forehead and temples, like dry grasses scattered over a skull. There was no beard upon his face, and the hard old lips were tightly drawn in a set expression, a little apart, so that the black shadow of the open mouth was visible between them. The long, nervous hands lay upon the counterpane together, the fingers of the one upon the wrist of the other feeling the sinking pulse, searching with their numbed extremities for a little flutter of motion in the dry veins. Thomas Craik lay motionless in his bed, not one outward sign betraying the tremendous conflict that was taking place in his still active brain. He was himself to the last, such as he had always been in the great moments of his life, apparently cool and collected, in reality filled with the struggle of strong, opposing passions.

He was not alone. Two great physicians were standing in silence, side by side, before the magnificent chimney-piece, beneath which a soft fire of dry wood was burning steadily with a low and unvarying musical roar. An attendant sat upright upon a carved chair at the foot of the bed, not taking his eyes from the sick man's face.

The room was large and magnificent in its furniture and appointments. The high wainscot had been carved in rare woods after the designs of a great French artist. The walls above were covered with matchless Cordova leather from an Italian palace. The ceiling was composed of rich panels that surrounded a broad canvas from the hand of a famous Spanish master, dead long ago. The chimney-piece was enriched with old brass work from Cairo, and with exquisite tiles from Turkish mosques. Priceless eastern carpets of which not one was younger than the century, covered the inlaid wooden floor. Diana of Poitiers had slept beneath the canopy of the princely bedstead; it was said that Louis the Fourteenth had eaten off the table that was placed beside it, and Benvenuto Cellini had carved the silver bell which stood within reach of the patient's hand. There was incongruity in the assemblage of different objects, but the great value of each and all saved the effect from vulgarity, and lent to the whole something of the odd harmony peculiar to certain collections.

It was the opinion of the two doctors that Tom Craik was dying. They had done what they could for him and were waiting for the end. As to his malady it was sufficiently clear to both of them that his vitality was exhausted and that even if he survived this crisis he could not have long to live. They agreed that the action of the heart had been much impaired by a life of constant excitement and that the nerves had lost their elasticity. They had taken pains to explain to his sister, Mrs. Sherrington Trimm, that there was very little to be done and that the patient should be advised to make his last dispositions, since a little fatigue more or less could make no material difference in his state, whereas he would probably die more easily if his mind were free from anxiety. Totty had spent the day in the house and intended to return in the evening. She bore up very well under the trial, and the physicians felt obliged to restrain her constant activity in tending her brother while she was in the room, as it seemed to make him nervous and irritable. She had their fullest sympathy, of course, as persons who are supposed to be sole legatees of the dying very generally have, but so far as their professional capacity was concerned, the two felt that it went better with the patient when his faithful sister was out of the house.

From time to time inquiries were made on the part of acquaintances, generally through their servants, but they were not many. Though the other persons in the room scarcely heard the distant ringing of the muffled bell, and the careful opening and shutting of the street door, the feeble old man never failed to catch the sound of both and either with his eyes or half-uttered words asked who had called. On receiving the answer he generally moved his head a little wearily and his lids drooped again.

"Is there anybody you expect? Anybody you wish to see?" one of the physicians once asked, bending low and speaking softly. He suspected that something was disquieting the dying man's mind.

But there was no answer, and the lids drooped again. It was now dusk and it would soon be night. Many hours might pass before the end came, and the doctors consulted in low tones as to which of them should remain. Just then the faint and distant rattle of the bell was heard. Immediately Tom Craik stirred, and seemed to be listening attentively. The two men ceased speaking and they could hear the front door softly open in the street below, and close again a few seconds later. One of the physicians glanced at the patient, saw the usual look of inquiry in his face and quickly left the room. When he returned he held a card in his hand, which he took to the bedside after looking at it by the fireside. Bending down, he spoke in a low tone.

"Mr. George Winton Wood has called," he said.

Tom Craik's sunken eyes opened suddenly and fixed themselves on the speaker's face.

"Any message?" he asked very feebly.

"He said he had only just heard of your illness, and was very sorry — would call again."

A strange look of satisfaction came into the old man's colourless face, and a low sigh escaped his lips as he closed his eyes again.

"Would you like to see him?" inquired the doctor.

The patient shook his head without raising his lids, and the room was still once more. Presently the other physician departed and the one who was left installed himself in a comfortable chair from which he could see the bed and the door. During half an hour no sound was heard save the muffled roar of the wood fire. At last the sick man stirred again.

"Doctor — come here," he said in a harsh whisper.

"What is it, Mr. Craik?"

"Send for Trimm at once."

"Mrs. Trimm, did you say?"

"No — Sherry Trimm himself — make my will — see? Quick."

The physician stared at his patient for a moment in very considerable surprise, for he thought he had reason to suppose that Thomas Craik's will had been made already, and now he half suspected that the old man's mind was wandering. He hesitated.

"You think I'm not able, do you?" asked Craik, his rough whisper rising to a growl. "Well, I am. I'm not dead yet, so get him quickly."

The doctor left the room without further delay, to give the necessary orders. When he returned, Mr. Craik was lying with his eyes wide open, staring at the fire.

"Give me something, can't you?" he said with more energy than he had shown that day.

The doctor began to think that it was not yet all up with his patient, as he mixed something in a glass and gave it to him. Craik drank eagerly and moved his stiffened lips afterwards as though he had enjoyed the taste of the drink.

"I may not jockey the undertaker," he grumbled, "but I shall last till morning, anyhow."

Nearly half an hour elapsed before Sherrington Trimm reached the house, but during all that time Thomas Craik did not close his eyes again. His face looked less waxen, too, and his sight seemed to have recovered some of the light that had been fading out of it by degrees all day. The doctor watched him with interest, wondering, as doctors must often wonder, what was passing in his brain, what last, unspent remnant of life's passions had caused so sudden a revival of his energy, and whether this manifestation of strength were the last flare of the dying lamp, or whether Tom Craik, to use his own words, would jockey the undertaker, as he had jockeyed many another adversary in his stirring existence.

The door opened, and Sherrington Trimm entered the room. He was a short, active man, slightly inclined to be stout, bald and very full about the chin and neck, with sharp, movable blue eyes, and a closely-cut, grizzled moustache. His hands were plump, white and pointed, his feet were diminutive and his dress was irreproachable. He had a habit of turning his head quickly to the right and left when he spoke, as though challenging contradiction. He came briskly to the bedside and took one of Craik's wasted hands in his, with a look of honest sympathy.

"How are you, Tom?" he inquired, suppressing his cheerful voice to a sort of subdued chirp.

"According to him," growled Craik, glancing at the doctor, "I believe I died this afternoon. However, I want to make my will, so get out your tools, Sherry, and set to. Please leave us alone," he added, looking up at the physician.

The latter went out, taking the attendant with him.

"Your will!" exclaimed Sherry Trimm, when the door had closed behind the two. "I thought —— "

"Bad habit, thinking things. Don't. Put that drink where I can reach it — so. There's paper on the table. Sit down."

Trimm saw that he had better not argue the matter, and he did as he was bidden. He was indeed very much surprised at the sudden turn of affairs, for he was perfectly well aware that Tom Craik had made a will some years previously in which he left his whole fortune to his only sister, Trimm's wife. The lawyer wondered what his brother-in-law intended to do now, and as the only means of ascertaining the truth seemed to be to obey his orders, he lost no time in preparing to receive the dictation.

"This the last will and testament of me, Thomas Craik," said the sick man, sharply. "Got that? Go on. I do hereby revoke and annul all former wills made by me. That's correct isn't it? No, I'm not wandering —not a bit. Very important that clause — very. Go ahead about the just debts and funeral expenses. I needn't dictate that."

Trimm wrote rapidly on, nervously anxious to get to the point.

"Got that? Well. I bequeath all my worldly posses-sions, real and personal estate of all kinds — go on with the stock phrases — include house and furniture, trinkets and everything."

Trimm's hand moved quickly along the ruled lines of the foolscap.

"To whom?" he asked almost breathlessly, as he reached the end of the formal phrase.

"To George Winton Wood," said Craik with an odd snap of the lips. "His name's on that card, Sherry, beside you, if you don't know how to spell it. Go on. Son of Jonah Wood of New York, and of Fanny Winton deceased, also of New York. No mistake about the identity, eh? Got it down? To have and to hold—and all the rest of it. Let's get the signature—look sharp! Get in the witness clause right—that's the most important—don't forget to say, in our presence and in the presence of each other—there's where the hitch comes in about proving wills. All right. Ring for the doctor and we'll have the witnesses right away. Make the date clear."

Sherrington Trimm had not recovered from his sur-prise, as he pressed the silver button of the bell. The physician entered immediately.

"Can you be the other witness yourself, Sherry? Rather not? Doctor, just send for Stubbs, will you please? He'll do, won't he?"

Trimm nodded, while he and the physician set a small invalid's table upon the sick man's knees, and spread upon it the will, of which the ink was not yet dry. Trimm dipped the pen in the ink and handed it to Mr. Craik.

"Let me drink first," said the latter. He swallowed the small draught eagerly, and then looked about him.

"Will you sign?" asked Trimm nervously.

"Is Stubbs here? Wait for him. Here, Stubbs — you see — this is my will. I'm going to sign it, and you're a witness."

"Yes, sir," said the butler, gravely. He moved forward cautiously so that he could see the document and recognise it if he should ever be called upon to do so.

The sick man steadied himself while the doctor thrust his arm behind the pillows to give him more support. Then he set the pen to the paper and traced his name in large, clear characters. He did not take his eyes from the paper until the doctor and the servant had signed as witnesses. Then his head fell back on the pillows.

"Take that thing away, Sherry, and keep it," he said, feebly, for the strength had gone out of him all at once. "You may want it to-morrow — or you may not."

Mechanically he laid his fingers on his own pulse, and then lay quite still. Sherrington Trimm looked at the doctor with an expression of inquiry, but the latter only shrugged his shoulders and turned away. After such a manifestation of energy as he had just seen, he felt that it was impossible to foresee what would happen. Tom Craik's nerves might weather the strain after all, and he might recover. Mr. Trimm folded the document neatly, wrapped it in a second sheet of paper and put it into his pocket. Then he prepared to take his leave. He touched the sick man's hand gently.

"Good-night, Tom," he said, bending over his brother-in-law. "I will call in the morning and ask how you are."

Craik opened his eyes.

"Tell nobody what I have done, till I'm dead," he answered in a whisper. "Good-night."

Mr. Trimm felt no inclination to divulge the contents of the will. He was a very shrewd and keen man, who could certainly not be accused of having ever neglected his own interest, but he was also scrupulously honest, not only with that professional honesty which is both politic and lucrative, but in all his thoughts and reasonings with himself. At the present moment, his position was not an agreeable one. It is true that neither he nor his wife were in need of Craik's money, for they had plenty of their own; but it is equally certain that during several years past they had confidently expected to inherit the old man's fortune, if he died before them. Trimm had himself drawn up the will by which his wife was made the heir to almost everything Craik possessed. There had been a handsome legacy provided for this same George Winton Wood, but all the rest was to have been Totty's. And now Trimm had seen the whole aspect of the future changed by a stroke of the pen, apparently during the last minutes of the old man's life. He knew that the testator was in full possession of his senses, and that the document was as valid as any will could be. Conscientious as he was, if he had believed that Craik was no longer sane, he would have been quite ready to take advantage of the circumstance, and would have lost no time in consulting the physician with a view to obtaining evidence in the case that would arise. But it was evident that Craik's mind was in no way affected by his illness. The thing was done, and if Craik died it was irrevocable. Sherry and Totty Trimm would never live in the magnificent house of which they had so often talked.

"Not even the house!" he whispered to himself as he went down stairs. "Not even the house!"

For a legacy he would not have cared. A few thou-

sands were no object to him, and he was unlike his wife
in that he did not care for money itself.   The whole
fortune, or half of it, added to what the couple already
had, would have made in their lives the difference
between luxury and splendour; the possession of the
house alone, with what it contained, would have given
them the keenest pleasure, but in Trimm's opinion a
paltry legacy of ten thousand dollars, or so, would not
have been worth the trouble of taking.   Of course it was
possible that Tom Craik might recover, and make a third
will.   Trimm knew by experience that a man who will
once change his mind completely, may change it a dozen
times if he have time.   But Craik was very ill and there
seemed little likelihood of his ever getting upon his
legs again.

Trimm had known much of his brother-in-law's affairs
during the last twenty years, and he was far less surprised at the way in which he had now finally wound
them up, before taking his departure from life, than
most people would have been.   He knew better than any
one that Craik was not so utterly bad-hearted as he was
generally believed to be, and he knew that as the man
grew older he felt twinges of remorse when he thought
of Jonah Wood.   That he cordially detested the latter
was not altogether astonishing, since he had so greatly
injured him, but the natural contrariety of his nature
forced him into an illogical situation.   He hated Wood
and yet he desired to make him some sort of restitution,
not indeed out of principle or respect for any law, human
or divine, but as a means of pacifying his half-nervous,
half-superstitious conscience.   He could not have done
anything openly in the matter, for that would have been
equivalent to acknowledging the unwritten debt, so that
the only way out of his difficulty lay in the disposal of
his fortune after his death.   But although he suffered
something very like remorse, he hated Jonah Wood too
thoroughly to insert his name in his will.   There was
nothing to be done but to leave money to George.   It

had seemed to him that a legacy of a hundred thousand dollars would be enough to procure his own peace of mind, and having once made that arrangement he had dismissed the subject.

But as he lay in this illness, which he believed was to be his last, further change had taken place in his view of the matter. He was naturally suspicious, as well as shrewd, and the extreme anxiety displayed by his sister had attracted his attention. They had always lived on excellent terms, and Totty was distinctly a woman of demonstrative temperament. It was assuredly not surprising that she should show much feeling for her brother and spend much time in taking care of him. It was quite right that she should be at his bedside in moments of danger, and that she should besiege the doctors with questions about Tom's chances of recovery. But in Tom's opinion there was a false note in her good behaviour and a false ring in her voice. There was something strained, something not quite natural, something he could hardly define, but which roused all the powers of opposition for which he had been famous throughout his life. It was a peculiarity of his malady that his mental faculties were wholly unimpaired, and were, if anything, sharpened by his bodily sufferings and by his anxiety about his own state. The consequence was that as soon as the doubt about Totty's sincerity had entered his mind, he had concentrated his attention upon it, had studied it and had applied himself to accounting for her minutest actions and most careless words upon the theory that she was playing a part. In less than twenty-four hours the suspicion had become a conviction, and Craik felt sure that Totty was overdoing her show of sisterly affection in order to hide her delight at the prospect of her brother's death. It is not too unjust to say that there was a proportion of truth in Mr. Craik's suppositions, and that Mrs. Sherrington Trimm's perturbation of spirits did not result so much from the dread of a great sorrow as from the prospect of a very great satisfaction when that sorrow should have spent itself. She was not in the least ashamed of her heartlessness, either. Was she not doing everything in her power to soothe her brother's last days, sacrificing to his comfort the last taste of gaiety she could enjoy until the mourning for him should be over, submitting to a derangement of her comfortable existence which was nothing short of distracting? It was not her fault if Tom had not one of those lovable natures whose departure from this life leaves a great void in the place where they have dwelt.

But from being convinced that Totty cared only for the money to the act of depriving her of it was a long distance for the old man's mind to pass over. He was just enough to admit that in a similar position he would have felt very much as she did, though he would certainly have acted his part more skilfully and with less theatrical exaggeration. After all, money was a very good thing, and a very desirable thing, as Thomas Craik knew, better than most people. After all, too, Totty was his sister, his nearest relation, the only one of his connections with whom he had not quarrelled at one time or another. The world would think it very natural that she should have everything, and there was no reason why she should not, unless her anxiety to get it could be called one. He considered the case in all its bearings. If, for instance, that young fellow, George Wood, whom he had not seen since he had been a boy, were to be put in Totty's place, what would he feel, and what would he do? He would undoubtedly wish that Tom Craik might die speedily, and his eyes would assuredly gleam when he thought of moving into the gorgeous house, a month after the funeral. That was only human nature, simple, unadorned, everyday human nature. But the boy supposed that he had no chance of getting anything, and did not even think it worth while to ring at the door and ask the news of his dying relation. Of course not; why should he? And yet, thought the sour old man, if George Wood could guess how near he was to being made a millionaire, how nimbly his feet would move in the appropriate direction, with what alacrity he would ring the bell, with what an accent of subdued sympathy he would question the servant! Truly, if by any chance he should take it into his head to make inquiries, there would be an instance of disinterested good feeling, indeed. He would never do that. Why then should the money be given to him rather than to Totty?

But the idea had taken possession of the old man's active brain, and would not be chased away. As he thought about it, too, it seemed as though he might die more easily if such full restitution were made. No one could tell anything about the future state of existence. Thomas Craik was no atheist, though he had never found time or inclination to look into the question of religion, and certain peculiarities in his past conduct had made any such meditations particularly distasteful to him. When once the end had come the money could be of no use to him, and if George Wood had it, Thomas Craik might stand a better chance in the next world. Totty had received her share of the gain, too, and had no claim to any more of it. He had managed her business with his own and had enriched her while enriching himself, with what had belonged to Jonah Wood, and to a great number of other people. At all events, if he left everything to George no one could accuse him hereafter — whatever that might mean — with not having done all he could to repair the wrong. He said to himself philosophically that one of two things must happen; either he was to die, and in that case he would do well to die with as clear a conscience as he could buy, or he was to recover, and would then have plenty of time to reflect upon his course without having deprived himself of what he liked.

At last, between the two paths that were open to him, he became confused, and with characteristic coolness he determined to leave the matter to chance. If George Wood showed enough interest in him to come to the door and make inquiries, he would change his will. If the young fellow did not show himself, Totty should have the fortune.

"That's what I call giving Providence a perfectly fair chance," he said to himself. A few hours after he had reached this conclusion George actually came to the house.

Then Tom Craik hesitated no longer. The whole thing was done and conclusively settled without loss of time, as Craik had always loved to do business.

It is probable that if George had guessed the importance of the simple act of asking after his relation's condition, he would have gone home without passing the door, and would have spent so much time in reflecting upon his course, that it would have been too late to do anything in the matter. The problem would not have been an easy one to solve, involving, as it did, a question of honesty in motive on the one hand, and a consideration of true justice on the other. If any one had asked him for his advice in a similar case he would have answered with a dry laugh that a man should never neglect his opportunities, that no one would be injured by the transaction, and that the money belonged by right to the family of the man from whom it had been unjustly taken. But though George could affect a cynically practical business tone in talking of other people's affairs he was not capable of acting upon such principles in his own case. To extract profit of any sort from what was nothing short of hypocrisy would have been impossible to him.

He had been unable to resist the temptation of asking the news, because he sincerely hoped that the old man was about to draw his last breath, and because there seemed to him to be something attractively ironical in the action. He even expected that Mr. Craik would understand that the inquiry was made from motives of hatred rather than of sympathy, and imagined with pleasure that the thought might inflict a sting and embitter his last moments. There was nothing contrary to George's feelings in that, though he would have flushed with shame at the idea that he was to be misunderstood and that what was intended for an insult was to be rewarded with a splendid fortune.

Very possibly, too, there was a feeling of opposition concerned in his act, for which he himself could not have accounted. He was not fond of advice, and Constance Fearing had seemed very anxious that he should not do what he had done. Being still very young, it seemed absurd to him that a young girl whom he scarcely knew and had only seen twice should interfere with his free will.

This contrariety was wholly unreasoning, and if he had tried to understand it, he would have failed in the attempt. He would certainly not have attributed it to the beginning of a serious affection, for he was not old enough to know how often love's early growth is hidden by what we take wrongly for an antagonism of feeling.

However all these things may be explained, George Wood felt that he was in a humour quite new to him, when he rang at Tom Craik's door. He was elated without knowing why, and yet he was full of viciously combative instincts. His heart beat with a pleasant alacrity, and his mind was unusually clear. He would have said that he was happy, and yet his happiness was by no means of the kind which makes men at peace with their surroundings or gentle toward those with whom they have to do. There was something overbearing in it, that agreed with his natural temper and that found satisfaction in what was meant for an act of unkindness.

He found his father reading before the fire. The old gentleman read, as he did everything else, with the air of a man who is performing a serious duty. He sat in a high-backed chair with wooden arms, his glasses carefully adjusted upon his nose, his head held high, his lips set in a look of determination, his long hands holding the heavy volume in the air before his sight and expressive in their solid grasp of a fixed and unalterable purpose. George paused on the threshold, wondering for the thousandth time that so much resolution of character as was visible in the least of his father's actions, should have produced so little practical result in the struggles of a long life.

"Won't you shut that door, George?" said Jonah Wood, not looking away from his book nor moving a muscle.

George did as he was requested and came slowly forward. He stood still for a moment before the fireplace, spreading his hands to the blaze.

"Tom Craik is dying," he said at last, looking at his father's face.

There was an almost imperceptible quiver in the strong hands that held the book. A very slight colour rose in the massive grey face. But that was all. The eyes remained fixed on the page, and the angle at which the volume was supported did not change.

"Well," said the mechanical voice, "we must all die some day."

CHAPTER VI.

The world was very much surprised when it was informed that Thomas Craik was not dead after all. During several weeks he lay in the utmost danger, and it was little short of a miracle that he was kept alive — one of those miracles which are sometimes performed upon the rich by physicians in luck. While he was ill George, who was disappointed to find that there was so much life in his enemy, made frequent inquiries at the house, a fact of which Mr. Craik took note, setting it down to the young man's credit. Nor did it escape the keen old man that his sister Totty's expression grew less hopeful, as he himself grew better, and that her fits of spasmodic and effusive rejoicing over his recovery were succeeded by periods of abstraction during which she seemed to be gazing regretfully upon some slowly receding vision of happiness.

Mrs. Sherrington Trimm was indeed not to be envied. In the first place all immediate prospect of inheriting her brother's fortune was removed by his unexpected convalescence; and, secondly, she had a suspicion that in the midst of his illness he had made some change in the disposition of his wealth. It would be hard to say how this belief had formed itself in her mind, for her husband was a man of honour and had scrupulously obeyed Craik's injunction to be silent in regard to the will. He found this the more easy, because what he liked least in his wife's character was her love of money. Having only one child, he deemed his own and Totty's fortunes more than sufficient, and he feared lest if she were suddenly enriched beyond her neighbours, she might launch into the career of a leader of society and take up a position very far from agreeable to his own more modest tastes. Sherry Trimm was an eminently sensible as well as an eminently honourable man. He possessed a very keen sense of the ridiculous, and he knew how easily a woman like Totty could be made the subject of ridicule, if she had her own way, and if she suddenly were placed in circumstances where the question of expenditure need never be taken into consideration. She had rarely lost an opportunity of telling him what she should do if she were enormously rich, and it was not hard to see that she confidently expected to possess such riches as would enable her to carry out what Sherry called her threats.

On the other hand Mr. Trimm's sense of honour was satisfied by his brother-in-law's new will. There is a great deal more of that sort of manly, honourable feeling among Americans than is dreamed of in European philosophy. Europe calls us a nation of business men, but it generally forgets that we are not a nation of shop-keepers, and that if we esteem a merchant as highly as a soldier or a lawyer it is because we know by experience that the hands which handle money can be kept as clean as those that draw the sword or hold the pen. In strong races the man ennobles the occupation, the occupation does not degrade the man. If Thomas Craik was dishonest, Jonah Wood and Sherrington Trimm were both as upright gentlemen as any in the whole world. It was not in Jonah Wood's power to recover what had been taken from him by operations that were only just within the pale of the law, because laws have not yet been made for such cases; nor was it Sherrington Trimm's vocation to play upon Tom Craik's conscience in the interests of semi-poetic justice. But Trimm was honourable enough and disinterested enough to rejoice at the prospect of seeing stolen money restored to its possessor instead of being emptied into his wife's purse, and he was manly enough to have felt the same satisfaction in the act, if his own circumstances had been far less flourishing.

But Totty thought very differently of all these things. She had in her much of her brother's nature, and the love of money, which being interpreted into American means essentially the love of what money can give, dominated her character, and poisoned the pleasant qualities with which she was undoubtedly endowed. She had, as a natural concomitant, the keenest instinct about money and the quarter from which it was to be expected. Something was wrong in her financial atmosphere, and she felt the diminution of pressure as quickly and as certainly as a good barometer indicates the approaching south wind when the weather is still clear and bright. It was of no use to question her husband, and she knew her brother well enough to be aware that he would conceal his purpose to the last. But there was an element of anxiety and doubt in her life which she had not known before. Tom Craik saw that much in her face and suspected that it was the result of his recovery. He did not regret what he had done and he made up his mind to abide by it.

Meanwhile George Wood varied the dreariness of his hardworking life by seeing as much as possible of the

Fearings. He went to the house in Washington Square as often as he dared, and before long his visits had assumed a regularity which was noticeable, to say the least of it. If he had still felt any doubt as to what was passing in his own heart at the end of the first month, he felt none whatever as the spring advanced. He was in love with Constance, and he knew it. The young girl was aware of the fact also, as was her sister, who looked on with evident disapproval.

"Why do you not send the man away?" Grace asked, one evening when they were alone.

"Why should I?" inquired Constance, changing colour a little though her voice was quiet.

"Because you are flirting with him, and no good can come of it," Grace answered bluntly.

"Flirting? I?" The elder girl raised her eyebrows in innocent surprise. The idea was evidently new to her, and by no means agreeable.

"Yes, flirting. What else can you call it, I would like to know? He comes to see you — oh yes, you cannot deny it. It is certainly not for me. He knows I am engaged, and besides, I think he knows that I do not like him. Very well — he comes to see you, then. You receive him, you smile, you talk, you take an interest in everything he does — I heard you giving him advice the other day. Is not that flirting? He is in love with you, or pretends to be, which is the same thing, and you encourage him."

"Pretends to be? Why should he pretend?" Constance asked the questions rather dreamily, as though she had put them to herself before and more than half knew the answer. Grace laughed a little.

"Because you are eminently worth while," she replied. "Do you suppose that if you were as poor as he is, he would come so often?"

"That is not very good-natured," observed Constance, taking up her book again. There was very little surprise in her tone, however, and Grace was glad to note the fact. Her sister was less simple than she had supposed.

"Good nature!" she exclaimed. "What has good nature to do with it? Do you think Mr. Wood comes here out of good nature? He wants to marry you, my dear. He cannot, and therefore you ought to send him away."

"If I loved him, I would marry him."

"But you do not. And, besides, the thing is absurd! A man with no position of any sort — none of any sort, I assure you — without fortune, and what is much worse, without any profession."

"Literature is a profession."

"Oh, literature — yes. Of course it is. But those miserable little criticisms he writes are not literature. Why does he not write a book, or even join a newspaper and be a journalist?"

"Perhaps he will. I am always telling him that he should. And as for position, he is a gentleman, whether he chooses to go into society or not. His father was a New Englander, I believe — but I have heard poor papa say very nice things about him — and his mother was a Winton and a cousin of Mrs. Trimm's. There is nothing better than that, I suppose."

"Yes — that odious Totty!" exclaimed Grace in a tone of unmeasured contempt. "She brought him here in the hope that one of us would take a fancy to him and help her poor relation out of his difficulties. Besides, she is the silliest, shallowest little woman I ever knew!"

"I daresay. I am not fond of her. But you are unjust to Mr. Wood. He is very talented, and he works very hard ——"

"At what? At those wretched little paragraphs? I could write a dozen of them in an hour!"

"I could not. One has to read the books first, you know."

"Well — say two hours, then. I am sure I could write a dozen in two hours. Such stuff, my dear! You are dazzled by his conversation. He does talk fairly well, when he pleases. I admit that."

"I am glad you leave him something," said Constance. "As for my marrying him, that is a very different matter. I have not the slightest idea of doing that. To be quite honest, the idea has crossed my mind that he might wish it —— "

"And yet you let him come?"

"Yes. I cannot tell him not to come here, and I like him too much to be unkind to him — to be cold and rude for the sake of sending him away. If he ever speaks of it, it will be time to tell him what I think. If he does not, it does him no harm — nor me either, as far as I can see."

"I do not know. It seems to me that to encourage a man and then drop him when he can hold his tongue no longer is the reverse of human kindness."

"And it seems to me, my dear, that you are beginning to argue from another side of the question. I did not understand that it was out of consideration for Mr. Wood —— "

"No, it was not," Grace admitted with a laugh. "I am cruel enough to wish that you would be unkind to him without waiting for him to offer himself. You are a very inscrutable person, Conny! I wish I could find out what you really think."

Constance made no answer, but smiled gently at her sister as she took up her book for the second time. She began to read as though she did not care to continue the conversation, and Grace made no effort to renew it. She understood enough of Constance's character to be sure that she could never understand it thoroughly, and she relinquished the attempt to ascertain the real state of things. If Constance had vouchsafed any reply, she would have said that she was in considerable perplexity concerning her own thoughts. For the present, however, her doubts gave her very little trouble. She possessed one of those calm characters which never force their owners to be in a hurry about a decision, and she was now, as always, quite willing to wait and see what course her inclinations would take.

Calmness of this sort is often the result of an inborn distrust of motives in oneself and in others, combined with an almost total absence of impatience. The idea that it is in general better to wait than to act, gets the upper hand of the whole nature and keeps it, perhaps throughout life, perhaps only until some strong and disturbing passion breaks down the fabric of indolent prejudice which surrounds such minds. Constance had thought of most of the points which her sister had brought up against George Wood, and was not at all surprised to hear Grace speak as she had spoken. On the contrary she felt a sort of mental pride in having herself discerned all the objections which stood in the way of her loving George. None of them had appeared to be insurmountable, because none of them were in reality quite just. She was willing to admit that her fortune might be what most attracted him, but she had no proof of the fact, and having doubted him, she was quite as much inclined to doubt her own judgment of him. His social position was not satisfactory, as Grace had said, but she had come to the conclusion that this was due to his distaste for society, especially since she had heard many persons of her acquaintance express their regret that the two Woods could not forget old scores. His literary performances were assuredly not of the first order, and she felt an odd sort of shame for him, when she thought of the poor little paragraphs he turned out in the papers, and compared the work with his conversation. But George had often explained to her that he was obliged to write his notices in a certain way, and that he occupied his spare time in producing matter of a very different description. In fact there were answers to every one of Grace's objections and Constance had already framed for herself the replies she was prepared to give her sister.

Her principal difficulty lay in another direction. Was the very decided liking she felt for George Wood the beginning of love, or was it not? That it was not love at the present time she was convinced, for her instinct told her truly that if she had loved him, she could not have discussed him so calmly. What she defined as her liking was, however, already so pronounced that she could see no objection to allowing it to turn into something warmer and stronger if it would, provided she were able to convince herself of George's sincerity. Her fortune was certainly in the way. What man in such circumstances, she asked herself, could be indifferent to the prospect of such a luxurious independence as was hers to confer upon him she married? She wished that some concatenation of events might deprive her of her wealth for a time long enough to admit of her trying the great experiment, on condition that it might be restored to her so soon as the question was decided in one way or the other. Nevertheless she believed that if she really loved him, she could forget to doubt the simplicity of his affection.

George, on his part, was not less sensitive upon the same point. His hatred of all sordid considerations was such that he feared lest his intentions might be misinterpreted wherever there was a question of money. On the other hand, he was becoming aware that his intercourse with Constance Fearing could not continue much longer upon its present footing. There existed no pretext of relationship to justify the intimacy that had sprung out of his visits, and even in a society in which the greatest latitude is often allowed to young and marriageable women, his assiduity could not fail to attract attention. The fact that the two young girls had a companion in the person of an elderly lady distantly connected with them did not materially help matters. She was a faded, timid, retiring woman who was rarely seen, and who, indeed, took pains to keep herself out of the way when there were any visitors, fearing always to intrude where she might not be wanted. George had seen her once or twice but was convinced that she did not know him by sight. He knew, however, that his frequent visits had been the subject of remark among the young girls' numerous acquaintance, for his cousin Totty had told him so with evident satisfaction, and he guessed from Grace's behaviour, that she at least would be glad to see no more of him. What Grace had told her sister, however, was strictly true. Constance encouraged him. George was neither tactless nor fatuous, and if Constance had shown that his presence was distasteful to her, he would have kept away, and cured himself of his half-developed attachment as best he could.

About this time an incident occurred which was destined to produce a very decided effect upon his life. One afternoon in May he was walking slowly down Fifth Avenue on his way to Washington Square when he suddenly found himself face to face with old Tom Craik, who was at that moment coming out of one of the clubs. The old man was not as erect as he had been before his illness, but he was much less broken down than George had supposed. His keen eyes still peered curiously into the face of every passer, and he still set down his stick with a sharp, determined rap at every step. Before George could avoid the meeting, as he would instinctively have done had there been time, he was conscious of being under his relation's inquiring glance. He was not sure that the latter recognised him, but he knew that a recognition was possible. Under the circumstances he could not do less than greet his father's enemy, who was doubtless aware of his many inquiries during the period of danger. George lifted his hat civilly and would have passed on, but the old gentleman stopped him, to his great surprise, and held out a thin hand, tightly encased in a straw-coloured glove — he permitted himself certain exaggerations of dress which somehow were not altogether incongruous in his case.

"You are George Wood?" he asked. George was

struck by the disagreeable nature of his voice and at the same time by the speaker's evident intention to make it sound pleasantly.

"Yes, Mr. Craik," the young man answered, still somewhat confused by the suddenness of the meeting.

"I am glad I have met you. It was kind of you to ask after me when I was down. I thank you. It showed a good heart."

Tom Craik was sincere, and George looked in vain for the trace of a sneer on the parchment that covered the worn features, and listened without detecting the least modulation of irony in the tones of the cracked voice. He felt a sharp sting of remorse in his heart. What he had meant for something very like an insult had been misunderstood, had been kindly received, and now he was to be thanked for it.

"I hate you, and I asked because I wanted to be told that you were dead "—he could not say that, though the words were in his mind, and he could almost hear himself speaking them. A flush of shame rose to his face.

"It seemed natural to inquire," he said, after a moment's hesitation. It had seemed very natural to him, as he remembered.

"Did it? Well, I am glad it did, then. It would not have seemed so to every young man in your position. Good day — good day to you. Come and see me if you care to."

Again the thin gloved hand grasped his, and George was left alone on the pavement, listening to the sharp rap of the stick on the stones as the old man walked rapidly away. He stood still for a moment, and then went on down the Avenue. The dry regular rapping of that stick was peculiarly disagreeable and he seemed to hear it long after he was out of earshot.

He was very much annoyed. More than that, he was sincerely distressed. Could he have guessed what had been the practical result of his inquiries during the illness, he would assuredly have even then turned and overtaken Tom Craik, and would have explained with savage frankness that he was no friend, but a bitter enemy who would have rejoiced to hear that death had followed and overtaken its victim. But since he could not dream of what had happened, it appeared to him that any explanation would be an act of perfectly gratuitous brutality. It was not likely that he should meet the old man often, and there would certainly be no necessity for any further exchange of civilities. He suffered all the more in his pride because he must henceforth accept the credit of having seemed kindly disposed.

Then he remembered how, at his second meeting with Constance Fearing, she had earnestly advised him not to do what had led to the present situation. It would have been different had he known her as he knew her now, had he loved her as he undoubtedly loved her to-day. But as things had been then, he hardly blamed himself for having been roused to opposition by his strong dislike of advice.

"I have received the reward of my iniquities," he said, as he sat down in his accustomed seat and looked at her delicate face.

"What has happened to you?" she asked, raising her eyes with evident interest.

"Something very disagreeable. Do you like to hear confessions? And when you do, are you inclined to give absolution to your penitents?"

"What is it! What do you want to tell me?" Her face expressed some uneasiness.

"Do you remember, when I first came here — the second time, I should say — when Tom Craik was in such a bad way, and I hoped he would die? You know, I told you I would go and leave a card with inquiries, and you advised me not to. I went — in fact, I called several times."

"You never told me. Why should you? It was foolish of me, too. It was none of my business."

"I wish I had taken your advice. The old man got

well again, but I have not seen him till to-day. Just now, as I walked here, he was coming out of his club, and I ran against him before I knew where I was. Do you know? He had taken my inquiries seriously. Thought I asked out of pure milk and water of human kindness, so to say — thanked me so nicely and asked me to go and see him! I felt like such a beast."

Constance laughed and for some reason or other the high, musical ring of her laughter did not give George as much satisfaction as usual.

"What did you do?" she asked, a moment later.

"I hardly know. I could not tell him to his face that he had not appreciated my peculiar style of humour, that I loathed him as I loathe the plague, and that I had called to know whether the undertaker was in the house. I believe I said something civil — contemptibly civil, considering the circumstances — and he left me in front of the club feeling as if I had eaten something I did not like. I wish you had been there to get me out of the scrape with some more good advice!"

"I? Why should I —— "

"Because, after all, you got me into it, Miss Fearing," George answered rather sadly. "So, perhaps, you would have known what to do this time."

"I got you into the scrape?" Constance looked as much distressed as though it were really all her fault.

"Oh, no — I am not in earnest, exactly. Only, I have such an abominably contrary nature that I went to Tom Craik's door just because you advised me not to — that is all. I had only seen you twice then — and —— " he stopped and looked fixedly at the young girl's face.

"I knew I was wrong, even then," Constance answered, with a faint blush. The colour was not the result of any present thought, nor of any suspicion of what George was about to say; it was due to her recollection of her conduct on that long remembered afternoon nearly four months earlier.

"No. I ought to have known that you were right. If you were to give me advice now —— "

"I would rather not," interrupted the young girl.

"I would follow it, if you did," said George, earnestly. "There is a great difference between that time and this."

"Is there?"

"Yes. Do you not feel it?"

"I know you better than I did."

"And I know you better — very much better."

"I am glad that makes you more ready to follow sensible advice ——"

"Your advice, Miss Fearing. I did not mean ——"

"Mine, then, if you like it better. But I shall never offer you any more. I have offered you too much already, and I am sorry for it."

"I would rather you gave me advice — than nothing," said George in a lower voice.

"What else should I give you?" Her voice had a ring of surprise in it. She seemed startled.

"What you will never give, I am afraid — what I have little enough the right to ask."

Constance laid down the work she held, and looked out of the window. There was a strange expression in her face, as though she were wavering between fear and satisfaction.

"Mr. Wood," she said suddenly, "you are making love to me."

"I know I am. I mean to," he answered, with an odd roughness, as the light flashed into his eyes. Then, all at once, his voice softened wonderfully. "I do it badly — forgive me — I never did it before. I should not be doing it now, if I could help myself — but I cannot. This once — this once only — Constance, I love you with all my heart."

He was timid, and women, whether old or young, do not like timidity. It was not that he lacked either force or courage by nature, nor any of those qualities whereby women are won. But the life he had led had kept him younger than he believed himself to be, and his solitary existence had given his ideal of Constance the opportunity of developing more quickly than the reality. He loved her, it is true, but as yet in a peaceful, unruffled way, which partook more of boundless admiration than of passion. An older man would have recognised the difference in himself. The girl's finer perceptions were aware of it without comprehending it in the least. Nevertheless it was an immense satisfaction to George to speak out the words which in his heart had so long been written as a motto about the shrine of his imagination.

Constance said nothing in answer, but rose, after a moment's pause, and went and stood before the fireplace, now filled with ferns and plants, for the weather was already warm. She turned her back upon George and seemed to be looking at the things that stood on the chimney-piece. George rose, too, and came and stood beside her, trying to see her face.

"Are you angry?" he asked softly. "Have I offended you?"

"No, I am not angry," she answered. "But — but — was there any use in saying it?"

"You do not love me at all? You do not care whether I come or go?"

She pitied him, for his disappointment was genuine, and she knew that he suffered something, though it might not be very much.

"I do not know what love is," she said thoughtfully. "Yes — I care. I like to see you — I am interested in what you do — I should be sorry never to see you again — but I do not feel — what is it one should feel, when one loves?"

"Is there any one — any man — whom you like better than you like me?"

"No," she answered with some hesitation, "I do not think there is."

"And there is a chance that you may like me better still — that you may some day even love me?"

"Perhaps. I cannot tell. I have not known you very long."

"It seems long to me — but you give me all I ask, more than I had a right to hope for. I thank you, with all my heart."

"There is little to thank me for. Do you think I mean more than I say?" She turned her head and looked calmly into his eyes. "Do you think I am promising anything?"

"I would like to think so. But what could you promise me? You would not marry-me, even if you loved me as I love you."

"You are wrong. If I loved you, I would marry you — if I were sure that your love was real, too. But it is not. I am sure it is not. You make yourself think you love me ——"

The young man's dark face seemed to grow darker still as she watched it. There was passion in it now, but of a kind other than loving. His over sensitive nature had already taken offence.

"Please do not go on, Miss Fearing," he said, in a low voice that trembled angrily. "You have said enough already."

Constance drew back in extreme surprise, and looked as though she had misunderstood him.

"Why — what have I said?" she asked.

"You know what you meant. You are cruel and unjust."

There was a short pause, during which Constance seemed to be trying to grasp the situation, while George stood at the other end of the chimney-piece, staring at the pattern in the carpet. The girl's first impulse was to leave the room, for his anger frightened and repelled her. But she was too sensible for that, and she thought she knew him too well to let such a scene pass without an explanation. She gathered all her courage and faced him again.

"Mr. Wood," she said with a firmness he had never seen in her, "I give you my word that I meant nothing in the least unkind. It is you who are doing me an injustice. I have a right to know what you understood from my words."

"What could you have meant?" he asked coldly. "You are, I believe, very rich. Every one knows that I am very poor. You say that I make myself think I love you——"

"Good heavens!" cried Constance. "You do not mean to say that you thought that! But I never said it, I never meant it—I would not think it——"

There was a little exaggeration in the last words. She had thought of it, and that recently, though not when she had spoken. It was enough, however. George believed her, and the cloud disappeared from his face. It was she who took his hand first, and the grasp was almost affectionate in its warmth.

"You will never think that of me?" he asked earnestly.

"Never—forgive me if any word of mine could have seemed to mean that I did."

"Thank you," he answered. "It is only my own folly, of course, and I am the one to be forgiven. Things may be different some day."

"Yes," assented Constance with a little hesitation, "some day."

A moment later George left the house, feeling as a soldier does who has been under fire for the first time.

CHAPTER VII.

Not long after the events last chronicled, the Fearings left New York for the summer, and George was left to his own meditations, to the society of his father and to the stifling heat of the great city. He had seen Constance again more than once before she and her sister had left town, and he had parted from her on the best of terms. To tell the truth, since his sudden exhibition of violent temper, she had liked him even better than before. His genuine anger had to some extent dissipated the cloud of doubt which always seemed to her to hang about his motives. The doubt itself was not gone, for as it had a permanent cause in her own fortune it was of the sort not easily driven away.

As for George himself, he considered himself engaged, of course in a highly conditional way, to marry Miss Constance Fearing. She had repeated, at his urgent solicitation, what she had said when he had first declared himself, to wit, that if she ever loved him she would marry him, and that there was no one whom she at present preferred to him. More than this, he could not obtain from her, and in his calm moments, which were still numerous, he admitted that she was perfectly fair and just in her answer. He, on his part, had declared with great emphasis that, however she might love him, he would not marry her until he was independent of all financial difficulties, and had made himself a name. On the whole, nothing could have seemed more improbable than that the marriage could ever take place. The distance between writing second-rate reviews at ten dollars a column, and being one of the few successful writers of the day is really almost as great as it looks to the merest outsider. Moreover, a friendship of several months' standing is generally speaking a bad foundation on which to build hopes of love. The very intimacy of intercourse forbids those surprises in which love chiefly delights. Friendly hands have taken the bandage from his eyes, and he has learned to see his way about with remarkable acuteness of perception.

Perhaps the most immediate and perceptible effect of the last few interviews with Constance was to be found in the work he turned out, and in the dissatisfaction it caused in quarters where it had formerly been considered excellent. It was beginning to be too good to serve its end, for the writer was beginning to feel that he could no longer efface his individuality and repress his own opinions as he had formerly done. He exceeded in his articles the prescribed length, he made vicious Latin quotations, and concocted savagely epigrammatic sentences, he inserted sharp remarks about prominent writers, where they were manifestly beside the purpose, besides being palpably unjust, there was a sting in almost every paragraph which did not contain a paradox, and, altogether, he made the literary editors who employed him very nervous.

"It won't do, Mr. Wood," one of them said. "The publishers don't like it. Several have written to me. The paper can't stand this kind of thing. I suppose the fact is that you are getting too good for this work. Take my advice. Either go back to your old style, or write articles over your own name for the magazines. They like quotations and snap and fine writing — authors and publishers don't, not a bit."

"I have tried articles again and again," George answered. "I cannot get them printed anywhere."

"Well — you just go ahead and try again. You'll get on if you stick to it. If you think you can write some of your old kind of notices, here's a lot of books ready. But seriously, Mr. Wood, if you write any more like the last dozen or so, I can't take them. I'm sorry, but I really can't."

"I'll have one more shot," said George, desperately, as he took up the books. He could not afford to lose the wretched pay he got for the work.

He soon saw that other managers of literary departments thought very much as this first specimen did.

"A little more moderation, Mr. Wood," said a second, who was an elderly æsthetic personage. "I hate violence in all its forms. It is so fatiguing."

"Very well," said George submissively.

He went to another, the only one whom he knew rather intimately, a pale, hardworking, energetic young fellow, who had got all manner of distinctions at English and

German universities, who had a real critical talent, and
who had risen quickly to his present position by his
innate superiority over all competitors in his own line.
George liked him and admired him. His pay was not
brilliant, for he was not on one of the largest papers, but
he managed to support his mother and two young sisters
on his earnings.

"Look here, Wood," he said one morning, "this is not
the way criticism is done. You are not a critic by
nature. Some people are. I believe I am, and I always
meant to be one. You do this sort of thing just as you
would do any writing that did not interest you, and you
do it fairly well, because you have had a good education,
and you know a lot of things that ordinary people do not
know. But it is not your strong point, and I do not
believe it ever will be. Try something else. Write
an article."

"That is what everybody tells me to do," George answered. He was disappointed, for he believed that what
he did was really good, and he had expected that the man
with whom he was now speaking would have been the
one of all others to appreciate his work. "That is what
they all tell me," he continued, "but they do not tell me
how to get my articles accepted. Have you a recipe for
that, Johnson?"

The pale young man did not answer at once. He was
extremely conscientious, which was one reason why he
was a good critic.

"I cannot promise much," he said at last. "But I
will tell you what I will do for you. If you will write
an article, or a short story — say five to eight thousand
words — I will read it and give you my honest opinion.
If I like it, I'll push it, and it may get into print. If I
don't, I'll tell you so, and I'll do nothing. You will
have to try again. But I am convinced that you are
naturally an author and not a critic."

"Thank you," said George gratefully. He knew what
the promise meant, from such a man as Johnson, who

would have to sacrifice his time to the reading of the manuscript, and whose opinion was worth having.

"Can you give me any work this week?" he asked, before he took his leave.

Johnson looked at him quietly, as though making up his mind what to say.

"I would rather not. You do not do it as well as you did, and I am responsible. If there is anything else I could do for you ——" He stopped.

"If you will be so kind as to read my article ——"

"Yes, of course. I said I would. I mean ——" Johnson looked away, and his pale face blushed to the roots of his hair. "I mean — if you should need twenty dollars while the article is being written, I can ——"

George felt a very peculiar emotion, and his voice was a little thick, as he took the other's hand.

"Thank you, Johnson, but I don't need it. You are awfully kind, though. Nobody ever did as much for me before."

When he left the room, the nervous flush had not yet disappeared from the literary editor's forehead, nor had the odd sensation quite subsided from George's own throat. If Tom Craik had offered him the loan of twenty dollars, he would have turned his back on him with a bitter answer. It was a very different matter when poor, overworked Johnson put his hand in his pocket and proffered all he could spare. For a minute George forgot all his disappointments and troubles in the gratitude he felt to the pale young man. Nor did he ever lose remembrance of the kindly generosity that had prompted the offer.

But as he walked slowly homewards the bitterness of his heart began to show itself in another direction. He thought of the repeated admonitions and parcels of advice which had been thrust upon him during the last few days, he thought of his poverty, of his failures, and he compared all these facts with his aspirations. He, a poor devil who seemed to be losing the power to earn a miserable ten dollars with his pen, he, whose carefully prepared articles had been rejected again and again, often without a word of explanation, he, the unsuccessful scribbler of second-rate notices, had aspired, and did still aspire, not only to marry Constance Fearing, but to earn for himself such a position as should make him independent of her fortune, so far as money was concerned, and which, in the direction of personal reputation, should place him in the first rank in his own country. Wonderful things happened, sometimes, in the world of letters; but, so far as he knew, they needed a considerable time for their accomplishment. He was well advanced in his twenty-sixth year already, and it was madness to hope to achieve fame in less than ten years at the least. In ten years, Constance would be two and thirty. He had not thought of that before, and the idea filled him with dismay. It seemed a great age, an absurd age for marriage. And, after all, there was not the slightest probability of her waiting for him. In the first place, she did not love him, or, at least, she said that she did not, and if her affection was not strong enough to declare itself, it could hardly be taken into consideration as an element in the great problem. The whole thing was ridiculous, and he would give up the idea — if he could.

But he could not. He recognised that the thought of Constance was the bright spot in his life, and that without her image he should lose half his energy. In the beginning, there had been a sort of complacent acquiescence in the growth of his love, which made it seem as though he had voluntarily set up an idol of his own choosing, which he could change at will. But the idol had begun to feed on his heart, and was already exerting its mysterious, dominating influence over his actions and beliefs. He began to concoct a philosophy of self-deception, in the hope of obtaining a good result. It seemed certain that he could never marry Constance — certain, at all events, while this mood lasted — but he could still dream of her and look forward to his union with her.

The great day would come, of course, when she would marry some one else, and when he should doubtless be buried in the ruin of his dreams, but until then he would sustain the illusion.

And what an illusion it was! The magnitude of it appalled him. Penniless, almost; dependent for his bread upon his ruined father; baffled at every turn; taught by experience that he had none of the power he seemed to feel — that was the list of his advantages, to be set in the balance against those possessed by Constance Fearing. George laughed bitterly to himself as he pursued his way through the crowded streets. It struck him that he must be a singularly unlucky man, and he wondered how men felt upon whom fortune smiled perpetually, who had never known what it meant to work hard to earn a dollar, to whom money seemed as common and necessary an element as air. He remembered indeed the time when, as a boy, he had known luxury, and existed in unbroken comfort, and the memory added a bitterness to his present case. Nevertheless he was not downhearted. Black as the world looked, he could look blacker, he fancied, and make the cheeks of fortune smart with the empty purse she had tossed in his face. His walk quickened, and his fingers itched for the pen. He was one of those men who harden and grow savage under defeat, reserving such luxuries as despondency for the hours of success.

Without the slightest hesitation, he set to work. He scarcely knew how it was that he determined to write an article upon critics and criticism; but when he sat down to his table the idea was already present, and phrases of direful import were seething in the fire of his brain. All at once he realised how he hated the work he had been doing, how he loathed himself for doing it, how he detested those who had doled out to him his daily portion. What a royal satisfaction it was to "sling ink," as the reporters called it! To heap his full-stocked thesaurus of abuse upon somebody and something, and most especially upon himself, in his capacity as one of the critics! To devote the whole profession to the perdition of an everlasting contempt, to hold it up as a target for the public wrath, to spit upon it, to stamp upon it, to tear it to rags, and to scatter the tatters abroad upon the tempest of his reprobation! The phrases ran like wildfire along the paper, as he warmed to his work, and dragged old-fashioned anathemas from the closets of his memory to swell the hailstorm of epithets that had fallen first. Anathema Maranatha! Damn criticism! Damn the critics! Damn everything!

It was a very remarkable piece of work when it was finished, more remarkable in some ways than anything he ever produced afterwards, and if he had taken it to Johnson in its original form, the pale young man's future career might have been endangered by a fit of sudden and immoderate mirth. Fortunately, George already knew the adage — is it not Hood's? — which says "it is the print that tells the tale." He was well aware that writing ink is to printers' ink as a pencil drawing to a painted canvas, and that what looks mild and almost gentle when it appears in an irregular handwriting upon a sheet of foolscap can seem startlingly forcible when impressed upon perfectly new and very expensive paper, in perfectly new and very expensive type. He read the article over.

"Perhaps it is a little strong," he said to himself, with a grim smile, as he reviewed what he had written. "I feel a little like Wellington revisiting Waterloo!"

Indeed, from the style of the discourse, one might have supposed that George had published a dozen volumes simultaneously, and that every critic in the civilised world had sprung up and rent him with one accord. "English Bards and Scotch Reviewers" was but milk and water, with very little milk, compared with his onslaught. The dead lay in heaps, as it were, in the track of his destroying charge, and he had hanged, drawn and quartered himself several times for his own satisfaction, gibbeting the quarters on every page. In his fury and unquenchable thirst for vengeance, he had quoted whole passages from notices he had written, only to tear them to pieces and make bonfires of their remains.

"I think I had better wait a day or two," he remarked, as he folded up the manuscript and put it into a drawer of his table.

It is characteristic of the profession and its necessities, that, after having crushed and dismembered all critics, past, present and to come, in the most complete and satisfactory manner, George Wood laid his hand upon the new volumes which he had last brought home and proceeded during several days with the task of reviewing them. Moreover, he did the work much better than usual, taking an odd delight in affecting the attitude of a gentle taster, and in using the very language he most despised, just for the sake of persuading himself that he was right in despising it. The two editors who had given him work to do that week were surprised to find that he had returned with such success to his former style of writing. They were still further surprised when an article entitled "Cheap Criticism" appeared, about six weeks later, in a well known magazine, signed with his name in full. They did not like it all.

George had recast the paper more than once, and at last, when he had regretfully "rinsed all the starch out of it," as he said to himself, he had taken it to Johnson.

"I did not know that any modern human being could use such violent language without swearing," said the pale young man, catching a phrase here and there as he ran his eye over the manuscript.

"Do you call that violent?" asked George, delighted to find that he had left his work more forcible than he had supposed. "I wish you could have seen the first copy! This looked like prayer and meditation compared with it."

"If you pray in that style," remarked Johnson, "your prayers will be at least heard, if they are not answered.

They will attract attention in some quarter, though perhaps not in the right one."

George's face fell.

"Do you think it is too red-hot?" he asked. "I have been spreading butter on the public nòse so long," he added, almost apologetically.

"Oleomargarine," suggested Johnson. "It is rather warm. That phrase — 'revelling in the contempt of appearing contemptible' — I say, Wood, that is not English, you know, and it's a scorcher, too."

"Not English!" exclaimed George, whose blood was up at once. "Why not?"

"Because it is Volapück, or Malay — or something else, I don't know what it is, though I admit its force."

"I do not see how I can put it, then. It is just what we all feel."

"Look here. You do not mean that your victim despises himself for appearing to be despicable, do you? He does, I dare say, but you wanted to hit him, not to show that he is still capable of human feeling. I think you meant to say that he rejoiced in his own indifference to contempt."

"I believe I did," said George, relinquishing the contest as soon as he saw he was wrong. "But 'revel' is not bad. Let that stand, at least."

"You cannot revel in indifference, can you?" asked Johnson pitilessly.

"No. That is true. But it was English, all the same, though it did not mean what I intended."

"I think not. You would not say an author appears green, would you? You would say he appears to be green. Then why say that a critic appears contemptible?"

"You are always right, Johnson," George answered with a good-natured laugh. "I should have seen the mistake in the proof."

"But that is the most expensive way of seeing mistakes. I will read this carefully, and I will send you word to-morrow what I think of it."

"What makes you so quick at these things?" asked George, as he rose to go.

"Habit. I read manuscript novels for a publishing house here. I do it in the evening, when I can find time. Yes — it is hard work, but it is interesting. I am both prophet and historian. The book is the reality which I see alternately from the point of view of the future and the past."

The result was that Johnson, who possessed much more real power than George had imagined, wrote a note, with which the manuscript was sent, and to George's amazement the paper was at once accepted and put into type, and the proofs were sent to him. Moreover the number of the magazine in which his composition appeared was no sooner published than he received a cheque, of which the amount at once demonstrated the practical advantages of original writing as compared with those of second-rate criticism.

With regard to the attention attracted by his article, however, George was bitterly disappointed. He was on the alert for the daily papers in which an account of the contents of the periodicals is generally given, and he expected at least a paragraph from each.

In the first one he took up, after an elaborate notice of articles by known persons, he found the following line : —

"Mr. George Winton Wood airs his views upon criticism in the present number."

That was all. There was not a remark, nor a hint at the contents of his paper, nothing to break the icy irony of the statement. He pondered long over the words, and then crammed the open sheet into the waste-paper basket. This was the first. There might be better in store for him. On the evening of the same day he found another.

"An unknown writer has an article upon criticism," said the oracle, without further comment.

This was, if possible, worse. George felt inclined to write to the editor and request that his name might be mentioned. It was a peculiarly hard case, as he had reviewed books for this very paper during the last two years, and was well known in the office. The third remark was in one of those ghastly-spritely medleys written under the heading of "Chit-Chat."

"By the way," inquired the reviewer, "who is Mr. George Winton Wood? And why is he so angry with the critics? And does anybody mind? And who is he, any way?"

Half a dozen similar observations had the effect of cooling George's hopes of fame very considerably. They probably did him good by eradicating a great deal of nonsense from his dreams. He had before imagined that in labouring at his book notices he had seen and known the dreariest apartment in the literary workhouse, forgetting that all he wrote appeared anonymously and that he himself was shielded behind the ægis of a prosperous newspaper's name. He had not known that a beginner is generally received, to use a French simile, like a dog in a game of ninepins, with kicks and execrations, unless he is treated with the cold indifference which is harder to bear than any attack could be. And yet, cruel as the method seems, it is the best one in most cases, and saves the sufferer from far greater torments in the future. What would happen if every beginner in literature were received at the threshold with cakes and ale, and were welcomed by a chorus of approving and encouraging critics? The nine hundred out of every thousand who try the profession and fail, would fail almost as certainly a little later in their lives, and with infinitely greater damage to their sensibilities. Moreover the cakes and ale would have been unworthily wasted, and the chorus of critics would have been necessarily largely leavened with skilful liars, which, it is to be hoped and believed, is not the case in the present condition of criticism, in spite of George Wood and his opinions. Is it better that boys should be allowed to remain in school two or three years without being examined, and that the ignorant ones should then be put to shame before their comrades? Or is it better that the half-witted should be excluded from the first, and separately taught? The question answers itself. We who, rightly or wrongly, have fought our way into public notice, have all, at one time or another, been made to run the gauntlet of abuse, or to swim the dead sea of indifference. The public knows little of our lives. It remembers the first book of which everybody talked and which, it foolishly supposed, represented our first experiment in print. It knows nothing of the many years of thankless labour in the columns of the daily press, it has never heard of our first paper in a magazine, nor of our pride at seeing our signature in a periodical of some repute, nor of the sovereign contempt with which the article and the name were received. The comfortable public has never dreamed of the wretched prices most of us received when we entered the ranks, and, to be honest, there is no reason why it should. It would be quite as sensible to found a society for the purpose of condoling with school-boys during their examinations, as to excite the public sympathy on behalf of what one may call undergraduate authors. The weeding at the beginning keeps the garden clean and gay — and amputations must be performed in good time, if the gangrene is to be arrested effectually.

George Wood, as has been said before, was not of the kind to be despondent, though he was easily roused to anger. The porcupine is an animal known to literature, as well as a beast of the field, and the quills of the literary porcupine can be very easily made to stand on end. George was one of the species and, on the whole, a very favourable specimen. Fortunately for those who had accorded so little appreciation to his early efforts, he was at that time imprisoned in the enclosure appropriated to unknown persons. He bristled unseen and wasted his wrath on the desert air. He had looked forward to the publication of his first article, as to an emancipation from slavery, whereas he soon discovered that he had only been advanced to a higher rank in servitude. That is what most men find out when they have looked forward to emancipation of any kind, and wake up to find that instead of being chained to one side of the wall, they are chained to the other.

George supposed that it would now be an easier matter to get some of his former work into print. He had four or five things in very tolerable shape, resting in a drawer where he had put them when last rejected. He got them out again, and again began to send them to periodicals, without consulting his friend Johnson. To his surprise, they were all returned without comment.

"Go and ask for a job," said Johnson, the omniscient, when he heard of the failure. "Suggestion on the part of the editor is the better part of valour in the writer."

"What do you mean?" asked George. He had supposed that there was nothing he did not know in this connection.

"They won't take articles on general subjects without a deal of interest and urging," answered the other. "Get introduced to them in person. I will do it with most of them. Then go to them and say, 'I am a very remarkable young man, though you do not seem to know it. I will write anything about anything in the earth or under the earth. Sanskrit, botany and the differential calculus are my especially strong points, but the North Pole has great attractions for me, I am strong in theology and political economy, and, if anything, I would rather spend a year in writing up the Fiji Islands than not. If you have nothing in this line, there is music and high art, in which I am sound, I have a taste for architecture and I understand practical lobster-fishing. Have you anything for me to do?' That is the way to talk to these men," Johnson added with a smile. "Try it."

George laughed.

"But that is not literature," he objected.

"Not literature? Everything that can be written about is literature, just as everything that can be eaten is man — in another form. You can learn as much English in writing up lobster-fishing, as in trying to compose a five-act tragedy, and you will be paid for it into the bargain. Besides, if you are ever going to write anything worth reading, you must see more and think less. Don't read books for a while; read things and people. Thinking too much, without seeing, is like eating too much — it makes your writing bilious."

"This is the critic's recipe for acquiring fame in letters!" exclaimed George.

"Fame in letters is a sort of stuffed bugbear. You can frighten children with it, but it belongs to the days of witches and hobgoblins. The object of literature nowadays is to amuse without doing harm. If you do that well you will be famous and rich."

"You are utterly cynical to-day, Johnson. Are you in earnest in what you advise me to do?"

"Perfectly. Try everything. Offer your services to write anything. Among all the magazines and weeklies there is sure to be one that is in difficulties because it cannot get some particular article written. Don't be too quick to say you understand the subject, if you don't. Say you will try it. A man may get up almost any subject in six weeks, and it is a good thing for the mind, once in a long time. Try everything, I say. Make a stir. Let these people see you — make them see you, if they don't want to. It is not time lost. You can use them all in your books some day. There is an age when it is better to wear out shoe-leather than pens — when the sweat of the brow is worth a dozen bottles of ink. Don't sit over your desk yelping your discontent, while your real brain is rusting. Confound it all! It is the will that does it, the stir, the energy, the beating at other people's doors, grinding up their stairs, making them feel that they must not lose the chance of using a man who can do so much, making them ashamed to send **you**

away. Do you think I got to be where I am without a
rough and tumble fight at the first? Take everything
that comes into your way, do it as well as you know how,
with all your might, and keep up a constant howl for
more. They will respect you in spite of themselves."

The pale young man's steel-blue eyes flashed, the
purple veins stood out on his white clenched hands and
there was a smile of triumph in his face and a ring of
victory in his voice. He had fought them all and had
got what he wanted, by talent, by industry, but above all
by his restless and untiring energy, and he was proud
of it.

To George Wood, in his poverty, it seemed very little,
after all, to be the literary editor of a daily paper. That
was not the position he must win, if he would marry
Constance Fearing.

CHAPTER VIII.

The summer passed quickly away without bringing
any new element into George's life. He did not reject
Johnson's advice, but he did not follow it to the letter.
His instinct was against the method suggested by his
friend, and he felt that he had not the assurance to follow it out. He was too sensitive and proud to employ
his courage in besieging persons who did not want him.
Nevertheless he found work to do, and his position was
improved, though his writings still failed to attract any
attention. He had imagined that there was but a step
from the composition of magazine articles to the making
of a book, but he soon discovered the fallacy of the idea,
and almost regretted the old days of "book-tasting."

Meanwhile, his thoughts dwelt much on Constance,
and he adorned the temple of his idol with everything
upon which, figuratively speaking, he could lay his
hands. Strange to say, her absence during the summer

was a relief to him. It made the weakness of his position and the futility of his hopes seem less apparent, and it gave him time to make at least a step in the direction of success. He wrote to her, as often as he dared, and twice in the course of the summer she answered with short letters that had in his eyes a suspicious savour of kindness rather than of anything even distantly approaching to affection. Nevertheless those were great days in his calendar on which these missives came. The notes were read over every morning and evening until Constance returned, and were put in a place of safety during the day and night.

George looked forward with the greatest anxiety to Miss Fearing's return. He had long felt that her sister's antagonism was one of the numerous and apparently insurmountable obstacles that barred his path, and he dreaded lest Grace's influence should, in the course of the long summer, so work upon Constance's mind as to break the slender thread that bound her to him. As regards Grace's intention he was by no means wrong. She lost no opportunity of explaining to Constance that her friendship for George Wood was little short of ridiculous, that the man knew he had no future and was in pursuit of nothing but money, that his writings showed that he belonged to the poorest class of amateurs, that men who were to succeed were always heard of from boyhood, at school, at college and in their first efforts and that Constance was allowing her good nature to get the better of her common-sense in encouraging such a fellow. In short there was very little that Grace left unsaid. But though George had foreseen all this, as Grace, on her part, had determined beforehand upon her course of action during the summer, neither Grace nor George had understood the effect that such talk would produce upon her whom it was meant to influence. There was in Constance's apparently gentle nature an element of quiet resistance which, in reality, it was not hard to rouse. Like many very good and very conscientious people, she

detested advice and abominated interference, even on the
part of those she loved best. Her attachment for her
sister was sincere in its way, though not very strong,
and it did not extend to a blind respect for Grace's opinions. Grace could be wrong, like other people, and Grace
was hasty and hot-tempered, prejudiced and not free
from a certain sort of false pride. These were assuredly
not the defects of Constance's character, at least in her
own opinion.

Her opposition was aroused and she began to show it.
Indeed, her two letters to George were both written immediately after conversations had taken place in which
Grace had spoken of him with more than usual bitterness. She felt as though she owed him some reparation
for the ill-treatment he got at her sister's hands, and this
accounted in part for the flavour of kindness which
George detected in her words. The situation was further
strained by the arrival of one of the periodicals which
contained an article by him. The sisters both read it,
and Constance was pleased with it. In an indirect way,
too, she felt flattered, for it looked as though George
were beginning to follow her advice.

"It is trash," said Grace authoritatively, as she threw
the magazine aside.

Constance allowed a full minute to elapse before she
answered, during which she seemed to be intently watching the sail of a boat that was slowly working its way up
the river. The two girls had paused between one visit
and another to rest themselves in a place they owned
upon the Hudson. The weather was intensely hot, and
it was towards evening.

"It is not trash," said Constance quietly. "You are
quite mistaken. You are completely blinded by your
prejudice."

Grace was very much surprised, for it was unlike Constance to turn upon her in such a way.

"I think it is trash for two reasons," she said, with a
short laugh. "First, because my judgment tells me it

is, and secondly because I know that George Wood could not possibly write anything else."

"You can hardly deny that you are prejudiced after that speech. Do you know what you will do, if you go on in this way? You will make me fall in love with Mr. Wood and marry him, out of sheer contrariety."

"Oh no!" laughed Grace. "You would not marry him. At the last minute you would throw him over, and then he would bring an action against you for breach of promise with a view to the damages."

Constance suddenly grew very pale. She turned from the window where she was standing, crossed the small room and stood still before her sister.

"Do you mean that?" she asked very coldly.

Grace was frightened, for the first time in her life, but she did her best to hide it.

"What difference does it make to you, whether I mean it or not?" she inquired with a rather scornful smile.

"This difference — that if you think such things, you and I may as well part company before we quarrel any further."

"Ah — you love him, then? I did not know." Grace laughed nervously.

"I do not love him, but if I did I should not be ashamed to say so to you or to the whole world. But I like him very, very much, and I will not hear him talked of as you talk of him. Do you understand?"

"Perfectly. Nothing could be clearer," said Grace with a contemptuous curl of the lip.

"Then I hope you will remember," Constance answered.

Grace did remember. Indeed, for some time she could think of nothing else. It seemed clear enough to her that something more than friendship was needed to account for the emotion she had seen in her sister's face. It was the first time in her recollection, too, that Constance had ever been really angry, and Grace was not inclined to rouse her anger a second time. She changed her tactics and ignored George Wood altogether, never mentioning him nor reading anything that he sent to Constance. But this mode of treating the question proved unsatisfactory, for it was clear that Wood wrote often, and there was nothing to prove that Constance did not answer all his letters. Fortunately the two sisters were rarely alone together during the rest of the summer, and their opportunities of disagreeing were not numerous. They were not in reality as fond of each other as the world thought, or as they appeared to be. Their natures were too different, and at the same time the difference was not of that kind in which each character seems to fill a want in the other. On the contrary the points in which they were unlike were precisely those which most irritated the other's sensibilities. They had never before quarrelled nor been so near to a quarrel as they were in the course of the conversation just recorded, but they were in reality very far from being harmonious.

The devoted affection of their mother had kept them together while she had lived, and, to some extent, had survived her, the memory of her still exercising a strong influence over both. Constance, too, was naturally very pacific, and rarely resented anything Grace said, in jest or in earnest. Grace was often annoyed by what she called her sister's sweetness, and it was that very quality which prevented the other from retaliating. She had now shown that she could turn, and fiercely, if once aroused, and Grace respected her the more for having shown that she had a temper.

Enough has been said to show that George's fear that Constance would think less well of him through Grace's influence, was without foundation. She even went so far as to send for him as soon as she returned to New York in the autumn. It was a strange meeting, for there was constraint on both sides, and at the same time each felt the necessity of showing the other that no change had taken place for the worse in their mutual relations.

Constance was surprised to find how very favourably George Wood compared with the men she had seen during the summer — men all more or less alike in her eyes, but nevertheless representing in her imagination the general type of what the gentleman is supposed to be, the type of the man of her own class, the mate of her own species. Grace had talked so much, in the early part of the season, of George's inferior social position, of his awkward manner, and, generally, of his defects, that Constance had almost feared to find that she had been deceived at first and that there was a little truth in her sister's words. One glance, one phrase of his, sufficed to set her mind at rest. He might have peculiarities. but they were not apparent in his way of dressing, of entering a room or of pronouncing the English language. He was emphatically what he ought to be, and she felt a keen pleasure in taking up her intercourse with him at the point where it had been interrupted more than four months earlier.

And now the exigencies of this history require that we should pass rapidly over the period that followed. It was an uneventful time for all concerned. George Wood worked with all his might and produced some very creditable papers on a variety of subjects, gradually attracting a certain amount of notice to himself, and advancing, as he supposed, as fast as was possible in his career. Success, of the kind he craved, still seemed very far away in the dim future, though there were not wanting those who believed that he might not wait long for it. Foremost among those was Constance Fearing. To her there was a vast difference between the anonymous scribbler of small notices whom she had known a year ago, and the promising young writer who appeared to her to have a reputation already, because most of her friends now knew who he was, had read one or more of his articles and were glad to meet him when occasion offered. She felt indeed that he had not yet found out his best talent, but her instinct told her that the time could not be very distant when it would break out of its own impulse and surprise the world by its brilliancy. That he actually possessed great and rare gifts she no longer doubted.

Next to Constance, the Sherrington Trimms were the loudest in their praise of George's doings. Totty could talk of nothing else when she came to the house in Washington Square, and her husband never failed to read everything George wrote, and to pat him on the back after each fresh effort. Even George's father began to relent and to believe that there might be something in literature after all. But he showed very little enthusiasm until, one day, an old acquaintance with whom he had not spoken for years, crossed the street and shook hands with him, congratulated him upon his boy's "doing so well." Then Jonah Wood felt that the load of anxiety he had borne for so many years was suddenly lifted from his shoulders. People thought his boy was "doing well"! He had not hoped to be told that spontaneously by any one for years to come. The dreary look began to fade out of his grey face, giving way to something that looked very like happiness.

George himself was the least appreciative of his own success. Even Johnson, who was sparing of praise in general, wrote occasional notes in his paper expressive of his satisfaction at his friend's work and generally containing some bit of delicate criticism or learned reference that lent them weight and caused them to be reprinted into other newspapers.

So the winter came and went again and the month of May came round once more. George was with Constance one afternoon almost exactly a year from the day on which he had first told her of his love. Their relations had been very peaceful and pleasant of late, though George was not so often alone with her as in former times. The period of mourning for the girls' mother was past and many people came to the house. George himself had gradually made numerous acquaintances and led a more social life than formerly, finding interest, as Johnson had predicted, in watching people instead of poring over books. He was asked to dinner by many persons who had known his father and were anxious to make amends for having judged him unjustly, and when they had once received him into their houses, they liked him and did what they could to show it. Moreover he was modest and reticent in regard to himself and talked well of current topics. Insensibly he had begun to acquire social popularity and to forget much of his boyish cynicism. -He fancied that he went into society merely because it sometimes gave him an opportunity of meeting Constance, but he was too natural and young not to like it for itself.

"Shall we not go out?" he asked, when he found her alone in the drawing-room.

Constance looked up and smiled, as though she understood his thought. He was afraid that Grace would enter the room and spoil his visit, as had happened more than once, and Constance feared the same thing. Neither had ever said as much to the other, but there was a tacit understanding between them, and their intimacy had developed so far that Constance made no secret of wishing to be alone with him when he came to the house. She smiled in spite of herself and George smiled in return.

"Yes. We can take a turn in the Square," she said. "It will be — cooler, you know." A soft laugh seemed to explain the hesitation, and George felt very happy.

A few minutes later they were walking side by side under the great trees. Instinctively they kept away from the Fearings' house — Grace might chance to be at the window.

"It was almost a year ago," said George, suddenly.

"What?"

"That I told you I loved you. You think differently of me now, do you not?"

"A little differently, perhaps," Constance answered.

Then, feeling that she was blushing, she turned her face away and spoke rapidly. "Yes and no. I think more of you — that is to say, I think better of you. You have done so much in this year. I begin to see that you are more energetic than I fancied you were."

"Does it seem to you as though what I have done has brought us any nearer together, you and me?"

"Nearer? Perhaps. I do not quite see how you mean." The blush had disappeared, and she looked puzzled.

"I mean because I have begun — only begun — to make something like a position for myself. If I succeed I hope we shall seem nearer yet — nearer and nearer, till there shall be no parting at all."

"I think you mistake a letter in the word — you talk as though you meant dearer, more than nearer — do you not?" Constance laughed, and blushed again.

"If I said that you were making love to me — to-day, as you said a year ago — would you answer that you meant it — as I did?"

"What impertinence!" exclaimed Constance still laughing lightly.

"No — but would you?"

"I cannot tell what I should do, if you said anything so outrageous!"

"I love you. Is that outrageous and impertinent?"

"N—o. You say it very nicely — almost too nicely. I am afraid you have said it before."

"Often, though I cannot expect you to remember the exact number of repetitions. How would you say it — if you were obliged to say it? I have a good ear for a tune. I could learn your music."

"Could you?" Constance hesitated while they paused in their walk and George looked into her eyes.

She saw something there that had not been present when he had first spoken, a year ago. He had seemed cold then, even to her inexperience. Now there was both passion and tenderness in his look, and there was sadness in his face.

"You do love me now," she said softly. "I can see it."

"And you, dear — will you not say the little words?"

Again she hesitated. Then she put out her hand and touched his very gently. "I hate you, sir," she said. But she pronounced the syllables with infinite softness and delicacy, and the music of her voice could not have been more sweet if she had said "I love you, dear." Then she laughed again.

"I could hear you say that very often, without being hurt," said George tenderly.

"I only wanted to show you how I should say those other words — if I would," she answered.

"Is that all? Well — if there is a just proportion between your hatred and your love and your way of expressing them, your love must be——" he stopped.

"Must be what?"

"As great as mine. I cannot find anything stronger than that to say — nor could you, if you knew."

"So you love me, then. I wonder how long it will last? When did it begin?"

"The second time I saw you."

"Love at second sight! How romantic — so much more original than at first sight, and so much more natural. No — you must not take my hand — there are people over there — and besides, there is no reason why you should. I told you I hated you. There — walk like a sensible being and talk about your work!"

"You are a strange creature, Constance."

"Am I? Why do you call me Constance? I do not call you George — indeed I do not like the name at all."

"Nor I, if you do not — you can call me Constantine if you like. That name would be more like yours."

"I do not like my own. It makes me think of the odiously good little girls in story books. Besides, what is it? Why am I called Constance? Is it for the town in Switzerland? I was never there. Is it for the virtue I least possess?"

"As your sister is called Grace," suggested George.

"Hush! Grace is a very graceful girl. Take it in that way, and leave her alone. Am I the English for Constantia? Come, give me an explanation! Talk! Say something! You are leaving the burden of the conversation to me, and then you are not even listening!"

"I was thinking of you — I always am. What shall I talk about? You are the only subject on which I could be at all eloquent."

"You might talk about yourself, for a change," suggested Constance.

"But you say you hate me, so that you would not find an account of me agreeable, would you?"

"I think my hatred could be made very accommodating, if you would talk pleasantly — even about yourself."

"I would rather make love to you than talk."

"I have no doubt you would, but that is just what I do not want you to do. Besides, you have done it before — without any result."

"That is no reason for not trying again, is it?"

"Why try it at all?"

"Love is its own reason," said George, "and it is the reason for most other things as well. I love you and I am not in search of reasons. I love you very, very much, with all my heart — so much that I do not know how to say it. My life is full of you. You are everywhere. You are always with me. In everything I have done since I have known you I have thought of you. I have asked myself whether this would please you, whether that would bring a smile to your dear face, whether these words or those would speak to your heart and be sweet to you. You are everything the world holds for me, the sun that shines, the air I breathe. Without the thought of you I could neither think nor work. If a man can grow great by the thought of woman's love, you can make me one of the greatest — if men die of broken hearts you can kill me — you are everything to me — life, breath and happiness."

Constance was silent. He spoke passionately, and there was an accent of truth in his low, vibrating voice, that went to her heart. For one moment she almost felt that she loved him in return, as she had often dreamed of loving. That he was even now more to her than any living being, she knew already.

"You like me," he said presently. "You like me, you are fond of me, you have often told me that I am your best friend, the one of whom you think most. You let me come when I will, you let me say all that is in my heart to say, you let me tell you that I love you ——"

"It is very sweet to hear," said Constance softly.

"And it is sweet to say as well — dearest. Ah, Constance, say it once, say that it is more than friendship, more than liking, more than fondness that you feel. What can it cost you to say it?"

"Would it make you very happy?"

"It would make this world heaven."

Constance stopped in her walk, drew back a little from his side, and looked at him.

"I will say it," she said quietly. "I love you — yes, I do. No — do not start — it is not much to hear, you must not be too hopeful. I will tell you the truth — so, as we stand — no nearer. It is not friendship nor fondness, nor mere liking. It is love, but it is not what it should be. Do you know why I tell you? Because I care too much for your respect to let you think I am a miserable flirt, to let you think that I am encouraging you and drawing you on, without having the least heart in the matter. You must think me very conscientious. Perhaps I am. Yes, I have encouraged you, I have drawn you on, because I like to hear you say what you so often say of late, that you love me. It is very sweet to hear, as I told you just now. And, do you know? I wish I could say the same things to you, and feel them. But I do not love you enough, I am not sure of my love, it is greater to-day and less to-morrow, and I will not give you little where you give me so much. You know my secret now.

You may hope, if you will. I am not deceiving you. I may love you more and more, and the day when I feel that it is all strong and true and whole and sound and unchangeable I will marry you. But I will not promise. I will not run the risk so long as I feel that my love may turn again into friendship next week — or next year. Do you see? Have you understood me? Is it all clear now?"

"I understand your words, dear, but not your heart. I thank you ——"

"No. Do not thank me. Come, let us walk on, slowly. Do you know that it has been the same with you, though you will not admit it? You did not love me a year ago, as you do now, did you?"

"No. That was impossible. I love you more and more every day, every week, every month."

"A year ago it would have been quite possible for you to have forgotten me and loved some other woman. You did not look at me as you do now. Your voice had not the same ring in it."

"I daresay not — I have changed. I can feel it."

"Yes, and it is because I have watched you changing in one way, that I am afraid I may change in the other."

George was very much surprised and at the same time was made very happy by what she had told him. He had indeed suspected the truth, and it was not enough to have heard her say the words "I love you" in the calm and reasoning tone she had used. But on the other hand, there was something brilliantly honest about her confession, that filled him with hope and delight. If a woman so true once loved with all her heart, she would love longer and better and more truly than other women can. So at least thought George Wood, as he walked by her side beneath the trees in Washington Square, and glanced from time to time at her lovely blushing face.

"I thank you, dear, with all my heart," he said after a long pause.

"There is little enough to thank me for. It seems to me that I could not have done less. Would it have been honest and right to let things go on as they were going without an explanation?"

"Perhaps not. But most women would have done nothing. I understand you better now, I think — if a man can ever understand a woman at all."

"I do not understand myself," Constance answered thoughtfully. "Promise me one thing," she added, looking up quickly into his face.

"Anything in the world," he said.

"Anything? Then promise me that what I have said to-day shall make no difference in the way we meet, and that you will behave just as you did before."

"Indeed I will. What difference could it make? I do not see."

"Well, it might. Remember that we are not engaged to be married —— "

"Oh, that? Of course not. I am engaged to you, but you are not engaged to me. Is that it?"

"Better not think of any engagement at all. It can do no good. Love me if you will, but do not consider yourself bound."

"If you will tell me how I can love you without feeling bound to you, perhaps I will try and obey your commands. It must be a very complicated thing." George laughed happily.

"Well, do as you will," said Constance. "Only be honest with me, as I have been with you. If a time comes when you feel that you love me less, tell me so frankly, and let there be an end. Will you?"

"Yes. I am not afraid. The day will never come."

"Never is thought to be an old-fashioned word, I believe — like always. Will you do something else to please me — something to pay me for my honesty?"

"Anything — everything."

"Write a book, then. It is time you did it."

George did not answer at once. There was nothing which he really wished more to accomplish than what Constance asked of him, and yet, in spite of years of literary work and endless preparation, there was nothing for which he really felt himself less fitted. He was conscious that fragments of novels were constantly floating through his brain and that scenes formed themselves and conversations arranged themselves spontaneously in his mind when he least expected it; but everything was vague and unsettled, he had neither plot nor plan, neither the persons of the drama nor the scene of their action, neither beginning nor continuation, nor end. To promise to write a book now, this very year, seemed like madness. And yet he was beginning to fear lest he should put off the task until it should be too late. He was in his twenty-seventh year, and in his own estimation was approaching perilously near to thirty.

"Why do you ask me to do it now?" he inquired.

"Because it is time, and because if you go on much longer with these short things you will never do anything else."

"I only do it as a preparation, as a step. Honestly, I do not feel that I know enough to write a good book, and I should be sorry to write a bad one."

"Never mind. Make a beginning. It can do no harm to try. You have written a great deal lately and you can leave the magazines alone for a while. Shall I tell you what I would like?"

"Yes — what?"

"I would like you to write your book and bring the chapters as you write them, and read them to me one by one."

"Would you really like that?"

"Indeed I would."

"Then I will do it. I mean that I will try, for I am sure I cannot succeed. But — you did not think of that — where can we read without being interrupted? I do not propose to give your sister the benefit —— "

"In Central Park — on fine days. There are quiet places there."

"Will you go there with me alone?" George asked in some surprise.

"Yes. Why not? Have I not told you that I love you — a little."

"I bless you for it, dear," said George.

And so they parted.

CHAPTER IX.

George felt like a man who has committed himself to take part in some public competition although not properly prepared for the contest, and during the night that succeeded his last meeting with Constance he slept little. He had promised to write a book. That was bad enough, considering that he felt so little fitted for the task. But, at least, if he had undertaken to finish the work, revise it and polish it and eliminate all the errors he could discover before bringing it to Miss Fearing in its final shape, he could have comforted himself with the thought that the first follies he committed would be known only to himself. He had promised, however, to read the chapters to Constance as he wrote them, one by one, and the thought filled him with dismay. The charming prospect of numberless meetings with her was marred by the fear of being ridiculous in her eyes. It was for her alone that the book was to be written. It would be a failure and he would not even attempt to publish it, but the certainty that the public would not witness his discomfiture brought no consolation with it. Better a thousand times to be laughed at by the critics than to see a pained look of disappointment in Constance's eyes. Nevertheless he considered his promise sacred, and, after all, it was Constance who had driven him to make it. He had protested his incapacity as well as he could. She would see that he had been right and would acknowledge the wisdom of waiting a little longer before making the great attempt.

At first, he felt as though he were in a nightmare, in

a dim labyrinth from which he had pledged himself to find an escape in a given time. His nerves, for the first time in his life, played him false. He grew suddenly hot, and then as suddenly cold again. Attempting to fix his imagination, monstrous faces presented themselves before his eyes in the dark, and he heard fragments of conversation in which there were long sentences that meant nothing. He lit a candle and sat up in bed, clasping his forehead with his long, smooth fingers, and beginning to feel that he knew what despair really meant.

This then was the result of years of preparation, of patient practice with the pen, of thoughtful reading and careful study. He had always felt that he lacked the imagination necessary for producing a novel, and now he felt sure of it. Johnson had told him that he was no critic, and he had believed Johnson, because Johnson was himself the best critic he knew. What then was he? A writer of short papers and articles. Yes, he could do that. How easily now, at this very moment, could he think of half a dozen subjects for such work, and how neatly he could put them into shape, develop them in a certain number of pages and polish them to the proper degree of brilliancy!

The morning dawned and found him still searching and beating his brain for a subject. As the light increased he felt more and more nervous. It was not in his nature to put off the beginning upon which he had determined, and he knew that on that day he must write the first words of his first book, or forfeit his self-respect for ever. There was an eminently comic side to the situation, but he could not see it. His dread of being ridiculous in the eyes of the woman he loved was great enough to keep him from contemplating the absurdity of his case. His sensations became intolerable; he felt like a doomed man awaiting his execution, whose only chance of a reprieve lay in inventing a plot for a novel. He could bear it no longer, and he got out of bed and opened his window. The fresh air of the May morning rushed in and suddenly filled the room with sweetness and his excited brain with a new sense of possibilities. He sat down at his table without thinking of dressing himself, and took up his pen. A sheet of paper lay ready before him, and the habit of writing was strong in itself — too strong to be resisted. In a few minutes that white sheet would be covered with words that would mean something, and those words would be the beginning of his book, of the novel he was about to write but of the contents of which he had not the remotest conception. This was not the way he had anticipated the commencement of the work that was to lay the first stone of his reputation. He had fancied himself sitting down to that first page, calm and collected, armed with a plot already thoroughly elaborated, charmed beforehand with the characters of his own invention, carried away from the first by the spirit of the action, cheered at every page by the certainty of success, because failure was to have been excluded by the multiplicity of his precautions. And here he was, without an idea in his brain or the least subject for an excuse, beginning a romance which was to be judged step by step by the person of all others most dear to him.

George dipped his pen into the ink a second time and then glanced at the calendar. It was the fifth of May.

"Well," he said aloud, "there is luck in odd numbers. Here goes my first novel!"

And thereupon, to his own great surprise, he began writing rapidly. He did not know what was coming, he hardly knew whether his hero had black hair or brown, and as for the heroine, he had not thought of her at all. But the hero was himself and was passing a night of great anxiety and distress in a small room, in a small house, in the city of New York. The reason of his anxiety and distress was a profound secret as yet, because George had not invented it, but there was no difficulty in depicting his state of mind. The writer had just spent that very night himself, and was describing it while the sun was yet scarcely risen. He chuckled viciously as he drove his pen along the lines and wrote out the ready phrases that rushed into his brain. It was inexpressibly comic to be giving all the details of his hero's suffering without having the smallest idea of what caused it; but, as he went on, he found that his silence upon this important point was lending an uncanny air of mystery to his first chapter, and his own interest was unexpectedly aroused.

It seemed strange, too, to find himself at liberty to devote as much space as he pleased to the elaboration of details that attracted his attention, and to feel that he was not limited in space as he had hitherto been in all he wrote. Of course, when he stopped to think of what he was to do next, he was as much convinced as ever that nothing could come of his attempt beyond this first chapter. The whole affair was like a sort of trial gallop over the paper, and doubtless when he read over what he had written he would be convinced of its worthlessness. He remembered his first fiery article upon the critics, and the wholesale cutting and pruning it had required before he could even submit it to Johnson. Then, however, he had written under the influence of anger; now, he was conscious of a new pleasure in every sentence, his ideas came smoothly to the surface and his own language had a freshness which he did not recognise. In old times he had studied the manner of great writers in the attempt to improve his own, and his style had been subject to violent attacks of Carlyle and to lucid intervals of Macaulay, he had worshipped at Ruskin's exquisite shrine and had offered incense in Landor's classic temple, he had eaten of Thackeray's salt and had drunk long draughts from Dickens's loving-cup. Perhaps each had produced its effect, but now he was no longer conscious of receiving influence from any of them. For the first time in his life he was himself, for better, for worse, to fail or to succeed.   His soul and his consciousness expanded together in a new and intoxicating life, as he struck those first reckless strokes in the delicious waters of the unknown.

He forgot everything, dress, breakfast, his father, the time of day and the time of year, and when he rose from his seat he had written the first chapter of his novel. For some occult reason he had stopped suddenly and dropped his pen.   He knew instinctively that he had reached his first halting-place, and he paused for breath, left the table and went to the window.   To his astonishment the sun was already casting shadows in the little brick yard, and he knew that it must be past noon.   He looked at himself and saw that he was not dressed, then he looked at his watch and found that it was one o'clock. He rubbed his eyes, for it had all been like a dream, like a vision of fairyland, like a night spent at the play. On the table lay many pages of closely-written matter, numbered and neatly put together by sheer force of habit.   He hardly knew what they contained, and he was quite unable to recall the words that opened the first paragraph.   But he knew the last sentence by heart, for it was still ringing in his brain, and strange to say, he knew what was to come next, though he seemed not to have known it so long as he held his pen.   While he dressed himself the whole book, confused in its details but clear in its general outline, presented itself to his contemplation, and he knew that he should write it as he saw it.   It would assuredly not be a good novel, it would never be published, and he was wasting his time, but it would be a book, and he should keep his promise to Constance.   He went downstairs and found his father at luncheon, with a newspaper beside him.

"Well, George," said the old gentleman, "I thought you were never going to get up."

"I am not quite sure that I have been to bed," answered the young man.   "But I know that I have been writing since it was daylight and have had no breakfast."

"That is a bad way of beginning the day," said Jonah Wood, shaking his head. "You will derange your digestion by these habits. It is idle to try such experiments on the human frame."

"It was quite an unwilling experiment. I forgot all about eating. I had some work that had to be done and so I put it through."

"More articles?" inquired his father with kindly interest.

"I believe I am writing a book," said George. "It is a new sensation and very exhilarating, but I cannot tell you anything about it till I have got on with it further."

"A book, eh? Well, I wish you success, George. I hope you are well prepared and that you will do nothing hasty or ill considered."

"No, indeed!" exclaimed George with a laugh.

Hasty and ill considered! Could any two epithets better describe the way in which he had gone to work? What rubbish it would be when it was finished, he thought, as he attacked the cold meat and pickles. He realised that he was desperately hungry, and unaccountably gay considering that he anticipated a total failure, and it was surprising that while he believed that he had been producing trash he should be in such a hurry to finish his meal in order to produce more. Nothing, however, seemed to be of the slightest importance, except to write as fast as he could in order to have plenty of manuscript to read to Constance at the first opportunity.

That night before going to bed he sat down in a comfortable chair, lit a pipe and read over what he had written. It must be very poor stuff, of course, he considered, because he had turned it out so quickly; but he experienced one of the great pleasures of his life in reading it over. The phrases sent thrills of satisfaction through him and his hand trembled as he took up one sheet after another. It was strange that he should be able to take such delight in what must manifestly be so bad. But, bad or not, the thing was alive, and the characters were his companions, whispering in his ear the words that they were to speak, and bringing with them their individual atmospheres, while a sort of secondary and almost unconscious imagination performed the scene-shifting in a smooth and masterly fashion.

Three days later, he sat beside Constance Fearing upon a wooden bench in a retired nook in Central Park. The weather was gloriously beautiful, and the whole world smelt of violets and sunshine. Everything was fresh and peaceful, and the stillness was broken only by the voices of laughing children who played together a hundred yards away from where the pair were sitting.

"And now, begin," said Constance eagerly, as George produced his folded manuscript.

"It is horrible stuff," he said. "I had really much rather not read it."

"Shall I go away?"

"No."

"Then read!"

A great wave of timidity came over the young man in that moment. He could not account for it, for he had often read to Constance the manuscript of his short articles. But this seemed very different. He let the folded sheets rest on his knee, and gazed into the distance, seeing nothing and wishing that he might sink through the earth into his own room. To judge from the sensation in his throat, he would not be able to read at all. Then all at once, he grew cold. He had undertaken to do this thing and he must carry it through, come what might. Constance would not laugh at him, and she would be just. He wished that she were Johnson, for it would be easier.

"I am waiting," she said with a gentle smile. George laughed.

"I never was so frightened in my life," he said. "I know what stage fright is, now."

Constance looked at him, and she liked his timidity

more than she had often liked his boldness. She felt
that she loved him a little more than before. Her voice
was very soft when she spoke.

"Are you afraid of me, dear?" she asked.

The blood came to George's face. It was the first
time she had ever used an endearing expression in
speaking to him.

"Not since you have said that," he answered, opening
the sheets.

He read the first chapter, and she did not interrupt
him. Occasionally he glanced at her face. It was very
grave and thoughtful, and he could not guess what was
passing in her mind.

"That is the end of the first chapter," he said at last.
"Do you like it?"

"Go on!" she exclaimed quickly without heeding his
question.

George did as he was bidden and read on to the end of
what he had brought. Whatever Constance might think
of the work, she was evidently anxious to hear it, and
this fact at least gave him a little courage. When he
had finished, he folded up the sheets quickly and returned
them to his pocket, without looking at his companion's
face. He did not dare ask her again for her opinion and
he waited for her to speak. But she said nothing and
leaned back in her seat, apparently contemplating the
trees.

"Would you like to walk a little?" George asked in
an unsteady voice. He now took it for granted that she
was not pleased.

"Do you want to know what I think of your three
chapters?"

"Yes, please," he answered nervously.

"They are very, very good. They are as much better
than anything you have ever done before, as champagne
is better than soda-water."

"Not really!" George exclaimed in genuine and overwhelming surprise. "You are not in earnest?"

"Indeed I am," Constance answered, with some impatience. "Do you think I would say such a thing if I were not sure of it? Do you not feel it yourself? Did you not know it when you were writing?"

"No — I thought, because it was written so fast it could not be worth much. Indeed, I think so still — I am afraid that you are —— "

"Mistaken?"

"Perhaps — carried away because you like me, or because you think I ought to write well."

"Nonsense. Promise me that you will not show this book to any one until it is quite finished. I want you to take my word for it, to believe in my judgment, because I know I am right. Will you?"

"Of course I will. To whom should I show it? I think I should be ashamed."

"You need not be ashamed if you go on in that way. When will you have written more?"

"Give me three days — that will give you three chapters at least and take you well into the story. You are not going out of town yet."

"I shall not go until it is finished," said Constance with great determination. She had made up her mind that George would write better if he wrote very fast, and she meant to urge him to do his utmost.

"But that may take a long time," he objected.

"No it will not," she answered. "You would not keep me in New York when it is too hot, would you?"

"I will do my best," said George.

He kept his word and three weeks later he sat in his room, in the small hours of the morning, writing the last page of his first novel. He was in a state of indescribable excitement, though he semed to be no longer thinking at all. The pen seemed to do the work of itself and he followed the words that appeared so quickly with a feverish interest. He had not the least idea how it would all look when it was done, but something told him that it was being done in the right way. His hand flew from side to side of the paper, and then stopped suddenly, why, he could not tell. It was not possible that there should be nothing more to say, no more to add, not one word to make the completion more complete. He collected his thoughts and read the page over carefully to the end. No — there was nothing wanting, and one word more would spoil the conclusion.

"I do not understand why, I am sure," he said to himself. "But that is the end, and there is no doubt about it. So here it goes! George — Winton — Wood — May 29th."

He pushed the sheet away from him. Rather theatrical, he thought, to sign his name to it, as though it were a real book, and as though the manuscript were worth keeping. He had done it all to please Constance, and Constance was pleased. In twenty-four days he had concocted a novel — and he had never in his life enjoyed twenty-four days so much. That was because he had seen Constance so often and because this wretched scroll had amused her. Would she like the last three chapters? Of course she would. He would take her the whole manuscript and make her a present of it. That was all it could be good for. To publish such stuff would be folly, even if any publisher could be found to abet such madness. On the whole, he would prefer to throw the whole into the fire. Nobody could tell. He might be famous some day in the far future, and then when he was dead and gone and could not interfere any longer, some abominable literary executor would get hold of this thing and print it, and show the world what an egregious ass the celebrated George Winton Wood had been when he was a very young man. But Constance could have it if she liked, on condition that it was never shown to anybody.

Thereupon George tumbled into bed and slept soundly until ten o'clock on the following morning, when he gathered up his manuscript, tied it up into a neat bundle and went to meet Constance at their accustomed trysting-place in the Park.

There were some very striking passages towards the conclusion of the book, and George read them as well as he could. Indeed as many of the best speeches were put into the mouth of the hero and were supposed to be addressed to the lady of his affections, George found it very natural to speak them to Constance and to give them a very tender emphasis. It was clear, too, that Constance understood the real intention of the love-making and, to all appearance, appreciated it, for the colour came and went softly in her face, and there was sometimes a little moisture in her eyes and sometimes a light that is not caused by mere interest in an everyday novel. George wrote better than he talked, as many men do who are born writers. There was music in his phrases, but it was the music of pure nature and not the rhythm of a studied prose. That was what most struck the attention of the young girl who sat beside him, drinking in the words which she knew were meant for her, and which she felt were more beautiful than anything she had heard before.

To tell the truth, though she had spoken her admiration very frankly and forcibly, she was beginning to doubt her own ability to judge of the work. If George's talent were really as great as it now seemed to her, how had it remained concealed so long? There had been nothing to compare with this in his numerous short writings. Was this because they had not been addressed to herself, or was it for this very reason that his novel was so much more fascinating? Or was it really because he had at last found out his strength and was beginning to use it like a giant? She could not tell. She confessed to herself that she had assumed much in setting up her judgment as a standard for him in the matter. The more he had read, the more she had been amazed at his knowledge of things and men, at his easy versatility and at the power he displayed in the more dramatic parts of the book. Of one thing she felt sure. The book would be read and would be liked by the class of people with whom she associated. What the critics might think or say about it was another matter.

She had been prepared for something well done at the last, but she had not anticipated the ending — that ending which had so much surprised the writer himself in his inexperience of his own powers. His voice trembled as he read the last page, and he was not even conscious of being ashamed of showing so much feeling about the creatures of his imagination. He was aware, as in a dream that Constance's small hand was tightly clasped in his while he was reading, and then, as his voice ceased, he felt her head resting against his shoulder.

She was looking down and he could only see that there was colour in her face, but as he gazed at the tiny fair curls that were just visible to him, he saw a crystal tear fall upon his rough sleeve and glisten in the May sunlight.

"You have dropped one of your diamonds," he said, softly. "Is it for me — or for the man in the book?"

She looked up into his face with a happy smile.

"You should know best," she answered.

Her face was very near to his, and though his came nearer, she did not draw hers away. George forgot the nurses and the children in the distance. If all his assembled acquaintances had been drawn up in ranks before him, he would have forgotten their presence too. His lips touched her cheek, not timidly, nor roughly either, though he felt for one moment that his blood was on fire. Then she drew back quickly and took her hand from his.

"It is very wrong of me," she said. "Perhaps I shall never love you enough for that."

"How can you say so? Was it for the man in the book, then, after all?"

"I do not know — forget it. It may come some day ——"

"Is it nearer than it was? Is it any nearer?" George asked, very tenderly.

"I do not know. I am very foolish. Your book moved me I suppose — it is so grand, that last part, where he tells her the truth, and she sees how noble he has been all through."

"I am glad you have liked it so much. It was written to amuse you, and it has done that, at all events. So here it is. Do you care to keep it?"

Constance looked at him in surprise, not understanding what he meant.

"Of course I want it," she answered. "After it is printed give it back to me."

"Printed!" exclaimed George, contemptuously. "Do you think anybody would publish it? Do you really think I would offer it to anybody?"

"You are not serious," said the young girl, staring at him.

"Indeed I am in earnest. Do you believe a novel can be dashed off in that way, in three or four weeks and be good for anything? Why, it needs six months at least to write a book!"

"What do you call this?" Constance asked, growing suddenly cold and taking the manuscript from his hands.

"Not a book, certainly. It is a scrawl of some sort, a little better than a dime novel, a little poorer than the last thrilling tale in a cheap weekly. Whatever it is, it is not a publishable story."

Constance could not believe her ears. She did not know whether to be angry at his persistent contempt of her opinion, or to be frightened at the possibility of his being right.

"We cannot both be right," she said at last, with sudden energy. "One of us two must be an idiot — an absolute idiot — and — well, I would rather not think that I am the one, you know."

George laughed and tried to take the manuscript back, but she held it behind her and faced him.

"What are you going to do with it?" he asked, when he saw that she was determined to keep it.

"I will not tell you.   Did you not say you had written it for me?"

"Yes, but for you alone."

"Not at all.   It is my property, and I will make any use of it I like."

"Please do not show it to any one," he said very earnestly.

"I promise nothing.   It is mine to dispose of as I see fit."

"Let me look over it at least — I am sure it is full of bad English, and there are lots of words left out, and the punctuation is erratic.   Give me that chance."

"No.   I will not.   You can do it on the proof.   You are always telling me of what you do on the proofs of things."

"Constance!   For Heaven's sake give it back to me and think no more about it."

"Do you love me?"

"You know I do ——"

"And do you want me to love you? — I may, you know."

"I want nothing else — but, Constance, I beg of you ——"

"Then apply your gigantic intellect to the contemplation of what concerns you.   To be short, mind your own business, and go home."

"Please ——"

"If you are not gone before I count five, I shall hate you.   I am beginning — one — two ——"

"Well, there is one satisfaction," said George, abandoning the contest, "if you send it to a publisher to read, you will never see it again, nor hear of it."

"I will stand over him while he reads it," said Constance, laughing.   "If you are good you can take me to the carriage — if not, go away."

George walked by her side and helped her into the brougham that waited for her a short distance from the place where they had sat.   He was utterly overcome by the novelty of the situation and did not even attempt to speak.

"It is a great book," said Constance, speaking through the open window after he had shut the door. "Tell him to go home."

"I do not care a straw what it is, so long as it has pleased you. Home, John!"

"Yes sir."

And away the carriage rolled. Constance had not determined what she should do with her prize, but she was not long in making up her mind. George had often spoken of his friend Johnson, and had shown her articles written by him. It struck her that he would be the very person to whom she might apply for help. George would never suspect her of having gone to him and, from all accounts, he was an extremely reticent and judicious personage. She told the coachman to drive her to the office of the newspaper to which Johnson belonged and to beguile the time she began to read the manuscript over again from the beginning. When the carriage stopped she did not know that she had been driving for more than an hour since she had left George standing in the road in the Park.

CHAPTER X.

Constance did not find Johnson without asking her way many times, and losing it nearly as often, in the huge new building which was the residence and habitation of the newspaper. Nor did her appearance fail to excite surprise and admiration in the numerous reporters, messengers and other members of the establishment who had glimpses of her as she passed rapidly on, from corridor to corridor. It happened that Johnson was in the room allotted to his department, which was not always the case at that hour, for he did much of his work at his home.

"Come in!" he said sharply, without looking up from his writing. "Well — what is it? Oh!" as he saw Miss Fearing standing before him. "I beg your pardon, madam!"

"Are you Mr. Johnson? Am I disturbing you?" Constance asked. She was beginning to be surprised at her own audacity, and almost wished she had not come.

"Yes madam. My name is Johnson, and my time is at your service," said the pale young man, moving forward his best chair and offering it to her.

"Thank you. I will not trouble you long. I have here a novel in manuscript —— "

Johnson interrupted her promptly.

"Excuse me, madam, but to avoid all misunderstanding, I should tell you frankly from the first that we never publish fiction —— "

"No, of course not," Constance broke in. "Let me tell my story."

Johnson bowed his head and assumed an attitude of attention.

"A friend of yours," the young girl continued, "has written this book. His name is Mr. George Winton Wood —— "

"I know him very well." Johnson wondered why George had not come himself, and wondered especially how he happened to dispose of so young and beautiful an ambassadress.

"Yes — he has often told me about you," said Constance. "Very well. He has written this novel, and I have read it. He thinks it is not worth publishing, and I think it is. I want to ask a great favour of you. Will you read it yourself?"

The pale young man hesitated. He was intensely conscientious, and he feared there was something queer about the business.

"Pardon me," he said, "does Mr. Wood know that you have brought it to me?"

"No indeed! I would not have him know it for the world!"

"Then I would rather not —— "

"But you must!" Constance exclaimed energetically. "It is splendid, and he wants to burn it. It will make his reputation in a day — I assure you it will! And besides, I would not promise him not to show it. Please, please, Mr. Johnson —— "

"Well, if you are quite sure there is no promise —— "

"Oh, quite, quite sure. And will you give me your opinion very soon? If you begin to read it you will not be able to lay it down."

Johnson smiled as he thought of the hundreds of manuscripts he had read for publishers. He had never found much difficulty in laying aside any of them.

"It is true," Constance insisted. "It is a great book. There has been nothing like it for ever so many years."

"Very well, madam. Give me the screed and I will read it. When shall I send — or would you rather —— "

He stopped, not knowing whether she wished to give her name. Constance hesitated, too, and blushed faintly.

"I am Miss Fearing," she said. "I live in Washington Square. Will you write down the address? Come and see me — or are you too busy?"

"I will bring you the manuscript the day after to-morrow, Miss Fearing."

"Oh please, yes. Not later, because I cannot go out of town until I know — I mean, I want to go to Newport as soon as possible. Come after five. Will you? I mean if it is not giving you really too much trouble —— "

"Not in the least, Miss Fearing," said the pale young man with alacrity. He was thinking that for the sake of conversing a quarter of an hour with such an exceedingly amiable young lady, he would put himself to vastly more trouble than was involved in stopping at Washington Square on his way up town in the afternoon.

"Thank you. You are so kind. Good-bye, Mr. Johnson." She held out her hand, but Johnson seized his hat and prepared to accompany her.

"Let me take you to the Elevated, Miss Fearing," he said.

"Thank you very much, but I have a carriage downstairs," said Constance. "If you would show me the way — it is so very complicated."

"Certainly, Miss Fearing."

Constance wondered why he repeated her name so often, whether it was a habit he had, or whether he was nervous, or whether he thought it good manners. She was not so much impressed with him at first sight as she had expected to be. He had not said anything at all clever, though it was true that there had not been many opportunities for wit in the conversation that had taken place. He belonged to a type with which she was not familiar, and she could not help asking herself whether George had other friends like him, who, if she knew them, would call her by her name half a dozen times in three minutes, and if he had many of them whether, in the event of her marrying him, she would be expected to know them all and to like them for his sake. Not that there was anything common or vulgar about this Johnson whom George praised so much. He spoke quietly, without any especial accent, and quite without affectation. He was dressed with perfect simplicity and good taste, there was nothing awkward in his manner — indeed Constance vaguely wished that he might have shown some little awkwardness or shyness. He was evidently a man of the highest education, and George said he was a man of the highest intelligence, but as Constance gave him her hand and he closed the door of the brougham, the impression came over her with startling vividness, that Mr. Johnson was emphatically not a man she would ask to dinner. She felt sure that if she met him in society she should feel a vague surprise at his being there, though she might find it impossible to say why he should not. On the other hand, though she was aware that she put herself in his power to some extent, since it was impossible that he should not guess that her interest in George Wood was the result of something at least a little stronger than ordinary friendship,

yet she very much preferred to trust this stranger rather
than to confide in any of the men she knew in society,
not excepting John Bond himself.

At five o'clock on the day agreed upon, Constance was
informed that "a gentleman, a Mr. Johnson," had called,
saying that he came by appointment.

"You are so kind," said Constance, as he sat down
opposite to her. He held the manuscript in his hand.
"And what do you think of it? Am I not right?"

"I am very much surprised," said the pale young man.
"It is a remarkable book, Miss Fearing, and it ought to
be published at once."

Constance had felt sure of the answer, but she blushed
with pleasure, a fact which did not escape Johnson's
quiet scrutiny.

"You really think Mr. Wood has talent?" she asked,
for the sake of hearing another word of praise.

"There is more talent in one of his pages than in the
whole aggregate works of half a dozen ordinarily successful writers," Johnson answered with emphasis.

"I am so glad you think so — so glad. And what is
the first thing to be done in order to get this published?
You see, I must ask your help, now that you have given
your opinion."

"Will you leave the matter in my hands, Miss Fearing?"

Constance hesitated. There was assuredly no one who
would be more likely to do the proper thing in the matter, and yet she reflected that she knew nothing or next
to nothing of the man before her, except from George's
praise of his intelligence.

"Suppose that a publisher accepts the book," she said
warily, "what will he give Mr. Wood for it?"

"Ten per cent on the advertised retail price," Johnson
answered promptly.

"Of every copy sold, I suppose," said Constance, who
had a remarkably good head for business. "That is not
much, is it? And besides, how is one to know that the

publisher is honest? One hears such dreadful stories about those people."

Johnson laughed a little.

"Faith is the evidence of things unseen, supported by reasonable and punctual payments," he said. "Publishers are not all Cretans, Miss Fearing. There be certain just men among them who have reputations to lose."

"And none of them would do better than that by the book? But of course you know. Have you ever published anything yourself? Forgive my ignorance——"

"I once published a volume of critical essays," Johnson answered.

"What was the title? I must read it — please tell me."

"It is not worth the trouble, I assure you. The title was that — *Critical Essays* by William Johnson."

"Thank you, I will remember. And will you really do your very best for Mr. Wood's book? Do you think it could be published in a fortnight?"

"A fortnight!" exclaimed Johnson, aghast at Constance's ignorance. "Three months would be the shortest time possible."

"Three months! Dear me, what a length of time!"

Johnson rapidly explained as well as he could the principal reasons why it takes longer to publish a book than to write one. He exchanged a few more words with Constance, promising to make every effort to push on the appearance of the novel, but advising her to expect no news whatever for several months. Then he took his leave.

Half an hour later Constance was at her bookseller's.

"I want a book called *Critical Essays*, by William Johnson," she said. "Have you got it, Mr. Popples?"

She waited some time before it was brought to her. Then she pretended to look through it carefully, examining the headings of the papers that were collected in it.

"Is it worth reading?" she asked carelessly.

"Excellent, Miss Fearing," answered the grey-haired

professional bookseller. He had known Constance since she had been a mere child with a passion for Mr. Walter Crane's picture-books. "Excellent," he repeated, emphatically. "A little dry perhaps, but truly excellent."

"Has it been a success, do you know?"

"Yes, I know, Miss Fearing," answered Mr. Popples, with a meaning smile. "I know very well. I happen to know that it did not pay for the printing."

"Did the author not even get ten per cent on the advertised retail price?" Constance inquired.

Mr. Popples stared at her for a moment, evidently wondering where she had picked up the phrase. He immediately suspected her of having perpetrated a literary misdeed in one volume.

"No, Miss Fearing. I happen to know that Mr. Johnson did not get ten per cent on the advertised retail price of his book; in point of fact, he got nothing at all for it, excepting a number of very flattering notices. But excuse me, Miss Fearing, if you were thinking of venturing upon publishing anything——" His voice dropped to a confidential pitch.

"I?" exclaimed Constance.

"Well, Miss Fearing, it could be done very discreetly, you know. Just a little volume of sweet verse? Is that it, Miss Fearing? Now, you know, that kind of thing would have a run in society, and if you would like to put it into my hands, I know a publisher——"

"But, Mr. Popples," interrupted Constance, recovering from her amusement so far as to be able to interrupt the current of the bookseller's engaging offers, "I never wrote anything in my life. I asked out of sheer curiosity."

Mr. Popples smiled blandly, without the least appearance of disappointment.

"Well, well, Miss Fearing, you are quite right," he said. "In point of fact those little literary ventures of young ladies very rarely do come to much, do they? To misquote the Laureate, Miss Fearing, we might say that

'Men must write and women must read'! Eh, Miss Fearing?"

The old fellow chuckled at his bad joke, as he wrapped up the volume of *Critical Essays* by William Johnson, and handed it across the table. There were only tables in Mr. Popples's establishment; he despised counters.

"Anything else to serve you, Miss Fearing? A novel or two, for the May weather? No? Let me take it to your carriage."

"Thanks. I am walking, but I will carry it. Good evening."

"Good evening, Miss Fearing. Your parasol is here. Walking this evening! In the May weather! Good evening, Miss Fearing."

And Mr. Popples bowed his favourite customer out of his establishment, with a very kindly look in his tired old spectacled eyes.

Constance had got what she had come for. If William Johnson, author of *Critical Essays*, a journalist and a man presumably acquainted with all the ins and outs of publishing, had made nothing by his successful book, George would be doing very well in obtaining ten per cent on the advertised retail price of every copy of his novel which was sold. Constance had been mistaken when she had doubted Johnson, but she did not regret her doubt in the least. After all, she had undertaken the responsibility of George's book, and she could not conscientiously believe everything she was told by strangers concerning its chances. Mr. Popples, however, was above suspicion, and had, moreover, no reason for telling that the *Critical Essays* had brought their author no remuneration. Johnson's face, too, inspired confidence, as well as George's own trust in him. Constance felt that she had done all she could, and she accordingly made her preparations for going out of town.

She was glad to get away, in order to study herself. The habit of introspection had grown upon her, for she had encouraged herself in it, ever since she had begun to feel that George was something more to her than a friend. Her over-conscientious nature feared to make some mistake which might embitter his life as well as her own. She was in constant dread of letting herself be carried away by the impulse of a moment to say something that might bind her to marry him, before she could feel that she loved him wholly as she wished to love him. On looking back, she bitterly regretted having allowed him to kiss her cheek on that morning in the Park. She had been under the influence of a strong emotion, produced by the conclusion of his book, and she seemed in her own eyes to have acted in a way quite unworthy of herself. Had she been able to carry her analysis further, she would have discovered that behind her distrust of herself she felt a lingering distrust of George. A year earlier she had thought it possible that he was strongly attracted by her fortune. Now, however, she would have scouted the idea, if it had presented itself in that shape. But it was present, nevertheless, in a more subtle form.

"He loves me sincerely," she said to herself. "He would marry me now, if I were a pauper. But would he have loved me from the first if I had been poor?"

It was not often that she put the question, even in this way, but as it belonged to that class of vicious inquiries which it is impossible to answer, it tormented her perpetually by suggesting a whole series of doubts, useless in themselves and mischievous in their consequences. She was convinced of two things. First, that she was unaccountably influenced by George's presence to say and do things which she was determined at other times that she would never say or do; and, secondly, that whether she loved him truly or not she could not imagine herself as loving any one else nearly so much. Under these circumstances, it was clearly better that she should not see him for a considerable time. She would thus withdraw herself from the sphere of his direct influence, and she would have leisure to study and weigh her own feelings, with a view to reaching a final decision. Nevertheless she looked forward to the moment of parting from him with something that was very like pain. Contrary to her expectations, the interview passed off with little show of emotion on either side.

They talked for some time about the book, Constance assuming an air of mystery as regards its future and George speaking of it with the utmost indifference. At the last minute, when he had risen to go and was standing beside her, she laid her hand upon his arm.

"You do not think I am heartless, do you?" she asked, looking at a particular button on his coat.

"No," George answered. "I think you are very sincere. I sometimes wish you would forget to be so sincere with yourself. I wish you would let yourself run away with yourself now and then."

"That would be very wrong. It would be very unfair and unjust to you. Suppose — only suppose, you know — that I made up my mind to marry you, and then discovered when it was too late that I did not love you. Would not that be dreadful? Is it not better to wait a little longer?"

"You shall never say that I have pressed you into a decision against your will," said George, betraying in one speech his youth, his ignorance of woman in general and his almost quixotic readiness to obey Constance in anything and everything.

"You are very generous," she answered, still looking at the button. "But I will not feel that I am spoiling your life — no, let me speak — to keep you in this position much longer would be doing that, indeed it would. In six months from now you will be famous. I know it, though you laugh at me. Then you will be able to marry whom you please. I cannot marry you now, for I do not love you enough. You are free, you must not feel that I want to bind you, do you understand. You will travel this summer, for you have told me that you are going to make several visits in country-houses. If you see any one you like better than me, do not feel that you are tied by any promises. It would not break my heart, if you married some one else."

In spite of her calmness there was a slight tremor in her voice which did not escape George's ear.

"I shall never love any one else," he said simply.

"You may. I may. But waiting must have a limit——"

"Say this, Constance," said George. "Say that if, by next May, you do not love me less than you do now, you will be my wife."

"No. I must love you more. If I love you better than now, it will show that my love is always to increase, and I will marry you."

"In May?"

"In May, next year. But this is no engagement. I make no promise, and I will take none from you. You are free, and so am I, until the first of May——"

"I shall never be free again, dear," said George, happily, for he anticipated great things of the strange agreement she proposed. He put his arm about her and drew her to him very tenderly. Another second and his lips would have touched her cheek, just where they had touched it once before. But Constance drew back quickly and slipped from his arm.

"No, no," she laughed, "that is not a part of the agreement. It is far too binding."

George's face was grave and sad. Her action had given him a sharp thrust of painful disappointment, and he did his best not to hide it. Constance looked at him a moment.

"Am I not right?" she asked.

"You are always right—even when you give me pain," he answered with a shade of bitterness.

"Have I given you pain now?"

"Yes."

"Did you think, from the way I behaved, that I would let you kiss me for good-bye?"

"Yes."

"You shall not say that I hurt you, and you shall not go away believing that I deceived you," said Constance, coming back to him.

She put her two hands round his neck and drew down his willing face. Then she kissed him softly on both cheeks.

"Forgive me," she said. "I did not mean to hurt you. Good-bye — dear."

George left the house feeling very happy, but persuaded that neither he nor any other man could ever understand the heart of woman, which, after all, seemed to be the only thing in the world worth understanding. He had ample time for reflection in the course of the summer, but without the reality before him the study of the problem grew more and more perplexing.

The weather grew very warm in the end of June, and George left New York. He had written much in the course of the year and had earned enough money to give himself a rest during the hot months. He tried to persuade his father to accompany him and to spend the time by the seaside while George himself made his promised visits. But Jonah Wood declared that he preferred New York in the summer and that nothing would induce him to waste money on such folly as travelling. To tell the truth, the old gentleman had grown accustomed to rigid economy in his little house in town, but he could not look forward with any pleasure to the discomforts of second-rate hotels in second-rate places. So George went away alone.

He had already begun another book. He did not look upon his first effort in the light of a book at all, but he had tasted blood, and the thirst was upon him, and he must needs quench it. This time, however, he set himself steadily to work to do the very best he could, labouring to repress his own vivacity and trying to keep out of the fever that was threatening to carry him away outside of himself. He limited his work strictly to a small amount every day, polishing every sentence and thinking out every phrase before it was set down. Working in this way he had written about half a volume by the end of August, when he found himself in a pleasant country-house by the sea in the midst of a large party of people. He had all but forgotten his first book, and had certainly but a very dim recollection of what it contained. He looked back upon its feverish production as upon a sort of delirious dream during which he had raved in a language now strange to his memory.

One afternoon, in the midst of a game of lawn-tennis, a telegram was brought to him.

"Rob Roy and Co. publish book immediately England and America. Have undertaken that you accept royalty ten per cent retail advertised price. Wire reply. C. F."

George possessed a very considerable power of concealing his emotions, but this news was almost too much for his equanimity. He thrust the despatch into his pocket and went on playing, but he lost the game in a shameful fashion and was roundly abused by his cousin Mamie Trimm, who chanced to be his partner. Mamie and her mother were stopping in the same house, by what Mrs. Sherrington Trimm considered a rather unfortunate accident, since Mamie was far too fond of George already. In reality, the excellent hostess had an idea that George loved the girl, and as the match seemed most appropriate in her eyes, she had brought them together on purpose.

As soon as possible he slipped away, put on his flannel jacket and went to the telegraph office, reading the despatch he had received over and over again as he hurried along the path, and trying to compose his answer at the same time. Constance's message seemed amazingly neat, businesslike and concise, and he wondered whether some one else had not been concerned in the affair. The phrase about the royalty did not sound like a woman's expression, though she might have copied it from the publisher's letter.

George had formerly imagined that if his first performance were really in danger of being published, he should do everything in his power to prevent such a catastrophe. He felt no such impulse now, however. Messrs. Rob Roy and Company were very serious people, great publishers, whose name alone gave a book a chance of success. They bore an exceptional reputation in the world of books, and George knew very well that they would not publish trash. But he was not elated by the news, however much surprised he might be. It was strange, indeed, that a firm of such good judgment should have accepted his novel, but it could not but be a failure, all the same. He would get the proofs as soon as possible, and he would do what he could to make the work decently presentable by inserting plentiful improvements.

His answer to Constance's telegram was short.

"Deplore catastrophe. Pity public. Thank publisher. Agree terms. Where are proofs?   G. W."

By the time the proofs were ready, George was once more in New York, though Constance had not yet returned. He was hard at work upon his second book and looked with some disgust at the package of printed matter that lay folded as it had come, upon his table. Nevertheless he opened the bundle and looked at them.

"Confound them!" he exclaimed. "They have sent me a paged proof instead of galleys!"

It was evident that he could not insert many changes, where the matter was already arranged in book form, and he anticipated endless annoyance in pasting in extensive "riders" of writing-paper in order to get room for the vast changes he considered necessary.

An hour later he was lying back in his easy-chair reading his own novel with breathless interest. He had not yet made a correction of any kind in the text. It was not until the following day that he was able to go over it all more calmly, but even then, he found that little could be done to improve it. When he had finished, he sent the proofs back and wrote a letter to Constance.

"I have read the book over," he wrote, among other things, "and it is not so bad as I supposed. I know that it cannot be good, but I am convinced that worse novels have found their way into print, if not into notice. I take back at least one-tenth of all I said about it formerly, and I will not abuse it in the future, leaving that office to those who will doubtless command much forcible language in support of their just opinion. Am I to thank you, too? I hardly know. There are other things for which I would rather be in a position to owe you thanks. However, the die is cast, you have made a skipping-rope of the Rubicon and have whisked it under my feet without my consent. Let the poor book take its chance. Its birth was happy, may its death at least be peaceful."

To this Constance replied three weeks later.

"I am glad to see that a disposition to repentance has set in. You are wise in not abusing my book any more. You ought to be doing penance in sackcloth and ashes before that bench in Central Park on which I sat when I told you it was good. The children would all laugh at you, and throw stones at you, and I should be delighted. I am not coming to town until it is published and is a success. Grace thinks I have gone into speculations, because I get so many letters and telegrams about it. I shall not tell you what the people who read the manuscript said about it. You can find that out for yourself."

George awoke one morning to find himself, if not famous, at least the topic of the day in more countries than one. A week had not elapsed before the papers were full of notices of his book and speculations as to his personality. No one seemed to consider that George Winton Wood, the novelist, could be the same man as G. W. Wood, the signer of modest articles in the magazines. The first review called him an unknown person of surprising talent, the second did not hesitate to describe him as a man of genius, and the third — branded him as a plagiarist who had stolen his plot from a forgotten novel of the beginning of the century and had somehow — this was not clear in the article — made

capital out of the writings of Macrobius, he was a vil-
lain, a poacher, a pickpocket novelist, a literary body-
snatcher, in fact in the eyes of all but the over-lax law,
little short of a thief. George knew that sort of style,
and he read the abuse over again and again with unmitigated delight. He had done as much himself in the
good old days when the editors would let him. He did
not show this particular notice to his father, however,
and only handed him those that were favourable — and
they were many. Jonah Wood sat reading them all day
long, over and over again.

"I am very glad, George," he said, repeatedly. "I
am very proud of you. It is splendid. But do you
think all this will bring you much pecuniary remuneration?"

"Ten per cent on the advertised retail price of each
copy," was George's answer.

He entered the railway station one day and was amazed
to see the walls of the place covered with huge placards,
three feet square, bearing the name of his book and his
own, alternately, in huge black letters on a white ground.
The young man at the bookstall was doing a thriving
business. George went up to him.

"That book seems to sell," he said quietly.

"Like hot cakes," answered the vendor, offering him
his own production. "One dollar twenty-five cents."

"Thank you," said George. "I would not give so
much for a novel."

"Well, there are others will, I guess," answered the
young man. "Step aside if you please and give these
ladies a chance."

George smiled and turned away.

CHAPTER XI.

Sherrington Trimm had kept Mr. Craik's secret as well as he could, but although he had not told his wife anything positive concerning the will that had been so hastily drawn up, he had found it impossible not to convey to Totty such information about the matter as was manifestly negative. She had seen very soon that he considered the inheritance of her brother's money as an illusion, upon which he placed no faith whatever, and she had understood that in advising her not to think too much about it, he meant to do more than administer one of his customary rebukes to her covetousness. At last, she determined to know the truth and pressed him with the direct question.

"So far as I know, my dear," he answered, gravely, "you will never get that money, so you may just as well put the subject out of your mind, and be satisfied with what you have."

Neither diplomacy nor cajolery nor reproaches could force anything more definite than this from Sherrington Trimm's discreet lips, though Totty used all her weapons, and used them very cleverly, in her untiring efforts to find out the truth. Was Tom going to leave his gold to a gigantic charity? Sherry's round, pink face grew suddenly stony. Was it a hospital or an asylum for idiots? — he really might tell her! His expression never changed. Totty was in despair, and her curiosity tormented her in a way that would have done credit to the gad-fly which tortured Io of old. Neither by word, nor look, nor deed could Sherry be made to betray his brother-in-law's secret. He was utterly impenetrable, as soon as the subject was brought up, and Totty even fancied that he knew beforehand when she was about to set some carefully-devised trap for him, so ready was he to oppose her wiles.

On the other hand since old Mr. Craik had recovered, his sister had shown herself more than usually anxious to please him. In this she argued as her husband had done, saying that a man who had changed his will once might very possibly change it again. She therefore spared no pains in consulting Tom's pleasure whenever occasion offered, and she employed her best tact in making his life agreeable to him. He, on his part, was even more diverted than she intended that he should be, and he watched all her moves with inward amusement. There had never been any real sympathy between them. He had been the first child, and several others had died in infancy during a long series of years, Totty, the youngest of all, alone surviving, separated from her brother in age by nearly twenty years. From her childhood, she had always been trying to get something from him, and whenever the matters in hand did not chance to clash with his own interests, he had granted her request. Indeed, on the whole, and considering the man's grasping character, he had treated her with great generosity. Totty's gratitude, however, though always sincere, was systematically prophetic in regard to favours to come, and Tom had often wondered whether anything in the world would satisfy her.

Of late she seemed to have developed an intense interest in the means of prolonging life, and she did not fail to give him the benefit of all the newest theories on the subject. Tom, however, did not feel that he was going to die, and was more and more irritated by her officious suggestions. One day she took upon herself to be more than usually pressing. He had been suffering from a slight cold, and she had passed an anxious week."

"There is nothing for you, Tom," she said, "but a milk cure and massage. They say there is nothing like it. It is perfectly wonderful —— "

Her brother raised his bent head and looked keenly at her, while a sour smile passed over his face.

"Look here, Totty," he answered, "don't you think I should keep better in camphor?"

"How can you be so unkind!" exclaimed Totty, blushing scarlet. She rarely blushed at all, and her brother's amusement increased, until it reached its climax and broke out in a hard, rattling laugh.

After this, Mrs. Trimm grew more cautious. She talked less of remedies and cures and practised with great care a mournfully sympathetic expression. In the course of a week or two this plan also began to wear upon Craik's nerves, for she made a point of seeing him almost every day.

"I say, Totty," he said suddenly. "If anybody is dead, tell me. If you think anybody is going to die, send for the doctor. But if they are all alive and well, don't go round looking like an undertaker's wife when the season has been too healthy."

"How can you expect me to look gay?" Totty asked with a sad smile. "Do you think it makes me happy to see you going on in this way?"

"Which way?" inquired Mr. Craik with a pleased grin.

"Why, you won't have massage, and you won't take the milk cure, and you won't go to Aix, and you won't let me do anything for you, and — and I'm so unhappy! Oh Tom, how unkind you are!"

Thereupon Mrs. Trimm burst into tears with much feeling. Tom Craik looked at her for some seconds and then, being in his own house, rang the bell, sent for the housekeeper and a bottle of salts, and left Totty to recover as best she might. He knew very well that those same tears were genuine and that they had their source in anger and disappointment rather than in any sympathy for himself, and he congratulated himself upon having changed his will in time.

The old man watched George Wood's increasing success with an interest that would have surprised the latter, if he had known anything of it. It seemed as if, by assuring him the reversion of the fortune, Tom Craik had given him a push in the right direction. Since that time, indeed, George's luck had begun to turn, and now, though still unconscious of the wealth that awaited him, he was already far on the road to celebrity and independence. The lonely old man of business found a new and keen excitement in following the doings of the young fellow for whom he had secretly prepared such an overwhelming surprise. He was curious to see whether George would lose his head, whether he would turn into the fatuous idol of afternoon tea-parties, or whether he would fall into vulgar dissipation, whether he would quarrel with his father as soon as he was independent, or whether he would spend his earnings in making the old gentleman more comfortable.

Tom Craik cared very little what George did, provided he did something. What he most regretted was that he could not possibly be present to enjoy the surprise he had planned. It amused him to think out the details of his future. If, for instance, George took to drinking and gambling, losing and wasting at night what he had laboured hard to earn during the day, what a moment that would be in his life when he should be told that Tom Craik was dead, and that he was master of a great fortune. The old man chuckled over the idea, and fancied he could see George's face when, having lost more than he could possibly pay, his young eyes heavy with wine, his hand trembling with excitement, he would be making his last desperate stand at poker in the quiet upper room of a gambling club. He would lose his nerve, show his cards, lose and sink back in his chair with a stare of horror. At that moment the door would open and Sherry Trimm would come in and whisper a few words in his ear. Tom Craik liked to imagine the young fellow's bound of surprise, the stifled cry of amazement that would escape from his lips, the doubts, the fears that would beset him until the money was his, and then the sudden cure that would follow. Yes, thought Tom, there was no such cure for a spendthrift as a fortune, a real fortune. To make a man love money,

give it to him all at once in vast quantities — provided
he is not a fool. And George was no fool. He had
already proved that.

There was something satanic in Mr. Craik's speculations. He knew the world well. It amused him to
fancy George, admired and courted as a literary lion,
but feared by all judicious mammas, as only young, poor
and famous literary lions are feared. How the sentimental young ladies would crowd about him and offer
him tea, cake and plots for his novels! And how the
ring of mothers would draw their daughters away from
him and freeze him with airs politely cold! How two
or three would be gathered together in one corner of the
room to say to each other that two or three others in the
opposite corner were foolishly exposing their daughters
to the charms of an adventurer, for his books bring him
in nothing, my dear, not a cent — Mr. Popples told me
so! And how the compliment would be returned upon
the two or three, by the other two or three, with usuri-
ous compound interest. Enter to them, thought Craik,
another of their tribe — what do you think, my dears?
Tom Craik left all that money to George Wood, house,
furniture, pictures, horses and carriages — everything!
Just think! I really must go and speak to the dear
fellow! And how they would all be impelled, at the
same moment, by the same charitable thought! How
they would all glide forward, during the next quarter of
an hour, impatient to thaw with intimacy what they had
lately wished to freeze with politeness, and how, a little
later, each would say to her lovely daughter as they
went home — you know Georgey Wood — for it would be
Georgey at once — is such a good fellow, so famous and
yet so modest, so unassuming when you think how
enormously rich he is. Is he rich, mamma? Why,
yes, Kitty — or Totty, or Dottie, or Hattie, or Nelly —
he has all Tom Craik's money, and that gem of a house
to live in, and the pictures and everything, and your
cousin — or your aunt — Totty is furious about it — but

he is such a nice fellow. There would not be much
difficulty about getting a wife for the "nice fellow"
then, thought Thomas Craik.

And one or other of these things might have actually
happened, precisely as Thomas Craik foresaw if that
excellent and worthy man, Sherrington Trimm had not
unexpectedly fallen ill during the spring that followed
George Wood's first success. His illness was severe and
was undoubtedly caused by too much hard work, and was
superinduced by a moderate but unchanging taste for
canvas-backs, truffles boiled in madeira and an especial
brand of brut champagne. Sherry recovered, indeed,
but was ordered to Carlsbad in Bohemia without delay.
Totty found that it was quite impossible for her to
accompany him, considering the precarious state of her
brother's health. To leave Tom at such a time would
be absolutely heartless. Sherrington Trimm expressed
a belief that Tom would last through the summer and
perhaps through several summers, as he never did a
stroke of work and was as wiry as hairpins. He might
have added that his brother-in-law did not subsist upon
cryptogams and brut wines, but Sherry resolutely avoided
suggesting to himself that the daily consumption of
those delicacies was in any way connected with his late
illness. His wife, however, shook her head, and quoting glibly three or four medical authorities, assured him
that Tom's state was very far from satisfactory. Mamie
might go with her father, if she pleased, but Totty
would not leave the sinking ship.

"Till the rats leave it," added Mr. Trimm viciously.
His wife gave him a mournfully severe glance and left
him to make his preparations.

So he went abroad, and was busy for some time with
the improvement of his liver and the reduction of his
superfluous fat, and John Bond managed the business in
his stead. John Bond was a very fine fellow and did
well whatever he undertook, so that Mr. Trimm felt no
anxiety about their joint affairs. John himself was de-

lighted to have an opportunity of showing what he could do and he looked forward to marrying Grace Fearing in the summer, considering that his position was now sufficiently assured. He was far too sensible a man to have any scruples about taking a rich wife while he himself was poor, but he was too independent to live upon Grace's fortune, and as she was so young he had put off the wedding until he felt that he was making enough money to have all that he wanted for himself without her aid. When they were married she could do what she pleased without consulting him, and he would do as he liked without asking her advice or assistance. He considered that marriage could not be happy where either of the couple was dependent upon the other for necessities or luxuries, and that domestic peace depended largely on the exclusion of all monetary transactions between man and wife. John Bond was a typical man of his class, tall, fair, good-looking, healthy, active, energetic and keen. He had never had a day's illness nor an hour's serious annoyance. He had begun life in the right way, at the right end and in a cheerful spirit. There was no morbid sentimentality about him, no unnecessary development of the imagination, no nervousness, no shyness, no underrating of other people and no overrating of himself. He knew he could never be great or famous, and that he could only be John Bond as long as he lived. John Bond he would be, then, and nothing else, but John Bond should come to mean a great deal before he had done with the name. It should mean the keenest, most hardworking, most honest, most reliable, most clean-handed lawyer in the city of New York. There was a breezy atmosphere of truth, soap and enterprise about John Bond.

Before going abroad Sherrington Trimm asked Tom Craik whether he should tell his junior partner of the existence of a will in favour of George Wood. Mr. Craik hesitated before he answered.

"Well, Sherry," he said at last, "considering the uncertainty of human life, as Totty says, and considering that you are more used to Extra Dry than to Carlsbad waters, you had better tell him. There is no knowing what tricks that stuff may play with you. Let it be in confidence."

"Of course," said Mr. Trimm. "I would rather trust John Bond than trust myself."

The same day he imparted the secret to his partner. The latter nodded gravely and then fell into a fit of abstraction which was very rare with him. He knew a great deal of the relations existing between Constance and George Wood, and in his frank, lawyer-like distrust of people's motives, he had shared Grace's convictions about the man, though he had always treated him with indifference and always avoided speaking of him.

There are some people whose curiosity finds relief in asking questions, even though they obtain no answers to their inquiries. Totty was one of these, and she missed her husband more than she had thought possible. There had been a sort of satisfaction in tormenting him about the will, accompanied by a constant hope that he might one day forget his discretion in a fit of anger and let out the secret she so much desired to learn. Now, however, there was no one to cross-examine except Tom himself, and she would as soon have thought of asking him a direct question in the matter as of trying to make holes in a mill-stone with a darning-needle. Her curiosity had therefore no outlet and as her interest was so directly concerned at the same time, it is no wonder that she fell into a deplorably unsettled state of mind. For a long time not a ray of light illuminated the situation, and Totty actually began to grow thin under the pressure of her constant anxiety. At last she hit upon a plan for discovering the truth, so simple that she wondered how she had failed to think of it before.

Nothing indeed could be more easy of execution than what she contemplated. Her husband kept in a desk in his room a set of duplicate keys to the deed boxes in his office. Among these there must be also the one that opened her brother's box. These iron cases were kept in a strong room that opened into a small corridor between Sherrington Trimm's private study and the outer rooms where the clerks worked. Totty had her own box there, separate from her husband's and she remembered that there was one not far from hers on which was painted her brother's name. She would have no difficulty in entering the strong room alone, on pretence of depositing a deed. Was she not the wife of the senior partner, and had she not often done the same thing before? If her brother had made a new will, it must be in that box, where he kept such papers as possessed only a legal value. One glance would show her all she wanted to know, and her mind would be at rest from the wearing anxiety that now made her life almost unbearable.

She opened the desk and had no difficulty in finding the key to her brother's box. It was necessary to take something in the nature of a deed, to hold in her hand as an excuse for entering the strong room, for she did not want to take anything out of it, lest John Bond, who would see her, should chance to notice the fact and should mention it to her husband when he came back. On the other hand, it would not do to deposit an empty envelope, sealed and marked as though it contained something valuable. Mrs. Trimm never did things by halves nor was she ever so unwise as to leave traces of her tactics behind her. A palpable fraud like an empty envelope might at some future time be used against her. To take any document away from the office, even if she returned the next day, would be to expose herself to a cross-examination from Sherrington when he came home, for he knew the state of her affairs and would know also that she never needed to consult the papers she kept at the office. There was nothing for it but to have a real document of some sort. Totty sat down and thought the matter over for a quarter of an hour. Then she ordered her carriage and drove down town to the office of a broker who sometimes did business for her and her husband.

"I have made a bet," she said, with a little laugh, "and I want you to help me to win it."

The broker expressed his readiness to put the whole New York Stock Exchange at her disposal in five minutes, if that were of any use to her.

"Yes," said Totty. "I have bet that I will buy a share in something — say for a hundred dollars — that I will keep it a year and that at the end of that time it will be worth more than I gave for it."

"One way of winning the bet would be to buy several shares in different things and declare the winner afterwards. One of the lot will go up."

"That would not be fair," said Totty with a laugh. "I must say what it is I have bought. Can you give me something of the kind — now? I want to take it away with me, to show it."

The broker went out and returned a few minutes later with what she wanted, a certificate of stock to the amount of one hundred dollars, in a well-known undertaking.

"If anything has a chance, this has," said the broker, putting it into an envelope and handing it to her. "Oh no, Mrs. Trimm — never mind paying for it!" he added with a careless laugh. "Give it back to me when you have done with it."

But Totty preferred to pay her money, and did so before she departed. Ten minutes later she was at her husband's office. Her heart beat a little faster as she asked John Bond to open the strong room for her. She hoped that something would happen to occupy him while she was within.

"Let me help you," he said, entering the place with her. The strong room was lighted from above by a small skylight over a heavy grating, the boxes being arranged on shelves around the walls. John Bond went straight to the one that belonged to Totty and moved it forward a little so that she could open it. She held her envelope ostentatiously in one hand and felt for her key in her pocket with the other. She knew which was hers and which was her brother's, because Tom's had a label fastened to it, with his name, whereas her own had none.

"Thanks," she said, as she turned the key in the lock and raised the lid. "Please do not stay here, Mr. Bond, I want to look over a lot of things so as to put this I have brought into the right place."

"Well—if I cannot be of any use," said John. "I have rather a busy day. Please call me to shut the room when you have finished."

Totty breathed more freely when she was alone. She could hear John cross the corridor and enter the private office. A moment later everything was quiet. With a quick, stealthy movement, she slipped the other key into the box labelled "T. Craik," turned it and lifted the cover. Her heart was beating violently.

Fortunately for her the will was the last paper that had been put with the others and lay on the top of them all. The heavy blue envelope was sealed and marked "Will," with the date. Totty turned pale as she held it in her hands. She had not the slightest intention of destroying it, whatever it might contain, but even to break the seal and read it looked very like a criminal act. On the other hand, when she realised that she held in her hand the answer to all her questions, and that by a turn of the fingers she could satisfy all her boundless curiosity, she knew that it was of no use to attempt resistance in the face of such a temptation. She realised, indeed, that she would not be able to restore the seal, and that she must not hope to hide the fact that somebody had tampered with the will, but the thought could not deter her from carrying out her intention. As she turned, her sleeve caught on the corner of the box which she had inadvertently left open and the lid fell with a sharp snap. Instantly John Bond's footstep was heard in the corridor.

Totty had barely time to withdraw the key from her brother's box and to bury the will under her own papers when John entered the room.

"Oh!" he exclaimed in evident surprise, "I thought I heard you shut your box, and that you had finished."

"No," said Totty in an unsteady voice, bending her pale face over her documents. "The lid fell, but I opened it again. I will call you when I come out."

John returned to his work without any suspicion of what had happened. Then Totty extracted a hairpin from the coils of her brown hair and tried to lift the seal of the will from the paper to which it was so firmly attached. But she only succeeded in damaging it. There was nothing to be done but to tear the envelope. Still using her hairpin she slit open one end of the cover and drew out the document.

When she knew the contents, her face expressed unbounded surprise. It had never entered her head that Tom could leave his money to George Wood of all people in the world.

"What a fool I have been!" she exclaimed under her breath.

Then she began to reflect upon the consequences of what she had done, and her curiosity being satisfied, her fears began to assume serious proportions. Was it a criminal act that she had committed? She gazed rather helplessly at the torn envelope. It would be impossible to restore it. It would be equally impossible to put the will back into the box, loose and unsealed, without her husband's noticing the fact the next time he had occasion to look into Tom Craik's papers. He would remember very well that he had sealed it and marked it on the outside. The envelope, at least, must disappear at once. She crumpled it into as small a compass as possible and put it into her pocket. It would be very simple to burn it as soon as she was at home. But how to dispose of the will itself was a much harder matter. She dared not destroy that also, for that might turn out to be a deliberate theft, or fraud, or whatever the law called such deeds. On the other hand, her brother might ask for it at any time and if it were not in the box it could not be forthcoming, and her husband would get into trouble. It would be easy for Tom to suspect that Sherrington Trimm had destroyed the will, in order that his wife, as next of kin and only heir-at-law should get the fortune. She thought that, as it was, Tom had shown an extraordinary belief in human nature, though when she thought of her husband's known honesty she understood that nobody could mistrust him. He himself would doubtless be the first to discover the loss. What would he do? He would go to Tom and make him execute a duplicate of the will that was lost. Meanwhile, and in case Tom died before Sherrington came back, Totty could put the original in some safe place, where she could cause it to be found if necessary — behind one of those boxes, for instance, or in some corner of the strong room. Nothing that was locked up between those four walls could ever be lost. If Tom died, she would of course be told that a will had been made and was missing. John Bond would come to her in great distress, and she would come down to the office and help in the search. The scheme did not look very diplomatic, but she was sure that there was nothing else to be done. It was the only way in which she could avoid committing a crime while avoiding also the necessity of confessing to her husband that she had committed an act of supreme folly.

She folded the paper together and looked about the small room for a place in which to hide it. As she was looking she thought she heard John Bond's step again. She had no time to lose for she would not be able to get rid of him if he entered the strong room a third time. To leave it on one of the shelves would be foolish, for it might be found at any time. She could see no chink or crack into which to drop it, and John was certainly coming. Totty in her desperation thrust the paper into the bosom of her dress, shut up her own box noisily and went out.

She thought that John Bond looked at her very curiously when she went away, though the impression might

well be the result of her own guilty fears. As a matter
of fact he was surprised by her extreme pallor and was
on the point of asking if she were ill. But he reflected
that the strong room was a chilly place and that she
might be only feeling cold, and he held his tongue.

The paper seemed to burn her, and she longed to be
in her own house where she could at least lock it up
until she could come to some wise decision in regard to
it. She leaned back in her carriage in an agony of nervous fear. What if John Bond should chance to be the
one who made the discovery? He probably knew of the
existence of the will, and he very probably had seen it
and knew where it was. It was strange that she had
not thought of that. If, for instance, it happened that
he needed to look at some of her brother's papers that
very day, would he not notice the loss and suspect her?
After all, he knew as well as any one what she had to
gain by destroying the will, if he knew what it contained. How much better it would have been to put it
back in its place even without the envelope! How
much better anything would be than to feel that she
might be found out by John Bond!

She was already far up town, but in her distress she
did not recognise her whereabouts, and leaning forward
slightly looked through the window. As fate would
have it, the only person near the carriage in the street
was George Wood, who had recognised it and was trying
to get a glimpse of herself. When he saw her, he bowed
and smiled, just as he always did. Totty nodded hastily
and fell back into her seat. A feeling of sickening
despair came over her, and she closed her eyes.

CHAPTER XII.

George Wood's reputation spread rapidly. He had arrested the attention of the public, and the public was both ready and willing to be amused by him. He had finished the second of his books soon after the appearance of the first, and he had found no difficulty in selling the manuscript outright upon his own terms. It was published about the time when the events took place which have been described in the last chapter, and it obtained a wide success. It was, indeed, wholly different from its predecessor in character and presented a strong contrast to it. The first had been full of action, passionate, strange, unlike the books of the day. The second was the result of much thought and lacked almost altogether the qualities that had given such phenomenal popularity to the first. It was a calm book, almost destitute of plot and of dramatic incidents. It had been polished and adorned to the best of the young writer's ability, he had put into it the most refined of his thoughts, he had filled it with the sayings of characters more than half ideal. He had believed in it while he was writing it, but he was disappointed with it when it was finished. He had intended to bind together a nosegay of sweet-scented flowers about a central rose, and when he had finished, his nosegay seemed to him artificial, the blossoms looked to him as though they were without stems, tied to dry sticks, and the scent of them had no freshness for his nostrils. Nevertheless he knew that he had given to his work all that he possessed of beauty and refinement in the storehouse of his mind, and he looked upon the venture as final in deciding his future career. It is worse to meet with failure on the publication of a second book, when the first has taken the world by surprise, than it is to fail altogether at the very beginning. Many a polished scholar has produced one good volume;

many a refined and spiritual intelligence has painted one
lovely scene and dropped the brushes for ever, or taken
them up only to blotch and blur incongruous colours
upon a spiritless outline, searching with blind eyes for
the light that shone but once and can never shine again.
Many have shot one arrow in the air and have hit the
central mark, whose fingers scarce knew how to hold the
bow.   The first trial is one of half-reasoned, half-inspired
talent; the second shows the artist's hand; the third
and all that follow are works done in the competition
between master and master, to which neither apprentice
nor idle lover of the art can be admitted.   He whose
first great effort has been successful, and whose second
disappoints no one but himself, may safely feel that he
has found out his element and known his own strength.
He will perhaps turn out only a dull master at his craft
as years go on, or he may be but a second-rate artist, but
his apprenticeship has been completed and he will henceforth be judged by the same standard as other artists and
masters.

George Wood had followed his own instinct in lavish-
ing so much care and thought and pains upon the book that
was now to appear, and his instinct had not deceived him,
though when he saw the result he feared that he had
made the great false step that is irretrievable.   Though
many were ready to accept his work on any terms he
was pleased to name, yet he held back his manuscript for
many weeks, hesitating to give it to the world.   The
memory of his first enthusiasms blended in his mind with
the beauties of tales yet untold and darkened in his eyes
the polish of the present work.   Constance admired it
exceedingly, saying that, although nothing could ever be
to her like the first, this was so different in every way,
and yet so good, that no unpleasant comparisons could
be made between the two.   Then George took it to Johnson who kept it a long time and would give no opinion
about it until he had read every word it contained.

"This settles it," he said at last.

"For better or for worse?" George asked, looking at the pale young man's earnest face.

"For better," Johnson answered without hesitation. "You are a novelist. It is not so broad as a church-door, nor so deep as a well — but it will serve. You will never regret having published it."

So the book went to the press and in due time appeared, was tasted, criticised and declared to be good by a majority of judges, was taken up by the public, was discussed, liked and obtained a large sale. . George was congratulated by all his friends in terms of the greatest enthusiasm and he received so many invitations to dinner as made him feel that either his digestion or his career, or both, must perish in the attempt to cope with them. The dinner-party of to-day, considered as the reward of merit and the expression of good feeling, is no novelty in the history of the world's society. Little Benjamin was expected to eat twelve times as much as any of his big brothers because Joseph liked him, and the successful man of to-day is often treated with the same kindly, though destructive liberality. No one would think it enough to ask him to tea and overwhelm him with the praises of a select circle of fashionable people. He must be made to eat in order that he may understand from the fulness of his own stomach the fulness of his admirer's heart. To heap good things upon the plate of genius has been in all times considered the most practical way of expressing the public admiration — and in times not long past there was indeed a practical reason for such expression of goodwill, in that genius was liable to be very hungry even after it had been universally acknowledged. The world has more than once bowed down from a respectful distance, to the possessor of a glorious intelligence, who in his heart would have preferred a solid portion of bread and cheese to the perishable garlands of flowers scattered at his feet, or to the less corruptible monuments of bronze and stone upon which his countrymen were ready to lavish their gold after he was dead of starvation.

A change has come over the world of late, and it may be that writers themselves have been the cause of it. It is certain that since those who live by the pen have made it their business to amuse rather than to admonish and instruct their substance has been singularly increased and their path has been made enviably smooth. Their shadows not only wax and follow the outlines of a pleasant rotundity, but they are cast upon marble pavements, inlaid floors and Eastern carpets, instead of upon the dingy walls and greasy. mud of Grub Street. The star of the public amuser is in the ascendant, and his "Part of Fortune " is high in the mid-heaven.

It has been said that nothing succeeds like success, and George very soon began to find out the truth of the saying. He was ignorant of the strange possibilities of wealth that were in store for him, and the present was sufficient for all his desires, and far exceeded his former hopes. The days were gone by when he had looked upon his marriage with Constance Fearing as a delicious vision that could never be realised, and to contemplate which, even without hope, seemed to be a dangerous piece of presumption. He had now a future before him, brilliant, perhaps, but assuredly honourable and successful. At his age and with his health and strength the possibility of his being broken down by overwork or illness did not present itself to him, and, if it had, he could very well have afforded to disregard it in making his calculations. The world's face showed him one glorious catalogue of hopes and he felt that he was the man to realise them all.

And now, too, the first of May was approaching again and he looked forward to receiving a final answer from Constance. Her manner had changed little towards him during the winter, but he thought that little had been for the better. He never doubted, now, that she was most sincerely attached to him nor that it depended on anything but her own fancy, to give a name to that attachment and call it love. Surely the trial had lasted

long enough, surely she must know her own mind now,
after so many months of waiting. It was two years
since he had first told her that he loved her, a year had
passed away since she had admitted that she loved him
a little, and now the second year, the one she had asked
for as a period of probation had spent itself likewise,
bringing with it for George the first great success of his
life and doubling, trebling his chances of happiness.
His growing reputation was a bond between them, of
which they had forged every link together. Her praise
had stimulated his strength, her delicate and refined
taste had often guided the choice of his thoughts, his
power of language had found words for what was in the
hearts of both. George could no more fancy himself as
working without consulting Constance than he could
imagine what life would be without sight or hearing.
Her charm was upon him and penetrated all he did, her
beauty was the light by which he saw other women, her
voice the music that made harmony of all other sounds.
He loved her now, as women have rarely been loved, for
love had taken root in his noble and generous nature, as
a rare seed in a virgin soil, beautiful from the first and
gaining beauty as it grew in strength and fulness of
proportion. His heart had never been disturbed before,
by anything resembling true passion, there were no
reminiscences to choke the new growth, no dry and
withered stems about which the new love must twine
itself until its spreading leaves and clasping tendrils
made a rich foliage to cover the dead tree. He, she,
the world, love, reputation, were all young together, all
young and fresh, and full of the power to grow. To
think that the prospect of such happiness should be
blighted, the hope of such perfect bliss disappointed
was beyond the power of George's imagination.

The time was drawing near when he was to have his
answer. He had often done violence to himself of late
in abstaining from all question of her love. Earlier in
the year he had once or twice returned to his old way of

talking with her, but she had seemed displeased and had put him off, answering that the first of May was time enough and that she would tell him then. He had no means of knowing what was passing in her mind, for she was almost always the same Constance he had known so long, gentle, sympathising, ready with encouragement, enthusiastic concerning what he did well, suggestive when he was in doubt, thoughtful when his taste did not agree with hers. Looking back upon those long months of intimacy George knew that she had never bound herself, never uttered a promise of any sort, never directly given him to understand that she would consent to be his wife. And yet her whole life seemed to him to have been one promise since he had known her and it was treason, in his judgment, to suspect her of insincerity.

In the last days of April, he saw less of her than usual, though he could scarcely tell why. More than once, when he had hoped to find her alone, there had been visitors with her, or her sister had been present, and he had not been able to exchange a word with her without being overheard. Indeed, when Grace was established in the room he generally made his visits as short as possible. There was something in the atmosphere of the house, too, that filled him with evil forebodings. Constance often seemed abstracted and preoccupied; there appeared to be a better understanding between the sisters in regard to himself than formerly, and Grace's manner had changed. In the old days of their acquaintance she had taken little pains to conceal her dislike after she had once made up her mind that George loved her sister, her greeting had been almost haughty, her words had been few and generally ironical, her satisfaction at his departure needlessly apparent. During the last month she had relaxed the severity of her behaviour, instead of treating him more harshly as he had expected and secretly hoped. With the unerring instinct of a man who loves deeply, concerning every

one except the object of his love, George had read the
signs of the times in the face of his old enemy, and
distrusted her increasing benignity. She, at least, had
come to the conclusion that Constance would not marry
him, and seeing that the necessity for destruction was
decreasing, she allowed the sun of her smiles to pene-
trate the dark storm-clouds of her sullen anger. George
would have preferred any convulsion of the elements to
this threatened calm.

Constance Fearing was in great distress of mind. She
had not forgotten the date, nor had she any intention of
letting it pass without fulfilling her engagement and
giving George the definite answer he had so patiently
expected. The difficulty was, to know what that answer
should be. Her indecision could not be ascribed to her
indolence in studying the question. It had been constantly before her, demanding immediate solution and
tormenting her with its difficulties throughout many
long months. Her conscientious love of truth had forced
her to examine it much more closely than she would
have chosen to do had she yielded to her inclinations.
Her own happiness was no doubt vitally concerned, but
the consideration of absolute loyalty and honesty must
be first and before all things. The tremendous importance of the conclusion now daily more imminent appalled
her and frightened her out of her simplicity into the
mazes of a vicious logic; and she found the labyrinth of
her difficulties further complicated in that its ways were
intersected by the by-paths of her religious meditations.
When her reason began to grow clear, she suddenly
found it opposed to some one of a set of infallible rules
by which she had undertaken to guide her whole existence. To-day she prayed to heaven, and grace was
given her to marry George. To-morrow she would examine her heart and ascertain that she could never love
him as he deserved. Could she marry him when he was
to give so much and she had so little to offer? That
would be manifestly wrong; but in that case why had

her prayer seemed to be answered so distinctly by an impulse from the heart? She was evidently not in a state of grace, since she was inspired to do what was wrong. Selfishness must be at the bottom of it, and selfishness, as it was the sin about which she knew most, was the one within her comprehension which she the most sincerely abhorred. But if her impulse to marry George was selfish, was it not the direct utterance of her heart, and might this not be the only case in life in which she might frankly follow her own wishes? George loved her most truly. If she felt that she wished to marry him, was it not because she loved him? There was the point, again, confronting her just where she had begun the round of self-torture. Did she love him? What was the test of true love? Would she die for him? Dying for people was theatrical and out of fashion, as she had often been told. It was much more noble to live for those one loved than to die for them. Could she live for George? What did the words mean? Had she not lived for him, said her heart, during the last year, if not longer? What nonsense, exclaimed her reason — as if giving a little encouragement and a great deal of advice could be called living for a man! It meant more than that, it meant so much to her that she felt sure she could never accomplish it. Therefore she did not love him, and it must all come to an end at once.

She reproached herself bitterly for her weakness that had lasted so long. She was a mere flirt, a heartless girl who had ruined a man's life and happiness recklessly, because she did not know her own mind. She would be brave now, at last, before it was quite too late. She would confess her fault and tell him how despicable she thought herself, how she repented of her evil ways, how she would be his best and firmest friend, his sister, anything that she could be to him, except his wife. He would be hurt, pained, heartbroken for a while, but he would see how much better it had been to speak the truth.

But in the midst of her passionate self-accusation, the

thought of her own state after she should have put him away for ever, presented itself with painful distinctness. Whether she loved him or not, he was a part of her life and she felt that she could not do without him. For one moment she allowed herself to think of his face if she told him that she consented to their union at last, she could see the happy smile she loved so well and hear the vibrating tones of the voice that moved her more than other voices. Then, to her inexpressible shame, there arose before her visions of another kind, and notably the face of Johnson, the hardworking critic. All at once George seemed to be surrounded by a host of people whom she did not know and whom she did not want to know, men whom, as she remembered to have thought before, she would not have wished to see at her table, yet friends of his, faithful friends — Johnson was one at least — to whom he owed much and whom he would not allow to slip out of his existence because he had married Constance Fearing. She blushed scarlet, though she was alone, and passionate tears of anger at herself burst from her eyes. To think of that miserable consideration, she must be the most contemptible of women. Truly, the baseness of the human heart was unfathomable and shoreless as the ocean of space itself! Truly, she did not love him, if she could think such thoughts, and she must tell him so, cost what it might.

The last night came, preceding the day on which she had promised to give him her decisive answer. She had written him a word to say that he was expected, and she sat down in her own room to fight the struggle over again for the last time. The morrow was to decide, she thought, and yet it was impossible to come to any conclusion. Why had she not set the period at two years instead of one? Surely, in twelve months more she would have known her own mind, or at least have seen what course to pursue. Step by step she advanced once more into the sea of her difficulties, striving to keep her intelligence free from prejudice, and yet hoping that her heart would speak clearly. But it was of no use, the labyrinth was more confused than ever, the light less, and her strength more unsteady. If she thought, it seemed as though her thoughts would drive her mad, if she prayed, her prayers were confused and senseless.

"I cannot marry him, I cannot, I cannot!" she cried at last, utterly worn out with fatigue and anxiety.

She threw herself upon her pillows and tried to rest, while her own words still rang in her ears. She slept a little and she uttered the same cry in her sleep. By force of conscious and unconscious repetition of the phrase, it became mechanised and imposed itself upon her will. When the morning broke, she knew that she had resolved not to marry George Wood, and that her resolution was irrevocable.

To tell him so was a very different matter. She grew cold as she thought of the scene that was before her, and became conscious that her nerves were not equal to such a strain. She fancied that the decision she had reached had been the result of her strength in her struggle with herself. In reality she had succumbed to her own weakness and had abandoned the contest, feeling that it was easier to do anything negative rather than to commit herself to a bondage from which she might some day wish to escape when it should be too late. With a little more firmness of character she would have been able to shake off her doubts and to see that she really loved George very sincerely, and that to hesitate was to sacrifice everything to a morbid fear of offending her now over-delicate conscience. Even now, if she could have known herself, she would have realised that she had by no means given up all love for the man who loved her, nor all expectation of ultimately becoming his wife. She would have behaved very differently if she had been sure that she was burning her ships and cutting off all possibility of a return, or if she had known the character of the man with whom she had to deal. She had passed through a sort of nervous crisis, and her resolution was in the main, a concession to her desire to gain time. In making it she had thrown down her arms and given up the fight. The reaction that followed made it seem impossible for her to face such a scene as must ensue.

At first it struck her that the best way of getting out of the difficulty would be to write to George and tell him her decision in as few words as possible, begging him to come and see her a week later, when she would do her best to explain to him the many and good reasons which had contributed to the present result. This idea, however, she soon abandoned. It would seem most unkind to deal such a blow so suddenly and then expect him to wait so long before enlightening him further upon the subject. Face him herself, she could not. She might be weak, she thought, and she was willing to admit it; it was only to add another unworthiness to the long list with which she was ready to accuse herself. She could not, and she would not tell George herself. The only person who could undertake to bear her message was Grace.

She felt very kindly disposed to Grace, that morning. There was a satisfaction in feeling that she could think of any one without the necessity of considering the question of her marriage. Besides, Grace had opposed her increasing liking for George from the beginning, and had warned her that she would never marry him. Grace had been quite right, and as Constance was feeling particularly humble just then, she thought it would be agreeable to her pride, if she confessed the superiority of Grace's judgment. She could accuse herself before her sister of all her misdeeds without the fear of witnessing George's violent grief. Moreover it would be better for George, too, since, he would be obliged to contain himself when speaking to her sister as he would certainly not control his feelings in an interview with herself. To be short, Constance was willing in that moment to be called a coward, rather than face the man she had wronged. Her courage had failed her altogether and she was being carried rapidly down stream from one concession to another, while still trying to give an air of rectitude and self-sacrifice to all her actions. She was preparing an abyss of well-merited self-contempt for herself in the future, though her present satisfaction in her release from responsibility had dulled her real sense of right and had left only the artificialities of her morbid conscience still sensitive to the flattery of imaginary self-sacrifice.

An hour later she was alone with her sister. She had greeted her in an unusually affectionate way on entering the room, and the younger girl immediately felt that something had taken place. She herself was smiling, and cordial in her manner.

"Grace, dearest," Constance began, after some little hesitation, "I want to tell you. You have talked so much about Mr. Wood — you know, you have always been afraid that I would marry him, have you not?"

"Not lately," answered Grace with a pleasant smile.

"Well — do you know? I have thought very seriously of it, and I had decided to give him a definite answer to-day. Do you understand? I have treated him abominably, Grace — oh, I am so sorry! I wish it could all be undone — you were so right!"

"It is not too late," observed Grace. Then, seeing that there were tears in her sister's eyes, she drew nearer to her and put her arm round her waist in a comforting way. "Do not be so unhappy, Conny," she said in a tone of deep sympathy. "Men do not break their hearts nowadays —— "

"Oh, but he will, Grace! I am sure he will — and the worst of it is that I must — you know —— "

"Not at all, dear. If you like I will break it to him —— "

"Oh, Grace, what a darling you are!" cried Constance, throwing both her arms round her sister's neck and kissing her. "I did not dare to ask you, and I could not, I could not have done it myself! But you will do it very kindly, will you not? You know he has been so good and patient."

There was an odd smile on Grace's strong face when she answered, but Constance was not in a mood to notice anything disagreeable just then.

"I will break it to him very gently," said the young girl quietly. "Of course you must tell me what I am to say, more or less — an idea, you know. I cannot say bluntly that you have sent word that you have decided not to marry him, can I?"

"Oh no!" exclaimed Constance, suddenly growing very grave. "You must tell him that I feel towards him just as I always did —— "

"Is that true?"

"Of course. I always told him that I did not love him enough to marry him. You may as well know it all. A year ago, he proposed again — well, yes, it was not the first time. I told him that if on the first of May — this first of May — I loved him better than I did then, I would marry him. Well, I have thought about it, again and again, all the time, and I am sure I do not love him as I ought, if I were to marry him."

"I should think not," laughed Grace, "if it is so hard to find it out!"

"Oh, you must not laugh at me," said Constance earnestly. "It is very, very serious. Have I done right, Grace? I wish I knew! I have treated him so cruelly, so hatefully, and yet I did not mean to. I am so fond of him, I admire him so much, I like his ways — and all — I do still, you know. It is quite true. I suppose I ought to be ashamed of it — only, I am sure I never did love him, really."

"I have no idea of laughing at the affair," answered Grace. "It is serious enough, I am sure, especially for him."

"Yes — I want to make a confession to you. I want to tell you that you were quite right, that I have encouraged him and led him on and been dreadfully unkind. I am sure you think I am a mere flirt, and perfectly heartless! Is it not true? Well, I am, and it is of no use to deny it. I will never, never, do such a thing again — never! But after all, I do like him very much. I never could understand why you hated him so, from the first."

"I did not hate him. I do not hate him now," said Grace emphatically. "I did hate the idea of his marrying you, and I do still. I thought it was just as well that he should see that from the way one member of the family behaved towards him."

"He did see it!" exclaimed Constance in a tone of regret. "It is another of the things I inflicted on him."

"You? I should rather think it was I —— "

"No, it was all my fault, all, everything, from beginning to end — and you are a darling, Gracey dear, and it is so sweet of you. You will be very good to him? Yes — and if he should want to see me very much, after you have told him everything, I might come down for a minute. I should so much like to be sure that he has taken it kindly."

"If you wish it, you might see him — but I hardly think — well, do as you think best, dear."

"Thank you, darling — you know you really are a darling, though I do not always tell you so. And now, I think I will go and lie down. I never slept last night."

"Silly child!" laughed Grace, kissing her on both cheeks. "As though it mattered so much, after all."

"Oh, but it does matter," Constance said regretfully as she left the room.

When Grace Fearing was alone she went to the window and looked out thoughtfully into the fresh, morning air.

"I am very glad," she said aloud to herself. "I am very, very glad. But I would not have done it. No, not for worlds! I would rather cut off my right hand than treat a man like that!"

In that moment she pitied George Wood with all her heart.

CHAPTER XIII.

When George entered the drawing-room he was surprised to find Grace there instead of Constance, and it was with difficulty that he repressed a nervous movement of annoyance. .On that day of all others he had no desire to meet Grace Fearing, and though he imagined that her presence was accidental and that he had come before the appointed time he felt something more of resentment against the young girl than usual. He made the best of the situation, however, and put on a brave face, considering that, after all, when the happiness of a lifetime is to be decided, a delay of five minutes should not be thought too serious an affair.

Grace rose to receive him and, coming forward, held his hand in hers a second or two longer than would have been enough under ordinary circumstances. Her face was very grave and her deep brown eyes looked with an expression of profound sympathy into those of her visitor. George felt his heart sink under the anticipation of bad news.

"Is anything the matter, Miss Fearing?" he inquired anxiously. "Is your sister ill?"

"No. She is not ill. Sit down, Mr. Wood. I have something to say to you."

George felt an acute presentiment of evil, and sat down in such a position with regard to the light that he could see Grace's face better than she could see his.

"What is it?" he asked in a tone of constraint.

The young girl paused a moment, moved in her seat, which she had selected in the corner of a sofa, rested one elbow on the mahogany scroll that rose at the end of the old-fashioned piece of furniture, supported her beautifully moulded chin upon the half-closed fingers of her white hand and gazed upon George with a look of inquiring sympathy. There was nothing of nervousness nor

timidity in Grace Fearing's nature. She knew what she
was going to do and she meant to do it thoroughly,
calmly, pitilessly if necessary.

"My sister has asked me to talk with you," she began,
in her smooth, deep voice. "She is very unhappy and
she is not able to bear any more than she has borne
already."

George's face darkened, for he knew what was coming
now, as though it were already said. He opened his
lips to speak, but checked himself, reflecting that he did
not know the extent of Grace's information.

"I am very, very sorry," she continued, earnestly.
"I need not explain matters. I know all that has happened. Constance was to have given you a final answer
to-day. She could not bear to do so herself."

Grace paused an instant, and if George had been less
agitated than he was, he would have seen that her full
lips curled a little as she spoke the last words.

"She has thought it all over," she concluded. "She
does not love you, and she can never be your wife."

There was a long pause. Grace changed her position,
leaning far back among the cushions and clasping her
hands upon her knees. At the same time she ceased to
look at the young man's face, and let her sight wander
to the various objects on the other side of the room.

In the first moment, George's heart stood still. Then
it began to beat furiously, though it seemed as though
its pulsations had lost the power of propelling the blood
from its central seat. He kept his position, motionless
and outwardly calm, but his dark face grew slowly
white, leaving only black circles about his gleaming eyes,
and his scornful mouth gradually set itself like stone.
He was silent, for no words suggested themselves to his
lips, now, though they had seemed too ready a moment
earlier.

Grace felt that she must say something more. She
was perfectly conscious of his state, and if she had been
capable of fear she would have been frightened by the
magnitude of his silent anger.

"I have known that this would come," she said, softly. "I know Constance better than you can. A very long time ago, I told her that at the last minute she would refuse you. She is very unhappy. She begged me to say all this as gently as possible. She made me promise to tell you that she felt towards you just as she had always felt, that she hoped to see you very often, that she felt towards you as a sister———"

"This is too much!" exclaimed George in low and angry tones. Then forgetting himself altogether, he rose from his seat quickly and went towards the door.

Grace was on her feet as quickly as he.

"Stop!" she cried in a voice not loud, but of which the tone somehow imposed upon the angry man.

He turned suddenly and faced her as though he were at bay, but she met his look calmly and her eyes did not fall before his.

"You shall not go away like this," she said.

"Pardon me," he answered. "I think it is the best thing I can do." There was something almost like a laugh in the bitterness of his tone.

"I think not," replied Grace with much dignity.

"Can you have anything more to say to me, Miss Fearing? You, of all people? Are you not satisfied?"

"I do not understand you, and from the tone in which you speak, I would rather not. You are very angry, and you have reason to be — heaven knows! But you are wrong in being angry with me."

"Am I?" George asked, recovering some control of his voice and manner. "I am at least wrong in showing it," he added, a moment later. "Do you wish me to stay here?"

"A few minutes longer, if you will be so kind," Grace answered, sitting down again, though George remained standing before her. "You are wrong to be angry with me, Mr. Wood. I have only repeated to you my sister's words. I have done my best to tell you the truth as gently as possible."

"I do not doubt it. Your mission is not an easy one. Why did your sister not tell me the truth herself? Is she afraid of me?"

"Do you think it would have been any easier to bear, if she had told you?"

"Yes."

"Why?" Grace asked.

"Because it is better to hear such things directly than at second hand. Because it is easier to bear such words when they are spoken by those we love, than by those who hate us. Because when hearts are to be broken it is braver to do it oneself than to employ a third person."

"You do not know what you are saying. I never hated you."

"Miss Fearing," said George, who was rapidly becoming exasperated beyond endurance, "will you allow me to take my leave?"

"I never hated you," Grace repeated without heeding his question. "I never liked you, and I never was afraid to show it. But I respect you — no, do not interrupt — I respect you, more than I did, because I have found out that you have more heart than I had believed. I admire you as everybody admires you, for what you do so well. And I am sorry for you, more sorry than I can tell. If you would have my friendship, I would offer it to you — indeed you have it already, from to-day."

"I am deeply indebted to you," George answered very coldly.

"You need not even make a show of thanking me. I have done you no service, and I should regret it very much if Constance married you. Do not look surprised. My only virtue is honesty, and when I have such things to say you think that is no virtue at all. I thought very badly of you once. Forgive me, if you can. I have changed my mind. I have neither said nor done anything for a long time to influence my sister, not for nearly a year. Do you believe me?"

George was beginning to be very much surprised at

Grace's tone. He was too much under the influence of
a great emotion to reason with himself, but the truth-
fulness of her manner spoke to his heart. If she had
condoled with him, or tried to comfort him, he would
have been disgusted, but her straightforward confession
of her own feelings produced a different effect.

"I believe you," he said, wondering how he could sincerely answer such a statement with such words.

"Thank you, you are generous." Grace rose again,
and put out her hand. "Do you care to see her, before
you go?" she asked, looking into his eyes. "I will
send her to you, if you wish it."

"Yes," George answered, after a moment's hesitation.
"I will see her — please."

He was left alone for a few minutes. Though the sun
was streaming in through the window, he felt cold as he
had never felt cold in his life. His anger had, he
believed, subsided, but the sensation it had left behind
was new and strange to him. He turned as he stood
and his glance fell upon Constance's favourite chair, the
seat in which she had sat so often and so long while he
had talked with her. Then he felt a sudden pain, so
sharp that it might have seemed the last in life, and he
steadied himself by leaning on the table. It was as
though he had seen the fair young girl lying dead in
that place she loved. But she was not dead. It was
worse. Then his great wrath surged up again, sending
the blood tingling through his sinewy frame to the tips
of his strong fingers, and bringing a different mood with
it, and a sterner humour. He was a very masculine
man, incapable of being long crushed by any blow. He
was sorry, now, that he had asked to see her. Had he
felt thus five minutes earlier, he would have declined
Grace's offer and would have left the house, meaning
never to re-enter it. But it was too late and he could
no longer avoid the meeting.

At that moment the door opened, and Constance stood
before him. Her face was pale and there were traces

of tears upon her cheeks. But he was not moved to pity by any such outward signs of past emotion. She came and stood before him, and laid one delicate hand upon his sleeve, looking up timidly to his eyes. He did not move, and his expression did not change.

"Can you forgive me?" she asked in a trembling voice.

"No," he answered, bitterly. "Why should I forgive you?"

"I know I have not deserved your forgiveness," she said, piteously. "I have been very, very wrong — I have done the worst thing I ever did in my life — I have been heartless, unkind, cruel, wicked — but — but I never meant to be —— "

"It is small consolation to me to know that you did not mean it."

"Oh, do not be so hard!" she cried, the tears rising in her voice. "I did not mean it so. I never promised you anything — indeed I never did!"

"It must be a source of sincere satisfaction, to feel that your conscience is clear."

"But it is not — I want to tell you all — Grace has not told you — I like you as much as ever, there is no difference — I am still fond of you, still very fond of you!"

"Thanks."

"Oh, George, are you a stone? Will nothing move you? Cannot you see how I am suffering?"

"Yes. I see." He neither moved, nor bent his head. His lips opened and shut mechanically as though they were made of steel. She looked up again into his face and his expression terrified her.

She turned away, slowly at first, as though in despair. Then with a sudden movement she threw herself upon the sofa and buried her face in the cushions, while a violent fit of sobbing shook her light frame from head to foot. George stood still, watching her with stony eyes. For a full minute nothing was audible but the sound of her weeping.

"You are so cold," she sobbed. "Oh, George, you will break my heart!"

"You seem to be chiefly overcome by pity for yourself," he answered cruelly. "If you have anything else to say, I will wait. If not ———"

She roused herself and sat up, the tears streaming down her cheeks, her hands clasped passionately together.

"Oh, do not go! Do not go — it kills me to let you go."

"Do you think it would? In that case I will stay a little longer." He turned away and went to the window. For some minutes there was silence in the room.

"George ———" Constance began timidly. George turned sharply round.

"I am here. Can I do anything for you, Miss Fearing?"

"Cannot you say you forgive me? Can you not say one kind word?"

"Indeed, I should find it very hard."

Constance had recovered herself to some extent, and sat staring vacantly across the room, while the tears slowly dried upon her cheeks. Her courage and her pride were alike gone, and she looked the very picture of repentance and despair. But George's heart had been singularly hardened during the half-hour or more which he had spent in her house that day. Presently she began speaking in a slow, almost monotonous tone, as though she were talking with herself.

"I have been very bad," she said, "and I know it, but I have always told the truth. I never loved you enough, I never cared for you as you deserved. Did I not tell you so? Oh yes, very often — too often. I should not have told you even that I cared a little. You are the best friend I ever had — why have I lost you by loving you a little? It seems very hard. It is not that you must forgive, it is that I should have told you so that I should — you kissed me once — it was not your fault. I let you do it. There seemed so little harm — and

yet it was so wrong.   And once, because there was pain
in your face, I kissed you, as I would have kissed my
sister.   I was so fond of you — I am still, although you
are so cruel and cold.   I did think — I really hoped that
I should love you some day.   You do not believe me?
What does it matter!   You will, for I always told you
what was true — but that is it — I hoped, and I let you
see that I hoped.   It was very wrong.   Will you try —
only try to forgive me?"

"Do you not think it would be better if you would let
me leave you, Miss Fearing?" George asked, coming
suddenly forward.   "It can do very little good to talk
this matter over."

"Miss Fearing!" exclaimed the young girl with a
sigh.   "It is so long since you called me that!   Do you
want to go?   How should I keep you?   Only this, will
you think kindly of me, sometimes?   Will you sometimes
think that I helped you — only a little — to be what you
are?   Will you say 'Good-bye, Constance,' a little
kindly?"

George was moved in spite of himself, and his voice
was softer when he answered her.

"Of what use is it, to speak of these things?   You
know all that you have been to me in these years, better
than I can tell you.   It turns out that I have been nothing to you — well, then —— "

"Nothing to me!   Oh George, you have been everything — my best friend —— "   She stopped short.

His heart hardened again.   It seemed to him that
every word she spoke was in direct contradiction to her
action.

"Will you tell me one thing?" he asked, after a
pause during which she seemed to be on the point of
bursting into tears again.

"Anything you ask me," she answered.

"Have you come to this decision yourself, or has your
sister influenced you?"   His eyes sought hers and tried
to read her inmost thoughts.

"It is my own resolution," she answered without wavering. "Grace has not spoken of my marrying you for more than a year."

"I am glad that it is altogether from your own heart——"

"Can you think that I would have taken the advice of some one else?" Constance asked, reproachfully.

"I do not know. It matters very little, after all. Pardon me if I have been rude or hasty. My manners may have been a little ruffled by this—this occurrence. Good-bye."

She took his hand and tried to press it, looking again for his eyes. But he drew his fingers away quickly and was gone before she could detain him. For one moment she sat staring at the closed door. Then she once more hid her face in the deep soft cushions and sobbed aloud, more passionately than the first time.

"Oh, I know I ought to have married him, I know I really love him!" she moaned.

And so the first act of Constance Fearing's life comedy was played out and the curtain fell between her and the happiness to grasp which she lacked either the will or the passion, or both. She had acted her part with a sincerity so scrupulous that it was like a parody of truth. She had thought of marrying George Wood with delight, she had broken with him in the midst of what might be called a crisis of doubt, and she had parted from him with sincere and bitter tears, feeling that she had sacrificed all she held dear in the world to the ferocious Moloch of her conscience.

To follow the action of her intelligence any farther through the mazes of the labyrinth into which she had led it would be a labour so stupendous that no sensible person could for a moment contemplate the possibility of performing the task, and for the present Constance Fearing must be left to her tears, her meditations, and her complicated state of mind with such pity as can be spared for her weaknesses and such kind thoughts as may be bestowed by the charitable upon her gentle character. It will be easier to understand the strong passion and the bitter disappointment which agitated George Wood's powerful nature during the hours which followed the scenes just described.

His day was indeed not over yet, though he felt as though the sun had gone down upon his life before it was yet noon. He was neither morbid nor self-conscious, nor did he follow after the chimera intro-spection. He was simply and savagely angry with Constance, with himself, with the whole known and unknown world. For the time, he forgot who he was, what he was, and all that he had done or that he might be expected to do in the future. He knew that Con-stance had spoken the truth in saying that she had promised nothing. The greater madman he, to have ex-pected anything whatever! He knew that her whole life and conversation had been one long promise during nearly two years — the more despicably heartless and altogether contemptible she was, then, for since she had spoken what was true she had acted what was a lie from begin-ning to end. Forgive her? He had given her his only answer. Why should he forgive her? Were there any extenuating circumstances in her favour? Not one — and if there had been, he knew that he would have torn that one to tatters till it was unrecognisable to his sense of justice. Her tears, her pathetic voice, her timidity, even her pale face — they had all been parts of the play, harmonic chords in the grand close of lies that had ended her symphony of deception. She had even pre-pared his ears by sending Grace to him with her warm, sympathetic eyes, her rich, deep voice and her tale of spontaneous friendship. It was strange that he should have believed the other girl, even for one moment, but he admitted that he had put some faith in her words. How poor a thing was the strongest man when desper-ately hurt, ready to believe in the first mockery of sym-pathy that was offered him, ready to catch at the mere

shadow of a straw blown by the wind! Doubtless the
two sisters had concocted their comedy overnight and
had planned their speeches to produce the proper effect
upon his victimised feelings. He had singularly disappointed them both, in that case. They would have to
think longer and think more wisely the next time they
meant to deceive a man of his character. He remembered with delight every cold, hard word he had spoken,
every cruelly brutal answer he had given. He rejoiced
in every syllable saving only that "I believe you" he
had bestowed on Grace's asseverations of friendship and
esteem. And he had been weak enough to ask Constance
whether Grace had spoken the truth, as if they had not
arranged between them beforehand every sentence of each
part! That had been weakness indeed! How they would
laugh over his question when they compared notes! By
this time they were closeted together, telling each other
all he had said and done. On the whole, there could not
be much to please them, and he had found strings for
most of his short phrases after the first surprise was over.
He was glad that he disbelieved them both, and so thoroughly. If there had been one grain of belief in Constance left to him, how much he still might suffer. His
illusion had fallen, but it had fallen altogether with one
shock, in one general and overwhelming crash. There
was not one stone of his temple whole that it might be
set upon another, there was not one limb, one fragment
of his beautiful idol that might recall its loveliness. All
was gone, wholly, irrevocably, and he was glad that it
was all gone together. The ruin was so complete that
he could doubtless separate the memory of the past from
the fact of the present, and dwell upon it, live upon it,
as he would. If he met Constance now, he could behave
towards her as he would to any other woman. She was
not Constance any more. Her name roused no emotion
in his heart, the thought of her face as he had last seen
it was not connected with anything like love. Her false
face, that had been so true and honest once! He could
scorn the one and yet love the other.

If George had been less absorbed in his angry thoughts, or had known that there was anything unusual in his expression, he would not have walked up Fifth Avenue on his way from Washington Square. The times were changed since he had been able to traverse the thoroughfare of fashion in the comparative certainty of not meeting an acquaintance. Before he had gone far, he was conscious of having failed to return more than one friendly nod, and he was disgusted with himself for allowing his emotions to have got the better of his habitually quick perception. At the busy corner of Fourteenth Street he stopped upon the edge of the pavement, debating for a moment whether he should leave the Avenue and go home by the elevated road, or strike across Union Square and take a long walk in the less crowded parts of the city. Just then, a familiar and pleasant voice spoke at his elbow.

"Why, George!" exclaimed Totty Trimm. "How you look! What is the matter with you?"

"How do you do, cousin Totty? I do not understand. Is there anything the matter with my face?"

"I wish you could see yourself in the glass!" cried the little lady evidently more and more surprised at his unusual expression. "I wish you could. You are as white as a sheet, with great rings round your eyes. Where in the world have you been?"

"I? Oh, I have only been making a visit at the Fearings. I suppose I am tired."

"The Fearings?" repeated Totty, with a sweet smile. "How odd! I was just going there — walking, you see, because it is such a lovely afternoon. You won't come back with me? They won't mind seeing you twice in the same day, I daresay."

"Thanks," answered George, speaking hurriedly, and growing, if possible, paler than before. "I think it would be rather too much. Besides, I have a lot of work to do."

"Well — go in and see Mamie on your way up. She

is alone — got a horrid cold, poor child! She will be so glad and she will give you a cup of tea. You might put a little of that old whiskey of Sherry's into it. I am sure you are not well, George. You are looking wretchedly. Good-bye, dear boy."

Totty squeezed his hand warmly, gave him an earnest and affectionate look, and tripped away down the Avenue. George wondered whether she had guessed that there was anything wrong.

"I suppose I ought to have lied," he said to himself, as he crossed the thoroughfare. "They will — but I cannot do it so well. I ought to have told her that I had been to the club."

Totty Trimm had not only guessed that something was very wrong indeed. She had instinctively hit upon the truth. She, like many other people, had seen long ago that George was in love with Constance Fearing, and she had for a long time been glad of it. During the last three or four days, however, she had changed her mind in a way very unusual with her, and she had been hoping with all her heart that something would happen to break off a match that seemed to be very imminent. The matter had been so constantly in her thoughts that she referred to it everything she heard about the Fearings and about George. She had not really had the slightest intention of going to the house in Washington Square when she had met her cousin, but the determination had formed itself so quickly that she had spoken the truth in declaring it. She made up her mind to see Constance the moment she had seen George's face and had learned that he had been with her. She pursued her way with a light heart, and her nimble little feet carried her more lightly and smoothly than ever. She rang the bell and asked if the young ladies were at home.

"Yes ma'am," answered the servant, "but Miss Constance is not very well, and is gone to her room with a headache, and Miss Grace said she would see no one, ma'am."

"I just met Mr. Wood," objected Totty, "and he said he had been here this afternoon."

"Yes ma'am, and so he was, and it's since Mr. Wood left that the orders was given. Shall I take your card, Mrs. Trimm, ma'am?"

"No. It is of no use. You can tell the young ladies I called."

She descended the steps and went quickly back towards Fifth Avenue. There was great joy and triumph in her breast and her smile shed its radiance on the trees on the deserted pavement and on the stiff iron railings as she went along.

"That idiotic little fool!" said Mrs. Sherrington Trimm in her heart. "She loves him, and she has refused one of the best matches in New York because she fancies he wants her money!"

She reflected that if Mamie had the same chance, she should certainly not refuse George Winton Wood, and she determined that if diplomacy could produce the necessary situation, she would not be long in bringing matters to the proper point. There is no time when a man is so susceptible, so ready to yield to the charms of one woman as when he has just been jilted by another — so, at least, thought Totty, and her worldly experience was by no means small. And if the marriage could be brought about, why then —— Totty's radiant face expressed the rest of her thoughts better than any words could have done.

While she was making these reflections the chief figure in her panorama was striding up the Avenue at a rapid pace. Strange to say his cousin's suggestion, that he should go and see Mamie had proved rather attractive than otherwise. He did not care to walk the streets, since Totty had been so much surprised by his appearance. He might meet other acquaintances, and be obliged to speak with them. If he went home he would have to face his father, who would not fail to notice his looks, and who might guess the cause of his distress, for the old gentleman was well aware that his son was in love with Constance and hoped with all his heart that the marriage might not be far distant. Mamie would be alone, Mamie knew nothing of his doings, she was a good girl, and he liked her. To spend an hour with her would cost him nothing, as she would talk the greater part of the time, and he would gain a breathing space in which to recover from the shock he had received. She was indeed the only person whom he could have gone to see at that moment without positive suffering, except Johnson, and he was several miles from the office of Johnson's newspaper.

As he approached the Trimms' house his pace slackened, as though he were finally debating within himself upon the wisdom of making the visit. Then as he came within sight of the door he quickened his steps again and did not pause until he had rung the bell. A moment later he entered the drawing-room where Mamie Trimm was sitting in a deep easy-chair, among flowers near a sunlit window. She held a book in her hand.

"Oh George!" she cried, blushing with pleasure. "I am so glad — I am all alone."

"And what are you reading, all alone among the roses?" asked George kindly.

"What do you think?"

Then she held up the novel for him to see. It was the book he had just published.

CHAPTER XIV.

Mamie Trimm was one of those young girls of whom it is most difficult to give a true impression by describing them in the ordinary way. To say that her height was so many feet and so many inches — fewer inches than the average — that her hair was very fair, her eyes grey, her nose small, her mouth large, her complexion clear, her figure well proportioned, to say all this is to say nothing at all. A passport, in the days of passports, would have said as much, and the description would have just sufficed to point out Mamie Trimm if she had found herself in a company of tall women with black hair, large features and imposing presence. It would have been easier for a man to find her amongst a bevy of girls of her age, if he had been told that she possessed a charm of her own, which nobody could define. It would help him in his search, to be informed that she looked very delicate, but was not so in reality, that her figure was not only well proportioned, but was very exceptionally perfect and graceful, and that, but for her well-set grey eyes and her transparent complexion, her face could never have been called pretty. All these points may have combined to produce the aforesaid individuality that was especially hers. Little is known, I believe, of that fair young girl of whom Charles Lamb wrote to Landor — "Rose Aylmer has a charm that I cannot explain." Mamie Trimm was George Wood's Rose Aylmer.

He had known her all her life and there was between them that sort of intimacy which cannot exist at all unless it has begun in childhood. The patronising superiority of the schoolboy has found a foil in the clinging admiration of the little girl who is only half his age. The budding vanity of the young student has delighted in "explaining things" to the slim maiden of fourteen who believes all his words and worships all his ideas, the struggling, striving, hardworking beginner has found comfort in the unfailing friendship and devotion of the accomplished young woman whom he still thinks of as a child, and treats as a sister, not realising that the difference between fourteen and seven is one thing, while that between five or six and twenty, and eighteen or nineteen is quite another.

When a friendship of that kind has begun in childish

years it is not easily broken, even though the subsequent intercourse be occasionally interrupted. Of late, indeed, Constance Fearing had taken, and more than taken Mamie's place in George's life. He had seen his cousin constantly of course, but she had felt that he was not to her what he had been, that something she could not understand had come between them, and that she had been deprived of something that had given her pleasure. On the other hand, it was precisely at this time that she had made her first appearance in society and her life had been all at once made very full of new interests and new amusements. She had been received into the bosom of social institutions with enthusiasm, she had held her own with tact, she had danced at every ball, had received offers of marriage about once in three months, had refused them all systematically and was, on the whole, in the very prime of an American girl's social career. If her head had been turned by much admiration, she had concealed the fact very well, and the expression of her attractive face had not changed for the worse after two years of uninterrupted gaiety. She was still as innocently fond of George as she had been when a little girl and if the exigencies of continual amusement had deprived her of some of his companionship, she looked upon the circumstance with all the fatalism of the very young and the very happy, as a matter to be regretted when she had time for regrets, but inevitable and pre-destined. Her regrets, indeed, had not troubled her much until very lately, when George's growing reputation had begun to draw him into the current of society. She had seen then for the first time that there was another person, somewhat older than herself, in whose company he delighted as he had never delighted in her own, and her dormant jealousy had been almost awakened by the sight. It seemed to her that she had always had a prior right and claim upon her cousin's attention and conversation, and she did not like to find her right contested, especially by one so well able to maintain her conquests against all comers as was Constance Fearing. In her innocence, she had more than once complained to her mother that George neglected her, but hitherto her observations on the subject had received no sympathy from Mrs. Sherrington Trimm. Totty had no idea of allowing her only child to marry a penniless man of genius, and though, as has been set forth in the early part of this history she felt it incumbent upon her to do something for George, and encouraged his visits, she took care that he should meet Mamie as rarely as possible in her own house. As for Sherrington Trimm himself, he cared for none of these things. If Mamie loved George, she was welcome to marry him, if she did not there would be no hearts broken. George might come and go in his house and be welcome.

Mamie Trimm's undefinable charm doubtless covered a multitude of defects. She was of course very well educated, in the sense in which that elastic term is generally applied to all young girls of her class. It would be more true to say that she, like most of her associates, had been expensively educated. Nothing had been omitted which, according to popular social belief can contribute to the production of a refined and accomplished feminine mind. She had been taught at great pains a number of subjects of which she remembered little, but of which the transient knowledge had contributed something to the formation of her taste. She had been instructed in the French language with a care perhaps not always bestowed upon the subject in France, and the result was that she could read novels written in that tongue and, under great pressure of necessity, could converse tolerably in it, though the composition of the shortest note plunged her into a despair that would have been comic had it been less real. She possessed a shadowy acquaintance with German and knew a score of Italian words. In the department of music, seven years of study had given her some facility in playing simple dance music, and she was able to accompany a song tolerably, provided the movement were not too fast. On the other hand she danced to perfection, rode well and played a very fair game of lawn-tennis, and she got even more credit for these accomplishments than she deserved because her naturally transparent complexion and rather thin face had always made the world believe that her health was not strong.

In character she was neither very sincere, nor by any means unscrupulous. Her conscience was in a very natural state, considering her surroundings, and she represented very fairly the combination of her mother's worldly disposition with her father's cheerful, generous and loyal nature. She was far too much in love with life to be morbid, and far too sensible to invent imaginary trials. She had never thought of examining herself, any more than she would have thought of pulling off a butterfly's wings to see how they were fastened to its body. Her simplicity of ideas was dashed with a sprinkling of sentimentality which was natural enough at her age, but of which she felt so much ashamed that she hid it jealously from her father and mother and only showed a little of it to her most intimate friend when she had danced a little too long or suspected herself of having nearly accepted an offer of marriage. It was indeed with her, rather a quality than a weakness, for it sometimes made her feel that life did not consist entirely in waltzing a dozen miles every night and in talking over the race the next morning. The only visible signs of this harmless sentimentality were to be found in a secret drawer of her desk and took the shape of two or three dried flowers, a scrap of ribband and a dance programme in which the same initials were scrawled several times. She did not open the drawer at dead of night and kiss the flowers, nor hold the faded ribband to her hair, nor bedew the crumpled little bit of illuminated cardboard with her warm tears. On the contrary she rarely unlocked the receptacle unless it were to add some new memento to the collection, and on such occasions the

principal reason why she did not summarily eject the
representatives of older memories was that she felt a
sort of good-natured pity for them, as though they had
been living things and might be hurt by being thrown
away.   Her dainty room contained, indeed more than
one object given her by George Wood, from a collection
of picture-books that bore the marks of age and rough
usage, to her first tennis racquet, now battered and half
unstrung, and from that to a pretty toilet-clock set in
chiselled silver which her cousin had given her on her
last birthday, as a sort of peace-offering for his neglect.
It never would have entered her head, however, to hide
anything she had received from him in the secret drawer.
There was no sentimentality about her feelings for him,
and if there was a sentiment it was of the better and
stronger sort.   She felt that she had a right to like
George, and that his gifts had a right to be seen.   Once
or twice, of late, when she had been watching him
through the greater part of an evening while he talked
earnestly with Constance Fearing, Mamie had felt an
itching in her fingers to take everything he had given
her and to throw all into the street together; but she
had always been glad on the next day that she had not
yielded to the destructive impulse, and she had once
dreamed that, having carried out her dire intention
George had picked up the various articles in the street
and had brought them back to her, neatly packed in a
basket, with a sardonic smile on his grave face.   Since
then, she had thought more of Constance than of George's
old picture-books, the worn-out racquet, or the clock.

Mamie bore no malice against him, however, though
she was beginning to dislike the name of Fearing in a
way that surprised herself.   If George talked to her at
a party, she was always herself, graceful, winning and
happy; if he came to see her, the same words of welcome
rose to her lips and the same soft colour flashed through
the alabaster of her cheek, a colour which, as her mother
thought, should not have come so easily for one who was

already so dear. The careful Totty heard love's light tread afar off and caught the gleam of his weapons before it was yet day, her maternal anxiety had been stirred, and the devotion of the social tigress to her marriageable young had been roused almost to the point of self-sacrifice. Indeed, she had more than once interrupted some pleasant conversation of her own, in order to draw Mamie away from George, and more than once she had stayed at home when Mamie was tired with the dancing of the previous night lest in her absence George's evil genius should lead him to the house. Fortunately for her, no one had given her more constant and valuable assistance than George himself, which was the reason why Totty had not ceased to like him. Had he, on his part seemed as glad to be with Mamie, as Mamie to be with him, the claws of the tigress would have fastened upon him with sudden and terrible ferocity and would have accompanied him to the front door. There would now in all likelihood be a change in the tigress's view of the matter, and what had until lately seemed one of George's best recommendations, would soon be regarded in the light of a serious defect. The position of the invader had been very much changed since the day on which Totty Trimm had been left alone in the strong room for a quarter of an hour, and had brought away with her the last will and testament of Thomas Craik.

If George had ever in his life felt anything approaching to love for Mamie, he could not have failed to notice that Totty had done all in her power to keep the two apart during the past three years, in other words since Mamie had been of a marriageable age. But it had always been a matter of supreme indifference to him whether he were left alone with her or not, and to-day it had not struck him that Totty had never before proposed that he should go and spend an hour with her daughter when there was nobody about. Totty herself, if her heart had not been bursting with an anticipated triumph, would

have been more cautious, and would have thought twice
before making her suggestion with so much frankness.
In the moment of her meeting with him and guessing the
truth so many possibilities had suggested themselves to
her that she had not found time to reflect, and she had
for an instant entertained the idea of returning immediately from Washington Square to her own home, in
order to find George there and perform the part of the
skilful and interested consoler. A very little consideration showed her that this would be an unwise course to
pursue, and she had adopted a plan infinitely more diplomatic, of which the results will be seen and appreciated
before long. In the meantime George Wood was seated
beside Mamie and her flowers, listening to her talk, answering her remarks rather vaguely, and wondering why
he was alive, and since he was alive, why he was in that
particular place.

"You look tired, George," said the young girl, studying his face. "You look almost ill."

"Do I? I am all right. I have been doing a lot of
work lately. And you, Mamie — what is the matter?
Your mother told me just now that you had a bad cold.
I hope it is nothing serious."

"Oh, it is nothing. I wanted to read your book, and
I did not want to make visits, and I had just enough of
a cold to make a good excuse. A cold is so useful sometimes — it is just the same thing that your writing is to
you. Everybody believes it is inevitable, and then one
can do as one pleases. But you really do look dreadfully.
Have some tea — with a stick in it as papa calls it."

Mamie laughed a little at her own use of the slang
term, though her eyes showed that she was really made
anxious by George's appearance.

"Thank you," he answered. "I do not want anything,
but I am very tired, and when your mother told me you
were all alone at home I thought it would do me good to
come and stay with you a little while, if you would talk
to me."

"I am so glad you came. I have not seen much of you, lately." There was a ring of regret in her voice.

"You have been so gay. How can I get at you when you are racing through society all the year round from morning till night?"

"Oh, it is not that, George, and you know it is not! We have often been in the same gay places together, and you hardly ever come near me, though I would much rather talk with you than with all the other men."

"No you would not — and if you would, you are such a raving success, as they call it, this year, that you are always surrounded — unless you are sitting in corners with the pinks of desirability whose very shoe-strings are a cut above the 'likes o' me.' When are you going to marry, Mamie?"

"When somebody asks me, sir — she said," laughed the young girl.

"Who is somebody?"

"I do not know," answered Mamie with an infinitesimal sigh. "People have asked me, you know," she added with another laugh, "any number of them."

"But not the particular somebody who haunts your dreams?" asked George.

"He has not even begun to haunt me yet. You do, though. I dreamed of you the other night."

"You? How odd! What did you dream about me?"

"Such a funny dream!" said Mamie, leaning forward and smelling the roses beside her. It struck George as strange that the colour from the dark red petals should be thrown up into her face by the rays of the sun, though he knew something of the laws of incidence and reflection.

"I dreamed," continued Mamie, still holding the roses, "that I was very angry with you. Then I took all the things you ever gave me, the picture-books, and the broken doll, and the old racquet and the clock — by the by, it goes beautifully — and I threw them all out of my window into the street. And, of course, you were passing just at that moment, and you brought them all into the house in a basket, nicely done up in pink paper, and handed them back to me with that horrid smile you have when you are going to say something perfectly hateful."

"And then, what happened?" inquired George, who was amused in spite of himself.

"Oh, nothing. I suppose I woke just then. I laughed over it the next morning."

"But what made you so angry with me?"

"Nothing — that is — the usual thing. The way you always behave to me at parties."

George looked at her in silence for a second, before he spoke again.

"Do you mean to say that you really care," he asked, "whether I talk to you at parties, or not?"

"Of course I care!" exclaimed the young girl. "What a question!"

"I am sure I cannot see why. I am not a very amusing person. But since you would like me to talk to you, I will, as much as you please."

"It is too late now," answered Mamie, laying down the roses she had held so long. "Everything is over, or will be in a day or two, and you will not get a chance unless you come and stay with us this summer. Why do you never come and stay with us? I have often wondered."

"I was never asked," said George indifferently. "I could not well come without an invitation. And besides, I have generally been very busy in the summer."

"Did they never ask you?" inquired Mamie in evident surprise. "Mamma must have forgotten it."

"I daresay," George replied, rather dreamily. His thoughts were wandering from the conversation.

"She shall, this time," said Mamie with considerable emphasis. Then there was silence for some moments.

George did not know what she was thinking and cared very little to inquire. He was conscious that the surroundings in which he found himself were soothing to his humour, that Mamie's harmless talk was pleasant to his ear, and that if he had gone anywhere else on that afternoon, he might have committed some act of folly which would have had serious consequences. He was neither able nor anxious to understand his own state, since, whatever it might be, he desired to escape from it, and he was grateful for all external circumstances which helped his forgetfulness. He was no doubt conscious that it would be out of the question to recover from such a shock as he had received without passing through much suffering on his way to ultimate consolation. But he had been stunned and overcome by what had happened. The first passion of almost uncontrollable anger that swept over his nature had left him dull and almost apathetic for the time, bruised and willing to accept thankfully any peace that he could find.

Presently, Mamie turned the conversation to his books and talked enthusiastically of his success. She had read what he had written with greater care and understanding than he had expected of her, and she quoted whole passages from his novels, puzzling him sometimes with her questions, but pleasing him in spite of himself by her sincere and admiring appreciation. At last he rose to leave her.

"I wish you would stay," she said regretfully. But he shook his head. "Why not stay the rest of the afternoon?" she suggested. "We are not going out this evening and you could dine with us, just as you are."

This was altogether more than George wanted. He did not care to meet Totty again on that day.

"Then come again soon," said Mamie. "I have enjoyed it so much — and we are not going out of town for another fortnight."

"But you may not have another cold, Mamie," George observed.

"Oh, I will always have a cold, if you will come and sit with me," answered the young girl.

When George was once more in the street, he stared about him as though not knowing where he was. Then, when the full force of his disappointment struck him for the second time, he found it hard to believe that he had been spending an hour in careless conversation with his cousin. He looked at his watch mechanically, and saw that it was late in the afternoon. It was as though a dream had separated him from his last interview with Constance Fearing. Of that, at least, he had forgotten nothing; not a word of what she had said, or of what he had answered, had escaped his memory, every syllable was burned into the page of his day. Then came the great question, which had not suggested itself at first. Why had all this happened? What hidden reason was there in obedience to which Constance had so suddenly cast him off? Had she weakly yielded to Grace's influence? He had little faith in Grace's assurance that she had been silent, nor in Constance's confirmation of the statement. And Constance was weak. He had often suspected it, and had even wondered whether she would withstand the pressure brought to bear upon her and against himself. Yet her weakness alone did not explain what she had done. It had needed strength of some sort to face him, to tell him to his face what she had first told him through her sister's words. But her weakness had shown itself even then. She had wept and hidden her face and cried out that he was breaking her heart, when she was breaking his. George ground his heel upon the pavement.

Her heart, indeed! She had none. She was but a compound of nerves, prettiness and vanity, and he had believed her the noblest, bravest and best of women. He had lavished upon her with his lips and in his books such language as would have honoured a goddess, and she had turned out to be only a weak shallow-hearted girl, ready to break an honest man's heart, because she did not know her own mind. He cursed his ignorance of human nature and of woman's love, as he strode along the street toward his own home. Yet, rave as he would, he could not hate her, he could not get rid of the sharp pain that told him he had lost what he held most dear and was widowed of what he had loved best.

When he was at home and in his own room he became apathetic again. He had never known himself subject to such sudden changes of humour and at first he vaguely imagined that he was going to be ill, and that his nerves would break down. His father had not yet come home from the walk which was a part of his regular mode of life. George sat in his deep old easy-chair by the corner of his table and wondered whether all men who were disappointed in love felt it as he did. He tried to smoke and then gave it up in disgust. He rose from his seat and attempted to arrange the papers that lay in heaps about the place where he wrote, but his fingers trembled oddly and he felt alternately hot and cold. He opened a book and tried to read, but the effort to concentrate his attention was maddening. He felt as though he must be stifled in the little room that had always seemed a haven of rest before, and yet he did not know where to go. He threw open the window and stood looking at the rows of windows just visible above the brick wall at the back of the road. The shadows were deepening below and the sky above was already stained with the glow of evening. The prospect was not beautiful, but the cool air that fanned his face was pleasant to his senses, and he remained standing a long time, so long indeed that the stars began to shine overhead before he drew back and returned to his seat. Far down in his sensitive character there was a passionate love of all that is beautiful in the outer world. He hid it from every one, for some reason which he could not explain, but he occasionally let it show itself in his writings and the passages in which he had written of nature as it affected him, had not failed to be noticed for their peculiar grace and tenderness of execution. Since he had begun to write books all nature had become associated with Constance. He had often wondered what the connecting link could be, but had found no answer to the question. A star in the evening sky, a ray of moonlight upon rippling water, the glow of the sunset over drifted snow, the winnowed light of summer's afternoon beneath old trees, the scent of roses wet with dew, the sweet smell of country lanes when a shower had passed by — all these things acted like a charm upon him to raise the vision of Constance before his eyes. To-night he could not bear to look at the bright planet that was shining in that strip of exquisitely soft sky above the hard brick buildings.

That evening he sat with his father, a rather rare occurrence since he had gone so much into the world. The old gentleman had looked often at him during their meal but had said nothing about the careworn look of exhaustion that he saw in his son's face. It was nearly ten o'clock when Jonah Wood laid down his book by his side and raised his eyes. George had been trying to read also, and during the last half-hour he had almost succeeded.

"What is the matter with you, George?" asked his father.

George let his book fall upon his knee and stared at the lamp for a few seconds. He did not want sympathy from his father nor from any one else, but as he supposed that he would be unable to conceal his nervousness and ill temper for a long time to come, and as his father was the person who would suffer the consequences of both, he thought it better to speak out.

"I do not think there is anything the matter with my bodily condition," he answered at last. "I am afraid I am bad company, and shall be for a few days. This afternoon, Miss Fearing refused to marry me. I loved her. That is what is the matter, father."

Jonah Wood uncrossed his legs and crossed them again in the opposite way rather suddenly, which was his especial manner when he was very much surprised.

Mechanically, he took up his book again, and held it before his eyes. Then his answer came at last in a rather indistinct voice.

"I am sorry to hear that, George. I had thought she was a nice girl. But you are well out of it. I never did think much of women, anyhow, except your dear mother."

So far as words went, that was all the consolation George got from his father; but he knew better than to suppose that the old gentleman would waste language in condolence, whatever he might feel. That he felt something, and that strongly, was quite evident from the fact that although he conscientiously held his book before his eyes during the half-hour that followed, he never once turned over the page.

George rested little that night, and when at last he was sound asleep in the broad daylight, he was awakened by a knock at the door and a voice calling him. On looking out a note was handed to him, addressed in Totty Trimm's brisk, slanting, ladylike writing. He was told that an answer was expected and that the messenger was waiting.

"Dear George," Totty wrote, "I cannot tell you how amazed and distressed I am. I do hope there is not a word of truth in it, and that you will write me so at once. It is all over New York that Conny Fearing has jilted you in the most abominable way! Of course we all knew that you had been engaged ever so long. If it is true, she is a cruel, heartless, horrid girl, and she never deserved you. Do write, and do come and see me this afternoon. I shall not go out at all for fear of missing you. I am so, so sorry! In haste. — Your affectionate   TOTTY."

George swore a great oath, then and there. He had not mentioned the subject to any one but his father, so that either Constance or Grace must have told what had happened.

That the story really was "all over New York," as Totty expressed it, he found out very soon.

CHAPTER XV.

Totty had lost no time in spreading the report that everything was broken off between George Wood and Constance Fearing, and she had done it so skilfully that no one would have thought of tracing the story to her, even if it had proved to be false. She had cared very little what George himself thought about it, though she had not failed to see that he would lay the blame of the gossip on the Fearings. The two girls, indeed, could have no object in circulating a piece of news which did not reflect much credit upon themselves. What Totty wanted was in the first place that George should know that she was acquainted with his position, in order that she might play the part of the comforter and earn his gratitude. She could not of course question him directly, and she was therefore obliged to appear as having heard the tale from others; to manage this with success, it was necessary that the circumstances of the case should be made common property. Secondly, and here Totty's diplomatic instinct showed itself at its strongest, she was determined to prevent all possibility of a renewal of relations between Constance and George. In due time, probably in twenty-four hours at the latest, both Constance and Grace would know that all society was in possession of their secret. Having of course not mentioned it themselves to any one, they would feel sure that George had betrayed them in his anger, and would be proportionately incensed against him. If both parties should be so angry as to come to an explanation, which was improbable, neither would believe the other, the quarrel would grow and the breach would be widened. Totty herself would of course take George's part, as would the majority of his acquaintance, and he would be grateful for such friendly support at so trying a time.

Matters turned out very nearly as Mrs. Sherrington

Trimm had anticipated. There was, indeed, a slight variation in the programme, but she was not aware of it at the time, and if she had noticed it she would not have attached to it the importance it deserved. It chanced that Constance and Grace Fearing and George Wood had been asked with certain other guests to dine with a certain young couple lately returned from their wedding tour in Europe. The invitations had been sent and accepted on the last day of April, that is to say on the day preceding the one on which Constance gave George her definite refusal, and the dinner was to take place three or four days later. Now the young couple, who had bought a small place on the Hudson river, and were anxious to move into it as soon as possible, took advantage of those three or four days to go up to their country-house and to arrange it for themselves according to their ideas of comfort. They returned to town on the morning of their party and were of course ignorant of the gossip which had gone the rounds in their absence. Late on the afternoon of the day the husband came home from his club in great distress to tell his wife that Constance Fearing had thrown over George Wood and that the two were not on speaking terms. It was too late to make any excuse to their guests, so as to divide the party and give two separate dinners on different days. The worst of it was, that their table was small, the guests had been carefully arranged, and George Wood must inevitably sit beside either Constance or Grace. The young couple were in despair and spent all the time that was left in trying vainly to redistribute the places. There was nothing to be done but to put George next to Grace and to effect a total ignorance of the difficulty. At the last moment, however, the young hostess thought she could improve matters by speaking a word to George when he arrived. Constance and her sister, however, came before him.

"I am so sorry!" said the lady of the house quickly in the ear of the elder girl, as she drew her a little aside.

"Mr. Wood is coming — we have been out of town, and knew nothing about it — I do hope ——"

"I am very glad he is to be here," answered Constance. She was very pale and very calm.

"Oh dear!" exclaimed the hostess, growing very red. "I hope I have said nothing ——"

"Not at all," said Constance reassuring her. "There is a foolish bit of gossip in the air, I believe. The facts are very simple. Mr. Wood is a very old and good friend of mine. He asked me to marry him, and I could not. I like him very much and I hope we shall be as good friends as before. If there is any blame in the matter I wish to bear it. There he is."

The hostess felt better after this, but her curiosity was excited, and as George entered the room she went forward to meet him.

"I am so sorry," she said. "The Fearings are here and you will have to sit next to the younger one. You see we have only just heard — I am so sorry."

George Wood inclined his head a little. He was very quiet and grave.

"I may as well tell you at once," he said, "that there is not a word of truth in the story they are telling. I shall be very much obliged if you will deny it when you hear it mentioned. There never was any engagement between Miss Fearing and me."

"Well, I am very glad to hear it. Pray, forgive me," said the lady of the house.

George met Constance with his most impenetrably civil manner and they exchanged a few words which neither of them understood while they were speaking them, nor remembered afterwards. They both spoke in a low voice and the impression produced upon the many curious eyes that watched them was that they were on very good terms, though slightly embarrassed by the consciousness that they were being so much talked of.

At the dinner-table George found himself next to Grace. For some time he talked with his neighbour on his other side, then turned and inquired when Grace and her sister were going out of town, and what they intended to do during the summer. She, on her part, while answering his questions, looked at him with an air of cold and scornful surprise. Presently there was a brief burst of general conversation. Under cover of the numerous voices Grace asked a direct question.

"What do you mean by telling such a story as every one is repeating about my sister?" she asked.

George's eyes gleamed angrily for a moment and his answer came sharply and quickly.

"You would do better to ask that of yourself — or of Miss Fearing. I have said nothing."

"I do not intend to discuss the matter," Grace answered icily. "If the story were true it would hurt us and we should not tell it. But it is a lie, and a malicious lie." She turned her head away.

"Miss Fearing," George said, bending towards her a little, "I do not intend to be accused of such doings by any one. Do you understand? If you will take the trouble to ask the man on your left, he will tell you that I have denied the story everywhere during the last four days."

Grace looked at him again, and there was a change in her face. She was about to say something in reply, when the general talk, which had allowed them to speak together unheard, was interrupted by an unexpected pause.

"Do you prefer Bar Harbour to Newport, Miss Fearing?" George inquired in a tone which led every one to suppose that they had been discussing the comparative merits of watering-places.

The young girl smiled as she made an indifferent answer. She liked the man's coolness and tact in such small things. He was ready, imperturbable and determined, possessing three of the qualities which women like best in man. A little later another chance of exchanging a few words presented itself. This time Grace spoke less abruptly and coldly.

"If you have said nothing, who has told the tale?"
she asked.

"I do not know," George answered, keeping his clear
eyes fixed on hers. "If I knew, I would tell you. It
is a malicious lie, as you say, and it must have been set
afloat by a malicious person — by some one who hates
us all."

"Some one who hates my sister and me. It cannot
injure you in any way."

"That is true," said George. "It had not struck me
at first, because I was so angry at hearing the story.
Does your sister imagine that I have had anything to do
with it?"

"Yes," Grace answered, and her lip curled a little.
George misunderstood her expression and drew back
rather proudly. The fact was that Grace was thinking
how Constance accused herself every day of having been
heartless and cruel, declaring in her self-abasement that
even if George had chosen to tell the story he would have
had something very like a right to do so. Grace had no
patience with what she regarded as her sister's weakness.

To the delight of the young couple who gave the dinner it passed off very pleasantly. There had been no
apparent coldness anywhere, and they were persuaded
that none existed.

"Will you be kind enough to tell your sister what I
have told you?" said George to his neighbour as they
rose from the table.

"If you like," she answered indifferently. "Unless
you prefer to tell her yourself." The emphasis she put
on the last part of the sentence showed plainly enough
what her opinion was.

"I will," he said.

A little later in the evening he sat down by Constance
in a comparatively quiet corner of the small drawing-
room.

"Will you allow me to say a few words to you?" he
asked.

She looked at him in pathetic surprise, and if he had been a little more vain than he was, he would have seen that she was grateful to him for coming to her.

"I am always glad when you talk to me," she said, and her voice trembled perceptibly.

"You are very good," he answered in a tone that meant nothing. "I would not trouble you if it did not seem necessary. I have been talking about the matter to your sister at dinner. I wish you to know that I have had nothing to do with the invention of the story that is going the rounds of the town. I have denied it to every one, and I shall continue to deny it."

Constance glanced timidly at him, and then sighed as though she were relieved of a burden.

"I am very glad you have told me," she said.

"Do you believe me?" he asked.

"I have always believed everything you have told me, and I always shall. But if you had told some one what everybody is repeating, I should not have blamed you. It would have been almost true."

"I do not say things which are only almost true," said George very coldly.

Constance's face, which had regained some of its natural colour while she had been speaking with him, grew very white again, her lip trembled and there were tears in her eyes.

"Are you always going to treat me like this?" she asked, pronouncing the words with difficulty, as though a sob were very near.

If George had said one kind word at that moment, his history and hers might have been very different from that day onwards. But the wound he had received was yet too fresh, and moreover he was angry with her for showing a tendency to cry, and he hardened his heart.

"I trust," he answered in a chilly tone, "that we shall always meet on the best of terms."

A long silence followed, during which it was evident that Constance was struggling to maintain some appearance of outward calm. When she felt that she could command her strength, she rose and left him without another word. It was the only thing left for her to do. She could not allow herself to break down in a room full of people, before every one, and she could not stay where she was without bursting into tears. She had humbled herself to the utmost, she had been ready to offer every atonement in her power, and he had met her with a face of stone and a voice that cut her like steel.

That was the last time he saw her before the summer season. She and her sister left town suddenly the next day and George was left to his own devices and to the tender consolation that was showered upon him by Totty Trimm. But he was not easily consoled. As the days followed each other his face grew darker and his humour more gloomy. He could neither work nor read with any satisfaction and he found even less pleasure in the society of men and women than in his own. He would not have married Constance now, if she had offered herself to him, and implored him to take her. If it had been possible, he would gladly have gone abroad for a few months, in the hope of forgetting what had happened to him amidst the varied discomforts, amusements and interests of travelling. But he could not throw up certain engagements he had contracted, though at first it seemed impossible to fulfil them. He promised himself that as soon as he had accomplished his task he would start upon a journey without giving himself the trouble of defining its ultimate direction. For the present he remained sullenly in New York, sitting for hours at his table, a pen held idly between his fingers, his uneasy glance wandering from the paper before him to the wall opposite, from the wall to the window, from the window to his paper again. He was neither despondent nor hopeless. The more impossible he found it to begin his work, the more unyieldingly he forced himself to sit in his chair, the more doggedly he stuck to his determination. Writing had always seemed easy to him before, and he admitted no reason for its being hard now. With iron resolution he kept his place, revolving in his mind every situation and story of which he had ever heard and of which he believed he could make use. But though he turned, and twisted, and tormented every idea that presented itself, he could find neither plot nor scene nor characters in the aching void of his brain. Hour after hour, day after day, he did his best, growing thinner and more tired every day, feeling each afternoon more exhausted by the fruitless contest he was sustaining against the apathy of his intelligence. But when the stated time for work was past, and he pushed back the sheet of paper, sometimes as white as when he had taken it in the morning, sometimes covered with incoherent notes that were utterly worthless, when he felt that he had done his duty and could not be held responsible for the miserable result, when his head ached, his brow was furrowed, and his sight had become uncertain, then at last he gave himself up to the contemplation of his own wretchedness and to the pain of his utter desolation.

Totty did her best to attract him to her house as often as possible. He was vaguely surprised that she should stay so long in town, but he troubled himself very little about her motives, and as he never made any remark to her on the subject, she volunteered no explanation. She would have found it hard to invent one if she had been pressed to do so. It was hotter than usual at that season, and Mamie was greatly in need of a change. Totty could not plead a desire to make economies as a plausible excuse with any chance of being believed, and even Tom Craik, whose health usually supplied her with reasons for doing anything she wanted to do, had betaken himself to Newport. She seemed to have lost her interest in his movements and doings of late and had begun to express a pious belief that only heaven itself could interfere successfully when a man took such rash liberties with his health. Mr. Craik, indeed, lived by the book of arithmetic as Tybalt fought, his food was

weighed, his hours of sleep and half-hours of repose
were counted and regulated by untiring attendants, the
thickness of his clothing at each season was prescribed
by a great authority and his goings out and comings in
were registered for the latter's inspection, carriage-
makers invented vehicles for his use, upholsterers devised
systems of springs and cushions for his rest and when he
travelled he performed his journeys in his own car.   It
was hard to see where Totty could have been of use to
him, since he did not care for her conversation and
could buy better advice than she could give.

   If George had even suspected that Totty was responsible for the report spread concerning him and Constance,
he would have renounced his cousin's acquaintance and
would never have entered her house again, not even for
the sake of his old friendship with Sherry Trimm.   But
Totty's skill and tact had not been at fault.   In her own
opinion she had made one failure in her life and one
mistake.   She had failed to induce her brother to change
his will a second time, and she had committed a very
grave error in opening the will itself in the strong room
instead of bringing it home with her and lifting the seal
with a hot knife, so as to be able to restore it with all
its original appearance of security.   The question of the
will still disturbed her, but she was not a cowardly
woman, and, in particular, she was not afraid of her
husband.   If worst came to worst, she would throw herself upon his mercy, confess her curiosity, give him back
the document, clear her conscience and let him scold as
he pleased.   He would never tell any one, and Totty
was not afraid of making great personal sacrifices when
she could escape from a situation in no other way.   At
the present time the main thing of importance was to
please George, and to induce him to make her house his
own as much as possible.   If Sherrington, knowing
George's financial situation, came back and found him
engaged to marry Mamie, it would not be human in him
to bear malice against his wife for the part she had

played. Remorse she had none. She only regretted that she should have so far forgotten her caution as to do clumsily what she had done. She would neither fail nor make mistakes again.

She knew what she meant to do, and she knew how to do it. A man in George's situation is not easily affected by words no matter how skilfully put together nor how kindly uttered. He either does not hear them at all, or pays no attention to them, or puts no faith in them. It is more easy to soothe his humour by giving him agreeable surroundings than by talking to him. He has no appetite, but he may be tempted by new and exquisite dishes. He wants stimulants, and an especial brand of very dry champagne flatters his palate, exhilarates his nervous system and produces no evil consequences. He smokes more than is good for him, and in that case it is better that he should smoke the most delicate cigars imported directly from Havana, than that he should saturate his brain with nicotine from a vulgar pipe — Totty thought all pipes vulgar. The love-lorn wretch is uneasy, but he is less restless when he is left to himself for half an hour after dinner, in an absolutely perfect easy-chair, with an absolutely perfect light, and with all the newest and greatest reviews of the world at his elbow. He loathes the thought of conversational effort, but he can listen with a lazy satisfaction to the social chatter of a clever mother and her beautiful daughter, or his sensitive ears may even bear the reading aloud of the last really good novel. It is distressing to learn the next day that he does not remember the name of the hero nor the colour of the heroine's hair, and that he does not care to hear any more of the book. But it is no matter. Feminine invention is not at an end. It is late in May and there is a full moon. Would he enjoy a drive in the Park? He may smoke in the open carriage, if he pleases, for both the ladies like it. Or it will be Sunday to-morrow, and he never works on Sunday. Would it be very wrong to run out for the day on

board of Mr. Craik's yacht, instead of going to church?
Totty has the use of the yacht whenever she likes, and
she can take her prayer-book on board and read the service with Mamie while George lies on deck and meditates.
It is a steam-yacht, and it is no matter whether the
weather is calm or not. If he likes they can go up the
river with her instead. Or would he not care to have a
horse waiting for him at seven in the morning at the corner of the Park? There are all those horses eating their
heads off. It would be too early for Mamie to ride with
him, unless he positively insists upon it, but it could
not interfere with his day's work. He has forgotten to
write a letter? Poor fellow, when he has been working
all day long. It is a very important letter, and must be
posted to-night. There is the luxurious writing-table
with its perfect appliances, its shaded candles, the beautiful "Charta Perfecta," the smoothly-flowing ink that is
changed every morning, the very pens he always uses,
the spotless blotting-paper, wax and seals, if he needs
them, and postage-stamps ready and separated from each
other in the silver box — there is even a tiny sponge set
in a little stand on which to moisten them, lest the
coarse taste of the Government gum should offend the
flavour of the Turkish coffee he has been drinking. He
has an idea? He would like to make notes? There is
the library beyond that door. It is lighted. He has
only to shut himself in as long as he pleases. There is
a box of those cigars on the table. He has forgotten his
handkerchief? A touch of the bell, an order, and here
are two of dear Sherrington's, silk or linen, whichever
he prefers. The evening is hot? The windows are open
and there is a mint-julep with a straw in it by his side.
Or is it a little chilly? Everything is closed, the lamps
are all lighted, and the subtle perfume of Imperial tea
floats on the softened air. All is noiseless, perfect,
soothing, beyond description, and yet so natural that he
cannot feel as though it gave the least thought or trouble,
nor as if it were all skilfully prepared for his especial

benefit. He wonders why Sherry Trimm ever goes to the club, when he could spend his evenings in such a home, he closes his eyes, thinks of his unwritten book and asks himself whether the wheel of fortune will ever in its revolutions give him a right of his own to such supreme refinement of comfort.

It would have been strange, indeed, if George's humour had not been somewhat softened by so much luxury. He had liked what he could taste of it in his old days, when Totty had hardly ever asked him to dinner and had never expected to see him in the evening, in the days when he was a poor, unhappy nobody, and only a shabby relation of Mrs. Sherrington Trimm's. There had not been much done for his comfort then, when he came to the house, but the softness of the carpets, the elasticity of the easy-chairs and the harmony of all details had seemed delightful to him, and Totty had always been kind and goodnatured. But he had seen many things in the last two years, and was by no means so ready to be pleased as he had been when his only evening coat had been in a chronic state of repair. He had eaten terrapin and canvas-back off old Saxon china, and he had looked upon the champagne when it was of the most expensive quality. He had dined in grandeur with men whose millions were legion, and he had supped with epicures who knew what they got for their money. He had seen all sorts of society in his native city, all sorts of vulgar display, all sorts of unostentatious but enormously expensive luxury, all sorts of gilded splendour, and all sorts of faultless refinements in taste. But now, after he had dined and spent the evening with Totty half a dozen times in the course of a fortnight, he was ready to admit that he had never been in an establishment so perfect at all points, so quietly managed, so absolutely comfortable and so unpretentiously sybaritic in all its details. Totty and her husband were undoubtedly rich, but they were no richer than hundreds of people he knew. It was not money alone that produced the results he saw, and the certainty that the household was managed upon a sort of artistic principle of enjoyment gave him intense satisfaction. There was the same difference between Totty's way of living and that of most of her friends, that there is between a piece of work done by hand and the stereotyped copy of it made by machinery, the same difference there is between an illuminated manuscript and its lithographed fac-simile. The one is full of the individuality of the great artist, the other presents the perfection of execution without inspiration. The one charms, the other only pleases.

George appreciated most thoroughly at the end of the first week everything he ate, drank, felt and saw at his cousin's house, and what he heard was by no means as wearisome to his intellignce as he had supposed that it must be. Totty was far too clever a woman to flatter him openly, for she was keen enough to perceive that he was one of those men who feel a sort of repulsion for the work they have done and who put little faith in the judgment of others concerning it. She soon found out that he did not care to see his books lying upon the drawing-room table and that he suspected her of leaving them there with the deliberate intention of flattering him. They disappeared into the shelves of the library and were seen no more. But when George was reading the papers or a review — a form of rudeness in which she constantly encouraged him, she occasionally took the opportunity of introducing into her quiet conversation with Mamie some expression or some thought which he had used or developed in his writings. She avoided quotation, which she had always considered vulgar, and exercised her ingenuity in letting his favourite ideas fall from her lips in a perfectly natural manner. Though he was not supposed to be listening, he often heard her remarks, and was unconsciously pleased. The subtlety of the flatterer could go no further. Nor was that part of the talk which concerned himself neither directly nor indirectly by any means tiresome. Totty possessed very good powers of

conversation, and could talk very much better than most
women when she pleased. If she pretended to abhor the
name of culture and generally affected an air of indifference to everything that did not affect her neighbours or
herself, she did so with a wise premeditation and an
excellent judgment of her hearers' capacities. But her
own husband was fond of more intelligent subjects, and
was a man of varied experience and wide reading, who
liked to talk of what he read and saw. Totty's memory
was excellent, and as she gave herself almost as much
trouble to please Sherrington as she was now taking to
please George, she had acquired the art of amusing her
husband without any apparent exertion. What she said
was never very profound, unless she had got it by heart,
but the matter of it was generally clear and very fairly
well expressed.

As for Mamie, she was perfectly happy, for she was
unconsciously very much in love with George, and to see
him so often and in such intimacy was inexpressibly delightful. It was a pleasure even to see him sitting silent
in his chair, it was happiness to hear him speak and it
was positive joy to wait upon him. She had been more
disturbed than she had been aware by his evident devotion to Constance Fearing during the winter. The
gossip about the broken engagement had given her the
keenest pain, due to the fact, as she supposed, that Constance was totally unworthy of the man she had jilted.
But George's own assurance that no engagement had ever
existed had driven the clouds from her sky, although his
own subsequent conduct might well have aroused her
suspicions. Totty, however, took good care to explain
to her that the talk had been entirely without foundation
and that George's silence and gloomy ways were the result
of overwork. She hoped, she said, to induce him to
spend the summer with them and to give himself a long
rest.

CHAPTER XVI.

"Dear George," said Totty, one evening near the end of May, "I hate the idea of going away and leaving you here in the heat!"

"So do I," answered George, thoughtfully, as he turned in his chair and looked at his cousin's face.

"I am sure you will fall ill. There will be nobody to take care of you, no place where you can drop in to dinner when you feel inclined, and where you can do just as you like. And yet — you see how Mamie is looking! I cannot conscientiously keep her here any longer."

"Good heavens, Totty, you must not think of it! You do not mean to say you have been waiting here only on my account?"

Totty Trimm hesitated, withdrew one tiny foot, of which the point had projected beyond the skirt of her tea-gown, and then put out the other and looked at it curiously. They were both so small and pointed that George could not have told which was the right and which the left. She hesitated because she had not anticipated the question. George was not like other men. He would not be flattered by merely being informed that the whole Sherrington Trimm establishment had been kept up a month beyond the usual time, on a war footing, as it were, for his sole and express benefit. Most men would be pleased at being considered of enough importance to be told such a thing, though they might not believe the statement altogether. It was necessary that George should know that Totty was speaking the truth, if she answered his question directly. She hesitated and looked at the point of her little slipper.

"What does it matter?" she asked, suddenly, looking up and smiling at him affectionately.

It was very well done. The strongest asseverations could not have expressed more clearly her readiness to sacrifice everything she could to his comfort. George was touched.

"You have been very good to me, Totty. I cannot thank you enough." He took her hand and pressed it warmly.

"What is the use of having friends unless they will stand by you?" she asked, returning the pressure, while her face grew grave and sad.

Since she had written her first note after his disappointment, she had never referred to his troubles. He had answered her on that occasion as he answered every one, by saying that there had never been any engagement, and he had marvelled at her exceeding tact in avoiding the subject ever since. Her reference to it now, however, seemed natural, and did not hurt him.

"You have been more than a friend to me," he answered. "I feel as though you were my sister — only, if you were, I suppose I should be less grateful."

"No, you would not," said Totty with a smile of genuine pleasure produced of course by the success of her operations. "Do you want to do something to please me? Something to show your gratitude?"

"Whatever I can ——"

"Come and spend the summer with us — no, I do not mean you to make a visit of a month or six weeks. Pack up all your belongings, come down with us and be one of the family, till we are ready to come back to town. Make your headquarters with us, write your book, go away and make visits for a week when you like, but consider that our house is your home. Will you?"

"But, Totty, you would be sick of the sight of me ——" Visions of an enchanted existence by the river rose before George's eyes. He was to some extent intellectually demoralised, and every agreeable prospect in the future resolved itself into the thought of mental rest superinduced by boundless luxury and material comfort.

"What an idea!" exclaimed Totty indignantly. "Besides, if you knew how interested I am in making the proposal, you would see that you would be conferring a favour instead of accepting one."

She laughed softly when she had finished the sentence, thinking how very true her words were.

"I cannot understand how," George answered. "Please explain. I really cannot see how I shall be conferring a favour by eating your wonderful dinners and drinking that champagne of Sherry's."

Totty laughed again.

"I wish you would finish it! It would be ever so much better for his liver, if you would."

She wondered what George would think if he knew that a fresh supply of that particular brand of brut was already on its way from France, ordered in the hope that he might accept the invitation she was now pressing upon him.

"And as for the cook," she continued, "he will do nothing unless there is a man in the party. That is it, George. I have told you now. Dear Sherry is not coming back until the autumn, and Mamie and I feel dreadfully unprotected down there all by ourselves. Please, please come and take care of us. I knew you would come — oh, I am so glad! It is such a relief to feel that you will be with us!"

As indeed it was, since if George was under Totty's personal supervision there would be no chance of his returning to his former allegiance to Constance. George himself saw that her reasons were not serious, and considering the previous conversation and its earnest tone, he thought that he saw through Totty's playfulness and kindly wish to do a very friendly action.

"I will tell you what I will do," he said. "I will come for a month ——"

"No — I will not have you for a month, nor for two months — the whole summer or nothing."

So George at last consented, and left town two or three days later with Mrs. Sherrington Trimm and her daughter. He had felt that in some way he was acting weakly, and that he had yielded too easily to his cousin's invitation, but if he had been in any doubt about her sincere desire to keep him during the whole season, his anxiety was removed when as soon as he was established in his new quarters Totty immediately began to talk of plans for the months before them, in all of which George played a principal part, and Mamie took it for granted that there was to be no separation until they should all go back to New York together. During the first few days George allowed himself to be utterly idle and let the hours pass with an indifference to all thought which he had never known before.

He had been transported into a sort of fairyland, of which he had enjoyed occasional glimpses at other times, but which he had never had an opportunity of knowing intimately. It was unlike anything in his experience. Even the journey had not reminded him of other journeys, for it had been performed in that luxurious privacy which is dear to the refined American. Mr. Craik's yacht was permanently at his sister's disposal, and on the morning appointed for the departure she and Mamie and George had driven down to the pier at their leisure and had gone on board. It had been but a step from the perfectly appointed house in the city to the equally perfect dwelling on the water, and only one step more from the snowy deck of the yacht to the flower garden before the country mansion on the banks of the great river. Everything had been ready for them, on board and on shore, and George could not realise when the journey was over that he had been carried over a distance which he formerly only traversed in the heat and dust of a noisy train, or on the crowded deck of a river steamboat. He had passed the hot hours sitting under the cool shade of a double awning, in the most comfortable of chairs beside Mamie Trimm and opposite to her mother. There had been no noise, no tramping of sailors, no blowing of whistles, no shouting of orders. From time to time, indeed, he caught a glimpse of the captain's feet as he

paced the bridge, but that was all. At mid-day a servant
had appeared and Totty had glanced at him, glanced at
the table beside her and nodded. Immediately luncheon
had been served and George had recognised the touch
of the master in the two or three delicacies he had tasted,
and had found in his glass wine of the famous brand
which was said to have caused Sherry Trimm's sufferings. He had divided with Mamie a priceless peach,
which had no natural right to be ripe on the last day of
May, and Totty had selected for him a little bunch of
muscat grapes such as he might not have eaten in the
south before September. George tasted the ambrosia
and swallowed the nectar, and enjoyed the beautiful
scenery, the two pretty faces and the pleasant voices in
his ear, thinking, perhaps, of the old times when after
a desperate morning's work at reviewing trash, he had
sat down to a luncheon of cold meat, pickles and tea.
The thought of the contrast made the present more delightful.

The spell was not broken, and Totty's country-house
prolonged without interruption the series of exquisite
sensations which had been intermittent during the last
month in New York. If Totty had intended to play the
part of the tempter instead of being the chief comforter,
she could not have done it with a more diabolical skill.
She believed that a man could always be more easily
attacked by the senses than by his intelligence, and she
put every principle of her belief into her acts. She
partly knew, and partly guessed, the manner of George's
former life, the absence of luxury, the monotony of an
existence in which common necessities were always provided for in the same way, without stint but without
variety. Her art consisted in creating contrasts of unlike perfections, so that the senses, unable to decide
between the amount of pleasure experienced yesterday,
enjoyed to-day and anticipated to-morrow, should be kept
in a constant state of suspended judgment. She had
practised this system with her husband and it had often

succeeded in persuading him to let her have her own way, and she practised it continually for her own personal satisfaction, as being the only means of extracting all possible enjoyment from her existence.

George fell under the charm without even making an effort to resist it. Why, he asked himself dreamily, should he resist anything that was good in itself and harmless in its consequences? His life had all at once fallen in pleasant places. Should he disappoint Totty and give Mamie pain by a sudden determination to break up all their plans and return to the heat of the city? He could work here as well as anywhere else, better if there was any truth in the theory that the mind should be more active when the body is subject to no pain or inconvenience. A deal of ascoticism had been forced upon him since he had been seventeen years old, and he believed that a surfeit of luxuries would do him no harm now. He would get tired of it all, no doubt, and would be very glad to go back to his more simple existence.

Totty, however, was far too accomplished an Epicurean to allow her patient a surfeit of anything. She watched him more narrowly than he supposed and was ready with a change, not when she saw signs of fatigue in his manner, his face or his appetite, but before that, as soon as she had seen that he was pleased. She was playing a great game and her attention never relaxed. There was a fortune at stake of which he himself did not dream, and of which even she did not know the extent. She had everything in her favour. The coast was clear, for Sherrington was in Europe. The final scene was prepared, since Mamie was already in love with George. She herself was a past master of scene-shifting and her theatre was well provided with properties of every description. All that was necessary was that the hero should take a fancy to the heroine. But the very fact that it all looked so easy aroused Totty's anxiety. She said to herself that what appeared to be most simple was

often, in reality, most difficult, and she warned herself
to be careful and diffident of success.

Fortunately Mamie was all she could desire her to be.
She did not believe in beauty as a means of attracting a
disappointed man. Beauty could only draw his mind
into making comparisons, and comparisons must revive
recollection and reawaken regret. She had more faith
in Mamie's subtle charm of manner, voice and motion
than she would have had in all the faultless perfections
of classic features, queenly stature and royal carriage.
That charm of hers, gave her an individuality of her
own, such as Constance Fearing had never possessed, unlike anything that George had ever noticed in other girls
or women. Doubtless he might have too much of that,
too, as well as of other things, but Totty was even more
cautious of the effects she produced with Mamie than of
those she brought about by her minute attention to the
management of her house. And here her greatest skill
appeared, for she had to play a game of three-sided
duplicity. She had to please George, without wearying
him, to regulate the intercourse between the two so as to
suit her own ends, and to invent reasons for making
Mamie behave as she desired that she should without
communicating to the girl a word of her intentions. If
George appeared to have been enjoying especially a quiet
conversation with Mamie, he must be prevented from
talking to her again alone for at least twenty-four hours,
and even then he must be allowed to please himself in
the matter. This was not easy, for Mamie was by this
time blindly in love with him, and if she were not
watched would be foolish enough to bore him by her
frequent presence at his side. To keep her away from
him long enough to make him want her company needed
much diplomacy. If George went out for a turn in the
garden, and if Mamie joined him without an invitation,
Totty could not pursue the pair in order to protect George
from being bored. Hitherto also, Mamie had made no
confidences to her mother and did not seem inclined to

make any. Manifestly, if an accident could happen by which Mamie could be brought to betray herself to her careful parent, great advantages would ensue. The careful parent would then appear as the firm and skilful ally of the love-lorn daughter, the two would act in concert and great results might be effected. Totty was not only really fond of George, in her own way, but it would not have suited her that a hair of his head should be injured. Nevertheless, she nourished all sorts of malicious hopes against him at this stage. She wished that he might be thrown from his horse and brought home unhurt but insensible, or that he might upset his boat on the river under Mamie's eyes — in short that something might happen to him which should give Mamie a shock and throw her into her mother's arms.

Providence, however, did not come to Totty's assistance and she was thrown upon her own resources, aided in some small degree by an extraneous circumstance. The marriage of John Bond and Grace Fearing had been talked of for a long time, and Totty one morning learned that it was to take place immediately. She could not guess why they had chosen to be married in the very middle of the summer, when all their friends were out of town, and she had no inclination to go to the wedding, which was to be conducted without any great gathering or display of festivity. John Bond, as being Sherrington Trimm's partner and an old friend of Totty's, urged her of course to come down to town for the occasion and to bring Mamie, but the heat was intense, and as there would be nothing to see and no one present with whom she would care to talk, and nothing good to eat, and, on the whole, nothing whatever to do except to grin and look pleased, Totty made up her mind that she would have nothing to do with the affair, beyond sending Grace an expensive present. There were no regular invitations sent out, and George received no notice of what was happening. Totty, however, did not lose the opportunity of talking to Mamie about it all, with a view to sounding her views upon matrimony in general and upon her own future in particular.

"Johnnie Bond is such a fine fellow!" said Totty to her daughter, when they had been talking for some time.

Mamie admitted that he was a very fine fellow, indeed.

"Tell me, Mamie," said her mother, assuming a tone at once cheerful and confidential, "is not Johnnie Bond very nearly your ideal of what a husband ought to be?"

"Not in the least!" answered the young girl promptly. Totty looked very much surprised.

"No? Why, Mamie, I thought you always liked him so much!"

"So I do, in a way. But he is not at all in my style, mamma."

"What is your style, as you call it?" Totty seemed intensely interested as she paused for an answer. Mamie blushed, and looked down at a piece of work she was holding.

"Well — to begin with," she said, speaking quickly, "Mr. Bond is three-quarters lawyer and one-quarter idiot. At least I believe so. And all the rest of him is boating and tennis and — everything one does, you know — sport and all that. I never heard him make an intelligent remark in his life, though papa says he is as clever as they make them, for a lawyer of course. You know what I mean, mamma. He is one of those dreadfully earnest young men, who do everything with a purpose, as if it meant money, and they meant to get it. Oh, I could not bear to marry one of them! They are all exactly alike — so many steam engines turned out by the same maker!"

"Dear me, Mamie!" laughed Mrs. Trimm. "What very decided opinions you have!"

"I suppose Grace Fearing has decided opinions, too, in the opposite direction, or she would not have married him. I never can understand her, either, with those great dark eyes and that determined expression — she looks like a girl out of a novel, and I believe there is no

more romance about her than there is in a hat-stand!
There cannot be, if she likes Master Johnnie Bond — and
there is no reason why she should marry him unless she
does like him, is there?"

"None that I can see, but that is a very good one —
good enough for any one, I should think. You would
not care for Johnnie Bond, but you may care for some
one else. You have not told me what your ideal would
be like."

"Where is the use? You ought to know, mamma,
without being told."

"Of course I ought, child — only I am so stupid.
Would he be dark or fair?"

"Dark," answered the young girl, bending over her
work.

"And clever, I suppose? Of course. And slender,
and romantic to look at?"

"Oh, don't, mamma! Talk about something else."

"Why? I am not sure that we might not agree about
the ideal."

"No!" exclaimed Mamie with a little half scornful
laugh. "We should never agree about him, because I
would like him poor."

"You can afford to marry a poor man, if you please,"
said Totty, thoughtfully. "But would you not be afraid
that he loved your money better than yourself?"

"No indeed! I should love him, and then — I should
believe in him, of course."

"Then I do not see why you should not marry your
ideal after all, my dear. Come, darling — we both know
whom we are talking about. Why not say it to each
other? I would help you then. I am almost as fond of
him as you are."

Mamie blushed quickly and then turned pale. She
looked suspiciously at her mother.

"You are not in earnest, mamma," she said, after a
short pause.

"Indeed I am, child," answered Mrs. Trimm, meeting

her gaze fearlessly. "Do you think that I have not known it for a long time? And do you think I would have brought him here if I had not been perfectly willing that you should marry him?"

The young girl suddenly sprang up and threw her arms round her mother's neck.

"Oh mamma, mamma! This is too good! Too good! Too good!"

"Dear child!" exclaimed Totty, kissing her affectionately. "Is not your happiness always the first thing in my mind? Would I not sacrifice everything for that?"

"Yes—you are so sweet and dear. I know you would," said Mamie, sitting down beside her and resting her head upon her mother's plump little shoulder. "But you see—I thought that nobody knew, because we have always been together so much. And then I thought you would think what you just said, about the money, you know. But it is not true—I mean it would not be true. He would never care for that."

"No," answered Totty, almost forgetting herself. "I should think not! I mean—with his character—he is so honourable and fair—like your papa in that. But Mamie, darling, do you think he —— ?"

Totty stopped, conveying the rest of her question by means of an inquiringly sympathetic smile. Mamie shook her head a little sadly, and looked down.

"I am afraid he never will," she said, in a low voice. "And yet he should, for I—oh mother! I love him so —you will never know!"

She buried her face and her blushes in her hands upon her mother's shoulder. Totty patted her head affectionately and kissed her curls several times in a very motherly way. Her own face was suffused with smiles for she felt that she had done a very good day's work, and was surprised to think that it had been accomplished so easily. The fact was that Mamie was only too ready to speak of what filled her whole life, and had more than once been on the point of telling her mother all she felt. She had supposed, however, that she knew the ways of her mother's wisdom, and that George's poverty would always be an insuperable obstacle. She did not now in the least understand why Totty made so light of the question of money, and even in her great happiness at finding such ready sympathy she thought it very strange that she should have so completely mistaken her mother's character.

From that day, however, there was a tacit understanding between the two. Mamie was in that singular and not altogether dignified position in which a woman finds herself when she loves a man and has determined to win him, though she is not loved in return. There are doubtless many young women in the world who, whether for love or for interest, have wooed and won their present husbands, though the latter have never found it out, and would not believe it if it were told to them. Mamie differed from most of these, however, in that she was as modest as she was loving, and in her real distrust of her own advantages, which defect, or quality, was perhaps at the root of her peculiar charm. She knew that she was not beautiful, and she believed that beauty was a woman's strongest weapon. She had yet to learn that the way to men's hearts is not always through their eyes.

After her confession to her mother she began to discover the value of that ingenious lady's experience and tact. At first, indeed, she felt a modest hesitation in coolly doing what she was told, as a means of winning George's heart, but she soon found out that her mother was always right and that she herself was generally wrong.

"There is only one way of doing things," said Totty, one day, "and that is the right way. There is only one thing that a man really hates, and that is, being bored. And men are very easily bored, my dear. A man likes to have everything done for him in the most perfect way, but it spoils his enjoyment to feel that it is done espe-

cially for him and for nobody else. If you are afraid he
will catch cold, do not run after him with his hat, as
though he were an invalid. That is only an example,
Mamie. Men have an immense body of tradition to
sustain, and they do it by keeping up appearances as
well as they can. All men are supposed to be brave,
strong, honourable, enduring and generous. They are
supposed never to feel hot when we do, nor to catch
cold when we should. It is a part of their stage character never to be afraid of anything, and many of them
are far more timid than we are. I do not mean to say
that dear George has not all the qualities a man ought
to have. Certainly not. He is quite the finest fellow I
ever knew. But he does not want you to notice the fact.
He wants you to take it for granted, just as much as
little Tippy Skiffington does, who is afraid of a mouse
and would not touch a dog that had no muzzle on for all
he is worth, which is saying a great deal. Dear George
would not like it to be supposed that he cares for terrapin
and dry champagne any more than for pork and beans
— and yet the dear fellow is keenly alive to the difference. He does not want it to be thought he could ever
be bored by you or me, but he knows that we know that
he might be, and he expects us to use tact and to leave
him alone sometimes, even for a whole day. He will be
much more glad to see us the next time we meet him
and will show it by giving himself much more trouble
to be agreeable. It is not true that if you run away
men will follow you. They are far too lazy for that.
You must come to them, but not too often. What they
most want is amusement, and between their amusements,
to be allowed to do exactly what their high and mighty
intellects suggest to them, without comment. Never ask
a man where he has been, what he has seen, nor what he
has heard. If he has anything to tell, he will tell you,
and if he has not you only humiliate him by discovering
the emptiness of his thoughts. Always ask his opinion.
If he has none himself, he knows somebody who has, no

matter what the subject may be. The difference between men and women is very simple, my dear. Women look greater fools than they are, and men are greater fools than they look — except in the things they know how to do and do well."

"George is not a fool about anything!" said Mamie indignantly. She had been listening with considerable interest to her mother's homily.

"George, my dear," answered Totty, "is very foolish not to be in love with you at the present moment. Or, if he is, he is very foolish to hide it."

"I wish you would not talk like that, mamma! I am not half good enough for him."

Nevertheless Mamie consulted her mother and was guided by her. George would ride — should she accept his proposal and go with him or not? A word, a glance decided the matter for her, and George was none the wiser. He could not help thinking, however, that Mamie was becoming an extremely tactful young person, as well as a most agreeable companion. One day he could not resist his inclination to tell her so.

"How clever you are, Mamie!" he exclaimed after a pause in the conversation.

"I? Clever?" The girl's face expressed her innocent astonishment at the compliment.

"Yes. You are a most charming person to live with. How in the world did you know that I wanted to be alone yesterday, and that I wanted you to come with me to-day?" George laughed. "Do I not always ask you to come with me in precisely the same tone? Do I not always look as though I wanted you to come? How do you always know?"

Mamie was conscious that she blushed even more than she usually did when she was momentarily embarrassed. Indeed, the blush had two distinct causes on the present occasion. She had at first been delighted by the compliment he had paid her, and then, immediately afterwards, when he explained what he meant, she had felt her

shame burning in her face.   On the previous day, as
on the present afternoon, she had blindly followed her
mother's advice, given by an almost imperceptible motion
of the head and eyes that had indicated a negation
on the first occasion and assent on the second.   She
was silent now, and could find no words with which to
answer his question.

"How do you do it?" he asked again, wondering at
her embarrassment, and slackening the pace at which he
rowed, for they were in a boat together towards sunset.

Mamie's eyes suddenly filled with hot tears and she
hid her face with her small hands.

"Why, Mamie dear, what is it?" George asked, resting on his oars and leaning forward.

"O George," she sobbed, "if you only knew!"

CHAPTER XVII.

George did not forget Mamie's strange behaviour in
the boat, and he devoted much time to the study of the
problem it presented.   To judge from the girl's conduct
alone, she must be in love with him, and yet he did not
like the idea and took the greatest pains to keep it out of
his mind.   He was not in the humour in which it is a
pleasant surprise to a man to discover unexpected affection for himself in a quarter where he has not expected
to find it.   Moreover, if he had once made sure that
Mamie loved him, he would probably have thought it
his duty to go away as quickly as possible.   Such a
decision would have deprived him of much that he
enjoyed and it was desirable in the interests of his selfishness that it should be put off as long as possible.

At that time George began to feel the desire for work
creeping upon him once more.   During a few weeks only
had it been in his power to put away the habit of writ-

ing, and to close his eyes to all responsibility. Those
had been days when the whole world had seemed to be
upside down, as in a dream, while he himself moved in
the midst of a disordered creation, uncertainty, like a
soulless creature, without the capacity for independent
action nor the intelligence to form any distinct intention
from one moment to another. He took what he found
in his way without understanding, though not without
an odd appreciation of what was good, very much as
Eastern princes receive European hospitality. He was
grateful at least that his life should be made so smooth
for the time, for he was dimly conscious that anything
outwardly rough or coarse would have exasperated him to
madness. He believed that he thought a great deal about
the past, but when he attempted to give his meditations
a shape, they would accept none. In reality he was not
thinking, though the mirror of his memory was filled
with fleeting reflections of his former life, some clear
and startlingly vivid, others distorted and broken, but
all more or less beautified by the shadowy presence of a
being he had loved better than himself, and from whom
he was separated for ever.

With such a man, however, idleness was as impossible
as the desire for expression was irresistible. Since he
had written his first book, and had discovered what it was
that he was born to do, he had taken up a burden which
he could not lay down and had sworn allegiance to a
master from whom he could not escape. Not even the
bitter and overwhelming disappointment that had come
upon him could kill the desire to write. He was almost
ashamed of it at first, for he felt that though everything
he loved best in the world were dead before him, he
should be driven within a few weeks to take up his pen
again and open his inner eyes and ears to the play of his
mind's stage.

The power to do certain things is rarely separated
from the necessity for doing them, and the fact that they
are well done by no means proves that the doer has for-

gotten the blow that recently overwhelmed his heart in darkness and his daily life in an almost uncontrollable grief.   There are two lives for most men, whatever their careers may be, and the absence of either of these lives makes a man produce an impression of incompleteness upon those who know him.   When any one lives only by the existence of the heart, without active occupation, without manifesting inclination, taste or talent for outward things, we say that he has no interest in life, and is much to be pitied.   But we say that a man is heartless and selfish who appears to devote every thought to his occupation and every moment to increasing the chances of his success.   In the lives of great men we search with an especial pleasure for all that can show us the working of their hearts, and we remember with delight whatever we find that indicates a separate and inner chain of events, of which the links have been loves and friendships kept secret from the world.   The more nearly the two lives have coincided, the more happy we judge the man to have been, the more out of tune and discordant with each other, the more we feel that his existence must have seemed a failure in his own eyes; and when we are told only of his doings before the world, without one touch of softer feeling, we lay aside the book of his biography and say that it is badly written and that we are surprised to find that a man so uninteresting in himself should have exercised so much influence over his times.

George Wood had neither forgotten Constance, nor had he recovered from the wound he had received, and yet within a day or two of his resuming his work, he found that his love of it was not diminished nor his strength to do it abated.   It was not happiness to write, but it was satisfaction.   His hesitation was gone now, and his hand had recovered its cunning.   He no longer sat for hours before a blank sheet of paper, staring at the wall and racking his brain in the hope that a character of some sort would suddenly start into shape and

life from the chaotic darkness he was facing. Until the
first difficulties that attend the beginning of a book were
overcome, he had still a lingering and unacknowledged
suspicion that he could do nothing good without the daily
criticism and unfailing applause he had been accustomed
to receive from Constance during his former efforts.
When he was fairly launched, he felt proud of being
able to do without her. For the first time he was depend-
ing solely upon his own judgment, as he had always
relied upon his own ideas, and his judgment decided
that what he did was good.

From that time the arrangement of his day took again
the definite shape in which he had always known it, and
the mere distribution of his hours between work and rest
gave him back confidence in himself. He began to see
his surroundings from a more intelligent point of view,
and to take a keener interest in things and people.
Though he had by no means recovered from the first
great shock of his life, and though in his heart he was
as bitter as ever against her who had inflicted it, yet his
mind was already convalescent and was being rapidly
restored to its former vigour. There was power in his
imagination, strength in his language and harmony in
his style. What he thought took shape, and the shape
found expression.

He soon found that under these circumstances life was
bearable, and often enjoyable. Very gradually, as his
concentrated attention became absorbed in his own creations, the face of Constance Fearing appeared less often
in his dreams, and the heart-broken tones of her voice
rang less continually in his ears. He was not forgetting, but the physical impressions of sight and sound
upon his senses were wearing off. Occasionally indeed
they would return with startling force and vividness,
awakening in him for one moment the reality of all he
had suffered. At such times he could see again, as
though face to face, her expression at the instant when
she had seemed to relinquish the attempt to soften him,

and he could hear again the plaintive accents of her words and the painful cadence of her sobbing voice. But such visitations grew daily more rare and at last almost ceased altogether.

For what he had done himself he felt no remorse. His mind was not made like hers, and he would never be able to understand that she had done violence to her own heart in casting him off. He would learn perhaps some day to describe what she had done, to analyse her motives from his own point of view, but he would never be able to think of her as she thought of herself. In his eyes she would always be a little contemptible, even when time's charitable mists should have descended upon the past and softened all its outlines. He was cut off from her by one of the most impassable barriers which can be raised in the human heart, by his resentment against himself for having been deceived.

He did not ask himself whether he could ever love again. There was a strength in his present position, which almost pleased him. He had done with love and was free to speak of it as he chose, without regard for any one's feelings, without respect for the passion itself, if it suited his humour. There had been nothing boyish in the pure and passionate affection under which he had lived during two of the most important years in his life. He had felt all that a man can feel in the deep devotion to one spotless object. There would never again be anything so high and noble and untainted in all the years that were to come for him, and he knew it. The determination he had felt to be necessary in the first moment of his anger had carried itself out almost without any direction from his will. The Constance he had loved so dearly, was not the Constance who had refused to marry him, and who had dealt him such a cruel blow. The two were separated and he could still love the one, while hating and despising the other. But although he might meet the girl whose face and form and look and voice were those of her he had lost, this second Constance could never take the other's place. A word from her could not put fire into his heart, nor raise in his brain the vision of a magnificent inspiration. A touch from her hand could send no thrill of pleasure through his frame, there would be no joy in looking upon her fair face when next he saw it. She might say to him all that he had once said to her, she might appeal passionately to the love that was now dead, she might offer him her heart, her body and her soul. He wanted none of the three now. The break had been final and definite, love's path had broken off upon the edge of the precipice, and though she might stand on the old familiar way and beckon to him to come over and meet her, there was that between them which no man could cross.

Like all great passions the one through which George Wood had passed had produced upon him a definite effect, which could be appreciated, if not accurately measured. He was older in every way now than he had been two years and a half earlier, but older chiefly in his understanding of human nature. He knew, now, what men and women felt in certain circumstances, his instinct told him truly what it had formerly only vaguely suggested. The inevitable logic of life had taken him up as a problem, had dealt with him as with a subject fitted to its hand, and had forced upon him a solution of himself. Where he had entertained doubts, he now felt certainty, where he had hesitated in expressing the judgment of his tastes he now found his verdicts already considered and only awaiting delivery. Many months later, when the book he was now writing was published it was a new surprise to his readers. His first attempts had been noticeable for their beauty, his last book was remarkable for its truth.

Meanwhile his intimacy with Mamie grew unheeded by himself. During the many hours of each day in which he had no fixed occupation, he was almost constantly with her, and their conversation was at last only interrupted each evening to begin again the next afternoon, when he had done his work and came out of his room in search of relaxation. He had never found any explanation for her embarrassment on that day when he had been rowing her about on the river, and after a time he had ceased to seek for one. His brain was too busy with other things, and what he wanted when he was with her was rest rather than exercise for his curiosity in trying to solve the small enigmas of her girlish thoughts. She was a very pleasant companion, and that was all he cared to know. She brought about him an atmosphere of genuine and affectionate admiration that gave him confidence in himself and smoothed the furrows of his imagination when he had been giving that faculty more to do than was good for it.

Mamie, too, was happier than she had been a month earlier. She had no longer to suffer the humiliation of taking her mother's advice about what she should do, and she could enjoy George's company without feeling that she had been told to enjoy it in her own interest. As she learned to love him more and more, she was quick also to understand his ways. Signs that had formerly escaped her altogether were now as clear to her comprehension as words themselves. She knew, now, almost before he knew it himself, whether he wanted her to join him, or not, whether he preferred to talk or to be silent, whether he would like this question or that which she thought of asking him, or whether he would resent it and make her feel that she had made a mistake. One day, she ventured to mention Constance's name.

George had never visited the Fearings in their country-place, and was not aware until he came to stay with his cousin that they lived on the opposite shore of the river. Their house was not visible from the Trimms' side, as it was surrounded by trees, and the stream was at that point nearly two miles in width. Totty, however, who always had a view to avoiding any possibility of anything disagreeable, had very soon communicated the information to George in an unconcerned way, while pointing out and naming to him the various country-seats that could be seen from her part of the shore. George did not forget what he had been told, and if he ever crossed the river and rowed along the other bank, he was careful to keep away from the Fearings' land, in order to guard against any unpleasant meetings.

Now it chanced that on a certain afternoon he was pulling leisurely up stream towards a place where the current was slack, and where he occasionally moored the wherry to an old landing in order to rest himself and talk more at his ease. Mamie of course was seated in the stern, leaning back comfortably amongst her cushions and holding the tiller-ropes daintily between the thumb and finger of each hand. She could steer very well when it was necessary, and she could even row well enough to make some headway against the stream, but George had been accustomed to being alone in a boat, and gave her very little to do when he was rowing.

Mamie watched him idly, as his hands shot out towards her, crossed as he drew them steadily back and turned at the wrist to feather the oar as they touched his chest. Then her gaze wandered down stream towards the other shore, and she tried to make out the roof of the Fearings' house above the trees.

"George," she said suddenly, "will you be angry?"

"I am never angry," answered her cousin. "What are you going to do now? If you mean to jump out of the boat I will have a line ready."

"No. I am not going to jump out of the boat. But I am so afraid you will be angry, after all. It is something I want to ask you. I am sure you will not like it!"

"One way of not making me angry would be not to ask the question," observed George, with a quiet smile.

"But I want to ask you so much!" exclaimed the young girl, with an imploring look that made George's smile turn into a laugh. He had laughed more than once lately, in a very natural manner.

"Out with it, Mamie!" he cried, pulling his sculls

briskly through the water. "I shall not be very angry, I daresay, and I have fallen out of the habit of eating little girls, What is it?"

"Why do you never go and see the Fearings, George? You used to be there so much."

George's expression changed, though he continued to row with the same even stroke. His face grew very grave and he unconsciously glanced across the river toward the place at which Mamie had looked.

"I knew you would be angry!" she said in a repentant tone.

"No," George answered, "I am not angry. I am thinking."

He was, indeed, wondering how much of the truth the girl knew, and he was distrustful enough to fancy that she might have some object in putting the question. But Mamie was not diplomatic like her mother. She was simple and natural in her thoughts, and unaffected in her manner. He glanced at her again and saw that she was troubled by her indiscretion.

"Did your mother never tell you anything about it all?" he asked after a long pause.

"No. I only heard what everybody heard — last May, when the thing was talked about. I wondered — that is all — I wondered whether you had cared very much — for her."

Again there was a long silence, broken only by the even dipping of the oars and the soft swirl as they left the water.

"I did care," George answered at last. "I loved her very dearly."

He did not know why he made the confession. He had never said so much to any one except his own father. If he had guessed what Mamie felt for him, he would assuredly not have answered her question.

"Are you very unhappy, still?" asked the young girl in a dreamy voice.

"No. I do not think I am unhappy. I am different

from what I was — that is all. I was at first," he continued, without looking at his companion, of whose presence, indeed, he seemed scarcely conscious. "I was unhappy — yes, of course I was. I had loved her long. I had thought she would marry me. I found that she was indifferent. I shall never go and see her again. She does not exist for me any more — she is another person, whom I do not wish to know. I have loved and been disappointed, like many a better man, I suppose."

"Loved and been disappointed!" repeated the young girl in a very low voice, that hardly reached his ear. She was looking down, carelessly tying and untying the ends of the tiller-ropes.

"Yes. That is it," he said as though musing on something very long past. "You know now why I do not go there."

Then he quickened his stroke a little, and there was a sombre light in his dark eyes that Mamie could not see, for she was still looking down. She was glad that she had asked the question, seeing how he had answered it. There was something in his tone which told her that he was not mistaken about himself, and that the past was shut off from the present in his heart by a barrier it would be hard to break down.

"Do you think you can ever love again?" she asked, after a while, looking suddenly into his face.

"No," he answered, avoiding her eyes. "I shall never love any woman again — in the same way," he added after a moment's pause.

When he looked at her, she was very pale. He remembered all at once how she had changed colour and burst into tears some weeks earlier, sitting in that same place before him. Something was passing in her mind which he could not understand. He was very slow to imagine that she loved him. He was so dull of comprehension that he all at once began to fancy she might be more fond of Constance Fearing than he had guessed, that she might be her friend, as Totty was, and that the two had brought him to their country-house in the hope of soothing his anger, reviving his hopes, and bringing him once more into close relations with the young girl who had cast him off. The idea was ingenious in its folly, but his ready wrath rose at it.

"Are you very fond of her, Mamie?" he asked, bending his heavy brows and speaking in a hard metallic voice.

The blood rushed into the girl's face as she answered, and her grey eyes flashed.

"I? I hate her! I would kill her if I could!"

George was completely confused. His explanation of Mamie's behaviour had flashed upon him so suddenly that he had believed it the true one without an attempt to reason upon the matter. Now, it was destroyed in an instant by the girl's angry reply. When one young woman says that she hates another, it is tolerably easy to judge from her tone whether she is in earnest or not. Though he was still sorely puzzled, the cloud disappeared from George's face as quickly as it had come.

"This is a revelation!" he exclaimed. "I thought you and your mother were devoted to them both."

"It would be like me, would it not?" Mamie emphasised her words with an angry little laugh.

"It is not like you to hate people so savagely," George observed, looking at her closely.

"I should always hate anybody who hurt you — and I can hate, with all my heart!"

"Are you so fond of me as that?"

George thought that the girl was becoming every moment harder to understand. It had seemed a very natural question, since they had known each other and loved each other like brother and sister for so long. But he saw that there was something the matter. There was a frightened look in Mamie's grey eyes which he had never seen before, as though she had come all at once upon a great and unexpected danger. Then all the outline of her face softened wonderfully with a strange and gentle expression under the young man's gaze. She had never been pretty, save for her eyes and her alabaster skin. For one moment, now, she was beautiful.

"Yes," she said in an uncertain voice, "I am very fond of you — more fond of you than you will ever know."

Her secret was out, though she did not realise it. Then for the first time in George's life, though he was nearly thirty years of age, he looked on the face of a woman who loved him with all her heart, and he knew what love meant in another, as he had known it in himself.

The sun was going down behind the western hills and the dark water was very smooth and placid as he dipped his sculls noiselessly into the surface. He rowed evenly on for some minutes without speaking. Mamie was looking into the stream and drawing her white, ungloved hand along the glassy mirror.

"Thank you, Mamie," he said at last, very gently and kindly.

Again there was silence as they shot along through the purple shadows.

"And you, are you fond of me?" asked the young girl, looking furtively towards him, then blushing and gazing once more into the depths of the stream. George started slightly. He had not thought that the question would come.

"Indeed I am," he answered. He thought he heard a sigh on the rising evening breeze. "I grow more fond of you every day," he added quietly, though he felt that he was very far from calm.

So far as he had spoken, his words had been truthful. He was becoming more attached to Mamie every day, and she was beginning to take the place that Constance had occupied in his doings if not in his thoughts. But there was not a spark of love in his growing affection for her, and the discovery he had just made disturbed him exceedingly. He had never blamed himself for anything he had done in his intercourse with Constance

Fearing, but he accused himself now of having misled the innocent girl who loved him and of having then, by a careless question, drawn from her a confession of what she felt. It flashed upon him suddenly that he had taken Constance's place, and Mamie had taken his; that he had been thoughtless and cruel in all he had said and done during the last two months, and that she might well reproach him with having been heartless. A thousand incidents flooded his memory and crowded together upon his brain, and each brought with it a sting to his sense of honour. He had inadvertently done a great harm, and it had been done since his coming to the country. Before that, Mamie had felt for him exactly what he still felt for her, a simple, open-hearted affection. Remembering the brief struggle that had taken place in his mind before he had accepted Totty's invitation, he accused himself of having known beforehand what would happen, and of having weakly yielded because he had liked the prospect of leading so luxurious an existence. What surprised him, however, and threw all his reflections out of balance was that Totty herself should not have foreseen the disaster, Totty the diplomatic, Totty the worldly, Totty the covetous, who would as soon have given her daughter to one of her servants as to penniless George Wood! It was past comprehension. Yet, in spite of his distress, he could hardly repress a smile as he imagined what Totty's rage would be, should he marry Mamie and carry her off before the eyes of her horrified parent. Sherrington Trimm, himself, would be as well satisfied with him as with any other honest man, if he were sure of Mamie's inclinations.

Now, however, something must be done at once. He was not a weak creature, like Constance Fearing, to hesitate for months and years, practising a deception upon himself which he had not the courage to carry to the end. He even regretted the last words he had spoken, and which had been prompted by a foolish wish not to hurt the girl's feelings. It would have been better if he had left them unsaid. The situation must be defined, the harm arrested, if it could not be undone, and should it seem necessary, as it probably would, he himself must leave the place on the following morning. He opened his mouth to speak, but the blood rushed to his face and he could not articulate the words. He was overcome with shame and remorse and he would have chosen to do anything, to undergo any humiliation rather than this. But in a moment his strong nature gathered itself and grew strong, as it always did in the face of great difficulties. He hated hesitation and he would not hesitate, cost what it might. He was not cowardly, and he would not be afraid.

"Mamie," he said, suddenly, and he wondered how his voice could be so gentle, "Mamie, I do not love you."

He had expected everything, except what happened. Mamie looked into his eyes, and once again in the evening light the expression of her love transfigured her half pretty face and lent it a completeness of beauty such as he had never seen.

"Have you not told me that, dear?" she asked, half sadly, half lovingly. "It is not new. I have known it long."

George stared at her for a moment.

"I feared I had not said it clearly," he answered in low tones.

"Everything you have done and said has told me that, for two months past. Do not say it again."

"I must go away from this place. I will go to-morrow."

She looked up with startled eyes.

"Go away? Leave me? Ah, George, you will not be so unkind!"

The situation was certainly as strange as it was new, and George was very much confused by what was happening. His resolution to make everything clear was, however, as unbending as before.

"Mamie," he said, "we must understand each other.

Things must not go on as they have gone so long. If I were to stay here, do you know what I should be doing? I should be acting towards you as Constance Fearing acted with me, only it would be much worse, because I am a man, and I have no right to do such things, as women have."

"It is different," said the young girl, once more looking down into the water.

"No, it is not different," George insisted. "I have no right to act as though I should ever love you, to make you think by anything I do or say, that such a thing is possible. I am a brute, I know. Forgive me, Mamie, dear. It is so much better that everything should be clearly understood now. We have known each other so long, and so well——"

"Nothing that you can say will make it seem right to me that you should go away——"

"It is right, nevertheless, and if I do not do it, as I should, I shall never forgive myself——"

"I will forgive you."

"I shall hate myself——"

"I will love you."

"I shall feel that I am the most miserable wretch alive."

"I shall be happy."

CHAPTER XVIII.

George had rowed to a point where a deep indentation in the shore of the river offered a broad expanse of water in which there was but little current. He rested on his oars, bending his head and leaning slightly forward. It seemed very hard that he should suddenly be called upon to decide so important a question as had just arisen, at the very moment when he was writing the most difficult and interesting part of his book. To go away

was not only to deprive himself of many things which
he liked, and among those Mamie's own society had
taken the foremost place of late; it meant also to break
the current of his ideas and to arrest his own progress at
the most critical juncture. He remembered with loath-
ing the days he had spent in his little room in New
York, cudgelling his inert brain and racking his imagination for a plot, a subject, for one single character, for
anything of which he might make a beginning. And he
looked back to a nearer time, and saw how easily his mind
had worked amidst its new and pleasant surroundings.
It is no wonder that he hesitated. Only the artist can
understand his own interest in his art; only the writer,
and the writer of real talent, can tell what acute suffering it is to be interrupted in the midst of a piece of
good work, while its success is still uncertain in the
balance of his mind and while he still depends largely
upon outward circumstances for the peace and quiet
which are necessary to serious mental labour.

George was not heroic, though there was a touch of
quixotism in his nature. The temptation to stay where
he was, had a force he had not expected. Moreover,
whether he would or not, the expression he had twice
seen in Mamie's face on that afternoon, haunted him and
fascinated him. He experienced the operation of a charm
unknown before. He looked up and gazed at the young
girl as she sat far back in the stern of the boat. She
was not pretty, or at most, not more than half pretty.
Her mouth was decidedly far too large, and her nose
lacked outline. She had a fairly good forehead; he admitted that much, but her chin was too pointed and had
little modelling in it, while her cheeks would have been
decidedly uninteresting but for the extreme beauty of
her complexion. She was looking down, and he could
not see the grey eyes which were her best feature, but it
could not be denied that the long dark drooping lashes
and the strongly marked brown eyebrows contrasted
very well with the transparent skin. Her hair was not

bad, though it was impossible to say whether those little tangled ringlets were natural or were produced daily by the skilful appliance of artificial torsion. If her mouth was an exaggerated feature, at least the long, even lips were fresh and youthful, and, when parted, they disclosed a very perfect set of teeth. All this was true, and as George looked, he summed up the various points and decided that when Mamie wore her best expression, she might pass for a pretty girl.

But she possessed more than that. The catalogue did not explain her wonderful charm. It was not, indeed, complete, and as he glanced from her downcast face to the outlines of her shapely figure, he felt the sensation a man experiences in turning quickly from the examination of a common object, to the contemplation of one that is very beautiful. Psyche herself could have boasted no greater perfection of form and grac than belonged to this girl whose features were almost all insignificant. The triumph of proportion began at her throat, under the small ears that were set so close to the head, and the faultless lines continued throughout all the curves of beauty to the point of her exquisite foot, to the longest finger of her classic hand. Not a line was too short, not a line too long, there was no straightness in any one, and not one of them all followed too strong a curve.

George thought of Constance and made comparisons with a coolness that surprised himself. Constance was tall, straight, well grown, active; slight, indeed, but graceful enough, and gifted with much natural ease in motion. But that was all, so far as figure was concerned. George had seen a hundred girls with just the same advantages as Constance, and all far prettier than his cousin. Neither Constance nor any of them could compare with Mamie except in face. His eye rested on her now, when she was in repose, with untiring satisfaction, as his sight delighted in each new surprise of motion when she moved, whether on horseback, or walking, or at tennis. She represented to him the absolute ideal of refined animal life, combined with something spiritual that escaped definition, but which made itself felt in all she did and said.

When he thought of depriving himself for a long time of her society, he discovered that he admired her far more than he had suspected. It was admiration, but it was nothing more. He felt no pain at the suggestion of leaving her, but it seemed as though he were about to be robbed of some object familiar to him, to keep which was a source of unfailing, though indolent, satisfaction. He could not imagine himself angry, if some man of his acquaintance had married Mamie the next day, provided that he might talk to her as he pleased and watch her when he liked. There was not warmth enough in what he felt for her to kindle one spark of jealousy against any one whom she might choose for a husband.

But there was something added to the odd sort of attraction which the girl exercised over him, something which had only begun to influence him during the last quarter of an hour or less. She loved him, and he had just found it out. There is nothing more enviable than to love and be loved in return, and nothing more painful than to be loved to distraction by a person one dislikes. It may be said, perhaps, that nothing can be so disturbing to the judgment as to be loved by an individual to whom one feels oneself strongly attracted in a wholly different way. George Wood did not know exactly what was happening to him, and he did not feel himself able to judge his own case with any sort of impartiality; but his instinct told him to go away as soon as possible and to break off all intercourse with his cousin during some time to come. She had argued the question with him in her own way and had found answers to all he said, but he was not satisfied. It was his duty to leave Mamie, no matter at what cost, and he meant to go at once.

"My dear Mamie," he said at last, still unconsciously admiring the grace of her attitude, "I am very sorry for myself, but there is only one way. I cannot stay here any longer."

She raised her eyes and looked steadily at him.

"On my account?" she asked.

"Yes, and you know I am right."

"Because I have been foolish and — and — unmaidenly, I suppose."

"Dear child — how you talk!" George exclaimed. "I never said anything of the kind!" He was seriously embarrassed to find an answer to her statement.

"Of course you did not say it. But you probably thought it, which is the same thing. After all, it is true, you know. But then, have I not a right to be foolish, if I please? I have known you so long."

"Yes indeed!" George answered with alacrity, for he was glad to be able to agree with her in something. "It is a long time, as you say — ever since we were children together."

"Then you think there was nothing so very bad about what I said?"

"It was thoughtless — I do not know what it was. There was certainly nothing bad in it, and besides, you did not mean it, you know, did you?"

"Then why do you want to go away?" inquired Mamie, with feminine logic, and candour.

"Why because ——" George stopped as people often do, at that word, well knowing what he had been about to say, but now suddenly unwilling to say it. In fact, to say anything under the circumstances would have been a flagrant breach of tact. Since Mamie almost admitted that she had meant nothing, she had only been making fun of him and he could not well think of going away without seeming ridiculous in his own eyes.

"'Because,' without anything after it, is only a woman's reason," said the young girl with a laugh.

"Women's reasons are sometimes the best. At all events, I have often heard you say so."

"I am often laughing at you, when I seem most in earnest, George. Have you never noticed that I have a fine talent for irony? Do you think that if I were very much in love with you, I would tell you so? How conceited you must be!"

"No indeed!" George asseverated. "I would not imagine that you could do such a thing. When I told you I would go away, I was only entering into the spirit of the thing and carrying on your idea."

"It was very well done. I cannot help laughing at the serious face you made."

"Nor I, at yours," said the young man beginning to pull the boat slowly about.

Matters had taken a very unexpected turn and he began to feel his determination to depart oozing out of his fingers in a way he had not expected. His position, indeed, was absurd. He could not argue with Mamie the question of whether she had been in earnest or not. Therefore he was obliged to accept her statement, that she had been jesting. And if he did so, how could he humiliate her by showing that he still believed she loved him? In other words, by packing up his traps and taking a summary leave. He would only be making a laughing-stock of himself in her eyes. Nor was he altogether free from an unforeseen sensation of disappointment, very slight, very vague, and very embarrassing to his self-esteem. Look at it as he would, his vanity had been flattered by her confession, and it had also, in some way, appealed to his heart. To be loved by some one, as she had seemed to love, when that expression had passed over her face! The idea was pleasant, attractive, one on which he would dwell hereafter and which would stimulate his comprehension when he was describing scenes of love in his books.

"So of course you will stay and behave like a human being," said Mamie, after a short pause, as though she had summed up the evidence, deliberated upon it and were giving the verdict.

"I suppose I shall," George answered in a regretful tone, though he could not repress a smile.

"You seem to be sorry," observed the young girl with

a quick, laughing glance of her grey eyes. "If there are any other reasons for your sudden departure, it is quite another matter. The one you gave has turned out badly. You have not proved the necessity for ensuring my salvation by taking the next train."

"I would have gone by the boat," said George.

"Why?"

"Because the river would have reminded me to the last of this evening."

"Do you want to be reminded of it as much as that?" asked Mamie.

"Since it turns out to have been such a very pleasant evening, after all," George answered, glad to escape on any terms from the position in which his last thoughtless remark had placed him.

Mamie had shown considerable tact in the way by which she had recovered herself, and George was unconsciously grateful to her for having saved him from the necessity of an abrupt leave-taking, although he could not get rid of the idea that she had been more than half in earnest in the beginning.

"It was very well done," he said after they had landed that evening and were walking up to the house through the flower garden.

"Yes," Mamie answered. "I am a very good actress. They always say so in the private theatricals."

The evening colour had gone from the sky and the moon was already in the sky, not yet at the full. Mamie stood still in the path and plucked a rose.

"I can act beautifully," she said with a low laugh. "Would you like me to give you a little exhibition? Look at me — so — now the moonlight is on my face and you can see me."

She looked up into his eyes, and once more her features seemed to be transfigured. She laid one hand upon his arm and with the other hand raised the rose to her lips, kissed it, her eyes still fixed on his, then smiled and spoke three words in a low voice that seemed to send a thrill through the quiet air.

"I love you."

Then she made as though she would have fastened the flower in his white flannel jacket, and he, believing she would do it, and still looking at her, bent a little forward and held the buttonhole ready. All at once, she sprang back with a quick, graceful movement and laughed again.

"Was it not well done?" she cried, tossing the rose far away into one of the beds.

"Admirably," George answered. "I never saw anything equal to it. How you must have studied!"

"For years," said the young girl, speaking in her usual tone and beginning to walk by his side towards the house.

It was certainly very strange, George thought, that she should be able to assume such an expression and such a tone of voice at a moment's notice, if there were no real love in her heart. But it was impossible to quarrel with the way she had done it. There had been something so supremely graceful in her attitude, something so winning in her smile, something in her accent which so touched the heart, that the incident remained fixed in his memory as a wonderful picture, never to be forgotten. It affected his artistic sense so strongly that before he went to bed he took his pen and wrote it down, taking a keen pleasure in putting into shape the details of the scene, and especially in describing what escaped description, the mysterious fascination of the girl herself. He read it over in bed, was satisfied with it, thrust it under his pillow, and went to sleep to dream it over again just as it had happened, with one important exception. In his dream, the figure, the voice, the words, were all Mamie's, but the face was that of Constance Fearing, though it wore a look which he had never seen there. In the morning he laughed over the whole affair, being only too ready to believe that Mamie had really been laughing at him and that she had only been acting the little scene with the rose in the garden.

A few days later an event occurred which **again made** him doubtful in the matter. Since that evening he had felt that he had grown more intimate with his cousin than before. There had been no renewal of the dangerous play on her part, though both had referred to it more than once. Oddly enough it constituted a sort of harmless secret, which had to be kept from Mamie's mother and over which they could be merry only when they were alone. Yet, as far as George was concerned, though the bond had grown closer in those days, its nature had not changed, nor was he any nearer to being persuaded that his cousin was actually in love with him.

At that time, John Bond and his wife, having made a very short trip to Canada, returned to New York and came thence to establish themselves in the old Fearing house for the rest of the summer. John could not leave the business for more than ten days in the absence of his partner, and he did as so many other men do, who spend the hot months on the river, going to town in the morning and coming back in the evening. On Sundays only John Bond did not make his daily trip to New York.

Since his marriage, he and Grace had not been over to see the Trimms, though Mrs. Trimm had once been over to them on a week-day in obedience to the custom which prescribes that every one must call on a bride. There had been much suave coldness between Totty and the Fearings since the report of the broken engagement had been circulated, but appearances were nevertheless maintained, and Mr. and Mrs. Bond felt that it was their duty to return the visit as soon as possible. Constance accompanied them and the three sailed across the river late on one Sunday afternoon. The river is a great barrier against news, and as Totty had kept her house empty of guests, for some reason best known to herself, and had written to none of her many intimate friends that George Wood was spending the summer with her, the three visitors had no expectation of finding him among the party.

During the time which had followed her departure from

town, Constance Fearing had fallen into a listless habit of mind, from which she had found it hard to rouse herself even so far as to help in the preparations for her sister's marriage. When the ceremony was over, she had withdrawn again to her country-house in the sole company of the elderly female relation who has been mentioned already once or twice in the course of this history.

She was extremely unhappy in her own way, and there were moments when the pain she had suffered renewed itself suddenly, when she wept bitter tears over the sacrifice she had been so determined to make. After one of these crises she was usually more listless and indifferent than ever, to all outward appearance, though in reality her mind was continually preying upon itself, going over the past again and again, living through the last moments of happiness she had known, and facing in imagination the struggle she had imposed upon herself. She did not grow suddenly thin, nor fall ill, nor go mad, as women do who have passed through some desperate trial of the heart. She possessed, indeed, the sort of constitution which sometimes breaks down under a violent strain from without, but she had not been exposed to anything which could bring about so fatal a result. It was rather the regret for a lost interest in her life than the keen agony of separation from one she had loved, which affected her spirits and reacted very slowly upon her health. At certain moments the sense of loneliness made itself felt more strongly than at others, and she gave way to tears and lamentation, in the privacy of her own room, without knowing exactly what she wanted. She still believed that she had done right in sending George away, but she missed what he had taken with him, the daily incense offered at her shrine, the small daily emotions she had felt when with him, and which her sensitive temper had liked for their very smallness. There was no doubt that she had loved him a little, as she had said, for she had always been ready to acknowledge everything she felt. But it was questionable whether her love had increased or decreased since she had parted from him, and her fits of spasmodic grief were probably not to be attributed to genuine love-sickness.

On that particular Sunday afternoon chosen by the Bonds for their visit to Mrs. Sherrington Trimm, Constance was as thoroughly indifferent as usual to everything that went on. She was willing to join her sister and brother-in-law in their expedition rather than stay at home and do nothing, but her mind was disturbed by no presentiment of any meeting with George Wood.

It was towards evening, and the air was already cool by comparison with the heat of the day. Mrs. Trimm, her daughter and George were all three seated in a verandah from which they overlooked the river and could see their own neat landing-pier beyond the flower-garden. The weather had been hot and none of the three were much inclined for conversation. Suddenly Totty uttered an exclamation of surprise.

"Those people are coming here! Who are they, George? Can you see?"

George fixed his eyes on the landing and saw that the sail-boat had brought to. At the same moment the sails were quickly furled and a man threw a rope over one of the wooden pillars. A few seconds elapsed and three figures were seen upon the garden-walk.

"I wish you could see who they are, George," said Totty rather impatiently. "It is so awkward — not knowing."

"I think it is Miss Fearing," George answered slowly, "with her sister and John Bond."

He was the only one of the three who did not change colour a little as the party drew near. Mamie's marble forehead grew a shade whiter, and Totty's pretty pink face a little more pink. She was annoyed at being taken unawares, and was sorry that George was present. As for Mamie, her grey eyes sparkled rather coldly, and her large, even lips were tightly closed over her beautiful teeth. But George was imperturbable, and it would have been impossible to guess from his face what he felt. He observed the three curiously as they approached the verandah. He thought that Constance looked pale and thin, and he recognised in Grace and her husband that peculiar appearance of expensive and untarnished new-ness which characterises newly-married Americans.

"I am so glad you have come over!" Totty exclaimed with laudably hospitable insincerity. "It is an age since we have seen any of you!"

Mamie gave Constance her hand and said something civil, though she fixed her grey eyes on the other's blue ones with singular and rather disagreeable intensity.

"George has been talking to her about me, I suppose," thought Miss Fearing as she turned and shook hands with George himself.

Grace looked at him quietly and pressed his hand with unmistakable cordiality. Her husband shook hands energetically with every one, inquired earnestly how each one was doing, and then looked at the river. He felt rather uncomfortable, because he knew that every one else did, but he made no attempt to help the diffi-culty by opening the conversation. He was not a talka-tive man. Totty, however, lost no time in asking a score of questions, to all of which she knew the answers. George found himself seated between Constance and Grace.

"Have you been here long, Mr. Wood?" Constance asked, turning her head to George and paying no atten-tion to Totty's volley of inquiries.

"Since the first of June," George answered quietly, and then relapsed into silence, not knowing what to say. He was not really so calm as he appeared to be, and the suddenness of the visit had slightly confused his thoughts.

"I supposed that you were in New York," said Con-stance, who seemed determined to talk to him, and to no one else. "Will you not come over and see us?" she asked.

"I shall be very happy," George replied, without undue coldness, but without enthusiasm. "Shall you stay through the summer?"

"Certainly — my sister and John — Mr. Bond — are there, too. You see, it is so dreadfully hot in town, and he cannot leave the office, though there is nothing in the world to do, I am sure. By the way, what are you doing, if one may ask? I hope you are writing something. You know we are all looking forward to your next book."

George could not help glancing sharply at her face, which changed colour immediately. But he looked away again as he answered the question.

"The old story," he said. "A love story. What else should I write about? There is only one thing that has a permanent interest for the public, and that is love." He ended the speech with a dry laugh, not good to hear.

"Is it?" asked Constance with remarkable self-possession. "I should think there must be many other subjects more interesting and far easier to write upon."

"Easier, no doubt. I will not question your judgment upon that point, at least. More interesting to certain writers, too, perhaps. Love is so much a matter of taste. But more to the liking of the public — no. There I must differ from you. The great majority of mankind love, are fully aware of it, and enjoy reading about the loves of others."

Constance was pale and evidently nervous. She had clearly determined to talk to George, and he appeared to resent the advance rather than otherwise. Yet she would not relinquish the attempt. Even in his worst humour she would rather talk with him than with any one else. She tried to meet him on his own ground.

"How about friendship?" she asked. "Is not that a subject for a book, as well as love?"

"Possibly, with immense labour, one might make a book of some sort about friendship. It would be a very dull book to read, and a man would need to be very morbid to write it; as for the public it would have to undergo a surgical operation to be made to accept it. No. I think that friendship would make a very poor subject for a novelist."

"You do not think very highly of friendship itself, it seems," said Constance with an attempt to laugh.

"I do not know of any reason why I should. I know very little in its favour."

"Opinions differ so much!" exclaimed the young girl, gaining courage gradually. "I suppose you and I have not at all the same ideas about it."

"Evidently not."

"How would you define friendship?"

"I never define things. It is my business to describe people, facts and events. Bond is a lawyer and a man of concise definitions. Ask him."

"I prefer to talk to you," said Constance, who had by this time overcome her sensitive timidity and began to think that she could revive something of the old confidence in conversation. Unfortunately for her intentions, Mamie had either overheard the last words, or did not like the way things were going. She rose and pushed her light straw chair before her with her foot until it was opposite the two.

"What do you do with yourself all day long?" she asked as she sat down. "I am sure you are giving my cousin the most delightful accounts of your existence!"

"As a matter of fact, we were talking of friendship," said George, watching the outlines of Mamie's exquisite figure and mentally comparing them with Constance's less striking advantages.

"How charming!" Mamie exclaimed sweetly. "And you have always been such good friends."

With a wicked intuition of the mischief she was making, Mamie paused and looked from the one to the other. Constance very nearly lost her temper, but George's dark face betrayed no emotion.

"The best of friends," he said calmly. "What do you

think of this question, Mamie? Miss Fearing says she
thinks that a good book might be written about friendship. I answered that I thought it would be far from
popular with the public. What do you say?"

Constance looked curiously at Mamie, as though she
were interested in her reply. It seemed as though she
must agree with one or the other. But Mamie was not
easily caught.

"Oh, I am sure you could, George!" she exclaimed.
"You are so clever — you could do anything. For
instance, why do you not describe your friendship?
You two, you know you would be so nice in a book.
And besides, everybody would read it and it could not
be a failure." Mamie smiled again, as she looked at
her two hearers.

"I should think Mr. Wood might do something in a
novel with you as well as with me," said Constance.

George was not sure whether Mamie turned a shade
whiter or not. She was naturally pale, but it seemed to
him that her grey eyes grew suddenly dark and angry.

"You might put us both into the same book, George,"
she suggested.

"Both as friends?" asked Constance, raising her delicate eyebrows a little, while her nostrils expanded. She
was thoroughly angry by this time.

"Why, of course !" Mamie exclaimed with an air of
perfect innocence. "What could you suppose I meant?
I do not suppose he would be rude enough to fall in love
with either of us in a book. Would you, George?"

"In books," said George quietly, "all sorts of strange
things happen."

Thereupon he turned and addressed Grace, who was
on the other side of him, and kept up an animated conversation with her throughout the remainder of the visit.
It seemed to him to be the only way of breaking up an
extremely unpleasant situation. Constance was grateful to him for what he did, for she felt that if he had
chosen to forget his courtesy even for an instant he

would have found it easy to say many things which would have wounded her cruelly and which would not have failed to please his cousin. George, on his part, had acquired a clearer view of the real state of things.

"How I hate her!" Mamie said to herself, when Constance was gone.

"What a hateful, spiteful little thing she is!" thought Constance as she stepped into the boat.

CHAPTER XIX.

George was not altogether pleased by what had happened during the visit. He had expected that Constance would be satisfied with exchanging a few words of no import, and that she would make no attempt to lead him into conversation. Instead of this, however, she had seemed to be doing her best to make him talk, and had really been the one to begin the trouble which had ensued. If she had not allowed herself to refer in the most direct manner to the past, she would not have exposed herself to Mamie's subsequent attack. As for Mamie, though she had successfully affected a look of perfect innocence, and had spoken in the gentlest and most friendly tone of voice, there was no denying the fact that her speeches had made a visible impression upon Constance Fearing. The latter had done her best to control her anger, but she had not succeeded in hiding it altogether. It was impossible not to make a comparison between the two girls, and, on the whole, the comparison was in Mamie's favour, so far as self-possession and coolness were concerned.

"You were rather hard on Miss Fearing yesterday," George said on the following morning, when they were alone during the quarter of an hour he allowed to elapse between breakfast and going to work.

"Hard on her? What do you mean?" asked Mamie with well-feigned surprise.

"Why — I mean when you suggested that I should put you both into a book together. Oh, I know what you are going to say. You meant nothing by it, you had not thought of what you were going to say, you would not have said anything disagreeable for the world. Nevertheless you said it, and in the calmest way, and it did just what you expected of it — it hurt her."

"Well — do you mind?" Mamie inquired, with amazing frankness.

"Yes. You made her think that I had been talking to you about her."

"And what harm is there in that? You did talk about her a little a few days ago — on a certain evening. And, moreover, Master George, though you are a great man and a very good sort of man, and a dear, altogether, besides possessing the supreme advantage of being my cousin, you cannot prevent me from hating your beloved Constance Fearing nor from hurting her as much as I possibly can whenever we meet — especially if she sits down beside you and makes soft eyes at you, and tries to get you back!"

"Do not talk like that, Mamie. I do not like it."

Mamie laughed, and showed her beautiful teeth. There was a vicious sparkle in her eyes.

"You want to be taken back, I suppose," she said. "Tell me the truth — do you love her still?"

George suddenly caught her by the two wrists and held her before him. He was annoyed and yet he could not help being amused.

"Mamie, you shall not say such things! You are as spiteful as a little wild-cat!"

"Am I? I am glad of it — and I am not in the least afraid of you, or your big hands or your black looks."

George laughed and dropped her hands with a little shake, half angry, half playful.

"I really believe you are not!" he exclaimed.

"Of course not! Was she? Or were you afraid of her? Which was it? Oh, how I would have liked to see you together when you were angry with each other! She can be very angry, you know. She was yesterday. She would have liked to tear me to pieces with those long nails of hers. I hate people who have long nails!"

"You seem to hate a great many people this morning. I wish you would leave her alone."

"Oh, now you are going to be angry, too! But then, it would not matter."

"Why would it not matter?"

"Because I am only Mamie," answered the girl, looking up affectionately into his face. "You never care what I say, do you?"

"I do not know about that," George said. "What do you mean by saying that you are only Mamie?"

"Mamie is nobody, you know. Mamie is only a cousin, a little girl who wants nothing of George but toys and picture-books, a silly child, a foolish, half-witted little thing that cannot understand a great man — much less tease him. Can she?"

"Mamie is a witch," George answered with a laugh. There was indeed something strangely bewitching about the girl. She could say things to him which he would not have suffered his own sister to say if he had had one.

"I wish I were! I wish I could make wax dolls, like people I hate, as the witches used to do, and stick pins into their hearts and melt them before the fire, little by little."

"What has got into your head this morning, you murderous, revengeful little thing?"

"There are many things in my head," she answered, suddenly changing her manner, and speaking in an oddly demure tone, with downcast eyes and folded hands. "There are more things in my head than are dreamt of in yours — at least, I hope so."

"Tell me some of them."

"I dare do all that becomes — a proper little girl," said Mamie, laughing, "but not that."

"Dear me! I had no idea that you were such a desperate character."

"Tell me, George — if you did what I suggested yesterday and put us both into a book, Conny Fearing and me, which would you like best?"

"I would try and make you like each other, though I do not know exactly how I should go about it."

"That is not an answer. It is of no use to be clever with me, as I have often told you. Would you like me better than Conny Fearing? Yes — or no! Come, I am waiting! How slow you are."

"Which do you want me to say? I could do either — in a book, so that it can make no difference."

"Oh — if it would make no difference, I do not care to know. You need not answer me."

"All the better for me," said George with a laugh. "Good-bye — I am going to work. Think of some easier question."

George went away, wondering how it was all going to end. Mamie was certainly behaving in a very strange way. Her conduct during the visit on the previous afternoon had been that of a woman at once angry and jealous, and he himself had felt very uncomfortable. The extreme gentleness of her manner and expression while speaking with Constance had not concealed her real feelings from him, and he had felt something like shame at being obliged to sit quietly in his place while she wounded the woman he once loved so dearly, and of whom he still thought so often. He had done everything in his power to smooth matters, but he had not been able to do much, and his own humour had been already ruffled by the conversation that had gone before. He was under the impression that Constance had gone away feeling that he had been gratuitously disagreeable, and he was sorry for it.

Before very long, he had an opportunity of ascertaining what Constance felt and thought about his doings. On the afternoon of the Sunday following the one on which she had been to the Trimms', George had crossed to the opposite side of the river, alone, had landed near a thick clump of trees and was comfortably established in a shady spot on the shore with a book and a cigar. The day was hot and it was about the middle of the afternoon. Mamie and her mother had driven to the neighbouring church, for Totty was punctual in attending to her devotions, whereas George, who had gone with them in the morning, considered that he had done enough.

He was not sure to whom the land on which he found himself belonged, and he had some misgiving that it might be a part of the Fearing property. But he had been too lazy to pull higher up the stream when he had once crossed it, and had not cared to drop down the current as that would have increased the distance he would have had to row when he went home. He fancied that on such a warm day and at such a comparatively early hour, none of the Fearings were likely to be abroad, · even if he were really in their grounds.

Under ordinary circumstances he would have been safe enough. It chanced, however, that Constance had been unusually restless all day, and it had occurred to her that if she could walk for an hour or more in her own company she would feel better. The place where George was sitting was actually in her grounds, and she, knowing it to be a pretty spot, where there was generally a breeze, had naturally turned towards it. He had not been where he was more than a quarter of an hour when she came upon him. He heard a light step upon the grass, and looking up, saw a figure all in white within five paces of him. He recognised Constance, and sprang to his feet, dropping his book and his cigar at the same moment. Constance started perceptibly, but did not draw back. George was the first to speak.

"I am afraid I am trespassing here," he said quickly. "If so, pray forgive me."

"You are welcome," Constance answered, recovering herself. "It is one of the prettiest places on the river," she added a moment later, resting her hands upon the long handle of her parasol and looking out at the sunny water.

There was nothing to be done but to face an interview. She could hardly turn her back on him and walk away without exchanging a few phrases, and he, on his part, could not jump into his boat and row for his life as though he were afraid of her. Of the two she was the one best pleased by the accidental meeting. To George's surprise she seated herself upon the grass, against the root of one of the great old trees.

"Will you not sit down again?" she asked. "I disturbed you. I am so sorry."

"Not at all," said George, resuming his former attitude.

"Why do you say 'not at all' in that way? Of course I disturbed you, and I am disturbing you now, out of false politeness, because I am on my own ground and feel that you are a guest."

She was a little confused in trying to be too natural, and George felt the false note, and was vaguely sorry for her. She was much less at her ease than he, and she showed it.

"I came here out of laziness," he said. "It was a bore to pull that heavy boat any farther up, and I did not care to lose way by going farther down. I did not feel sure whether this spot was yours or not."

Constance said nothing for a moment, but she tapped the toe of her shoe rather impatiently with her parasol.

"You would not have landed here if you had thought that there was a possibility of meeting me, would you?"

The question was rather an embarrassing one and was put with great directness. It seemed to George that the air was full of such questions just now. He considered that his answer might entail serious consequences and he hesitated several seconds before speaking.

"It seems to me," he answered at last, "that although

I have but little reason to seek a meeting with you, I have none whatever for avoiding one."

"I hope not, indeed," said Constance, in a low voice. "I hope you will never try to avoid me."

"I have never done so."

"I think you have," said the young girl, not looking at him. "I think you have been unkind in never taking the trouble to come and see us during all these months. Why have you never crossed the river?"

"Did you expect that after what has passed between us I should continue to make regular visits?" George spoke earnestly, without raising or lowering his tone, and waited for an answer. It came with some hesitation.

"I thought that — after a time, perhaps, you would come now and then. I hoped so. I cannot see why you should not, I am sure. Are we enemies, you and I? Are we never to be friends again?"

"Friendship is a relation I do not understand," George answered. "I think I said as much the other day when you mentioned the subject."

"Yes. Somebody interrupted the conversation. I think," said Constance, blushing a little, "that it was your cousin. I wanted to say several things to you then, but it was impossible before all those people. Since we have met by accident, will you listen to me? If you would rather not, please say so and I will go away. But please do not say anything unkind. I cannot bear it and I am very unhappy."

There was something simple and pathetic in her appeal to his forbearance, which moved him a little.

"I will do whatever you wish," he said, in a tone that reminded her of other days. He folded his hands upon one knee and prepared to listen, looking out at the broad river.

"Thank you. I have longed for a chance of saying it to you, ever since we last met in New York. It has always seemed very easy to say until now. Yes. It is about friendship. Last Sunday I was trying to speak of it, and you were very unkind. You laughed at me."

"I am sincerely sorry, if I did. I did not know that you were in earnest."

"I was, and I am, very much in earnest. It is the only thing that can make my life worth living."

"Friendship?" asked George quietly. He meant to keep his word and say nothing that could hurt her.

"Your friendship," she answered. "Because I once made a great mistake, is there to be no forgiveness? Is it impossible that we should ever be good friends, see each other often and talk together as we did in the old days? Are you always to meet me with a stony face and hard, cruel words? Was my sin so great as that?"

"You have not committed any sin. You should not use such words."

"Oh, do not find fault with the way I say it — it is so hard to say it at all! Try and understand me."

"I do understand you, I think, but what you propose does not look possible to me. There has been that between us which makes it very hard to try such experiments. Do you not think so?"

"It may seem hard, but it is not impossible, if you will only try to think more kindly of me. Do you know what my mistake was — where I was most wrong? It was in not telling you — what I did — a year sooner. Let us be honest. Break through this veil there is between us, if it is only for to-day: What is formality to you or me? You loved me once — I could not love you. Is that a reason why you should treat me like a stranger when we meet, or why I should pick and choose my words with you, as though I feared you instead of — of being very fond of you? Think it all over, even if it pains you a little. You would have done anything for my sake once. If I had told you a year earlier — as I ought to have told you — that I could never love you enough to marry you, would you then have been so angry and have gone away from me as you did?"

"No. I would not," said George. "But there was that difference —— "

"Wait. Let me finish what I was going to say. It was not what I did, it was that I did it far too late. You would not have given up coming to see me, if it had all happened a year earlier. My fault lay in putting it off too long. It was very wrong. I have been very sorry for it. There is nothing I would not do for you — I am just what I always was in my feelings towards you — and more. Can I humiliate myself more than I have done before you? I do not think there are many women who would have done what I have done, what I am doing now. Can I be more humble still? Shall I confess it all again?"

"You have done all that a woman could or should," George said, and there was no bitterness in his voice. It seemed to him that the old Constance he had loved was slowly entering into the person of the young girl before him, whom he had of late treated as a stranger and who had been so really and truly one in his sight.

"And yet, will you not forgive?" she asked in a low and supplicating tone.

He gazed at the river and did not speak. He was not conscious that she was watching his face intently. She saw no bitterness nor hardness there, however, but only an expression of perplexity. The word forgiveness did not convey to him half what it meant to her. She attached a meaning to it, which escaped him. She was morbid and had taken an unreal view of all that had happened between them. His mind was strong, natural and healthy, and he could not easily understand why she should lend such importance to what he now considered a mere phrase, no matter how he had regarded it in the heat and anger of his memorable interview with her.

"Miss Fearing — " he began. He hardly knew why he called her by name, unless it was that he was about to make a categorical statement. So soon as the syllables had escaped his lips, however, he repented of having pronounced them. He saw a shade of pain pass over her face, and at the same time it seemed a childish way of indicating the distance by which they were now separated. It reminded him of George the Third's "Mr. Washington."

"Constance," he said after another moment's hesitation, "we do not speak in the same language. You ask me for my forgiveness. What am I to forgive? If there is anything to be forgiven, I forgive most freely. I was very angry, and therefore very foolish on that day when I said I would not forgive you. I am not angry now. What I feel is very different. I bear you no malice, I wish you no evil."

Constance was silent and looked away. She did not understand him, though she felt that he was not speaking unkindly. What he offered her was not what she wanted.

"Since we have come to these explanations," George continued after a pause, "I will try and tell you what it is that I feel. I called you Miss Fearing just now. Do you know why? Because it seems more natural. You are not the same person you once were, and when I call you Constance, I fancy I am calling some one else by the name of your old self, of the Constance I loved, and who loved me — a little."

"It is not I who have changed," said the young girl, looking down. "I am Constance still, and you are my best and dearest friend, though you be ever so unkind."

"A change there is, and a great one. I daresay it is in me. I was never your friend, as you understand the word, and you were mistaken in thinking that I was. I loved you. That is not friendship."

"And now, since I am another person — not the one you loved — can you not be my friend as well as — as you are of others? Why does it seem so impossible?"

"It is too painful to be thought of," said George in a low voice. "You are too like the other, and yet too different."

Constance sighed and twisted a blade of grass round her slender white finger. She wished she knew how to do away with the difference he felt so keenly.

"Do you never miss me?" she asked after a long silence.

"I miss the woman I loved," George answered. "Is it any satisfaction to you to know it?"

"Yes, for I am she."

There was another pause, during which George glanced at her face from time to time. It had changed, he thought. It was thinner and whiter than of old and there were shadows beneath the eyes and modellings — not yet lines — of sadness about the sensitive mouth. He wondered whether she had suffered, and why. She had never loved him. Could it be true that she missed his companionship, his conversation, his friendship, as she called it? If not, why should her face be altered? And yet it was strange, too. He could not understand how separation could be painful where there was no love. Nevertheless he was sorry that she should have suffered, now that his anger was gone.

"I am glad you loved me," she said at last.

"And I am very sorry."

"You should not say that. If you had not loved me — more than I knew — you would not have written, you would not be what you are. Can you not think of it in that way, sometimes?"

"What shall it profit a man if he gain the whole world and lose his own soul?" said George bitterly.

"You have not lost your soul," answered Constance, whose religious sensibilities were a little shocked, at once by the strength of the words as by the fact of their being quoted from the Bible. "You have no right to say that. You will some day find a woman who will love you as you deserve ——"

"And whom I shall not love."

"Whom you will love as well as you once loved me. You will be happy, then. I hope it may happen soon."

"Do you?" asked George, turning upon her quickly.

"For your sake I hope so, with all my heart."

"And for yours?"

"I hope I should like her very much," said Constance with a forced laugh, and looking away from him.

"I am afraid you will not," George answered, almost unconsciously. The words fell from his lips as a reply to her strained laughter which told too plainly her real thoughts.

"You should not ask such questions," she said, a moment later. "Do you find it hard to talk to me?" she asked, suddenly turning the conversation.

"I think it would be hard for you and me to talk about these things for long."

"We need not—if we meet. It is better that we should have said what we had to say, and we need never say it again. And we shall meet more often, now, shall we not?"

"Does it give you pleasure to see me?" There was a touch of hardness in the tone.

Constance looked down and the colour came into her thin face. Her voice trembled a little when she spoke.

"Are you going to be unkind to me again? Or do you really wish to know?"

"I am in earnest. Does it give you pleasure to see me?"

"After all I have said — oh, George, this has been the happiest hour I have spent since the first of May."

"Are you heartless or are you not?" asked George almost fiercely. "Do you love me that you should care to see me? Or does it amuse you to give me pain? What are you, yourself, the real woman that I can never understand?"

Constance was frightened by the sudden outbreak of passion, and turned pale.

"What are you saying? What do you mean?" she asked in an uncertain voice.

"What I say? What I mean? Do you think it is

pleasure to me to talk as we have been talking? Do you suppose that my love for you was a mere name, an idea, a thing without reality, to be discussed and dissected and examined and turned inside out? Do you fancy that in three months I have forgotten, or ceased to care, or learned to talk of you as though you were a person in a book? What do you think I am made of?"

Constance hid her face in her hands and a long silence followed. She was not crying, but she looked as though she were trying to collect her thoughts, and at the same time to shut out some disagreeable sight. At last she looked up and saw that his lean, dark face was full of sadness. She knew him well and knew how much he must feel before his features betrayed what was passing in his mind.

"Forgive me, George," she said in a beseeching tone. "I did not know that you loved — that you cared for me still."

"It is nothing," he answered bitterly. "It will pass."

Poor Constance felt that she had lost in a moment what she had gained with so much difficulty, the renewal of something like unconstrained intercourse. She rose slowly from the place where she had been sitting, two or three paces away from him. He did not rise, for he was still too much under the influence of the emotion to heed what she did. She came and stood before him and looked down into his face.

"George," she said slowly and earnestly, "I am a very unhappy woman — more unhappy than you can guess. You are dearer to me than anything on earth, and yet I am always hurting you and wounding you. This life is killing me. Tell me what you would have me do and say, and I will do it and say it — anything — do you understand — anything rather than be parted from you as I have been during these last months."

She meant every word she said, and in that moment, if George had asked her to be his wife she would have consented gladly. But he did not understand that she meant as much as that. He seemed to hesitate a moment and then rose quickly to his feet and stood beside her.

"You must not talk like that," he said. "I owe you much, Constance, very much, though you have made me very unhappy. I do not understand you. I do not know why you should care to see me. But I will come to you as often as you please if only you will not talk to me about what is past. Let us try and speak of ordinary things, of everyday matters. I am ashamed to seem to be making conditions, and I do not know what it all means, because, as I have said, I cannot understand you, and I never shall. Will you have me on those terms?"

He held out his hand as he spoke the last words, and there was a kindly smile on his face.

"Come when you will and as you will — only come!" said Constance, her face lighting up with gladness. She, at least, was satisfied, and saw a prospect of happiness in the future. "Come here sometimes, in the afternoon, it will be like —— "

She was going to say that it would be like the old time when they used to meet in the Park.

"It will be like a sort of picnic, you know," were the words that fell from her lips. But the blush on her face told plainly enough that she had meant to say something else.

"Yes," said George with a grim smile, "it will be like a sort of picnic. Good-bye."

"Good-bye — when will you come?" Constance could not help letting her hand linger in his as long as he would hold it.

"Next Sunday," George answered quickly. He reflected that it would not be easy to escape Mamie on any other day.

A moment later he was in his boat, pulling away into the midstream. Constance stood on the shore watching him and wishing with all her heart that she were sitting in the stern of the neat craft, wishing more than all that he might desire her presence there. But he did not.

He knew very well that he could have stayed another hour or two in her company if he had chosen to do so, but he had been glad to escape, and he knew it. The meeting had been painful to him in many ways, and it had made him dissatisfied and disappointed with himself. It had shown him what he had not known, that he loved the old Constance as dearly as ever, though he could not always recognise her in the strange girl who did not love him but who assured him that her separation from him was killing her. He had hoped and almost believed that he should never again feel an emotion in her presence, and yet he had felt many during that afternoon. Nor did he anticipate with any pleasure a renewal of the situation on the following Sunday, though he was quite sure that he had no means of avoiding it. If he had thought that Constance was merely making a heartless attempt to renew the old relations, he would have given her a sharp and decisive refusal. But she was undoubtedly in earnest and she was evidently suffering. She had gone to the length of reminding him that he owed the beginning of his literary career to her influence. It was true, and he would not be ungrateful. Courtesy and honour alike forbade ingratitude, and he only hoped that he might become accustomed to the pain of such meetings.

CHAPTER XX.

When George met Mamie on that evening, he hoped that she would ask no questions as to the way in which he had employed his afternoon, for he knew that if she discovered that he had been with Constance Fearing she would in all probability make some disagreeable observations about the latter, of a kind which he did not wish to hear. Without having defined the situation in his own mind, he felt that Mamie was jealous of Constance and would show it on every occasion. As a general rule she followed her mother's advice and asked him no questions when he had been out alone. But this evening her curiosity was aroused by an almost imperceptible change in his manner. His face was a shade darker, his voice a shade more grave than usual. After dinner, Totty stayed in the drawing-room to write letters and left the two together upon the verandah. It was very dark and they sat near each other in low straw chairs.

"What have you been doing with yourself?" Mamie asked, almost as soon as they were alone.

"Something that will surprise you," George answered. "I have been with Miss Fearing."

He had no intention of concealing the fact, for he saw that such a course would be foolish in the extreme. He meant to go and see Constance again, as he had promised her, and he saw that it would be folly to give a clandestine appearance to their meetings.

"Oh!" exclaimed Mamie, "that accounts for it all!" He could not see her face distinctly, but her tone told him that she was smiling to herself.

"Accounts for what?" he asked.

"For a great many things. For your black looks and your gloomy view of the dinner, and your general unsociability."

"I do not feel in the least gloomy or unsociable," George said drily. "You have too much imagination."

"Why did you go to see her?"

"I did not. I landed on their place without knowing it, and when I had been there a quarter of an hour, Miss Fearing suddenly appeared upon the scene. Is there anything else you would like to know?"

"Now you are angry!" Mamie exclaimed. "Of course. I knew you would be. That shows that your conversation with Conny was either very pleasant or very disagreeable. I am not naturally curious, but I would like to know what you talked about!"

"Would you?" George laughed a little roughly. "We did not talk of you — why should you want to know?"

"Oh, that mine enemy would write a book!" Mamie exclaimed, "and put into it an accurate report of your conversations, and send it to me to be criticised."

"Why are you so vicious? Let Miss Fearing alone, if you do not like her. She has done you no harm, and there is no reason why you should call her your enemy, and quote the Bible against her."

"I hate to hear you call her Miss Fearing. I know you call her Constance when you are alone with her."

"Mamie, you are a privileged person, but you sometimes go too far. It is of no consequence what I call her. Let us drop the subject and talk of something else, unless you will speak of her reasonably and quietly."

"Do you expect me to go with you when you make your next visit?"

"I shall be very glad if you will, provided that you will behave yourself like a sensible creature."

"As I did the other day, when she was here? Is that the way?" Mamie laughed.

"No. You behaved abominably——"

"And she has been complaining to you, and that is the reason why you are lecturing me, and making the night hideous with your highly moral and excellent advice. Give it up, George. It is of no use. I am bad by nature."

George was silent for a few minutes. It was clear that if he meant to see Constance from time to time in future matters must be established upon a permanent basis of some sort.

"Mamie," he said at last, "let us be serious. Are you really as fond of me as you seem to be? Will you do something, not to please me, but to help me?"

"Provided it is easy and I like to do it!" Mamie laughed. "Of course I will, George," she added a moment later in a serious tone.

"Very well. It is this. Forget, or pretend to forget, that there is such a person as Miss Fearing in the world.

Or else go and see her and be as good and charming as you know how to be."

"You give me my choice? I may do either?"

"It will help me if you will do either. I cannot hear her spoken of unkindly, and I cannot see her treated as you treated her the other day, without the shadow of a cause."

"I think there is cause enough, considering how she treated you. Oh, yes, I know what you will say — that there never was any engagement, and all the rest of it. It is very honourable of you, and I admire you men much for putting it in that way. But we all knew, and it is of no use to deny it, you know."

"You do not believe me? I give you my word of honour that there was no engagement. Do you understand? I made a fool of myself, and when I came to put the question I was disappointed. She was as free to refuse me as you are now, if I asked you to marry me. Is that clear?"

"Perfectly," said Mamie in a rather unnatural tone. "Since you give me your word, it is a different thing. I have been mistaken. I am very sorry."

"And will you do what I ask?"

"If you give me my choice, I will go and see her to-morrow. I will do it to please you — though I do not understand how it can help you."

"It will, nevertheless, and I shall be grateful to you."

The result of this conversation was that Mamie actually crossed the river on the following day and spent an hour with Constance Fearing to the great surprise of the latter, especially when she saw that her visitor was determined to be agreeable, as though to efface the impression she had made a few days earlier. Mamie was very careful to say nothing in the least pointed, nor anything which could be construed as an allusion to George.

Totty saw and wondered, but said nothing. She supposed that Mamie had made the visit because George had asked her to, and she was well satisfied that George should take the position of asking Mamie to do anything for him. That sort of thing, she said to herself, helps on a flirtation wonderfully.

As for George he did not look forward to his next meeting with Constance with any kind of pleasure. It was distinctly disagreeable, and he wished that something might happen to prevent it. He did not know whether Constance would tell Grace of his coming, but it struck him that he would not like to be surprised by Grace when he was sitting under the trees with her sister. Grace would assuredly not understand why he was there, and he would be placed in a very false position.

So far, he was right. Constance had not mentioned her meeting with George to any one, and had no intention of doing so. She, like George, said to herself that Grace would not understand, and it seemed wisest not to give her understanding a chance. Of late George had been rarely mentioned, and there was a tendency to coldness between the sisters if his name was spoken, even accidentally. Constance had at first been grateful for the other's readiness to help her on the memorable first of May, but as time went on, she began to feel that Grace was in some way responsible for her unhappiness and she resented any allusion to the past. Fortunately, Grace was very much occupied with her own existence at that time and was little inclined to find fault with other people's views of life. She had married the man she loved, and who loved her, for whom she had waited long, and of whom she was immensely proud. He was exactly suited to her taste and represented her ideal of man in every way. She would rather talk of him than of George Wood, and she preferred his company to her sister's when he was at home. They were a couple whose happiness would have become proverbial if it had been allowed to continue; one of those couples who are not interesting but to watch whom is a satisfaction, and whom it is always pleasant to meet. There was just the

right difference of age between them, there was just the
right difference in height, the proper contrast in complexion, both had much the same tastes, both were very
much in earnest, very sensible, and very faithful. It
was to be foreseen that in the course of years they would
grow more and more alike, and perhaps more and more
prejudiced in favour of their own way of looking at
things, that they would have sensible, good-looking
children, who would do all those things which they ought
to do and rejoice their parents' hearts, in short that they
would lead a peaceful and harmonious life and be in
every way an honour to their principles and a model to
all young couples yet unmarried. They were people to
whom nothing unusual would ever happen, people who,
if they had had the opportunity to invent gunpowder,
would have held a matrimonial consultation upon the
matter and would have decided that explosives should
be avoided with care, and had better not be invented at
all. Since their marriage they had both been less in
sympathy with Constance than before, and the latter was
beginning to suspect that it would not be wise for them
to live together when they returned to town. She was
in some doubt, however, about making any definite
arrangements. The elderly female relation who had
been a companion and a chaperon to the two young girls,
was on her hands, and had begun to show signs of turning into an invalid. It was impossible to turn her adrift,
though she was manifestly in the way at present, and
yet if Constance decided to live by herself, the good
lady was not the sort of person she needed. She gave a
good deal of thought to the matter, and turned it over in
every way, little suspecting that an event was about to
occur which would render all such arrangements futile.

On the Sunday afternoon agreed upon, George got into
the boat alone and pulled away into the stream without
offering any explanation of his departure to Mrs. Trimm
or to Mamie. He took it for granted that they intended
to go to church as usual and that he would not be missed.

Moreover, he owed no account of his doings to any one, as he said to himself, and would assuredly give none. He started at an early hour, but was surprised to see that Constance was at the place of meeting before him. As he glanced over his shoulder to see that he was rowing for the right point, he caught sight of her white serge dress beneath the trees.

"I have been watching you ever since you started," she said, holding out her hand to him. "Why do you always row instead of sailing? There is a good breeze, too."

"There are two reasons," he answered. "In the first place, the Trimms have no sail-boat, and secondly, if they had, I should not know how to manage it."

"My brother-in-law and Grace are out. Do you see their boat off there? Just under the bluff. They said they would probably go to your cousin's a little later. And now sit down. Do you know? I was afraid you would not come, until I saw your boat."

"What made you think that? Did I not promise that I would come?"

"Yes — I know. But I was afraid something would happen to prevent you — and then, when one looks forward to something for a whole week, it so often does not happen."

"That is true. But then, presentiments are always wrong. What have you been doing with yourself all the week?" George asked, feeling that since he had come so far, it was incumbent upon him to try and make conversation.

"Not much. I had one surprise — your cousin Mamie came over on Tuesday and made a long visit. I had not expected her, I confess, but she was in very good spirits and talked charmingly."

"She is a very nice girl," said George indifferently.

"Of course — I know. But when we were all over there the other day I thought — " she stopped suddenly and looked at George. "Is it forbidden ground?" she asked, with a slight change of colour.

"What? Mamie? No. Why should we not talk about her?"

"Well — I fancied she did not like me. She said one or two things that I thought were meant to hurt me. They did, too. I suppose I am very sensitive. After all, she looked perfectly innocent, and probably meant nothing by it."

"She often says foolish things which she does not mean," said George reflectively. "But she is a very good girl, all the same. You say she was agreeable the other day — what did you talk about?"

"She raved about you," said Constance. "She is a great admirer of yours. Did you know it?"

"I know she likes me," George answered coolly. "Her mother is a very old friend of mine and has been very kind to me. She saw that I was worn out with work, and insisted upon my spending the summer with them, as Sherry Trimm is abroad and they had no man in the house. So Mamie came over here to sing my praises, did she?"

"Yes, and she sang them very well. She is so enthusiastic — it is a pleasure to listen to her."

"I should think you would find that sort of thing rather fatiguing," said George with a smile.

"Strange to say I did not. I could bear a great deal of it without being in the least tired. But, as I told you, I was surprised by her visit. Do you know what I thought? I thought that you had made her come and be nice, because you had seen that I had been annoyed when we were over there. It would have been so like you."

"Would it? If I had done what you suppose, I would not tell you and I am very glad she came. I wish you knew each other better, and liked each other."

"We can, if you would be glad," said Constance. "I could go over there and ask her here, and see a great deal of her, and I could make her like me. I will if you wish it."

"Why should I put you to so much trouble, for a matter of so little importance?"

"It would be a pleasure to do anything for you," answered the young girl simply. "I wish I might."

George looked at her gravely and saw that she was very much in earnest. The readiness with which she offered to put herself to any amount of inconvenience at the slightest hint from him, proved she was looking out for some occasion of proving her friendship.

"You are very kind, Constance," he said gently. "I thank you very much."

A silence followed, broken only by the singing of the wind in the old trees. The sky was overcast and there were light squalls on the water. Presently George began to talk again and an hour passed quickly away, far more quickly and pleasantly than he had believed possible. They had many thoughts and ideas in common, and the first constraint being removed it was impossible that they should be long together without talking freely.

"Why not kill him?" said Constance in a critical tone. "It would solve many difficulties, and after all you do not want him any more."

They were talking of the book he was now writing. Insensibly they had approached the subject, and being once near it, George had not resisted the temptation to tell her the story.

"It would be so easy," she continued. "Take him out in a boat and upset him, you know. They say drowning is a pleasant death. A boat like my brother-in-law's — there it is. Do you see?"

Grace and her husband had been across to see Totty and were returning. The breeze was uncertain, and from time to time the boat lay over in a way that looked dangerous.

"Murder and sudden death!" said George with a light laugh. "Do you not think it would be more artistic to let him live? When I was a starving critic, that was one of my favourite attacks. At this point the author, for reasons doubtless known to himself, unexpectedly drowns his hero, and what might have proved a very fair story is brought to an abrupt close. You know the style. I used to do it very well. Do you not think they will say that?"

"What does it matter? Besides, it is only a suggestion, and this particular man is not the hero. I never liked him from the beginning, and I should be glad if he were brought to an awful end!"

"How heartless! But he is not so bad as you think. I never could tell a story well in this way, and you have not read the book. By Jove! I believe they have brought over Mamie and her mother. There are a lot of people in the boat."

He was watching the little craft rather anxiously. It struck him that he would rather not be found sitting under the trees with Constance, by that particular party of people.

"You do not think they will come here, do you?" he asked, turning to his companion. It seemed almost as natural as formerly that they should agree in not wishing to be interrupted by Grace, nor by any one else.

"Oh no!" Constance answered. "They will not come here. The buoy is anchored opposite the landing, much farther down, and John could not moor her to the shore. It is odd, though, that he should be running so free. He is losing way by coming towards us."

"I am sure they have seen us and mean to land here," said George in a tone that betrayed his annoyance.

Both watched the little boat in silence for some minutes.

"You are right," Constance said at last. "They are coming here. It is of no use to run away," she added, quite naturally. "They must have seen my white frock long ago. Yes, here they are."

By this time the boat was less than twenty yards from the shore and within speaking distance. She was a small, light craft, half-decked, and rigged as a cutter. John Bond was steering and the three ladies were seated in the middle. John let her head come to the wind and sang out —

"Wood! I say!"

"Hullo!" George answered, springing to his feet and advancing to the edge of the land.

"Can you take the ladies ashore in your boat?"

"All right!" George sprang into the light wherry, taking the painter with him, and pulled alongside of the party. In a moment the three ladies were over the side and crowded together in the stern.

"You will meet us at the house, dear, won't you?" said Grace to her husband just as George was turning his boat to row back.

"Yes, as soon as I can take her to her moorings," answered John, who was holding the helm up with one hand and loosening the sheet with the other.

As George rowed towards the land he faced the river and saw what happened. The three ladies were all looking in the opposite direction. The little cutter's head went round, slowly at first, and then more quickly as the wind filled the sail. At that moment a sharp squall swept over the water. George could see that John was trying to let the sheet go, but the rope was jammed and the sail remained close hauled, as it had been when he made the boat lie to. She had little ballast in her, and the weight of the ladies being out of her, left her far too light. George was not a practical sailor, and he turned pale as he saw the cutter lie over upon her side, though he supposed it might not be as dangerous as it looked. A moment later he stopped rowing. The little vessel had capsized and was floating bottom upwards. John Bond was nowhere to be seen.

"Can your husband swim?" he asked quickly of Grace. She started violently as she saw the look on his face, turned, caught sight of the sail-boat's keel and then screamed.

"Save him! Save him!" she cried in agony.

"Take the sculls, Mamie!" cried George as he sprang over the side into the river. He had not even thrown off his shoes or his flannel jacket.

George had calculated that he could reach the place where the accident had occurred much sooner by swimming than in the boat, which was long and narrow and needed some time to turn, and which moreover was moving in the opposite direction. He was a first-rate swimmer and diver and trusted to his strength to overcome the disadvantage he was under in being dressed. In a few seconds he had reached the cutter. John Bond was nowhere to be seen. Without hesitation he drew a long breath and dived under the boat. The unfortunate man had become entangled in the ropes and was under the vessel, struggling desperately to free himself. George laid hold of him just as he was making his last convulsive effort. But it was too late. The wet sail and the slack of the sheet had somehow fastened themselves about him. He grasped the arm with which George tried to help him, and his grip was like a steel vice, for John Bond was a very strong man and he was in his death agony. George now struggled for his own life, trying to free himself from the death clasp that held him, making desperate efforts to get his head under the side of the boat in order to breathe the air. But he could not loosen the dead man's iron hold. The effort to hold his breath could go no further, he opened his mouth, and made as though he were breathing, taking the cool fresh water into his lungs, while still exerting his utmost strength to get free. Then a delicious dreamy sleep seemed to come over him and he lost consciousness.

Mamie Trimm showed admirable self-possession. She brought her mother and Grace ashore in spite of their cries and entreaties, for she knew that they could do nothing, and she herself did not believe at first that anything serious had happened, and told them so as calmly as she could. She knew that George was an admirable swimmer and she had no fear for him, though as she reached the land she saw him dive under the capsized boat. He would reappear in thirty seconds at the most, and would probably bring John Bond up with him. She had great difficulty in making Grace go ashore, however, and without her mother's assistance she would have found it altogether impossible. The four women stood near together straining their sight, when nothing was to be seen. The struggles of the two men moved the light hull of the cutter during several seconds and then all was quiet.

With parted lips and blanched cheeks Constance Fearing stared at the water, leaning against the tree that was nearest to the edge. Grace would have fallen to the ground if Mrs. Trimm had not held her arms about her. Mamie stood motionless and white, expecting every moment to see George's dark head rise to the surface, believing that he could not be drowned.

At that moment a third boat, rowed by four strong pairs of arms shot past the wooded point at a tremendous speed, the water flying to right and left of the sharp prow, and churning in the wake, while the hard breathing of the desperate rowers could be heard.

"Jump on her keel, fellows!" roared a lusty voice. "There are four of us and we can right her. They're both under the stern!"

In an instant, as it seemed, the little cutter was lying on her side, and the four women could see the bodies of John Bond and George Wood clasped together and entangled in the sail, but partly drawn out of water by the lifting of the boat's side. Quicker than thought Mamie was in the wherry again and out on the water. The cutter had drifted in shore with the current during the two or three minutes in which all had happened. The girl saw that the rescuers needed help and was with them in an instant. What she did she never remembered afterwards, but for many days the strain upon her strength left her bruised and aching from head to foot. In less than a minute the bodies of the two men were in her boat and two of the newcomers were pulling her ashore. The others caught their own craft again and swam to land, pushing it before them.

With a cry that seemed to break her heart Grace fell upon her husband's corpse. He was dead, and she knew it, though two of the men did everything in their power to restore him. They were all gentlemen who lived by the river, and knew what to do in such cases.

On the other side the two young girls knelt beside the body of George Wood, both their faces as white as his, both silent, both helping to their utmost in the attempt to bring him to life. The men were prompt and determined in their action. One of them was a physician. For many minutes they moved George's arms up and down with a regular, cadenced motion, so as to expand and contract the lungs and produce an artificial breathing.

"I am afraid it is all up," said one in a low voice to his companion.

"Not yet," answered the other, who was the doctor. "I believe he is alive."

He was right. A minute later George's eyelids trembled.

"He is alive," said Constance in a strange, happy voice.

Mamie said nothing, but her great grey eyes opened wide with joy. Then all at once, with a smothered cry she threw herself upon him and kissed his dark face passionately, heedless of the two strangers as she was of the girl who was kneeling opposite to her.

Constance seized her by the arm and pushed her away from George with a strength no one would have suspected her of possessing.

"What is he to you, that you should do that?" she asked in a tone trembling with passion.

Mamie's eyes flashed angrily as she shook herself free and raised her head.

"I love him," she said proudly. "What are you to him that you should come between us?"

George opened his eyes slowly.

"Constance!" He could hardly articulate the name, and a violent fit of coughing succeeded the effort.

The two girls looked into each other's eyes. Both had heard the syllables, and both knew what they meant. In Constance's face there was pride, triumph, supreme happiness. In Mamie's closely-set lips and flashing eyes there was implacable hatred. She rose to her feet and drew back, slowly, while Constance remained kneeling on the ground. One moment more she remained where she was, gazing at her retreating rival. Then, with one more glance at George's reviving eyes, she sprang up and went to her sister's side.

Grace's grief was uncontrollable and terrible to see. During the night that followed it was impossible to make her leave her husband's body. She was far too strong to break down or to go mad, and she suffered everything that a human being can suffer without a moment's respite.

Constance never left her, though she could do nothing to soothe her fearful sorrow. Words were of no use, for Grace could not hear them. There was nothing to be done, but to wait and pray that she might become exhausted by the protracted agony.

It was late in the evening when the four gentlemen who had saved George's life brought him home with Mamie and her mother. There had been much to be thought of before he could think of returning. They had carried him to Constance's house at first, for he had been unable to walk, and they had given him some of the dead man's clothes in place of his own dripping garments, had chafed him and warmed him and poured stimulants down his throat. The doctor in the party had strongly urged him to spend the night where he was. But nothing could induce him to do that. As soon as he was strong enough to walk he insisted on recrossing the river.

Even Totty was terribly shocked and depressed by what had happened. She was not without heart and the tears came into her eyes when she thought of Grace's cruel bereavement.

"Oh, George," she said before they retired for the night, "you don't think anything more could have been done, do you? It was quite impossible to save him, was it not?"

A faint smile passed over the tired face of the man who had to all intents and purposes sacrificed his own life in the attempt to save John Bond, who had been as dead as he so far as his own sensations were concerned.

"I did what I could," he answered simply.

Mamie looked keenly into his eyes, as she bade him good-night. Her mother was already at the door.

"You love Constance Fearing still," she said in a tone that could not reach Totty's ears.

"I hope not," George answered with sudden coldness.

"When you opened your eyes, you said 'Constance' quite distinctly. We both heard it."

"Did I? That was very foolish. The next time I am drowned in the presence of ladies I will try and be more careful."

CHAPTER XXI.

The sudden death of John Bond caused an interruption in the lives of most of the people concerned in this history. George Wood had received one of those violent mental impressions from which men do not recover for many weeks. It was long before he could rid his dreams of the ever-repeated scene. When he closed his eyes the white sail of the little cutter rose before them, the sharp and sudden squall struck the canvas, and almost at the same instant he felt himself once more in the cool depths, struggling with a man already almost dead, striving with agonised determination to hold his breath, then abandoning the effort and losing consciousness, only to awake with a violent start and a short, smothered cry.

Even Totty, who was not naturally nervous, was haunted by terrible visions in the night and was a little pale and subdued during a fortnight after the accident. Mamie wore a strange expression, which neither George nor her mother could understand. Her lips were often tightly set together as though in some desperate effort, in which her eyelids drooped and her fingers grasped convulsively whatever they held. She was living over again that awful moment when she had clutched what she had believed to be the dead body of the man she loved, and almost unaided, she knew not how, had dragged it into the boat. There was another instant, too, which recalled itself vividly to her memory, the one in which the reviving man had pronounced Constance's name, and Constance had shown her triumph in her eyes.

As often happens in such cases, both George and Mamie had been less exhausted on the evening of the fatal day than they had been for several days afterwards. It was long before Mamie made any reference again to the first word he had spoken with returning consciousness. She often, indeed, stood gazing across the river, towards the scene of the tragedy and beyond the tall trees in the direction of the house that was hidden behind them, and George knew what was in her thoughts better than he could tell what was in his own. He had learned soon enough that he owed a large share of gratitude for the preservation of his life to Mamie herself. The young doctor who had done so much, had been to see him more than once and had repeated to him that if he had been left, even with his head above water, but without the immediate assistance necessary in such cases, during two or three minutes more, he would in all likelihood never have breathed again. The presence of a boat on the spot, and above all Mamie's exhibition of an almost supernatural strength in getting George into the wherry, had really saved his life. Without her, the four men who had acted so promptly would have been helpless. Their own craft was adrift and empty, and they had been unable to right the cutter so as to make use of her, light as she was. The doctor did not fail to say the same thing to Mamie, complimenting her on her presence of mind and extraordinary energy in a way that brought the colour to her pale cheeks. George felt that a new tie bound him to his cousin.

It was indeed impossible that where there was already so much genuine affection on the one side and so much devoted love on the other, such an accident should not increase both in a like proportion. Whether it were really true that Mamie had been the immediate means of saving George or not, the testimony was universally in favour of that opinion, and the girl herself was persuaded that without her help he would have perished. She had saved him at the moment of death, and she loved him ten times more passionately than before. As for him, he doubted his own power to reason in the matter. He had been fond of her before; he was devotedly attached to her now. His whole nature was full of gratitude and trust where she was concerned, and his relations with Constance Fearing began to take the appearance of an infidelity to Mamie. If he asked himself whether he felt or could ever feel for his cousin what he had felt so strongly for Constance, the answer was plain enough. It was impossible. But if he put the matter differently he found a different response in his heart. If, thought he, the two young girls were drowning before his eyes, as John Bond and he had been drowning before theirs, and if it were only possible to save one, which should it be? In that imaginary moment that was so real from his recent experience, when he was swimming forward with all his might to reach the spot in time, would he have struck out to the right and saved Mamie, or would he have turned to the left and drawn Constance ashore? There was no hesitation. Mamie should have lived and Constance might have died, though he would have risked his own life a hundred times to help her after the first was safe, and though the thought of her death sent a sharp pain through his heart. Was he then in love with both? That was an impossibility, he thought, an absurdity that could never be a reality, the creation perhaps of some morbid story-maker, evolved without experience from the elaboration of imaginary circumstances.

Since he had entered upon this frame of mind he had grown very cautious and reticent. He was playing with fire on both sides. That Mamie loved him with all her heart he now no longer doubted, and as for Constance, now that he had not seen her for some time and had found leisure to reflect upon her conduct, it seemed clear that the latter could not be explained upon any ordinary theory of friendship, and if so, she also loved him in her own strange way. He wished it had been easier to decide between the two, if he must decide at all. If there was to be no decision, he should lose no time in leaving the neighbourhood. To stay where he was would be to play a contemptibly irresponsible part. He was disturbing Constance's peace of mind, and he was not sure that at any moment he might not do or say something that would make Mamie believe that he loved her. He owed too much to these two beings, about whom his strongest affections were centred, he could not and would not give either the one or the other a moment's pain.

Totty was also not without her apprehensions in the matter. When she had somewhat recovered from the impression of the accident, she began to think it very odd that George should have been sitting alone with Constance under the trees on that Sunday afternoon. She remembered that he had disappeared mysteriously soon after luncheon, without saying anything of his intentions. She argued that he had certainly not met Constance by accident, and that if the meeting had been agreed upon the two must have met before. She knew that George had once loved the girl, and all she positively knew of the cause of the coldness between them was what she had learned from himself. She had undoubtedly refused him and he had been very angry, but that did not prevent his offering himself again, and did not by any means exclude the possibility of his being accepted. Totty was worldly-wise, and she understood young women of Constance's type better than most of them understand themselves. They imagine that in refusing men they are temporarily, and by an act of their own volition, putting them back from the state of love to the state of devoted friendship, in order to discover whether they themselves are in earnest. Many men bear the treatment kindly and reappear at the expected time with their second declaration, are accepted, happily married and forgotten promptly by designing mothers. Occasionally a man appears who is like George Wood, who raves, storms, grows thin and refuses to speak to the heartless little flirt who has wrecked his existence, until, on a summer's day he is unexpectedly forced into her society again, when he finds that he loves her still, tells her so and receives a kind answer, prompted by the fear of losing him altogether.

The prospect was not a pleasant one. If at the present juncture Constance were to succeed in winning George back, Totty was capable of being roused to great and revengeful wrath. Hitherto she had not even thought of such a catastrophe as probable, but the discovery that the two had been spending a quiet afternoon together under the trees strangely altered the face of the situation. If, however, George still felt anything for the girl, Totty had not failed to see that she also had gained something by the accident. It was a great point that Mamie should have saved George's life, and the longer Mrs. Trimm thought of it, the more sure she became that he had owed his salvation to the young girl alone, and that the four gentlemen who had appeared so opportunely had only been accessories to her action. George must be hard-hearted indeed if he were not grateful, and the natural way of showing his gratitude should be to fall in love without delay. But George was an inscrutable being, as was sufficiently shown by his secretly meeting Constance. Totty wondered whether she ought not to give him a hint, to convey tactfully to him the information that Mamie was deeply in love, to let him know that he was welcome to marry her. She hesitated to do this, however, fearing lest George should take to flight. She knew better than any one that he had been more attracted by the comfort, the quiet and the luxury of her home than by Mamie, when he had consented to spend the summer under the roof, and though Mamie herself had now grown to be an attraction in his eyes, she did not believe that the girl had inspired in him anything like the sincere passion he had felt for Constance.

Meanwhile those who had been most nearly affected by the calamity were passing through one of those periods of life upon which men and women afterwards look back with amazement, wondering how they could have borne so much without breaking under the strain. Grace was beside herself with grief. After the first few days of passionate weeping she regained some command over her actions, but the deep-seated, unrelenting pain, which no longer found vent in tears was harder to bear, inasmuch as it was more conscious of itself and of its own fearful proportions. For many days, the miserable woman never left her room, sitting from morning till evening in the same attitude, dry-eyed and motionless, gazing at the place where her dead husband had lain; and in that same place she lay all night, sleepless, waiting for the dawn, looking for the first grey light at the window, listening for his breathing, in the mad hope that it had all been but a dream which would vanish before the morning sun. Her heart would not break, her strong, well-balanced intelligence would not give way, though she longed for death or madness to end her sufferings.

At first Constance was always with her, but before long she understood that the strong woman preferred to be alone. All that could be done was to insist upon her taking food at regular intervals and to pray that her state might soon change. Once or twice Constance urged her to leave the place and to allow herself to be taken to the city, to the seaside, abroad, anywhere away from everything that reminded her of the past. But Grace stared at her with coldly wondering eyes.

"It is all I have left — the memory," she said, and relapsed into silence.

Constance consulted physicians without her sister's knowledge, but they said that there was nothing to be done, that such cases were rare but not unknown, that Mrs. Bond's great strength of constitution would survive the strain since it had resisted the first shock. And so it proved in the end. For on a certain morning in September, when Constance was seated alone in a corner of the old-fashioned garden, she had been startled by the sudden appearance of a tall figure in black, and of a face which she hardly recognised as being her sister's. She had been accustomed to seeing her in the dimness of a darkened room, wrapped in loose garments, her smooth brown hair hanging down in straight plaits. She was dressed now with all the scrupulous care of appearance that was natural to her, with perfect simplicity as became her deep mourning, but also with perfect taste. But the correctness of her costume only served to show the changes that had taken place during the past weeks. She was thin almost to emaciation, her smooth young cheeks were hollow and absolutely colourless, her brown eyes were sunken and their depth was accentuated by the dark rings that surrounded them. But she was erect as she walked, and she held her head as proudly as ever. Her strength was not gone, for she moved easily and without effort. Any one would have said, however, that, instead of being nearly two years younger than Constance, as she actually was, she must be several years older.

When Constance saw her, she rose quickly with the first expression of joy that had escaped her lips for many a day.

"Thank God!" she exclaimed. "At last!"

"At last," Grace answered quietly. "One thing only, Constance," she continued after a pause. "I will be myself again. But do not talk of going away, and never speak of what has happened."

"I never will, dear," answered the older girl.

There had been many inquiries made at the house by messengers from Mrs. Trimm, but neither she, nor Mamie nor George had ventured to approach the place upon which such awful sorrow had descended. They had been surprised at not learning that the two sisters had left their country-seat, and had made all sorts of conjectures concerning their delay in going away, but they gradually became accustomed to the idea that Grace might prefer to stay where she was.

"It would kill me!" Totty exclaimed with much emphasis.

"I could not do it," said Mamie, looking at George and feeling suddenly how hateful the sight of the river would have been to her if she had not seen his eyes open on that terrible day when he lay like dead before her.

"I would not, whether I could or not," George said. And he on his part wondered what he would have felt, had Constance or Mamie, or both, perished instead of John Bond. A slight shiver ran through him, and told him that he would have felt something he had never experienced before.

One morning when they were all at breakfast a note was brought to George in a handwriting he did not recognise, but which was oddly familiar from its resemblance to Constance's.

"Do see what it is!" exclaimed Totty before he had time to ask permission to read it.

His face expressed nothing as he glanced over the few lines the note contained, folded it again and put it into his pocket.

"Mrs. Bond wants me to go and see her," he said, in explanation. "I wonder why!"

"It is very natural," Totty answered. "She wants to thank you for what you did."

"Very unnecessary, considering the unfortunate result," observed George thoughtfully.

"Will you go to-day?" Mamie asked in the hope that he would suggest taking her with him.

"Of course," he answered shortly. As soon as breakfast was over he went to his work, without spending what he called his quarter of an hour's grace in the garden with his cousin.

George Wood was a nervous and sensitive man in spite of his strong organisation, and he felt a strong repugnance to revisiting the scene of the fatal accident. He had indeed been on the river several times since Bond had been drowned, and had taken Mamie with him, telling her that one ought to get over the first impression at once, lest one should lose the power of getting over them at all. But to row into the very water in which John had died and he himself had nearly lost his life, was as yet more than he cared to do when there was no definite object to be gained. Though the little wooded point of land was nearer to the house than the landing, he went to the latter without hesitation.

He was shocked at Grace's appearance when he met her in the great old drawing-room. Her face was very grave, almost solemn in its immobility, and her eyes looked unnaturally large.

"I fear I have given you a great deal of trouble, Mr. Wood," she said as she laid her thin cold fingers in his hand. He remembered that her grasp had formerly been warm and full of life.

"Nothing that you could ask of me would give me trouble," George answered earnestly. He had an idea that she wanted him to do her some service, in some way connected with the accident, but he could not imagine what it might be.

"Thank you," she said. He noticed that she continued to stand, and that she was apparently dressed for going out. "That is one reason why I asked you to come. I have not been myself and have seen no one until now. Let me thank you — as only I can — for your noble and gallant attempt to save my husband."

Her voice did not tremble nor did the glance of her deep eyes waver as she spoke of the dead man, but George felt that he had never seen nor dreamed of such grief as hers.

"I could not do less," he said hoarsely, for he found it hard to speak at all.

"No man ever did more. No man could do more," Grace said gravely. "And now, will you do me a great service? A great kindness?"

"Anything," George answered readily.

"It will be hard for you. It will be harder for me. Will you come with me to the place and tell me as well as you can, how it all happened?"

George looked at her in astonishment. Her eyes were fixed on his face and her expression had not changed.

"It is the only kindness any one can do for me," she said simply; and then without waiting for any further answer she turned towards the door.

George walked by her side in silence. They left the house and took the direction of the wooded point, never exchanging a word as they went. From time to time George glanced at his companion's face, wondering inwardly what manner of woman she might be who was able to suffer as she evidently had suffered, and yet could of her own accord face such an explanation of events as she had asked him to give her. In less than ten minutes they had reached the spot. Grace stood a few seconds without speaking, her thin face fixed in its unchangeable look of pain, her arms hanging down, her hands clasped loosely together.

"Now tell me. Tell me everything. Do not be afraid — I am very strong."

George collected his thoughts. He wished to make the story as short as possible, while omitting nothing that was of vital importance.

"I was rowing," he said, "and I saw what happened. The boat was lying to and drifting very slowly. Your husband put the helm up and she began to turn. At that moment the squall came. He tried to let out the sail — that would have taken off the pressure — but it seemed as though he could not. The last I saw of him was just as the boat heeled over. He seemed to be trying to get the sheet — the rope, you know — loose, so that it would run. Then the boat went over and I thought he had merely fallen overboard upon the other side. I asked you if he could swim. When you cried out, I jumped over and swam as hard as I could. Not seeing him I dived under. He seemed to be entangled in the ropes and the sail and was struggling furiously. I tried to drag him back, but he could not get out and caught me by the arm so that I could not move either. I did my best, but my breath would not hold out, and I could not get my head from under. He was not moving then, though he held me still. That is the last I remember, his grip upon my arm. Then I took in the water and it was all over."

He ceased speaking and looked at Grace. She was, if possible, paler than before, but she had not changed her position and she was gazing at the water. Many seconds elapsed, until George began to fear that she had fallen into a sort of trance. He waited a little longer and then spoke to her.

"Mrs. Bond!" She made no reply. "Are you ill?" he asked. She turned her head slowly towards him.

"No. I am not ill. Let us go back," she said.

They returned to the house as silently as they had come. Her step did not falter and her face did not change. When they reached the door, she stood still and put out her hand, evidently wishing him to leave her.

"You were very brave," she said. "And you have been very kind to-day. I hope you will come and see me sometimes."

George bowed his head silently and took leave of her. He had not the heart to ask for Constance, and, indeed, he preferred to be alone for a time. He had experienced a new and strange emotion, and his eyes had been opened concerning the ways of human suffering. If he had not seen and heard, he would never have believed that a woman capable of such calmness was in reality heartbroken. But it was impossible to look at Grace's face and to hear the tones of her voice without understanding instantly that the whole fabric of her life was wrecked. As she had told her sister, she had nothing left but the memory, and she had been determined that it should be complete, that no detail should be wanting to the very end. It was a satisfaction to remember that his last words — insignificant enough — had been addressed to her. She had wanted to know what his last movement had been, his last struggle for life. She knew it all now, and she was satisfied, for there was nothing more to be known.

As he rowed himself slowly across the river, George could not help remembering the Grace Fearing he remembered in old times and comparing her with the woman he had just left. The words she had spoken in praise of his courage were still in his ear with their ring of heartfelt gratitude and with the look that had accompanied them. There was something grand about her which he admired. She had never been afraid to show that she disliked him when she had feared that he might marry her sister. When Constance had at last determined upon her answer, it had been Grace who had conveyed it, with a frankness which he had once distrusted, but which he remembered and knew now to have been real. She had never done anything of which she was ashamed and she had been able now to thank him from her heart, looking fearlessly into his eyes. She would have behaved otherwise if she had ever deceived him. She would have said too much or too little, or she might have felt bound to confess at such a moment that she had formerly done him a wrong. A strange woman she was, he thought, but a strong one and very honest. She had never hesitated in her life, and had never regretted anything she had done — it was written in her face even now. He did not understand why she wished to see him often, for he could have supposed that his mere presence must call up the most painful memories. But he determined that if she remained some time longer he would once or twice cross the river and spend an hour with her. The remembrance of to-day's interview would make all subsequent meetings seem pleasant by comparison.

The circumstances of the afternoon had wearied him, and he was glad to find himself again in the midst of more pleasant and familiar associations. In answer to Totty's inquiries as to how Grace looked and behaved during his visit, he said very little. She looked very ill, she behaved with great self-possession, and she had wished to know some details about the accident. More than that George would not say, and his imperturbable face did not betray that there was anything more to be said. In the evening he found himself alone with Mamie on the verandah, Totty having gone within as usual, on pretence of writing letters. The weather was still pleasant, though it had grown much cooler, and Mamie had thrown a soft white shawl over her shoulders, of which George could see the outlines in the gloom.

"Tell me, what did she really do?" Mamie asked, after a long silence.

George hesitated a moment. He was willing to tell her many things which he would not have told her mother, for he felt that she could understand them and sympathise with them when Totty would only pretend to do so.

"Why do you want to know?" he asked, by way of giving himself more time to think.

"Is it not natural? I would like to know how a woman acts when the man she loves is dead."

"Poor thing!" said George. "There is not much to tell, but I would not have it known — do you understand? She made me walk with her to the place where it happened and go over the whole story. She never said a word, though she looked like death. She suffers terribly — so terribly that there is something grand in it."

"Poor Grace! I can understand. She wanted to know all there was to be known. It is very natural."

"Is it? It seemed strange to me. Even I did not like to go near the place, and it was very hard to tell her all about it — how poor Bond gripped my arm, and then the grip after he was dead."

He shuddered and was silent for a moment.

"I said it all as quickly and clearly as I could," he added presently. "She thanked me for telling her, and for what I had done to save her husband. She said she hoped I would come again sometimes, and then I left."

"You did not see Constance, I suppose?"

"No. She did not appear. I fancy her sister told her not to interrupt us and so she kept out of the way. It was horribly sad — the whole thing. I could not help thinking that if it had not been for you, the poor creature would never have known how it happened. I should not have been alive to tell the tale."

"Are you glad that you were not drowned?" Mamie asked in a rather constrained voice.

"For myself? I hardly know. I cannot tell whether I set much value on life or not. Sometimes it seems to be worth living, and sometimes I hardly care."

"How can you say that, George!" exclaimed the young girl indignantly. "You, so young and so successful."

"Whether life is worth living or not — who knows? It has been said to depend on climate and the affections."

"The climate is not bad here — and as for the affections ——" Mamie broke off in a nervous laugh.

"No," George said as though answering an unspoken

reproach. "I do not mean that. I know that you are all very fond of me and very good to me. But look at poor John Bond. He always seemed to you to be an uninteresting fellow, and I used to wonder why he found life worth living. I know now. He was loved — loved as I fancy very few men have ever been. If you could have seen that poor woman's face to-day, you would understand what I mean."

"I can understand without having seen it," said Mamie in a smothered voice.

"No," said George, pursuing his train of thought, tactless and manlike. "You cannot understand — nobody can, who has not seen her. There is something grand, magnificent, queenly in a sorrow like that, and it shows what she felt for the man and what he knew she felt. No wonder that he looked happy! Now I, if I had been drowned the other day — if you had not saved me — of course people would have been very sorry, but there would have been no grief like that."

He was silent. Then a sharp short sob broke the stillness, and as he turned his head he saw that Mamie had risen and was passing swiftly through the door into the drawing-room. He rose to his feet and then stood still, knowing that it was of no use to follow her.

"What a brute I am!" he thought as he sat down again.

Several minutes passed. He could hear the sound of subdued voices within, and then a door was opened and closed. A moment later Totty came out and looked about. She was dazzled by the light and could not see him. He rose and went forward.

"Here I am," he said.

She laid her hand upon his arm and looked at his face as she spoke, very gently.

"George, dear — things cannot go on like this," she said.

"You are quite right, Totty," he answered. "I will go away to-morrow."

"Sit down," said Totty. "Have you got one of those cigars? Light it. I want to have a long talk with you."

Totty Trimm had determined to bring matters to a crisis.

CHAPTER XXII.

George felt that his heart was beating faster as he prepared to hear what Totty had to say. He knew that the moment had come for making a decision of some sort, and he was annoyed that it should be thrust upon him, especially by Totty Trimm. He could not be sure of what she was about to say, but he supposed that it was her intention to deliver him a lecture upon his conduct towards Mamie, and to request him to make it clear to the girl, either by words or by an immediate departure, that he could never love her and much less marry her, considering his relatively impecunious position. It struck him that many women would have spoken in a more severe tone of voice than his cousin used, but this he attributed to her native good humour as much as to her tact. He drew his chair nearer to hers, nearer than it had been to Mamie's, and prepared to listen.

"George, dear boy," said Totty, "this is a very delicate matter. I really hardly know how to begin, unless you will help me." A little laugh, half shy, half affectionate, rippled pleasantly in the dusky air. Totty meant to show from the first that she was not angry.

"About Mamie?" George suggested.

"Yes," Totty answered with a quick change to the intonation of sadness. "About Mamie. I am very much troubled about her. Poor child! She is so unhappy —you do not know."

"I am sincerely sorry," said George gravely. "I am very fond of her."

"Yes, I know you are. If things had not been precisely as they are ——" She paused as though asking his help.

"You would have been glad of it. I understand." George thought that she was referring to his want of fortune, as she meant that he should think. She wanted to depress him a little, in order to surprise him the more afterwards.

"No, George dear. You do not understand. I mean that if you loved her, instead of being merely fond of her, it would be easier to speak of it."

"To tell me to go away?" he asked, in some perplexity.

"No indeed! Do you think I am such a bad friend as that? You must not be so unkind. Do you think I would have begged you so hard to come and stay all summer with us, that I would have left you so often together ——"

"You cannot mean that you wish me to marry her!" George exclaimed in great astonishment.

"It would make me very happy," said Totty gently.

"I am amazed!" exclaimed George. "I do not know what to say — it seems so strange!"

"Does it? It seems so natural to me. Mamie is always first in my mind — whatever can contribute to her happiness in any way — and especially in such a way as this ——"

"And she?" George asked.

"She loves you, George — with all her heart." Totty touched his hand softly. "And she could not love a man whom we should be more glad to see her marry," she added, putting into her voice all the friendly tenderness she could command.

George let his head sink on his breast. Totty held his hand a moment longer, gave it an infinitesimal squeeze and then withdrew her own, sinking back into her chair with a little sigh as though she had unburdened her heart. For some seconds neither spoke again.

"Cousin Totty," George said at last, "I believe you

are the best friend I have in the world. I can never thank you for all your disinterested kindness."

Totty smiled sweetly in the dark, partly at the words he used and partly at the hopes she founded upon them.

"It would be strange if I were not," she said. "I have many reasons for not being your enemy, at all events. I have thought a great deal about you during the last year. Will you let me speak quite frankly?"

"You have every right to say what you think," George answered gratefully. "You have taken me in when I was in need of all the friendship and kindness you have given me. You have made me a home, you have given me back the power to work, which seemed gone, you have —— "

"No, no, George, do not talk of such wretched things. There are hundreds of people who would be only too proud and delighted to have George Winton Wood spend a summer with them — yes, or marry their daughters. You do not seem to realise that — a man of your character, of your rising reputation — not to say celebrity — a man of your qualities is a match for any girl. But that is not what I meant to say. It is something much harder to express, something about which I have never talked to you, and never thought I should. Will you forgive me, if I speak now? It is about Constance Fearing."

George looked up quickly.

"Provided you say nothing unkind or unjust about her," he answered without hesitation.

"I?" ejaculated Totty in surprise. "Am I not so fond of her, that I wanted you to marry her? I cannot say more, I am sure. Constance is a noble-hearted girl, a little too sensitive perhaps, but good beyond expression. Yes, she is good. That is just the word. Scrupulous to a degree! She has the most finely balanced conscience I have ever known. Dr. Drinkwater — you know, our dear rector in New York — says that there is no one who does more for the poor, or who takes a greater interest in the church, and that she consults him upon everything, upon every point of duty in her life — it is splendid, you know. I never knew such a girl — and then, so clever! A Lady Bountiful and a Countess Matilda in one! Only — no, I am not going to say anything against her, because there is simply nothing to be said — only I really do not believe that she is the wife for you, dear boy. I do not pretend to say why. There is some reason, some subtle, undefinable reason why you would not suit each other. I do not mean to say that she is vacillating or irresolute. On the contrary, her sensitive conscience is one of the great beauties of her character. But I have always noticed that people who are long in deciding anything irritate you. Is it not true? Of course I cannot understand you, George, but I sometimes feel what you think, almost as soon as you. That is not exactly what I mean, but you understand. That is one reason. There are others, no doubt. Do you know what I think? I believe that Constance Fearing ought to marry one of those splendid young clergymen one hears about, who devote their lives to doing good, and to the poor — and that kind of thing."

"I daresay," said George, as Totty paused. The idea was new to him, but somehow it seemed very just. "At all events," he added, "she ought to marry a better man than I am."

"Not better — as good in a different way," suggested Totty. "An especially good man, rather than an especially clever one."

"I am not especially clever," George answered. "I have worked harder than most men and have succeeded sooner. That is all."

"Of course it is your duty to be modest about yourself. We all have our opinions. Some people call that greatness — never mind. The principle is the same. Tell me — you admire her, and all that, but you do not honestly believe that you and she are suited to each other, do you?"

Totty managed her voice so well that she made the

question seem natural, and not at all offensive. George considered his reply for a moment before he spoke.

"I think you are right," he said. "We are not suited to each other."

Totty breathed more freely, for the moment had been a critical one.

"I was sure of it, though I used to wish it had been otherwise. I used to hope that you would marry her, until I knew you both better — until I saw there was somebody else who was — well — in short, who loves you better. You do not mind my saying it."

"I am sorry if it is true —— "

"Why should you be sorry? Could anything be more natural? I should think that a man would be very glad and very happy to find that he is dearly loved by a thoroughly nice girl —— "

"Yes, if —— "

"No! I know what you are going to say. If he loves her. My dear George, it is of no use to deny it. You do love Mamie. Any one can see it, though she would die rather than have me think that she believed it. I do not say it is a romantic passion and all that. It is not. You have outgrown that kind of thing, and you are far too sensible, besides. But I do say that you are devotedly attached to her, that you seek her society, that you show how much you like to be alone with her — a thousand things, that we can all see."

"All" referred to Totty herself, of course, but George was too much disturbed to notice the fact. He could find nothing to say and Totty continued.

"Not that I blame you in the least. I ought to blame myself for bringing you together. I should if I were not so sure that it is the best thing for your happiness as well as for Mamie's. You two are made for each other, positively made for each other. Mamie is not beautiful, of course — if she were I would not give you a catalogue of her advantages. She is not rich —— "

"You forget that I have only my profession," said George, rather sharply.

"But what a profession — besides if it came to that, we should always wish our daughter to live as she has been accustomed to live. That is not the question. She is not beautiful and she is not rich, but you cannot deny it, George, she has a charm of her own, a grace, a something that a man will never be tired of because he can never find out just what it is, nor just where it lies. That is quite true, is it not?"

"Dear cousin Totty, I deny nothing ——"

"No, of course not! You cannot deny that, at least — and then, do you know? You have the very same thing yourself, the something undefinable that a woman likes. Has no one ever told you that?"

"No indeed!" exclaimed George, laughing a little in spite of himself.

"I am quite serious," said Totty. "Mamie and you are made for each other. There can be no doubt about it, any more than there can be about your loving each other, each in your own way."

"If it were in the same way ——"

"It is not so different. I was thinking of it only the other day. Suppose that several people were in danger at once — in that dreadful river, for instance — you would save her first."

George glanced sharply at his cousin. The same idea had crossed his own mind.

"How do you know that?" he asked.

"Is it not true?"

"Yes — I suppose it is. But I cannot imagine how you guessed ——"

"Do you think I am blind?" asked Totty, almost indignantly. "Do you think Mamie does not know it as well as I do? After all these months of devotion! You must think me very dull — the only wonder is that you should not yet have told her so."

George wondered why she took it for granted that he had not.

"What I should have to tell her would be very hard to say, as it ought to be said," he answered thoughtfully.

Totty's manner changed again and she turned her head towards him, lowering her voice and speaking in a tone of sincere sympathy.

"Oh, I know how hard it must be!" she said. "Most of all for you. To say, 'I love you,' and then to add, 'I do not love you in the same way as I once loved another.' But then, must one add that? Is it not self-evident? Ah no! There is no love like the first, indeed there is not!"

Totty sighed deeply, as though the recollection of some long buried fondness were still dear, and sweet and painful.

"And yet, one does love," she continued a little more cheerfully. "One loves again, often more truly, if one knew it, and more sincerely than the first time. It is better so — the affection of later years is happier and brighter and more lasting than that other. And it is love, in the best sense of the word, believe me it is."

If there had been the least false note of insincerity in her voice, George would have detected it. But what Totty attempted to do, she did well, with a consummate appreciation of details and their value which would have deceived a keener man than he. Moreover, he himself was in great doubt. He was really so strongly attracted by Mamie as to know that a feather's weight would turn the scale. But for the recollection of Constance he would have loved her long ago with a love in which there might have been more of real passion and less of illusion. Mamie was in many ways a more real personage in his appreciation than Constance. Totty had defined the difference between the two very cleverly by what she had said. The more he thought of it, the more ideal Constance seemed to become.

But there was another element at work in his judgment. He was obliged to confess that Totty was right in another of her facts. During the long months of the summer he had undoubtedly acted in a way to make ordinary people believe that he loved Mamie. He had more than once shown that he resented Totty's presence, and Totty had taken the hint and had gone away, with a readiness he only understood now. He had been very much spoiled by her, but had never supposed that she desired the marriage. It had been enough for him to show that he wished to talk to Mamie without interruption and he had been immediately humoured as he was humoured in everything in that charming establishment. Totty, however, and, of course, poor Mamie herself, had put an especial construction upon all his slightest words and gestures. To use the language of the world, he had compromised the girl, and had made her believe that he was to some extent in love with her, which was infinitely worse. It was very kind of Totty to be so tactful and diplomatic. Honest Sherry Trimm would have asked him his intentions in two words and would have required an answer in one, a mode of procedure which would have been far less agreeable.

"You owe her something, George," Totty said after a long pause. "She saved your life. You must not break her heart — it would be a poor return."

"God forbid! Totty, do you think seriously that I have acted in a way to make Mamie believe I love her?"

"I am sure you have — she knew it long ago. You need hardly tell her, she is so sure of it."

"I am very glad," George answered. "What will cousin Sherry say to this?"

"Oh, George! How can you ask? You know how fond he is of you — he will be as glad as I if ——"

"There shall be no 'ifs,'" George interrupted. "I will ask Mamie to-morrow."

He had made up his mind, for he detested uncertainties of all sorts. He felt that however he might compare Mamie with Constance, he was on the verge of some sort of passion for the former, whereas the latter represented something never to be realised, something which, even if offered him now, he could not accept without misgiv-

ings and doubts. Since he had made Mamie believe that
he loved her, no matter how unintentionally the result
had been produced, and since he felt that he could love
her in return, and be faithful to her, and, lastly, since
her father and mother believed that the happiness of her
life depended upon him, it seemed most honourable to
disappoint no one, and if it turned out that he was
making a sacrifice he would keep it to himself throughout his natural life.

Totty held her breath for a moment after he had made
his statement, fearing lest she should utter some invol-
untary exclamation of delight, too great even for the
occasion. Then she rose and came to his side, laid her
hands upon his shoulders and touched his dark forehead
with her salmon-coloured lips. George remembered that
a humming-bird had once brushed his face with its wings,
and the one sensation reminded him of the other.

"God bless you, my dear son!" said Totty in accents
that would have carried the conviction of sincerity to an
angel's heart.

George pressed her hand warmly, but with an odd
feeling that the action was not spontaneous. He felt as
though he were doing something that was expected of
him, and was doing it as well as he could, without enthusiasm. He looked up in the gloom and felt that
something warm fell upon his face.

"Why, cousin Totty, you are crying!" he exclaimed.

"Happy tears," answered Mrs. Sherrington Trimm in
a voice trembling with emotion. Then she turned and
swiftly entered the drawing-room, leaving him alone in
the verandah in the darkness.

"So the die is cast, and I am to marry Mamie," he
thought, as soon as she was gone.

In the first moments it was hard to realise that he had
bound himself by an engagement from which he could
not draw back, and that so soon after he had broken with
Constance Fearing. Five months had not gone by since
the first of May, since he had believed that his life was

ruined and his heart broken. What had there been in his love for Constance which had made it unreal from first to last, real only in the moment of disappointment? He found no answer to the question, and he thought of Mamie, his future wife. Yes, Totty was right. So far as it was possible to judge they were suited to each other in all respects except in his own lack of fortune. "Suited" was the very word. He would never feel what he had felt for the other, the tenderness, the devotion, the dependence on her words for his daily happiness — he might own it now, the sweet fear of hurting her or offending her, which he had only half understood. Constance had dominated him during their intercourse, and until he had seen her real weakness. With Mamie it would be different. She clung to him, not he to her. She looked up to him as a superior, he could never worship her as an idol. He was to occupy the shrine henceforth and he was to play the god and smile upon her when she offered incense. There could not be two images in two shrines, smiling and burning perfumes at each other. George smiled at the idea. But there was to be something else, something he had only lately begun to know. He was to be devotedly loved by some one, tenderly thought of, tenderly treated by one who now, at least, held the first place in his heart. That was very different from what he had hitherto received, the perpetual denial of love, the repeated assurances of friendship. He thought of that wonderful expression which he had seen two or three times on Mamie's face, and he was happy. There was nothing he would not do, nothing he would not sacrifice for the sake of receiving such love as that.

He slept peacefully through the night, undisturbed by visions of future trouble or dreams of coming disappointment. Nor had his mood changed when he awoke in the morning and gazed through the open windows at the trees beyond the river, where Constance's house was hidden. Would Constance be sorry to hear the news? Probably not. She would meet him with renewed offers of eternal friendship, and would in all probability come to the wedding. She had never felt anything for him. His lip curled scornfully as he turned away.

Early in the morning Totty entered her daughter's room. There was nothing extraordinary in the visit, and Mamie, who was doing her hair, did not look round, though she greeted her mother with a word of welcome. Totty kissed her with unwonted tenderness, even considering that she was usually demonstrative in her affections.

"Dear child," she said, "I just came in to see how you had slept. You need not go away," she added, addressing the maid. "You are a little pale, Mamie. But then you always are and it is becoming to you. What shall you wear to-day? It is very warm again — you might put on white, almost."

"Conny Fearing always wears white," Mamie answered.

"Why, she is in mourning of course," said Mrs. Trimm with some solemnity.

"Is she? For her brother-in-law? Well, she always did, which is the same thing, exactly. She had on a white frock on the day of the accident. I can see her now!"

"Oh then, by all means wear something else," said Totty with alacrity. "You might try that striped flannel costume — or the skirt with a blouse, you know. That is new."

"No," said Mamie with great decision. "I do not believe it is warm at all and I mean to wear my blue serge."

"Well," answered Mrs. Trimm, "perhaps it is the most becoming thing you have."

"Positively, mamma, I have not a thing to wear!" exclaimed Mamie, by sheer force of habit.

"I am sure I have not," answered her mother with a laugh.

"Oh you, mamma! You have lots of things."

Totty did not go away until she had assured herself that Mamie was at her best. She knew that it would have been folly to give the girl any warning of what was about to take place, and she was aware that Mamie's taste in dress was even better than her own, but she had been unable to resist the desire to see her and to go over in her own heart the circumstances of her triumph. She knew also that Mamie would never forgive her if she should discover that her mother had known of George's intention before George had communicated it to herself, but it seemed very hard to be obliged to wait even a few hours before showing her intense satisfaction at the result of her diplomacy.

During breakfast she was unusually cheerful and talkative, whereas George was exceptionally silent and spoke with an evident effort. Mamie herself had to some extent recovered her spirits, though she was very much ashamed of having made such an exhibition of her feelings on the previous evening. She offered a lame explanation, saying that she had felt suddenly cold and had run up to her room to get something warmer to put on; seeing it was so late, she had not thought it worth while to come down again. Then she changed the subject as quickly as she could and was admirably seconded by her mother in her efforts to make conversation. George's face betrayed nothing. It was impossible to say whether he believed her story or not.

"I suppose you are going to work all the morning," observed Mrs. Trimm as they rose from the table.

"I am not sure," George answered, looking steadily at her for a second. "At all events I will have a turn in the garden before I set to. Will you come, Mamie?" he asked, turning to his cousin.

For some minutes they walked away from the house in silence. George was embarrassed and had not made up his mind what he should say. He did not look at his cousin's face, but as he glanced down before him he was conscious of her graceful movement at his side. Perfect

motion had always had an especial charm for him, and at
the present moment he was glad to be charmed. Presently they found themselves in a shady place beneath
certain old trees, out of sight of the garden. George
stopped suddenly, and Mamie stopping also, looked at
him in some little surprise.

"Mamie," he said, in the best voice he could find, "do
you love me?"

"Better than anything in the world," answered the
young girl. Her lips grew slowly white and there was
a startled look in her fearless grey eyes.

"You saved my life. Will you take it — and keep
it?"

He looked to her for an answer. A supreme joy came
into her face, then shivered like a broken mirror under
a blow, and gave way to an agonised fear.

"Oh, do not laugh at me!" she cried, in broken and
beseeching tones.

"Laugh at you, dear? God forbid! I am asking you
to be my wife."

"Oh no! It is not true — you do not love me — it
never can be true!" But as she spoke, the day of happiness dawned again in her eyes — as a summer sun rising through a sweet shower of raindrops — and broke
and flooded all her face with gladness.

"I love you, and it is quite true," he answered.

The girl had for months concealed the great passion of
her life as well as she could; she had borne, with all
the patience she could command, the daily bitter disappointment of finding him always the same towards her;
she had suffered much and had hidden her sufferings
bravely, but the sudden happiness was more than she
could control. As he held her in his arms, he felt her
weight suddenly as though she had fallen, and he saw
her eyelids droop and her long straight lips part slowly
over her gleaming teeth. She was not beautiful, and he
knew it as he looked at her white unconscious face.
But she loved him as he had never been loved before, and

in that moment he loved her also. Supporting her with
one arm, he held up her head with his other hand and
kissed her again and again, with a passion he had never
felt. Very slowly the colour returned to her lips, and
then her eyes opened. There was no surprise in them,
for she was hardly conscious that she had fainted.

"Have I been long so?" she asked faintly as the look
of life and joy came back.

"Only a moment, darling," he answered.

"And it is to be so for ever — oh, it is too much, too
good, too great. How can I believe so much in one
day?"

It was long before they turned back again towards the
house. The sun rose higher and higher, and the winnowed light fell upon them through the leaves reddened
by the autumn colours that were already spreading over
the woods, from tree to tree, from branch to branch, from
leaf to leaf, like one long sunset lasting many days.
But they sat side by side not heeding the climbing sun
nor the march of the noiseless hours. Their soft voices
mingled lovingly with each other and with the murmur
of the scarcely stirring breeze. Very reluctantly they
rose at last to return, their arms twined about each other
until they saw the gables of the house rising above them
out of the rich mass of red, and orange, and yellow, and
brown, and green that crowned the maples, the oaks and
the sycamores. One last long kiss under the shade,
and they were out upon the hard brown earth of the
drive, in sight of the windows, walking civilly side by
side with the distance of half a pace between them.
Totty, the discreet, had watched for them until she had
caught a glimpse of their figures through the shrubbery
and had then retired within to await the joyful news.

Mamie disappeared as soon as they entered the house,
glad to be alone if she could not be with the man she
loved. But George went straight to her mother in the
little morning-room where she generally sat. She looked
up from her writing, as though she had been long

absorbed in it, then suddenly smiled and held out her hand. George pressed it with more sincerity than he had been able to find for the same demonstration of friendliness on the previous evening.

"I am very glad I took your advice," he said. "I am a very happy man. Mamie has accepted me."

"Has she taken the whole morning to make up her mind about so simple a matter?" asked Totty archly.

"Well, not all the morning," George answered. "We had one or two ideas to exchange afterwards. Totty — no, I cannot call my mother-in-law Totty, it is too absurd! Cousin Charlotte — will that do? Very well, cousin Charlotte, you must telegraph for Sherry's — I beg his pardon, for Mr. Trimm's consent. Where is he?"

"Here — see for yourself," said Totty holding up to his eyes a sheet of paper on which was written a short cable.

"Trimm. Carlsbad, Bohemia. Mamie engaged George Wood. Wire consent. Totty."

"You see how sure I was of her. I wrote this while you were out there — it is true, you gave me time."

"Sure of her, and of your husband," said George, surprised by the form of the message.

"Oh, I have no doubts about him," answered Mrs. Trimm with a light laugh. "He thinks you are perfection, you know."

The reply came late that night, short, sharp and business-like.

"Fix wedding-day. Returning. Sherry."

It was read by Totty with a sort of delirious scream of triumph, the first genuine expression she had permitted herself since her efforts had been crowned with success.

"It is too good to be believed," said Mamie aloud, as she laid her head on the pillow.

"I would never have believed it," said George thoughtfully, as he turned from his open window where he had been standing an hour.

CHAPTER XXIII.

"We had better say nothing about it for the present," said Totty to George on the following day. "It will only cause complications, and it will be much easier when we are all in town."

The two were seated together in the little morning-room, discussing the future and telling over what had happened. George was in a frame of mind which he did not recognise, and he seemed laughable in his own eyes, though he was far from being unhappy. His surprise at the turn events had taken had not yet worn off and he could not help being amused at himself for having known his own mind so little. At the same time he was grateful to Totty for the part she had played and was ready to yield to all her wishes in the matter. With regard to announcing the engagement, she told him that it was quite unnecessary to do so yet, and that, among other reasons, it would be better in the eyes of the world to publish the social banns after Sherrington had returned from abroad. Moreover, if the engagement were made known at once, it would be in accordance with custom that George should leave the house and find a lodging in the nearest town.

"I cannot tell why, I am sure," said Mrs. Trimm, "but it is always done, and I should be so sorry if you had to leave us just now."

"It would not be pleasant," George answered, thoughtfully. He had wished to inform Constance as soon as possible.

So the matter was decided, somewhat to his dissatisfaction in one respect, but quite in accordance with his inclinations in all others. And it was thereupon further agreed that as soon as the weather permitted, they would all return to town, and make active preparations for the wedding. Totty could see no reason whatever why the day should not be fixed early in November. She declared emphatically that she hated long engagements, and that in this case especially there could be no object in putting off the marriage. She assured Mamie that by using a little energy everything could be made ready in plenty of time, and she promised that there should be no hitch in the proceedings.

The week that followed the events last narrated slipped pleasantly and quickly away. As George had said at once, he was a very happy man; that is to say, he believed himself to be so, because the position in which he found himself was new, agreeable and highly flattering to his vanity. He could not but believe that he was taken into the family of his cousin solely on his own merits. Being in total ignorance of the fortune between which and himself the only barrier was the enfeebled health of an invalid old man, he very naturally attributed Totty's anxiety to see him marry her daughter to the causes she enumerated. He was still modest enough to feel that he was being very much overrated, and to fear lest he might some day prove a disappointment to his future wife and her family; for the part of the desirable young man was new to him, and he did not know how he should acquit himself in the performance of it. But the delicious belief that he was loved for himself, as he was, gave energy to his good resolutions and maintained at a genial warmth the feelings he entertained for her who loved him.

He must not be judged too harshly. In offering to marry Mamie, he had felt that he was doing his duty as an honourable man, and he assured himself as well as he could that he was able to promise the most sincere affection and unchanging fidelity in return for her passionate love. It was in one respect a sacrifice, for it meant that he must act in contradiction to the convictions of his whole life. He had always believed in love, and he had frequently preached that true and mutual passion was the only foundation for lasting happiness in marriage.

At the moment of acceding to Mrs. Trimm's very clearly expressed proposal, George had felt that Mamie would be to him hereafter what she had always been hitherto, neither more nor less. He did not wish to marry her, and if he agreed to do so, it was because he was assured that her happiness depended upon it, and that he had made himself responsible for her happiness by his conduct towards her. Being once persuaded of this, and assured that he alone had done the mischief, he was chivalrous enough to have married the girl, though she had been ugly, ill-educated and poor, instead of being rich, refined and full of charm, and to all outward appearances he would have married her with as good a grace and would have behaved towards her afterwards with as much consideration as though he had loved her. But the fact that Mamie possessed so many real and undeniable graces and advantages had made the sacrifice seem singularly easy, and the twenty-four hours that succeeded the moment of forming the resolution, had sufficed to destroy the idea of sacrifice altogether. Hitherto, George had fought against the belief that he was loved, and had done his best to laugh at it. Now, he was at liberty to accept that belief and to make it one of the chief pleasures of his thoughts. It flattered his heart, as Totty's professed appreciation of his fine qualities flattered his intelligence. In noble natures flattery produces a strong desire to acquit the debt which seems to be created by the acceptance of undue praise. Men of such temper do not like to receive and give nothing in return, nor can they bear to be thought braver, more generous or more gifted than they are. Possessing that high form of self-esteem which is honourable pride, they feel all the necessity of being in their own eyes worthy of the estimation they enjoy in the opinion of other men. The hatred of all false positions is strong in them and they are not quick to believe that they are justly valued by the world.

George found it easy to imagine that he loved the

young girl, when he had once admitted the fact that she loved him. It was indeed the pleasantest deception he had ever submitted to, or encouraged himself in accepting. He hid from himself the fact that his heart had never been satisfied, considering that it was better to take the realities of a brilliant future than to waste time and sentiment in dreaming of illusions. There was nothing to be gained by weighing the undeveloped capabilities of his affections against the manifestations of them which had hitherto been thrust upon his notice. He was doing what he believed to be best for every one as well as for himself, and no good could come of a hypercriticism of his sensibilities. Mamie was supremely happy, and it was pleasant to feel that he was at once the cause and the central figure in her happiness. The course of true love should run pleasantly for her at least, and its course would not be hard for him to follow.

A fortnight passed before he thought of fulfilling his promise and visiting Grace. The attraction was not great, but he felt a certain curiosity to know how she was recovering from the shock she had sustained. Once more he crossed the river and walked up the long avenue to the old house. As he was passing through the garden he unexpectedly came upon Constance, who was wandering idly through the deserted walks.

"It is so long since we have met!" she exclaimed, with an intonation of gladness, as she put out her hand.

"Yes," George answered. "I came once to see your sister, but you were not with her. How is she?"

"She is well — as well as any one could expect. I have tried to persuade her to go away, but she will not, though I am sure it is bad for her to stay here."

"But you cannot stay for ever.' It is already autumn — it will soon be winter."

"I cannot tell," Constance answered indifferently enough. "I confess that I care very little whether we pass the winter here or in town, provided Grace is contented."

"You ought to consider yourself to some extent. You look tired, and you must weary of all this sadness and dismal solitude. It stands to reason that you should need a change."

"No change would make any difference to me," said Constance, walking slowly along the path and swinging her parasol slowly from side to side.

"Do you mean that you are ill?" George asked.

"No indeed! I am never really ill. But it is a waste of breath to talk of such things. Come into the house. Grace will be so glad to see you; she has been anticipating your visit for a long time."

"Presently," said George. "The afternoons are still long and it is pleasant here in the garden."

"Do you want to talk to me?" asked the young girl, with the slightest intonation of irony.

"I wish to tell you something — something that will surprise you."

"I am not easily surprised. Is it about yourself?"

"Yes — it is not announced yet, but I want you to know it. You will tell no one, of course. I am going to be married."

"Indeed!" exclaimed Constance, with a slight start.

"Yes. I am sure you will be glad to hear it. I am engaged to be married to my cousin, Mamie Trimm."

Constance was looking so ill, already, that it could not be said that she turned pale at the announcement. She walked quietly on, gazing before her steadily at some distant object.

"It is rather sudden, I suppose," said George in a tone that sounded unpleasantly apologetic in his own ears.

"Rather," Constance answered with an effort. "I confess that I am astonished. You have my best congratulations."

She paused, and reflected that her words were very cold. She felt an odd chill in herself as well as in her language, and tried to shake it off.

"If you are happy, I am very glad," she said. "It was not what I expected, but I am very glad."

"Thanks. But, Constance, what did you expect — something very different? Why?"

"Nothing — nothing — it is very natural, of course. When are you to be married?" All the coldness had returned to her voice as she put the question.

"I believe it is to be in November. It will certainly be before Christmas. Mr. Trimm is expected to-morrow or the next day. He cabled his consent."

"Yes? Well, I am glad it has all gone so smoothly. I feel cold — is it not chilly here? Let us go in and find Grace."

She began to walk more quickly and in a few moments they reached the house, not having exchanged any further words. As they entered the door she stopped and turned to her companion.

"Grace is in the drawing-room," she said. "She wants to see you alone — so, good-bye. I hope with all my heart that you will be happy — my dear friend. Good-bye."

She turned and left him standing in the great hall. He watched her retreating figure as she entered the staircase which led away to the right. He had expected something different in her reception of the news, and did not know whether to feel disappointed or not. She had received the announcement with very great calmness, so far as he could judge. That at least was a satisfaction. He did not wish to have his equanimity disturbed at present by any great exhibition of feeling on the part of any one but himself. As he opened the door before him he wondered whether Constance were really glad or sorry to learn that he was to be married.

Grace rose and came towards him. He could not help thinking that she looked like a beautiful figure of fate as she stood in the middle of the room and held out her hand to take his. She seemed taller and more imposing since her husband's death and there was something interesting in her face which had not been there in old times, a look of greater strength, combined with a profound sadness, which would have attracted the attention of any student of humanity.

"I am very glad to see you — it is so good of you to come," she said.

"I could not do less, since I had promised — even apart from the pleasure it gives me to see you. I met your sister in the garden. She told me she hoped that you would be induced to go away for a time."

Grace shook her head.

"Why should I go away?" she asked. "I am less unhappy here than I should be anywhere else. There is nothing to take me to any other place. Why not stay here?"

"It would be better for you both. Your sister is not looking well. Indeed I was shocked by the change in her."

"Really? Poor child! It is not gay for her. I am very poor company. You thought she was changed, then?"

"Very much," George answered, thoughtfully.

"And it is a long time since you have seen her. Poor Constance! It will end in my going away for her sake rather than my own. I wonder what would be best for her, after all."

"A journey — a change of some sort," George suggested. He found it very hard to talk with the heart-broken young widow, though he could not help admiring her, and wondering how long it would be before she took another husband.

"No," Grace answered. "That is not all. She is unsettled, uncertain in all she does. If she goes on in this way she will turn into one of those morbid, introspective women who do nothing but imagine that they have committed great sins and are never satisfied with their own repentance."

"She is too sensible for that ——"

"No, she is not sensible, where her conscience is concerned. I wish some one would come and take her out of herself — some one strong, enthusiastic, who would shake her mind and heart free of all this nonsense."

"In other words," said George with a smile, "you wish that your sister would marry."

"Yes, if she would marry the right man — a man like you."

"Like me!" George exclaimed in great surprise.

"Yes — since I have said it. I did not mean to tell you so. I wish she would marry you after all. You will say that I am capricious and you will laugh at the way in which I have changed my mind. I admit it. I made a mistake. I misjudged you. If it were all to be lived over again, instead of paying no attention to what happened, as I did during the last year, I would make her marry you. It would have been much better. I made a great mistake in letting her alone."

"I had never expected to hear you say that," said George, looking into her brown eyes and trying to read her thoughts.

"I am not given to talking about myself, as you may have noticed, but I once told you that my only virtue was honesty. What I think, I say, if there is any need of saying anything. I told you that I never hated you, and it is quite true. I disliked you and I did not want you for a brother-in-law. In the old days, more than a year ago, Constance and I used to quarrel about you. She admired everything you did, and I saw no reason to do so. That was before you published your first book, when you used to write so many articles in the magazines. She thought them all perfection, and I thought some of them were trash and I said so. I daresay you think it is not very complimentary of me to tell you what I think and thought. Perhaps it is not. There is no reason why I should make compliments after what I have said. You have written much that I have liked since, and you have made a name for yourself. My judgment may be worthless, but those who can judge have told me that some things you have done will live.

But that is not the reason why I have changed my mind about you. If you were still writing those absurd little notices in the papers, I should think just as well of you, yourself, as I do now. You are not what I thought you were — a clever, rather weak, vain creature without the strength of being enthusiastic, nor the courage to be cynical. That is exactly what I thought. You will forgive me if I tell you so frankly, will you not? I found out that you are strong, brave and honourable. I do not expect that you will ever think again of marrying my sister, but if you do I shall be glad, and if you do not, I shall always be sorry that I did not use all my influence in making Constance accept you. That is a long speech, but every word of it is true, and I am glad I have told you just what I think."

George was silent for some seconds. There were assuredly many people in the world from whom he would have resented such an exposition of opinion in regard to himself. But Grace was not one of these. He respected her judgment in a way he could not explain, and he felt that all she had said confirmed his own ideas about her character.

"I am glad you have told me," he answered at length. "I have changed my mind about you, too. I used to feel that you were the opposing barrier between your sister and me, and that but for you we should have been happily married long ago. I hated you accordingly, with a fine unreasoning hatred. You were very frank with me when you came to give me her decision. I believed you at the moment, but when I was out of the house I began to think that you had arranged the whole thing between you, and that you were the moving power. It was natural enough, but my common sense told me that I was wrong within a month of the time. I have liked your frankness, in my heart, all along. It has been the best thing in the whole business."

"You and I understand each other," said Grace, leaning back in her seat and watching his dark face from beneath her heavy, drooping lids. "It is strange. I never thought we should, and until lately I never thought it would be pleasant if we did."

George was struck by the familiarity of her tone. She had always been the person of all others who had treated him with the most distant civility, and whose phrases in speaking with him had been the coldest and the most carefully chosen. He had formerly wondered how her voice would sound if she were suddenly to say something friendly.

"You are very good," he answered presently. "With regard to the rest — to what you have said about your sister. I have done my best to put the past out of my mind, and I have succeeded. When I met her in the garden just now, I told her what has happened in my life. I am to be married very soon. I did not mean to tell any one but Miss Fearing until it was announced publicly, but I cannot help telling you, after what you have said. I am going to marry my cousin in two months."

Grace did not change her position nor open her eyes any wider. She had expected to hear the news before long.

"Yes," she said, "I thought that would happen. I am very glad to hear it. Mamie is thorough and will suit you much better than Constance ever could. I wish that Constance were half as natural and enthusiastic and sensible. She has so much, but she has not that."

"No enthusiasm?" asked George, remembering how he had lived upon her appreciation of his work.

"No. She has changed very much since you used to see her every day. You had a good influence over her, you stirred her mind, though you did not succeed in stirring her heart enough. She cares for nothing now, she never talks, never reads, never does anything but write long letters to Dr. Drinkwater about her poor people — or her soul, I do not quite know which. No, you need not look grave, I am not abusing her. Poor child, I wish I could do anything to make her forget that same soul of

hers, and those eternal hospitals and charities! Your
energy did her good. It roused her and made her think.
She has a heart somewhere, I suppose, and she has plenty
of head, but she smothers them both with her soul."

"She will get over that," said George. "She will out-
grow it. It is only a phase."

"She will never get over it, until she is married,"
Grace answered in a tone of conviction.

"It is very strange. You talk now as if you were her
mother instead of being her younger sister."

"Her younger sister!" Grace exclaimed with a sigh.
"I am a hundred years older than Constance. Older in
everything, in knowing the meanings of the two great
words — happiness and suffering."

"Indeed, you may say that," George answered in a low
voice.

"I sometimes think that they are the only two words
that have any meaning left for me, or that should mean
anything to the rest of the world."

The settled look of pain deepened upon her face as she
spoke, not distorting nor changing the pure outlines, but
lending them something solemn and noble that was almost
grand. George looked at her with a sort of awe, and the
great question of the meaning of all life and death rose
before him, as he remembered her husband's death grip
upon his arm, and the moment when he himself had
breathed in the cool water and given up the struggle.
He had opened his eyes again to this world to see all
that was to result of pain and suffering from the death
of the other, whose sight had gone out for ever. They
had been together in the depths. The one had been
drowned and had taken with him the happiness of the
woman he had loved. The other, he himself, had been
saved and another woman's life had been filled with sunshine. Why the one, rather than the other? He, who
had always faced life as he had found it, and fought with
whatever opposed him, asked himself whether there were
any meaning in it all. Why should those two great

things, happiness and suffering, be so unevenly distributed? Was poor John Bond a loss to humanity in the aggregate? Not a serious one. Did he, George Wood, care whether John Bond were alive or dead, beyond the decent regret he felt, or ought to feel? No, assuredly not. Would Constance have cared, if he had not chanced to be her sister's husband, did Totty care, did Mamie care? No. They were all shocked, which is to say that their nerves, including his own, had been painfully agitated. And yet this man, John Bond, for whom nobody cared, but whom every one respected, had left behind him in one heart a grief that was almost awe-inspiring, a sorrow that sought no expression, and despised words, that painted its own image on the woman's face and spread its own solemn atmosphere about her. A keen, cool, sharp-witted young lawyer, by the simple act of departing this world, had converted a pretty and very sensible young woman into a tragic muse, had lent her grandeur of mien, had rendered her imposing, had given her a dignity that momentarily placed her higher than other women in the scale of womanhood. Which was the real self? The self that was gone, or the one that remained? Had a great sorrow given the woman a fictitious importance, or had it revealed something noble in her which no one had known before? Whichever were true, Grace was no longer the Grace Fearing of old, and George felt a strange admiration for her growing up within him.

"You are right, I think," he said after a long pause. "Happiness and suffering are the only words that have or ought to have any meaning. The rest — it is all a matter of opinion, of taste, of fashion, of anything you please excepting the heart."

"Constance will tell you that right and wrong are the two important words," said Grace. "And she will tell you that real happiness consists in being able to distinguish between the two, and that the only suffering lies in confounding the wrong with the right."

"Does religion mean that we are to feel nothing?"
George asked.

"That is what the religion of people who have never
felt anything seems to mean. Pay no attention to your
sorrows and distrust all your joys, because they are of no
importance compared with the welfare of your soul. It
matters not who lives or who dies, who is married, or
who is betrayed, provided you take care of your soul, of
your miserable, worthless, selfish little soul and bring
it safe to heaven!"

"That must be an odd sort of religion," said George.

"It is the religion of those who cannot feel. It is
good enough for them. I do not know why I am talking
in this way, except that it is a relief to be able to talk
to some one who understands. When are you to be
married?"

"I hope it may be in November."

"By-the-bye, what will Mr. Craik think of the marriage? He ought to do something for Mamie, I suppose."

"Mr. Craik is my own familiar enemy," said George.
"I never take into consideration what he is likely to do
or to leave undone. He will do what seems right in his
own eyes, and that will very probably seem wrong in the
eyes of others."

"Mrs. Trimm doubtless knows best what can be done
with him. What did Constance say, when you told her
of your engagement?"

"Very little. What she will say to you, I have no
doubt. That she hopes I shall be happy and is very glad
to hear of the marriage."

"I wonder whether she cares," said Grace thoughtfully. George thought it would be more discreet to say
nothing than to give his own opinion in the matter.

"No one can tell," Grace continued. "Least of all,
herself. I have once or twice thought that she regretted
you and wished you would propose again. And then, at
other times, I have felt sure that she was only bored —

bored to death with me, with her surroundings, with Dr. Drinkwater, the poor and her soul. Poor child, I hope she will marry soon!"

"I hope so," said George as he rose to leave. "Will you be kind enough not to say anything about the engagement until it is announced? That will be in a fortnight or so."

"Certainly. Come and see me when it is out, unless you will come sooner. It is so good of you. Good-bye."

He left the house and walked down the garden in the direction of the trees, thinking very much more of Grace and of her conversation than of Constance. Apart from her appearance, which had a novel interest for him, and which excited his sympathy, he hardly knew whether he had been attracted or repelled by her uncommon frankness of speech. There was something in it which he did not recognise as having belonged to her before in the same degree, something more like masculine bluntness than feminine honesty. It seemed as though she had caught and kept something of her dead husband's manner. He wondered whether she spoke as she did in order to remind herself of him by using words that had been familiar in his mouth. He was engaged in these reflections when he was surprised to meet Constance face to face as he turned a corner in the path.

"I thought you were indoors," he said, glancing at her face as though expecting to see some signs of recent distress there.

But if Constance had shed tears she had successfully effaced all traces of them, and her features were calm and composed. The truth of the matter was that she feared lest she had betrayed too much feeling in the interview in the garden, and now, to do away with any mistaken impression in George's mind, she had resolved to show herself to him again.

"Are you in your boat?" she asked. "I thought that as it was rather chilly, and if you did not mind, I would ask you to row me out for ten minutes in the sun. Do you mind very much?"

"I shall be delighted," said George, wondering what new development of circumstances had announced itself in her sudden desire for boating.

A few minutes later she was seated in the stern and he was rowing her leisurely up stream. To his surprise, she talked easily, touching upon all sorts of subjects and asking him questions about his book in her old, familiar way, but never referring in any way to the past, nor to his engagement, until at her own request he had brought her back to the landing. She insisted upon his letting her walk to the house alone.

"Good-bye," she said, "and so many thanks. I am quite warm now — and I am very, very glad about the engagement and grateful to you for telling me. I hope you will ask me to the wedding!"

"Of course," George answered imperturbably and then, as he pulled out into the stream he watched her slight figure as she followed the winding path that led up from the landing to the level of the grounds above. When she had reached the top, she waved her hand to him and smiled.

"I would not have him think that I cared — not for the whole world!" she was saying to herself as she made the friendly signal and turned away.

CHAPTER XXIV.

Sherrington Trimm arrived on the following afternoon, rosier and fresher than ever, and considerably reduced in weight. After the first general and affectionate greeting he proceeded to interview each member of the family in private, as though he were getting up evidence for a case. It was characteristic of him that he spoke to Mamie first. The most important point in his estimation was to ascertain whether the girl were really in love, or whether she had only contracted a passing attachment for George Wood. Knowing all that he did, and all that he supposed was unknown to his wife, he could not but regard the match with complacency, so far as worldly advantages were concerned. But if he had been once assured that his daughter's happiness was really at stake, he would have given her as readily to George, the comparatively impecunious author, as to Mr. Winton Wood, the future millionaire.

"Now, Mamie," he said, linking his arm in hers and leading her into the garden, "now, Mamie, tell us all about it."

Mamie blushed faintly and gave her father a shy glance, and then looked down.

"There is not much to tell," she answered. "I love him, and I am very happy. Is not that enough?"

"You are quite sure of yourself, eh?" Mr. Trimm looked sharply at her face. "And how long has this been going on?"

"All my life — though — well, how can I explain, papa? You ought to understand. One finds out such things all at once, and then one knows that they have always been there."

"I suppose so," said Sherry. "You did not know that 'it,' as you call it, was there when I went away."

"Oh yes, I did."

"Well, did you know it a year ago?"

"No, perhaps not. Oh, papa, this is like twenty questions." Mamie laughed happily.

"Is it? Never played the game — cannot say. And you have no doubts about him, have you?"

"How can anybody doubt him!" Mamie exclaimed indignantly.

"It is my business to doubt," said Sherry Trimm with a twinkle in his eye. "'I am the doubter and the doubt' — never knew what it meant till to-day."

"Then go away, papa!" laughed the young girl.

"And let George have a chance. I suppose that is

what you mean. On the whole, perhaps I could do
nothing better. But I will just see whether he has any
doubts, and finish my cigar with him."

Thereupon Sherrington Trimm turned sharply on his
heel and went in search of George. He found him standing on the verandah pensively examining a trail of ants
that were busily establishing communication between
the garden walk and a tiny fragment of sponge cake
which had fallen upon the step during afternoon tea.

"George," said Sherry in business-like tones, through
which, however, the man's kindly good nature was
clearly appreciable, "do you mind telling me in a few
words why you want to marry my daughter?"

George turned his head, and there was a pleasant smile
upon his face. Then he pointed to the trail of ants.

"Mr. Sherrington Trimm," he said, "do you mind
explaining to me very briefly why those ants are so particularly anxious to get at that piece of cake?"

"Like it, I suppose," Sherry answered laconically.

"That is exactly my case. I have gone to the length
of falling very much in love with Mamie, and I wish to
marry her. I understand that her views coincide with
mine and that you make no objections. I think that the
explanation is complete."

"Very well stated. Now, look here. The only thing
I care for on earth is that child's happiness. She is not
like all girls. You may have found that out, by this
time. If you behave yourself as I think you will, she
will be the best wife to you that man ever had. If you
do not — well, there is no knowing what she will do, but
whatever it is, it will surprise you. I do not know
whether hearts break nowadays as easily as they used
to, and I am not prepared to state positively that Mamie's
heart would break under the circumstances. But if you
do not treat her properly, she will make it pretty deuced
hot for you, and by the Eternal, so will I, my boy. I
like to put the thing in its proper light."

"You do," laughed George, "with uncommon clearness. I am prepared to run all risks of that sort."

"Hope so," returned Sherry Trimm, smoking thoughtfully. "Now then, George," he resumed in a more confidential tone, after a short pause, "there is a little matter of business between you and me. We are old friends, and I might be your father in point of age, and now about to become your father-in-law in point of fact. How about the bread and butter? I have no intention of giving Mamie a fortune. No, no, I know you are aware of that, but there are material considerations, you know. Now, just give me an idea of how you propose to live."

"If I do not lose my health, we can live very comfortably," George answered. "I think I can undertake to say that we should need no help. It would not be like this — like your way of living, of course. But we can have all we need and a certain amount of small luxury."

"Hum!" ejaculated Sherry Trimm in a doubting tone. "Not much luxury, I am afraid."

"A certain amount," George answered quietly. "I have earned over ten thousand dollars during the last year and I have kept most of it."

"Really!" exclaimed the other. "I did not know that literature was such a good thing. But you may not always earn as much, next year, or the year after."

"That is unlikely, unless I break down. I do not know why that should happen to me."

"You do not look like it," said Sherry, eyeing George's spare and vigorous frame, and his clear, brown skin.

"I do not feel like it," said George.

"Well, look here. I will tell you what I will do. I have my own reasons for not giving you a house just now. But I will give Mamie just half as much as you make, right along. I suppose that is fair. I need not tell you that she will have everything some day."

"You may give Mamie anything you like," George answered indifferently. "I shall never ask questions. If I fall ill and cannot work for a long time together, you will have to support her, and my father will support me."

"I daresay we could spare you a crust, my boy," said Sherrington Trimm, laying his small hand upon George's broad, bony shoulder and pushing him along. "I do not want to keep you any longer, if you have anything to do."

George sauntered away in the direction of the garden, and Sherry Trimm went indoors to find his wife. Totty met him in the drawing-room, having just returned from a secret interview with her cook, in the interests of Sherry's first dinner at home.

"Totty, look here," he said, selecting a comfortable chair and sitting down. He leaned back, crossed his legs, raised his hands and set them together, thumb to thumb and finger to finger, but said nothing more.

"I am looking," said Totty with a sweet smile. She seated herself beside him. "I have already looked. You are wonderfully better — I am so glad."

"Yes. Those waters have screwed me up a peg. But that is not what I mean. When I say, look here, I mean to suggest that you should concentrate your gigantic intellect upon the consideration of the matter in hand. You have made this match, and you are responsible for it. Will you tell me why you have made it?"

"How do you mean that I have made it?" asked Totty evasively.

"Innocence, thy name is Charlotte!" exclaimed Sherry, looking at the ceiling. "You brought George here, you knew that Mamie liked him and that he would like her, not on the first day, nor on the second, but inevitably on the third or fourth. You knew that on the fifth day they would love each other, that they would tell each other so on the sixth, and that the seventh day, being one of rest, would be devoted to obtaining our consent. You knew also that George was, and is, a penniless author — I admit that he earns a good deal — and yet you have done all in your power to make Mamie marry him. The fact that I like him has nothing to do with it."

"Nothing to do with it! Oh, Sherry, how can you say such things!"

"Nothing whatever. I would have liked lots of other young fellows just as well. What especial reason had you for selecting this particular young fellow? That is what I want to get at."

"Oh, is that all? Mamie loved him, my dear. I knew it long ago, and as I knew that you would not disapprove, I brought him here. It is not a question of money. We have more than we can ever need. It is not as if we had two or three sons to start in the world, Sherry."

She lent an intonation of sadness to the last words, which, as she was aware, always produced the same effect upon her husband. He had bitterly regretted having no son to bear his honourable name.

"That is just it," he answered sadly. "Mamie is everything, and everything is for her. That is the reason why we should be careful. She is not like a great many oirls. She has a heart and she will break it, if she is not happy."

"That is the very reason. You do not seem to realise that she is madly in love."

"No doubt, but was she madly in love, as you call it, when you brought them here?"

"Long before that —— "

"Then why did you never tell me — we might have had him to the house all the time —— "

"Because I supposed, as every one else did, that he meant to marry Constance Fearing. I did not want to spoil his life, and I thought that Mamie would get over it. But the thing came to nothing. In fact, I begin to believe that there never was anything in it, and that the story was all idle gossip from beginning to end. He is on as good terms as ever with her and goes over there from time to time to console poor Grace."

"Oh!" ejaculated Sherry in a thoughtful tone.

"You need not say 'oh,' like that. There is nothing

to be afraid of. It is perfectly natural that the poor woman should like to see him, when he nearly died in trying to save her husband. They say she is in a dreadful state, half mad, and ill, and so changed!"

"Poor John!" exclaimed Sherry sadly. "I shall never see his like again." He sighed, for he had been very fond of the man, besides looking upon him as a most promising partner in his law business.

"It was dreadful!" Mrs. Trimm shuddered as she thought of the accident. "I cannot bear to talk about it," she added.

A short pause followed, during which Totty wore a very sad expression, and Sherry examined attentively a ring he wore upon his finger, in which a dark sapphire was set between two very white diamonds.

"There is one thing," he said suddenly. "The sooner we pull up stakes the better. I do not propose to spend best part of my life in the cars. The weather is cool and we will go back to town. So pack up your traps, Totty, and let us be off. Have you written to Tom?"

"No," said Totty. "I would not announce the engagement till we were settled in town."

Sherrington Trimm departed on the following morning, alleging with truth that the business could not be allowed to go to pieces. Totty and the two young people were to return two or three days later, and active preparations were at once made for moving. Totty, indeed, could not bear the idea of allowing her husband to remain alone in New York. It was possible that at any moment he might discover that the will was missing from her brother's box. She might indeed have been spared much anxiety in this matter had she known that although Sherry had sealed and marked the document himself, it was not he who had placed it in the receptacle where it had been found by his wife. Sherry had handed it across the table to John Bond, telling him to put it in Craik's deed-box, and had seen John leave the room with it, but had never seen it since. It was not, indeed, until much later that he had communicated to his partner the contents of the paper. If it could not now be found, Sherry would suppose that John had accidentally put it into the wrong box and a general search would be made. Then it would be thought that John had mislaid it. In any case poor John was dead and could not defend himself. Sherry would go directly to Tom Craik and get him to sign a duplicate, but he would never, under any conceivable combination of circumstances, connect his wife with the disappearance of the will, nor mention the fact in her presence. Totty, however, was ignorant of these facts, and lived in the constant fear of being obliged to explain matters to her husband. Though she had thought much of the matter she had not hit upon any expedient for restoring the document to its place. She kept it in a small Indian cabinet which her brother had once given her, in which there was a hidden drawer of which no one knew the secret but herself. This cabinet she had brought with her and had kept all through the summer in a prominent place in the drawing-room, justly deeming that things are generally most safely hidden when placed in the most exposed position, where no one would ever think of looking for them. On returning to New York the cabinet was again packed in one of Totty's own boxes, but the will was temporarily concealed about her person, to be restored to its hiding-place as soon as she reached the town house.

Before leaving the neighbourhood George felt that it was his duty to apprise Constance and her sister of his departure, but he avoided the necessity of making a visit by writing a letter to Grace. It seemed to him more fitting that he should address his note to her rather than to her sister, considering all that had happened. He urged that both should return to New York before the winter began, and he inserted a civil message for Constance before he concluded.

Mamie took an affectionate leave of the place in which she had been so happy. During the last hours of the day preceding their return to town, George never left her side, while she wandered through the walks of the garden and beneath the beautiful trees, back to the house, in and out of the rooms, then lingered again upon the verandah and gazed at the distant river. He watched the movements of her faultless figure as she sat down for the last time in the places where they had so often sat together, then rose quickly, and, linking her arm in his, led him away to some other well-remembered spot.

"I have been so happy here!" she said for the hundredth time.

"You shall be as happy in other places, if I can make you so," George answered.

"Shall we? Shall I?" she asked, looking up into his face. "Who can tell! One is never so sure of the future as one is of the past — and the present. Shall we take it all with us to our little house in New York? How funny it will seem to be living all alone with you in a little house! I shall not give you champagne every day, George. You need not expect it! It will be a very little house, and I shall do all the work."

"If you will allow me to black the boots, I shall be most happy," said George. "I know how."

"Imagine! You, blacking boots!" exclaimed Mamie indignantly.

"Why not? But seriously, we can do a great deal more than you fancy — provided, as you say, that we do not go in for champagne every day, and keep horses and all that."

"I think we shall have more champagne and horses than other things," Mamie answered with a laugh. "Mamma is going to keep a carriage for me, as well as my dear old riding horse, and papa told me not to let you buy any wine, because there was some of that particular kind you like on the way out. Between you and me, I do not think they really expect us to be in the least economical, though mamma is always talking about it."

She was very happy and it was impossible for her to cloud the future by the idea of being deprived of any of the luxury to which she had always been accustomed. She knew in her heart that she was both willing and able to undergo any privation for George's sake, but it would have been unlike her to talk of what she would or could do when there was no immediate prospect of doing it. Her chief thought was to make her husband's house comfortable, and if she knew something of the art from having watched her mother, she knew also that comfort, as she understood it, required a very free use of money. George knew it, too, since he had been brought up in luxury and had been deprived of it at the age when such things are most keenly felt. The terrible, noiseless, hourly expenditure that he had seen in Totty's house made the exiguity of his own resources particularly apparent to his judgment.

"Good-bye, dear old place!" cried the young girl, as they stood on the verandah at dusk, before going in to dress for dinner. She threw kisses with her fingers at the garden and at the trees.

George stood by her side in silence, gazing out at the dim outline of the distant hills beyond the river.

"Are you not sorry to leave it all?" Mamie asked.

"Very sorry," he answered, as though not knowing what he said. Then he stooped, and kissed her small white face, and they both went in.

That night George sat up late in his room, looking over the manuscript that had grown under his hand during the summer months. It was all but finished and he intended to write the last chapter in New York, but it interested him to look through it before leaving the surroundings in which it had been written. What most struck him in the work was the care with which it was done. It was not a very imaginative book, but it was remarkable for its truth and clearness of style. He wondered at the coldness of certain scenes, which in his first conception of the story had promised to be the most dramatic. He wondered still more at the success with which he had handled points which in themselves seemed to be far from attractive to the novelist. His conversations were better than they had formerly been, but the love scenes were unsatisfactory, and he determined that he would re-write some of them. The whole book looked too truthful and too little enthusiastic to him, now, though he fancied that he had passed through moments of enthusiasm while he was writing it. On the whole, it was a disappointment to himself, and he believed that others would be disappointed likewise. He asked himself what Johnson would think of it, and made up his mind to abide by his opinion. Vaguely too, as one sometimes longs to see again a book once read, he wished that he might have Constance's criticism and advice, though he was conscious at the same time that it was not the sort of story she would have liked.

Two days later, he found himself once more in his little room in his father's house. The old gentleman received the news of the engagement in silence. He had guessed that matters would terminate as they had, and the prospect had given him little satisfaction. He thought that the alliance would probably cut him off from his son's society, and he was inwardly hurt that George should seem indifferent to the fact. But he said nothing. From the worldly point of view the marriage was a brilliant one, and it meant that George must ultimately be a rich man. His future at least was provided for.

George found Johnson hard at work, as usual, and if possible paler and more in earnest than before. He had taken a week's holiday during the hottest part of the summer, but with that exception had never relaxed in his astounding industry since they had last met.

"How particularly sleek you look," he said, scrutinising George's face as the latter sat down.

"I feel sleek," George answered with a slight laugh. "I believe that is what is the matter with the book I have been writing since I saw you. I am not satisfied with it, and I want your opinion. I sat up all last night to write the last chapter in my old den. I think it is better than the rest."

"That is a pity. It will look like a new silk hat on a beggar — or like a wig on a soup-tureen, as the Frenchmen say. But I daresay you are quite wrong about the rest of it. You generally are. For a man who can write a good story in good English when he tries, you have as little confidence as I ver saw in any one. The public does not write books and does not know how they are written. It will never find out that you wrote the beginning in clover and the end in nettles."

"Oh — the public!" exclaimed George. "One never knows what it will do."

"One may guess, sometimes. The public consists of a vast collection oɪ individuals collected in a crowd around the feet of four great beasts. There is the ignorant beast and the learned beast, the virtuous beast and the vicious beast. They are all four beasts in their way, because they all represent an immense accumulation of prejudice, in four different directions and having four different followings, all pulling different ways. You cannot possibly please them all and it is quite useless to try."

"I suppose you mean that the four beasts are the four kinds of critics. Is that it?"

"No," Jonnson answered. "That is not it at all. If we critics had more real influence with the public, the public would be all the better for it. As it is, the real critic is dying out, because the public will not pay enough to keep him alive. It is sad, but I suppose it is natural. This is the age of free thought, and the phrase, if you interpret it as most people do, means that all men are to consider themselves critics, whether they know anything or not. Have you brought your manuscript with you?"

"No. I wanted to ask first whether you would read it."

"You need not be so humble, now that you are a celebrity," said Johnson with a laugh. "You do not look the part, either. What has happened to you?"

"I am going to be married," George answered. "I am to marry my cousin, Miss Trimm."

"Not Sherrington Trimm's daughter!"

"The same, if it please you."

"I congratulate you on leaving the literary career," said Johnson with a sardonic smile. "I suppose you will never do another stroke of work. Well — it is a pity."

"I have to work for my living as I have done for years," George answered. "Do you imagine that I would live upon other people's money?"

"Do you really mean to go on working?"

"Of course I do, as long as I can hold a pen. I should if I were rich in my own right, for love of the thing."

"Love of the thing is not enough. Are you ambitious?"

"I do not know. I never thought about it. To me, the question is whether a thing is well done or not, for its own sake. The success of it means money, which I need, but apart from that I do not think I care very much about it. I may be mistaken. I value your opinion, for instance, and if I knew other men like you, I should value theirs."

"You will never succeed to any extent without ambition," Johnson answered with great energy. "It is everything in literature. You must feel that you will go mad if you are not first, if you are not acknowledged to be better than any one else during your lifetime. You must make people understand that you are a dangerous rival, and you must have the daily satisfaction of knowing that they feel it. Literature is like the storming of a redoubt, you must climb upon the bodies of the slain and be the first to plant your flag on the top. You must lie awake all night, and torment yourself all day to find some means of doing a thing better than other people. To be first, always, all your life, without fear of competition, to be Cæsar or to be nothing! I wish I could make you feel what I feel!"

"I think I would rather not," said George. "It must be very disturbing to the judgment to be always comparing oneself with others instead of trying to do the best one can in an independent way."

"You will never succeed without ambition." Johnson repeated confidently.

"Then I am afraid I shall never succeed at all, for I have not a spark of that sort of ambition. I do not care a straw for being thought better than any one else, nor for being a celebrity. I want to satisfy myself, my own idea of what is a good book, and I am afraid I never shall. I suppose that is a sort of ambition too."

"It is not the right sort."

George knew his friend very well and was familiar with most of his ideas. He respected his character, and he valued his opinion more than that of any man in his acquaintance, but he could never accept his theories as infallible. He felt that if he ever succeeded in writing a book that pleased him he would recognise its merits sooner than any one, and but for the necessity of earning a livelihood he would have systematically destroyed all his writings until he had attained a satisfactory result. That a certain amount of reputation might be gained by publishing what he regarded as incomplete or inartistic work was to him a matter of indifference, except for the material advantages which resulted from the transaction. Such, at least, was his belief about himself. That he was able to appreciate flattery when it was of a good and subtle quality, only showed him that he was human, but did not improve his own estimation of his productions.

A week later, Johnson returned the manuscript with a note in which he gave his opinion of it.

"It will sell," he wrote. "You are quite mistaken

about yourself, as usual. You told me the other day that you had no ambition. Your book proves that you have. You have taken the subject treated by Wiggins in his last great novel. It made a sensation, but in my opinion you have handled it better than he did, though he is called a great novelist. It was a very ambitious thing to do, and it is wonderful that, while taking a precisely similar situation, there should not be a word in your work that recalls his. After this, do not tell me that you have no ambition, for it is sheer nonsense. As for the last chapter, I should not have known that it was not written under the same circumstances as all the rest."

George laughed aloud to himself. He knew the name of Wiggins well enough, but he had never read one of the celebrated author's books, and if he had he would assuredly not have taken his plot.

"But Johnson could not know that," he said to himself, "and I have written just such stuff about other people."

The book went to the publisher and he thought no more of it. During the time that followed, his days were very fully occupied. Between making the necessary preparations for his approaching marriage, and the pleasant duty of spending a certain number of hours with Mamie every day, he had very little time to call his own, although nothing of any importance happened to vary the course of his life. At the beginning of November Constance Fearing and her sister returned to town, and at about the same time he was informed by Sherrington Trimm that it would be necessary for him to visit Mr. Thomas Craik, as he was about to become that gentleman's nephew by marriage.

"Of course, I know all about the old story, George," said Sherry. "But if I were you I would at least try and be civil. The fact is, I have reason to know that he is haunted by a sort of half-stagey, half-honest remorse for what he did, and he is very much pleased with the marriage, besides being a great admirer of your books."

"All right," said George, "I will be civil enough."

Sherry Trimm had conveyed exactly the impression which he had desired to convey. He had made George believe by his manner that he was himself anxious to keep his relations with Mr. Craik on a pleasant footing, doubtless on account of the money, and he had effectually deterred George from quarrelling with his unknown benefactor, while he had kept the question of the will as closely secret as ever.

CHAPTER XXV.

George had never been inside Mr. Craik's house, and the first impression made upon him by the sight of the old gentleman's collected spoil was a singular one. The sight of beautiful objects had always given him pleasure, but, on the other hand, his mind resented and abhorred alike disorder and senseless profusion. He had no touch in his composition of that modern taste which delights in producing a certain tone of colour in a room, by filling it with all sorts of heterogeneous and useless articles, of all periods and collected out of all countries. It was not sufficient in his eyes that an object should be of great value, or of great beauty, or that it should possess both at once; it was necessary also that it should be so placed as to acquire a right to its position and to its surroundings. A Turkish tile, a Spanish-Moorish dish, an Italian embroidery and an old picture might harmonise very well with each other in colour and in general effect, but George Wood's uncultivated taste failed to see why they should all be placed together, side by side upon the same wall, any more than why a periwig should be set upon a soup-tureen, as Johnson had remarked. He felt from the moment he entered the house as if he were in a bazaar of bric-à-brac, where everything was put up for sale, and in which each object must have somewhere a label tied or pasted to it, upon which letters and figures mysteriously shadowed forth its variable price to the purchaser while accurately defining its value to the vendor.

It must not be supposed, however, that because George Wood did not like the look of the room in which he found himself, it would not have been admired and appreciated by many persons of unquestioned good taste. The value there accumulated was very great, there was much that was exceedingly rare and of exquisite design and workmanship, and the vulgarity of the effect, if there were any, was of the more subtle and tolerable kind.

George stood in the midst of the chamber, hat in hand, waiting for the owner of the collection to appear. A door made of panels of thin alabaster set in rich old gilt carvings, was opposite to him, and he was wondering whether the light actually penetrated the delicate marble as it seemed to do, when the chiselled handle turned and the door itself moved noiselessly on its hinges. Thomas Craik entered the room.

The old gentleman's head seemed to have fallen forward upon his shoulders, so that he was obliged to look sideways and upwards in order to see anything above the level of his eyes. Otherwise he did not present so decrepit an appearance as George had expected. His step was sufficiently brisk, and though his voice was little better than a growl, it was not by any means weak. He was clothed in light-coloured tweed garments of the newest cut, and he wore a red tie, and shoes of varnished leather. The corner of a pink silk handkerchief was just visible above the outer pocket of his coat, and he emanated a perfume which seemed to be combined out of Cologne water and Russian leather.

"Official visit, eh?" he said with an attempt at a pleasant smile. "Glad to see you. Sorry you have waited so long before coming. Take a seat."

"Thanks," answered George, sitting down. "I am glad to see that you are quite yourself again, Mr. Craik."

"Quite myself, eh? Never was anybody else long enough to know what it felt like. But I have not forgotten that you came to ask — no, no, I remember that. Going to marry Mamie, eh? Glad to hear it. Well, well."

Thomas Craik rubbed his emaciated hands slowly together and looked sideways at his visitor.

"Yes," said George, "I am going to marry Miss Trimm——"

"Call her Mamie, call her Mamie — own niece of mine, you know. No use standing on ceremony."

"I think it is as well to call her Miss Trimm until we are married," George observed, rather coldly.

"Oh, you think so, do you? Well, well. Not to her face, I hope?"

George thought that Mr. Craik was one of the most particularly odious old gentlemen he had ever met. He changed the subject as quickly as he could.

"What a wonderful collection of beautiful things you have, Mr. Craik," he said, glancing at a set of Urbino dishes that were fastened against the wall nearest to him.

"Something, something," replied Mr. Craik, modestly. "Fond of pretty things? Understand majolica?"

"I am very fond of pretty things, but I know nothing about majolica. I believe the subject needs immense study. They say you are a great authority on all these things."

"Oh, they say so, do they? Well, well. Books are more in your line, eh? Some in the other room if you like to see them. Come?"

"Yes indeed!" George answered with alacrity. He thought that if he must sustain the conversation for five minutes longer, it would be a relief to be among things he understood. Tom Craik rose and led the way through the alabaster door by which he had entered. George found himself in a spacious apartment, consisting of two rooms which had been thrown into one by building an

arch in the place of the former wall of division. There
were no windows, but each division was lighted by a
large skylight of stained glass, supported on old Bohe-
mian iron-work. To the height of six feet from the floor,
the walls were lined with bookcases, the books being
protected by glass. Above these the walls were completely covered with tapestries, stuffs, weapons, old
plates and similar objects.

"Favourite room of mine," remarked Mr. Craik,
backing up to the great wood fire, and looking about
him with side glances, first to the right and then to the
left. "Look about you, look about you. A lot of books
in those shelves, eh? Well, well. About three thousand. Not many but good and good, as books should be,
inside and out. Eh? Like that?"

"Yes," said George, moving slowly round the room,
stooping and then standing erect, as he glanced rapidly
at the titles of the long rows of volumes. The born man
of letters warmed at the sight of the familiar names and
felt less inimically inclined towards the master of the
house.

"I envy you such books to read and such a place in
which to read them," he said at last.

"I believe you do," answered Mr. Craik, looking
pleased. "You look as if you did. Well, well. May
be all yours some day."

"How so?" George inquired, growing suddenly cold
and looking sharply at the old man.

"May leave everything to Totty. Totty may leave
everything to Mamie. Fact is, any station may be the
last. May have to hand in my checks at any time.
Funny world, isn't it? Eh?"

"A very humorous and comic world, as you say,"
George answered, looking at the old man with a rather
scornful twist of his naturally scornful mouth.

"Humorous and comic? I say, funny. It's shorter.
What would you do if you owned this house?"

"I would sell it," George answered with a dry laugh,

"sell it, except the books, and live on the interest of the proceeds."

"And you would do a very sensible thing, Mr. George Winton Wood," returned Tom Craik approvingly. All at once he dropped his detached manner of speaking and grew eloquent. "You would be doing a very sensible thing. A man of your age can have no manner of use for all this rubbish. If you ever mean to be a collector, reserve that expensive taste for the time when you have plenty of money, but can neither eat, drink, sleep, make love nor be merry in any way — no, nor write novels either. The pleasure does not consist in possessing things, it lies in finding them, bargaining for them, fighting for them and ultimately getting them. It is the same with money, but there is more variety in collecting, to my mind, at least. It is the same with everything, money, love, politics, collecting, it is only the fighting for what you want that is agreeably exciting. It has kept me alive, with my wretched constitution, when the doctors have been thinking of sending for the person in black who carries a tape measure. I never had any ambition. I never cared for anything but the fighting. I never cared to be first, second or third. I do not believe that your ambitious man ever succeeds in life. He thinks so much about himself that he forgets what he is fighting for. You can easily make a fool of an ambitious man by offering him a bait, and you may take the thing you want while he is chasing the phantom of glory on the other side of the house. I hope you are not ambitious. You have begun as if you were not, and you have knocked all the stuffing out of the rag dolls the critics put up to frighten young authors. I have read a good deal in my day, and I have seen a good deal, and I have taken a great many things I have wanted. I know men, and I know something about books. You ought to succeed, for you go about your work as though you liked it for the sake of overcoming difficulties, for the sake of fighting your subject and getting the better of it. Stick

to that principle. It prolongs life. Pick out the hardest
thing there is to be done, and go at it, hammer and tongs,
by hook or by crook, by fair means or foul. If you cannot do it, after all, nobody need be the wiser; if you
succeed every one will cry out in admiration of your industry and genius, when you have really only been
amusing yourself all the time — because nothing can be
more amusing than fighting. You are quite right. Ambition is nonsense and the satisfaction of possession is
bosh. The only pleasure is in doing and getting. If, in
the inscrutable ways of destiny, you ever own this
house, sell it, and when you are old, and crooked, and
cannot write any more, and people think you are a driv-
elling idiot and are sitting in rows outside your door,
waiting for dead men's shoes — why then, you can prolong your life by collecting something, as I have done.
The desire to get the better of a Jew dealer in a bargain
for a Maestro Georgio, or the determination to find the
edition which has been heard of but never seen, will
make your blood circulate and your heart beat, and your
brain work. I have half a mind to sell the whole thing
myself for the sake of doing it all over again, and keeping somebody waiting ten years longer for the money.
I might last ten years more if I could hit upon something new to collect."

The old man ceased speaking and looked up sideways
at George, with a keen smile, very unlike the expression
he assumed when he meant to be agreeable. Then he
relapsed into his usual way of talking, jerking out short
sentences and generally omitting the subject or the verb,
when he did not omit both. It is possible that he had
delivered his oration for the sake of showing George
that he could speak English as well as any one when he
chose to do so.

"Like my little speech? Eh?" he inquired.

"I shall not forget it," George answered. "Your ideas
cannot be accused of being stale or old fashioned, whatever else may be said of them."

"Put them into a book, will you? Well, well. Daresay printer's ink has been wasted on worse — sometimes."

George did not care to prolong his visit beyond the bounds of strict civility, though he had been somewhat diverted by his relation's talk. He asked a few questions about the books and discovered that Tom Craik was by no means the unreading edition-hunter he had supposed him to be. If he had not read all the three thousand choice volumes he possessed, he had at least a very clear idea of the contents of most of them.

"Buying an author and not reading him," he said, "is like buying a pig in a poke and then not even looking at the pig afterwards. Eh?"

"Very like," George answered with a short laugh. Then he took his leave. The old man went with him as far as the door that led out of the room in which they had first met.

"Come again," he said. "Rather afraid of draughts, so I leave you here. Good day to you."

George took the thin hand that was thrust out at him and shook it with somewhat less repulsion that he had felt a quarter of an hour earlier. The sight of the books had softened his heart a little, as it often softens the enmities of literary men when they least expect it. He turned away and left the house, wondering whether, after all, old Tom Craik had not been judged more harshly than he deserved. The man of letters is slow to anger against those who show any genuine fondness for his profession.

He walked down the avenue, thinking over what he had seen and heard. It chanced that after walking some time he stepped aside to allow certain ladies to pass him and on looking round saw that he was in the door of Mr. Popples's establishment. A thought struck him and he went in.

"Mr. Popples ——"

"Good morning, Mr. Winton Wood ——" Mr. Popples thought that the two names sounded better together.

"Good morning, Mr. Popples. I want to ask you a confidential question." George laughed a little.

"Anything, Mr. Winton Wood. Something in regard to the sales, no doubt. Well, in point of fact, sir, it is just as well to ask now and then how a book is going, just for the sake of checking the statement as we say, though I will say that Rob Roy and Company——"

"No, no," George interrupted with a second laugh. "They treat me very well. You know Mr. Craik, do you not?"

"Mr. Craik!" exclaimed the bookseller, with a beaming smile. "Why, dear me! Mr. Craik is your first cousin once removed, Mr. Winton Wood! Of course I know him." He prided himself on knowing the exact degree of relationship existing between his different customers, which was equivalent to knowing by heart the genealogy of all New York society.

"You are a subtle flatterer," George answered. "You pretend to know him only because he is my cousin."

"A great collector," returned the other, drawing down the corners of his mouth and turning up his eyes as though he were contemplating an object of solemn beauty. "A great collector! He knows what a book is, old or new. He knows, he knows—oh yes, he knows very well."

"What I want to know is this," said George. "Does Mr. Craik buy my books or not? Do you happen to remember?"

"Well, Mr. Winton Wood," answered Mr. Popples, "the fact is, I do happen to remember, by the merest chance. The fact is, to be honest, quite honest, Mr. Craik does not buy your books. But he reads them."

"Borrows them, I suppose," observed George.

"Well, not that, exactly, either. The fact is," said the bookseller, lowering his voice to a confidential whisper, "Mrs. Sherrington Trimm buys them and sends them to him. He buys mostly valuable books," he added, as though apologising for Mr. Craik's stinginess.

"Thank you, Mr. Popples," said George, laughing for the third time, and turning away.

"Oh, not at all, Mr. Winton Wood. Anything, anything. Walking this mor——"

But George was already out of the shop and the bookseller did not take the trouble to pronounce the last syllable, as he readjusted his large spectacles and took up three or four volumes that lay on the edge of the table.

"It cannot be said," George thought, as he walked on, "that I am very much indebted to Mr. Thomas Craik—not even for ten per cent on one dollar and twenty-five."

George would have been very much surprised to learn that the man who would not spend a dollar and a quarter in purchasing one of his novels had left him everything he possessed, and that the document which was to prove his right was reposing in that Indian cabinet of Mrs. Trimm's, which he had so often admired. It seemed as though Totty had planned everything to earn his gratitude, and he was especially pleased that she should have made her miserly brother read his books. It showed at once her own admiration for them and her desire that every one belonging to her should share in it.

Having nothing especial to do until a later hour, George thought of going to see Constance and Grace. They had only been in town two days, but he was curious to know whether Mrs. Bond had begun to look like herself again, or was becoming more and more absorbed in her sorrow as time went on. He had not been to the house in Washington Square since the first of May, and so many events had occurred in his life since that date that he felt as though he were separated from it by an interval of years instead of months. The time had passed very quickly. It would soon be three years since he had first gone up those steps with his cousin one afternoon in the late winter. As he approached the familiar door, he thought of all that had happened in the time, and he was amazed to find how he had changed. Six months earlier he had descended those steps with the certainty that the better and sweeter part of his life was behind him, and that his happiness had been destroyed by a woman's caprice. It had been a rough lesson but he had survived the ordeal and was now a far happier man than he had been then. In the flush of success, he was engaged to marry a young girl who loved him with all her heart, and whom he loved as well as he could. The world was before him now, as it had not been then, when he had felt himself dependent for his inspiration upon Constance's attachment, and for the help he needed upon his daily converse with her. If his heart was not satisfied as he had once dreamed that it might be, his hopes were raised by the experience of self-reliance. It had once seemed bitter to work alone; he had now ceased to desire any companionship in his labours. Mamie was to be his wife, not his adviser. She was to look up to him, and he must make himself worthy of her trust as well as of her admiration. He would work for her, labour to make her happy, to the extreme extent of his strength, and he would be proud of the part he would play. She would be the mother of children, graceful and charming as herself, or angular, tough and hard-working as he was, and he and she would love them. But there the relation was to cease, and he was glad of it. He owed much to Constance, and was ready to acknowledge the whole debt, but neither Constance herself, nor any other woman could take the same place in his life again. Least of all, she herself, he thought, as he rang the bell of her house and waited for admittance. In the old days his heart used to beat faster than its wont before he was fairly within the precincts of the Square. Now he was as unconscious of any emotion as though he were standing before his own door.

Grace received him alone in the old familiar drawing-room. She happened to be sitting in the place Constance used to choose when George came to see her, and he took his accustomed seat, almost unconscious of the associations it had once had for him.

"Constance is gone out," Grace began. "I am sure she will be sorry. It is kind of you to come so soon."

"You are no better," George answered, looking at her, and not heeding her remark. "I had hoped that you might be, but your expression is the same. Why do you not go abroad, and make some great change in your life?"

"I am very well," Grace replied with a faint smile which only increased the sadness of her look. "I do not care to go away. Why should I? It could make no difference."

"But it would. It would make all the difference in the world. Your sorrow is in everything, in all you see, in all you hear, in every familiar impression of your life — even in me and the sight of me."

"You are mistaken. It is here." She pressed her hand to her breast with a gesture almost fierce, and fixed her deep brown eyes on George's face for an instant. Then she let her arm fall beside her and looked away. "The worst of it is that I am so strong," she added presently. "I shall never break down. I shall live to be an old woman."

"Yes," George answered, thoughtfully, "I believe that you will. I can understand that. I fancy that you and I are somewhat alike. There are people who are unhappy, and who fade away and go out like a lamp without oil. They are said to die of broken hearts though they have not felt half as much happiness or sorrow as some tougher man and woman who live through a lifetime of despair and disappointment."

"Are you very happy?" Grace asked rather suddenly.

"Yes, I am very happy. I suppose I have reason to be. Everything has gone well with me of late. I have had plenty of success with what I have done, I am engaged to be married —— "

"That is what I mean," said Grace, interrupting him. "Are you happy in that? I suppose I have no right to ask such a question, but I cannot help asking it. You ought to be, for you two are very well matched. Do you know? It is a very fortunate thing that Constance refused you. You did not really love her any more than she loved you."

"What makes you say that?"

"If you were really in love, your love died a rather easy death. That is all."

"That is true," George answered, smiling in spite of himself.

"Do you remember the first of May as well as you did three months ago? Perhaps. I do not say that you have forgotten it altogether. When I told you her decision, you did not act like a man who has received a terrible blow. You were furiously, outrageously angry. You wished that I had been a man, that you might have struck me."

"I believed that I had cause to be angry. Besides, I have extraordinary natural gifts in that direction."

"Of course you had cause. But if you had loved her — as some people love — you would have forgotten to be angry for once in your life and you would have behaved very differently."

"I daresay you are right. As I came here to-day I was thinking over it all. You know I have not been here since that day. In old times I could feel my heart beating faster as I came near the house, and when I rang the bell my hand used to tremble. To-day I walked here as coolly as though I had been going home, and when I was at the door I was much more concerned to know whether you were better than to know whether your sister was in the house or not. Such is the unstability of the human heart."

"Yes — when there is no real love in it," Grace answered. "And the strongest proof that there was none in yours is that you are willing to own it. What made you think that you were so fond of her? How came you to make such a mistake?"

"I cannot tell. I would not talk to any one else as I am talking to you. But we understand each other, she is your sister and you never believed in our marriage. It began very gradually. Any man would fall in love with her, if he had the chance. She was interested in me. She was kind to me, when I got little kindness from any one —— "

"And none at all from me, poor man!" interrupted Grace.

"Especially none from you. It was she who always urged me to write a book, though I did not believe I could; it was to her that I read my first novel from beginning to end. It was she who seized upon it and got it published in spite of my protests — it was she who launched me and made my first success what it was. I owe her very much more than I could ever hope to repay, if I possessed any means of showing my gratitude. I loved her for her kindness and she liked me for my devotion — perhaps for my submission, for I was very submissive in those days. I had not learned to run alone, and if she would have had me I would have walked in her leading-strings to the end of my life."

"How touching!" exclaimed Grace, and the first genuine laughter of which she had been capable for three months followed the words.

"No, do not laugh," said George gravely. "I owe her everything and I know it. Most of all, I owe her the most loyal friendship and sincere gratitude that a man can feel for any woman he does not love. It is all over now. I never felt any emotion at meeting her since we parted after that abominable dinner-party, and I shall never feel any again. I am sure of that."

"I am sorry I laughed. I could not help it. But I am very glad that things have ended in this way, though, as I told you when I last saw you, I wish she would marry. She has grown to be the most listless, unhappy creature in the world."

"What can be the matter?" George asked. "Is it

not the life you are leading together? You are so lonely."

"I came back on her account," Grace answered wearily. "For my own sake I would never have left that dear place again. I have told her that I will do anything she pleases, go anywhere, live in any other way. It can make no difference to me. But she will not hear of leaving New York. I cannot mention it to her. She grows thinner every day."

"It is very strange. I am very sorry to hear it."

They talked together for some time longer and then George went away, inwardly wondering at his own conduct in having spoken of Constance so freely to her sister. It was not unnatural, however. Grace treated him as an old friend, and circumstances had suddenly brought the two into relations of close intimacy. As she had been chosen by Constance to convey the latter's refusal, it might well be supposed that she was in her sister's confidence, and George had said nothing which he was not willing that Grace should repeat. He had not been gone more than half an hour when Constance entered the room, looking pale and tired.

"I have been everywhere to find a wedding present for the future Mrs. Wood," she said, as she let herself sink down upon the sofa. "I can find nothing, positively nothing that will do."

"He has just been here," said Grace indifferently.

Constance changed colour and glanced quickly at her sister. She looked as though she had checked herself in the act of saying something which she might have regretted.

"What did you talk about?" she asked quietly, after a moment's pause. "I wish I had been here. I have not seen him since he came to announce his engagement."

"Yes. He was sorry to miss you, too. He was not particularly agreeable — considering how well he can talk when he tries. I am very fond of him now. I am

sorry I misjudged him formerly, and I told him so
before he came to town."

"You have discovered that you misjudged him, then,"
said Constance, as calmly as she could.

"Yes," Grace answered with perfect unconcern. "I
am always glad to see him. By-the-bye, we talked
about you."

"About me?"

"Yes. What is the matter? Is there any reason why
we should not talk about you?"

"Oh, none whatever — except that he loved me once."

"He said nothing but what was perfectly fair and
friendly. I asked him if he was happy in the prospect
of being married so soon, and then very naturally we
spoke of you. He said that he owed you the most loyal
friendship and sincere gratitude, that you had launched
him in his career by sending his first novel to the publisher without his consent, that without you, he would
not have been what he is — he said it seemed natural,
on looking back, that he should have loved you, or
thought that he loved you —— "

"Thought that he loved me?" Constance repeated in
a low voice.

"Yes. Considering how quickly he has recovered,
his love can hardly have been much more sincere than
yours. What is the matter, Conny dear? Are you ill?"

Constance had hidden her face in the cushions and
was sobbing bitterly, in the very place she had occupied
when she had finally refused George Wood, and almost
in the same attitude.

"Oh Grace!" she moaned. "You will break my heart!"

"Do you love him, now?" Grace asked in a voice that
was suddenly hard. She had not had the least suspicion of the real state of the case. Constance nodded
in answer, still sobbing and covering her face. Grace
turned away in disgust.

"What contemptible creatures we women can be!"
she said in an undertone, as she crossed the room.

CHAPTER XXVI.

George was in the habit of going to see Mamie every afternoon, and the hours he spent with her were by far the most pleasant in his day. Mrs. Trimm had thoroughly understood her daughter's nature when she had told George that the girl possessed that sort of charm which never wearies men because they can never find out exactly where it lies. It was not easy to imagine that any one should be bored in Mamie's society. George returned day after day, expecting always that he must ultimately find the continual conversation a burden, but reassured each time by what he felt after he had been twenty minutes in the house. As he was not profoundly moved himself it seemed unnatural that these long meetings should not at last become an irksome and uninteresting duty, the conscientious performance of which would react to the disadvantage of his subsequent happiness. The spontaneity which had given so much freshness to their intercourse while they were living under the same roof, was gone now that George found himself compelled to live by rules of consideration for others, and he was aware of the fact each time he entered Mamie's presence. Nevertheless her manner and voice exercised such a fascination over him as made him forget after a quarter of an hour that he and she were no longer in the country, and that he was no longer free to see her or not see her, as he pleased, independently of all formality and custom. Nothing could have demonstrated Mamie's superiority over most young women of her age more clearly than this fact. The situation of affianced couples after their engagement is announced is very generally hard to sustain with dignity on either side, but is more especially a difficult one for the man. It is undoubtedly rendered more easy by the enjoyment of the liberty granted among Anglo-Saxons in such

cases. But that freedom is after all only a part of our
whole system of ideas, and as we all expect it from the
first, we do not realise that our position is any more
fortunate than that of the young French gentleman, who
is frequently not allowed to exchange a single word with
his bride until he has been formally affianced to her,
and who may not talk to her without the presence of a
third person until she is actually his wife. Under our
existing customs a young girl must be charming indeed
if her future husband can talk with her three hours
every day during six weeks or two months and go away
each time feeling that his visit has been too short.
Neither animated conversation nor frequent correspond-
ence have any right to be considered as tests of love.
Love is not to be measured by the fluent use of words,
nor by an easy acquaintance with agreeable topics, nor
yet by lavish expenditure in postage-stamps. George
knew all this, and was moreover aware in his heart that
there was nothing desperately passionate in his affection; he was the more surprised, therefore, to find that
the more he saw of Mamie Trimm, the more he wished
to see of her.

"Do you think," he said to her, on that same afternoon in November, "that all engaged couples enjoy their
engagement as much as we do?"

"I am sure they do not," Mamie answered. "Nobody
is half as nice as we are!"

They were seated in a small boudoir that adjoined the
drawing-room. The wide door was open and they could
hear the pleasant crackling of the first wood fire that
was burning in the larger room, though they could not
see it. The air without was gloomy and grey, for the
late Indian summer was over, and before long the first
frosts would come and the first flakes of snow would be
driven along the dry and windy streets. It was early
in the afternoon, however, and though the light was cold
and colourless and hard, there was plenty of it. Mamie
was established in a short but very deep sofa, something

resembling a divan, one small foot just touching the
carpet, the other hidden from view, her head thrown
back and resting against the tapestry upon the wall, one
arm resting upon the end of the lounge, the little classic
hand hanging over the edge, so near to George that he
had but to put out his own in order to touch it. He was
seated with his back to the door of the drawing-room,
clasping his hands over one knee and leaning forward as
he gazed at the window opposite. He smiled at Mamie's
answer.

"No, I am sure other people do not enjoy sitting
together and talking during half the day, as we do," he
said. "I have often thought so. It is you who make
our life what it is. It will always be you, with your
dear ways —— "

He stopped, seeking an expression which he could not
find immediately.

"Have I dear ways?" Mamie asked with a little
laugh. "I never knew it before — but since you say
so —— "

"It is only those who love us that know the best of
us. We never know it ourselves."

"Do you love me, George?" The question was put
to him for the thousandth time. To her it seemed
always new and the answer was always full of interest,
as though it had never been given before.

"Very dearly." George laid his hand upon her slender fingers and pressed them softly. He had abandoned
the attempt to give her an original reply at each repetition of the inquiry.

"Is that all?" she asked, pretending to be disappointed, but smiling with her grey eyes.

"Can a man say more and mean it?" George inquired
gravely. Then he laughed. "The other day," he continued, "I was in a train on the Elevated Road. There
was a young couple opposite to me — the woman was a
little round fat creature with a perpetual smile, pretty
teeth, and dressed in grey. They were talking in low

tones, but I heard what they said. Baby language was
evidently their strong point. He turned his head towards
her with the most languishing lover-like look I ever saw.
'Plumpety itty partidge, who does 'oo love?' he asked.
'Zoo!' answered the little woman with a smile that went
all round her head like the equator on a globe."

Mamie laughed as he finished the story.

"That represented their idea of conversation, what you
call 'dear ways.' My dear ways are not much like that
and yours are quite different. When I ask you if you
love me, you almost always give the same answer. But
then, I know you mean it dear, do you not?"

"There it is again!" George laughed. "Of course I
do—only, as you say, my imagination is limited. I
cannot find new ways of saying it. But then, you do
not vary the question either, so that it is no wonder if
my answers are a little monotonous, is it?"

"Are my questions monotonous? Do I bore you with
them, George?"

"No, dear. I should be very hard to please if you bored
me. It is your charm that makes our life what it is."

"I wish I believed that. What is charm? What do
you mean by it? It is not an intellectual gift, it is not
a quality, a talent, nor accomplishment. I believe you
tell me that I have it because you do not know what else
to say. It is so easy to say to a woman 'You are full of
charm,' when she is ugly and stupid and cannot play on
the piano, and you feel obliged to be civil. I am sure
that there is no such thing as charm. It is only an imaginary compliment. Why not tell me the truth?"

"You are neither ugly nor stupid, and I am sincerely
glad that you leave the piano alone," said George. "I
could find any number of compliments to make, if that
were my way. But it is not, of course. You have lots
of good points, Mamie. Look at yourself in the glass if
you do not believe it. Look at your figure, look at your
eyes, at your complexion, at your hands—listen to your
own voice——"

"Do not talk nonsense, George. Besides, that is only a catalogue. If you want to please me you must compare all those things to beautiful objects. You must say that my eyes are like — gooseberries, for instance, my figure like — what shall I say?"

"Like Psyche's," suggested George.

"Or like an hour-glass, and my hands like stuffed gloves, and my skin like a corn starch pudding, and my voice like the voice of the charmer. That is the way to be complimentary. Poetry must make use of similes and call a spade an ace — as papa says. When you have done all that, and turned your catalogue into blank verse, tell me if there is anything left which you can call charm."

"Charm," George answered, "is what every man who loves a woman thinks she has — and if she has it all men love her. You have it."

"Dear me!" exclaimed the young girl. "Can you get no nearer to a definition than that?"

"Can you define anything which you only feel and cannot see — heat for instance, or cold?"

"Heat makes one hot, and cold makes one shiver," answered Mamie promptly.

"And charm makes a woman loved. That is as good an answer as yours."

"I suppose I must be satisfied, especially as you say that it can only be felt and not seen. Besides, if it makes you love me, why should I care what it is called? Do you know what it really is? It is love itself. It is because I love you so much, so intensely, that I make you love me. There is no such thing as charm. Charm is either a woman's love, or her readiness to love — one or the other."

Mamie laughed softly and moved the hand that was hanging over the end of the sofa, as though seeking the touch of George's fingers. He obeyed the little signal quite unconsciously.

"Who can that be?" Mamie asked, after a moment's

pause. She thought that she had heard a door open and that some one had entered the drawing-room. George listened a few seconds.

"Nobody," he said. "It was only the fire."

While the two had been talking, some one had really entered the large adjoining room as Mamie had suspected. Thomas Craik was not in the habit of making visits in the afternoon, but on this particular day he had found the process of being driven about in a closed brougham more wearisome than usual, and it had struck him that he might find Totty at home and amuse himself with teasing her in some way or other. Totty was expected every moment, the servant had said, and the discreet attendant had added that Mr. George and Miss Mamie were in the boudoir together. Mr. Craik said that he would wait in the drawing-room, to which he was accordingly admitted. He knew the arrangement of the apartment and took care not to disturb the peace of the young couple by making any noise. It would be extremely entertaining, he thought, to place himself so as to hear something of what they said to each other; he therefore stepped softly upon the thick carpet and took up what he believed to be a favourable position. His hearing was still as sharp as ever, and he did not go too near the door of the inner room lest Totty, entering suddenly, should suppose that he had been listening.

"So you think that I only love you because you love me," said George. "You are not very complimentary to yourself."

"I did not say that, though that was the beginning. You would never have begun to love me — George, I am sure there is some one in the next room!"

"It is impossible. Your mother would have come directly to us, and the servants would not have let any caller go in while she was out. Shall I look?"

"No — you are quite right," Mamie answered. "It is only the crackling of the fire." She was holding his hand and did not care to let it drop in order that he might satisfy her curiosity. "What was I saying?"

"Something very foolish — about my not loving you."

Thomas Craik listened for a while to their conversation, eagerly at first and then with an expression of weariness on his parchment face. He had been afraid to sit down, for fear of making a noise, and he found himself standing before a table, on which, among many other objects was placed the small Indian cabinet he had once given to his sister. Many years had passed since he had sent it to her, but his keen memory for details had not forgotten the secret drawer it contained, nor the way to open it. He looked at it for some time curiously, wondering whether Totty kept anything of value in it. Then it struck him that if she really kept anything concealed there, it would be an excellent practical joke to take out the object, whatever it might be, and carry it off. The idea was in accordance with that part of his character which loved secret and underhand dealings. The scene which would ensue when he ultimately brought the thing back would answer the other half of his nature which delighted in inflicting brutal and gratuitous surprises upon people he did not like. He laid his thin hands gently on the cabinet and proceeded to open it as noiselessly as he could.

Mamie's sharp ears were not deceived this time, however. She bent forward and whispered to George.

"There is somebody there. Go on tiptoe and look from behind the curtain. Do not let them see you, or we shall have to go in, and that would be such a bore."

George obeyed in silence, stood a moment peering into the next room, concealed by the hangings and then returned to Mamie's side. "It is your Uncle Tom," he whispered with a smile. "He is in some mischief, I am sure, for he is opening that Indian cabinet as though he did not want to be heard."

"I will tell mamma, when she comes in — what fun it will be!" Mamie answered. "He must have heard us before, so that we must go on talking — about the weather." Then raising her voice she began to speak of their future plans.

Meanwhile Mr. Craik had slipped back the part of the cover which concealed the secret drawer, and had opened the latter. There was nothing in it but the document which Totty kept there. He quickly took it out and closed the cabinet again. Something in the appearance of the paper attracted his attention, and instead of putting it into his pocket to read at home and at his leisure, as he had intended to do, he unfolded it and glanced at the contents.

He had always been a man able to control his anger, unless there was something to be gained by manifesting it, but his rage was now far too genuine to be concealed. The veins swelled and became visible beneath the tightly drawn skin of his forehead, his mouth worked spasmodically and his hands trembled with fury as he held the sheet before his eyes, satisfying himself that it was the genuine document and not a forgery containing provisions different from those he had made in his own will. As soon as he felt no further doubt about the matter, he gave vent to his wrath, in a storm of curses, stamping up and down the room, and swinging his long arms as he moved, still holding the paper in one hand.

Mamie turned pale and grasped George by the arm. He would have risen to go into the next room, but she held him back with all her strength.

"No — stay here!" she said in a low voice. "You can do no good. He knew we were here — something must have happened! Oh, George, what is it?"

"If you will let me go and see ——"

But at that moment, it became evident to both that Tom Craik was no longer alone. Totty had entered the drawing-room. As the servant had said, she had been expected every moment. Her brother turned upon her furiously, brandishing the will and cursing louder than before. In his extreme anger he was able to lift up his head and look her in the eyes.

"You damned infernal witch!" he shouted. "You abominable woman! You thief! You swindler! You —— "

"Help! help!" screamed Totty. "He is mad — he means to kill me!"

"I am not mad, you wretch!" yelled Tom Craik, pursuing her and catching her with one hand while he shook the will in her face with the other. "Look at that — look at it! My will, here in your keeping, without so much as a piece of paper or a seal to hold it — you thief! You have broken into your husband's office, you burglar! You have broken open my deed-box — look at it! Do you recognise it? Stand still and answer me, or I will hold you till the police can be got. Do you see? The last will and testament of me Thomas Craik, and not a cent for Charlotte Trimm. Not one cent, and not one shall you get either. He shall have it all, George Winton Wood, shall have it all. Ah — I see the reason why you have kept it now — If I had found it gone, you know I would have made it over again! Cheaper, and wiser, and more like you to get him for your daughter — of course it was, you lying, shameless beast!"

"What is the meaning of this?" George asked in ringing tones. He had broken away from Mamie with difficulty and she had followed him into the room, and now stood clinging to her mother. George pushed Tom Craik back a little and placed himself between him and Totty, who was livid with terror and seemed unable to speak a word. The sudden appearance of George's tall, angular figure, and the look of resolution in his dark face brought Tom Craik to his senses.

"You want to know the meaning of it," he said. "Quite right. You shall. When I was dying — nearly three years ago, I made a will in your favour. I left you everything I have in the world. Why? Because I pleased. This woman thought she was to have my money. Oh, you might have had it, if you had been less infernally greedy," he cried, turning to Totty. "This will was deposited in my deed-box at Sherry Trimm's office. Saw it there, on the top of the papers with my own eyes the last time I went; and Sherry was

in Europe then. So you took it, and no one else. Poor
Bond did not, though as he is dead, you will say he did.
It will not help you. So you laid your trap — oh yes!
I know those tricks of yours. You broke off George
Wood's marriage with the girl he loved, and you laid
your trap — very nicely done — very. You gave him
Sherry's wines, and Sherry's cigars to make him come.
I know all about it. I was watching you. And you
made him come and spend the summer up the river — so
nice, and luxurious, and quiet for a poor young author.
And you told nobody he was there — not you! I can see
it all now, the moonlight walks, and the rides and the
boating, and Totty indoors with a headache, or writing
letters. It was easy to get Sherry's consent when it was
all arranged, was it not? Devilish easy. Sherry is an
honest man — I know men — but he knew on which side
his daughter's bread was buttered, for he had drawn up
the will himself. He did not mind if George Winton
Wood, the poor author, fell in love with his daughter,
any more than his magnanimous wife was disturbed by
the prospect. Not a bit. The starving author was to
have millions — millions, woman! as soon as the old
brother was nailed up and trundled off to Greenwood!
And he shall have them, too. It only remains to be
seen whether he will have your daughter."

Craik paused for breath, though his invalid form was
as invigorated by his extreme anger as to make it appear
that he might go on indefinitely in the same strain. As
for George he was at first too much amazed by the story
to believe his ears. He thought Craik was mad, and
yet the presence of the will which the old man repeatedly
thrust before his eyes and in which he could not help
seeing his own name written in the lawyer's large clear
hand, told him that there was a broad foundation of
truth in the tale.

"Defend yourself, Totty," he said as quietly as he
could. "Tell him that this story is absurd. I think
Mr. Craik is not well —— "

"Not well, young man?" Craik asked, looking up at him with a bitter laugh. "I am as well as you. Here is my will. There is the cabinet. And there is Charlotte Sherrington Trimm. Send for her husband. Ask him if it is not a good case for a jury. You may be in love with the girl, and she may be in love with you, for all I know. But you have been made to fall in love with each other by that scheming old woman, there. The only way she could get the money into the family was through you. She is lawyer enough to know that there may be a duplicate somewhere, and that I should make one fast enough if there were not. Besides, to burn a will means the State's Prison, and she wants to avoid that place, if she can."

The possibility and the probability that the whole story might be true, flashed suddenly upon George's mind, and he turned very pale. The recollection of Totty's amazing desire to please him was still fresh in his mind, and he remembered how very unexpected it had all seemed, the standing invitation to the house, the extreme anxiety to draw him to the country, the reckless way in which Totty had left him alone with her daughter, Totty's manner on that night when she had persuaded him to offer himself to Mamie — the result, and the cable message she had shown him, ready prepared, and taking for granted her husband's consent. By this time Totty had sunk into a chair and was sobbing helplessly, covering her face with her hands and handkerchief. George walked up to her, while old Tom Craik kept at his elbow, as though fearing that he might prove too easily forgiving.

"How long have you known the contents of that will?" George asked steadily, and still trying to speak kindly.

"Since — the end — of April," Totty sobbed. She felt it impossible to lie, for her brother's eyes were fixed on her face and she was frightened.

"You did, did you? Well, well, that ought to settle it," said Craik, breaking into a savage laugh. "I fancy it must have been about that time that she began to like you so much," he added looking at George.

"About the first of May," George answered coldly. "I remember that on that day I met you in the street and you begged me to go and see Mamie, who was alone."

"I like men who remember dates," chuckled the old man at his elbow.

"I have been very much deceived," said George. "I believed it was for myself. It was for money. I have nothing more to say."

"You have not asked me whether I knew anything," said Mamie, coming before him. Her alabaster skin was deadly white and her grey eyes were on fire.

"Your mother knows you too well to have told you," George answered very kindly. "I have promised to marry you. I do not suspect you, but I would not break my word to you, even if I thought that you had known."

"It is for me to break my word," answered the young girl proudly. "No power on earth shall make me marry you, now."

Her lips were tightly pressed to her teeth as she spoke and she held her head high, though her eyes rested lovingly on his face.

"Why will you not marry me, Mamie?" George asked. He knew now that he had never loved her.

"I have had shame already," she answered. "Shame in being thrust upon you, shame in having thrust myself upon you — though not for your money. You never knew. You asked me once how I knew your moods, and when you wanted me and when you would choose to be alone. Ask her, ask my mother. She is wiser than I. She could tell from your face, long before I could, what you wished — and we had signals and signs and passwords, she and I, so that she could help me with her advice, and teach me how to make myself wanted by the man I loved. Am I not contemptible? And when I told you that I loved you — and then made you believe that I was only acting, because there was no response — shame? I have lived with it, fed on it, dreamed of it, and to-day is the crown of all — my crown of shame. Marry you? I would rather die!"

"Whatever others may have done, you have always been brave and true, Mamie," said George. "It may be better that we should not marry, but there has been no shame for you in this matter."

"I am not so sure," said Tom Craik with a chuckle and an ugly smile. "She is cleverer than she looks ——"

George turned upon the old man with the utmost violence.

"Sir!" he cried savagely. "If you say that again I will break your miserable old bones, if I hang for it!"

"Like that fellow," muttered Craik with a more pleasant expression than he had yet worn. "Like him more and more."

"I do not want to be liked by you, and you know why," George answered, for he had caught the words.

"Oh, you don't, don't you? Well, well. Never mind."

"No I do not. And what is more, I will tell you something, Mr. Craik. When you were ill and I called to inquire, I came because I hoped to learn that you were dead. That may explain what I feel for you. I have not had a favourable opportunity of explaining the matter before, or I would have done so."

"Good again!" replied the old gentleman. "Like frankness in young people. Eh, Totty? Eh, Mamie? Very frank young man, this, eh?"

"Furthermore, Mr. Craik," continued George, not heeding him, "I will tell you that I will not lift a finger to have your money. I do not want it."

"Exactly. Never enjoyed such sport in my life as trying to force money on a poor man who won't take it. Good that, what? Eh, Totty? Don't you think this is fun? Poor old Totty — all broken up! Bear these little things better myself."

Totty was in a fit of hysterics and neither heard nor heeded, as she lay in the deep chair, sobbing, moaning and laughing all at once. George eyed her contemptuously.

"Either let us go," he said to Craik, "and, if you have exhausted your wit, that would be the best thing; or else let Mrs. Trimm be taken away. I shall not leave you here to torment these ladies."

"Seat in my carriage? Come along!" answered Mr. Craik with alacrity.

George led Mamie back into the little room beyond. As they went, he could hear the old man beginning to rail at his sister again, but he paid no attention. He felt that he could not leave Mamie without another word. The young girl followed him in silence. They stood together near the window, as far out of hearing as possible. George hesitated.

"What is it, George?" asked Mamie. "Do you want to say good-bye to me?" She spoke with evident effort.

"I want to say this, dear. If you and I can help it, not a word of what has happened to-day must ever be known. I have been deceived, most shamefully, but not by you. You have been honest and true from first to last. The best way to keep this secret, is for us two to marry as though nothing had happened. Nobody would believe it then. I am afraid that Mr. Craik will tell some one, because he is so angry."

"I have told you my decision," Mamie answered firmly, though her lips were white. "I have nothing more to say."

"Think well of what you are doing. One should not come to such decisions when one is angry. Here I am, Mamie. Take me if you will, and forget that all those things have been said and done."

For one moment, Mamie hesitated.

"Do you love me?" she asked, trying to read his heart in his eyes.

But the poor passion that had taken the place of love

was gone. The knowledge that he had been played with and gambled for, though not by the girl herself, had given him a rude shock.

"Yes," he answered, bravely trying to feel that he was speaking the truth. But there was no life in the word.

"No, dear," said Mamie simply. "You never loved me. I see it now."

He would have made some sort of protest. But she drew back from him, and from his outstretched hand.

"Will you let me be alone?" she asked.

He bowed his head and left the room.

CHAPTER XXVII.

When George had seen old Tom Craik enter his carriage and drive away from the house, he breathed more freely. He could not think very connectedly of what had happened, but it seemed to him that the old man had played a part quite as contemptible as that which Totty herself had sustained so long. He would assuredly not have believed that the terrific anger of which he had witnessed the explosion was chiefly due to the discovery of what was intended to be a good action. Craik had never liked to be found out, and it was especially galling to him to be exposed in the act of endeavouring to make amends for the past. But for this consideration, he would have been quite capable of returning the will to its place in the cabinet, and of leaving the house quietly. He would have merely sent for a lawyer and repeated the document with a new date, to deposit it in some place to which his sister could not possibly gain access. But his anger had been aroused in the first moment by the certainty that Totty had understood his motives and must secretly despise him for making such a restitution of ill-gotten gain. George could not have comprehended this, and he feared that the old man should do some irreparable harm if he were left any longer with the object of his wrath. The look in Craik's eyes had not been reassuring, and it was by no means sure that the whole affair had not finally unsettled his intellect.

There was little ground for any such fear, however, as George would have realised if he could have followed Mr. Craik to his home, and seen how soon he repented of having endangered his health by giving way to his wrath. An hour later he was in bed and his favourite doctor was at his side, watching every pulsation of his heart and prepared to do battle at the first attack of any malady which should present itself.

George himself was far less moved by what had occurred than he would have believed possible. His first and chief sensation was a sickening disgust with Totty and with all that recent portion of his life in which she had played so great a part. He had been deceived and played with on all sides and his vanity revolted at the thought of what might have been if Craik's discovery had not broken through the veil of Totty's duplicity. It made him sick to feel that while he had fancied himself courted and honoured and chosen as a son-in-law for his own sake and for the sake of what he had done in the face of such odds, he had really been looked upon as an object of speculation, as a thing worth buying at a cheap price for the sake of its future value. Beyond this, he felt nothing but a sense of relief at having been released from his engagement. He had done his best to act honestly, but he had often feared that he was deceiving himself and others in the effort to do what seemed honourable. He did not deny, even now, that what he had felt for Mamie might in good time have developed into a real love, but he saw clearly at last that while his senses had been charmed and his intelligence soothed, his heart had never been touched.

Doubts about Mamie herself would present themselves, though he drove them resolutely away. It was natural that he should find it hard to realise in her that which he had never felt during their long intercourse, and while his instinct told him that the young girl had been innocent of all her mother's plotting and scheming, he said to himself that she would easily recover from her disappointment. If he was troubled by any regret it was rather that he should not have left her mother's house as soon as he had seen that she was interested, than that he should have failed to love her as he had tried to do. On the other hand he admitted that his conduct had been excusable, considering the pressure which Totty had brought to bear upon him.

The most unpleasant point in the future was the explanation which must inevitably take place between himself and Sherrington Trimm. It would be hard to imagine a meeting more disagreeable to both parties as this one was sure to be. There could be no question about Trimm's innocence in the whole affair, for his character was too well known to the world to admit the least suspicion. But it would be a painful matter to meet him and talk over what had happened. If possible, the interview must be avoided, and George determined to attempt this solution by writing a letter setting forth his position with the utmost clearness. He turned up the steps of a club to which he belonged and sat down to the task.

What he said may be summed up in a few words. He took it for granted that Trimm would be acquainted with what had occurred, by the time the letter reached him. It only remained for him to repeat what he had said to Mamie herself, to wit, that if she would marry him, he was ready to fulfil his engagement. He concluded by saying that he would wait a month for the definite answer, after which time he intended to go abroad. He sealed the note and took it with him, intending to send it to Trimm's house in the evening. As luck would have it, however, he met Trimm himself in the hall of the club. He had stopped on his way up town to refresh himself with a certain mild drink of his own devising.

"Hilloa, George!" he cried in his cheery voice. "What is the matter?" he asked anxiously as he saw the expression on the other's face.

"Have you been at home yet?" George asked.

"No."

"Something very disagreeable has happened. I have just written you a note. Will you take it with you and read it after you have heard what they have to say?"

"Confound it all!" exclaimed Sherry Trimm. "I am not fond of mystery. Come into a quiet room and tell me all about it."

"I would rather that you found it out for yourself," said George, drawing back.

Sherry Trimm looked keenly at him, and then took him by the arm.

"Look here, George," he said, "no nonsense! I do not know what the trouble is, but I see it is serious. Let us have it out, right here."

"Very well," George answered. "Your wife has made trouble," he said, as soon as they were closeted in one of the small rooms. "You drew up Mr. Craik's will, and you kept his secret. When you had gone abroad, your wife got the will out of the deed-box in your office and took it home with her. She kept it in that Indian cabinet and Mr. Craik found it there this afternoon, and made a fearful scene. Unfortunately your wife could not find any answer to what he said, and thereupon Mamie declared that she would not marry me."

Sherrington Trimm's pink face had grown slowly livid while George was speaking.

"What did Tom say?" he asked quietly.

"He hinted that his sister had not been wholly disinterested in her kindness to me," said George. "Unfortunately Mamie and I were present. I did the best I could, but the mischief was done."

Sherrington said nothing more, but began to walk up
and down the small room nervously, pulling at his short
grizzled moustache from time to time. Like every one
else who had been concerned in the affair, he grasped
the whole situation in a moment.

"This is a miserable business," he said at last in a
tone that expressed profound humiliation and utter
disgust.

George did not answer, for he was quite of the same
opinion. He stood leaning against a card-table, drum-
ming with his fingers on the green cloth behind him.
Sherry Trimm paused in his walk, and struck his
clenched fist upon the palm of his other hand. Then he
shook his head and began to pace the floor again.

"An abominable business," he muttered. "I cannot
see that there is anything to be done, but to beg your
pardon for it all," he said, suddenly turning to George.

"You need not do that," George answered readily.
"It is not your fault, Cousin Sherry. All I want to
say, is what I had already written to you. If Mamie
will change her mind and marry me, I am ready."

Trimm looked at him sharply.

"You are a good fellow, George," he said. "But I
don't think I could stand that. You never loved her as
you ought to love to be happy. I saw that long ago and
I guessed that there had been something wrong. You
have been tricked into the whole thing — and — just go
away and leave me here, will you? I cannot stand this."

George took the outstretched hand and shook it warmly.
Then he left the room and closed the door behind him.
In that moment he pitied Sherrington Trimm far more
than he pitied Mamie herself. He could understand
the man's humiliation better than the girl's broken
heart. He went out of the club and turned homewards.
He had yet to communicate the intelligence to his
father, and he was oddly curious to see what the old
gentleman would say. An hour later he had told the
whole story with every detail he could remember, from

the day when Totty had told him to go and see Mamie to his recent interview with Sherry Trimm.

"I am sorry for you, George," said Jonah Wood. "I am very sorry for you."

"I think, on the whole, that is more than I can say for myself," George answered. "I am far more sorry for Mamie and her father. It is a relief to me. I would not have believed it, this morning."

"Do you mean that you were not in love?"

"Yes. I am just as fond of her as ever. There is nothing I would not do for her. But I do not want to marry her and I never did, till that old cat made me think it was my duty."

"I should think you would have known what your duty was, without waiting to be told. I would have told her mother that I did not love the girl, and I would have gone the next morning."

"You are so sensible, father!" George exclaimed. "I looked at it differently. It seemed to me that if I had gone so far as to make Mamie believe that I loved her, I ought to be able to love her in earnest."

"When you are older, you will know better," observed the old gentleman severely. "You have too much imagination. As for Mr. Craik, he will not leave you his money now. I doubt if he meant to."

George went and shut himself up in the little room which had witnessed so many of his struggles and disappointments. He sat down in his shabby old easy-chair and lit a short pipe and fell into a profound reverie. The unexpected had played a great part in his life, and as he reviewed the story of the past three years, he was surprised to find how very different his own existence had been from that of the average man. With the exception of his accident on the river and the scene he had witnessed to-day, nothing really startling had happened to him in that time, and yet his position at the present moment was as different from his position three years earlier as it possibly could be. In that time he had risen from total obscurity into the publicity of reputation, if not of celebrity. He was not fond of disturbing the mass of papers that encumbered his table, and there, deep down under the rest were still to be found rough drafts of his last poor little reviews. Hanging from one corner there was visible the corrected "revise" of one of his earliest accepted articles. At the other end, beneath a piece of old iron which he used as a paper-weight, lay the manuscript of his first novel, well thumbed and soiled, and marked at intervals in pencil with the names of the compositors who had set up the pages in type. There, upon the table, lay the accumulated refuse of three years of hard work, of the three years which had raised him into the public notice. Much of that work had been done under the influence of one woman, of one fair young girl who had bent over his shoulder as he read her page after page, and whose keen, fresh sight had often detected flaws and errors where he himself saw no imperfection. She had encouraged him, had pushed him, and urged him on, in spite of himself, until he had succeeded, beyond his wildest expectations. Then he had lost her, because he had thought that she was bound to marry him. He did not think so now, for he felt that in that case, too, he had been mistaken, as in the more recent one he had deceived himself. He had never been in love. He had never felt what he described in his own books. His blood had never raced through his veins for love, as it had often done for anger and sometimes for mere passing passion. Love had never taken him and mastered him and carried him away in its arms beyond all consideration for consequences. It was not because he was strong. He knew that whatever people might think of him, he had often been weak, and had longed to be made strong by a love he could not feel. He had been ready to yield himself to a belief in affections which had proved unreal and which had disappointed himself by their instability and by the ease with which he had recovered from them. Even in the solitude of his own room he was ashamed to own to his inner consciousness how little he had been moved by all that had happened to him in those three years.

He thought of Johnson, the pale-faced hard-working man, whose heart was full of unsatisfied ambition and who had distanced his competitors by sheer energy and enthusiasm. He envied the man his belief in himself and his certainty of slow but sure success. Slow, indeed, it must be. Johnson had toiled for many years at his writing to attain the position he occupied, to be considered a good judge and a ready writer by the few who knew him, to gain a small but solid reputation in a small circle. He had worked much harder than George himself, and yet to-day, George Wood was known and read where William Johnson had never been heard of. Of the two Johnson was by far the better satisfied with his success, though of the two he possessed by very much the more ambition, in the ordinary acceptation of the word.

Then George thought of Thomas Craik, and of his sneer at ambitious men. He had said that there was no pleasure in possession, but only in getting, getting, getting, as long as a man had breath; that the wish to excel other men in anything was a drawback and a disadvantage, and that nothing in the world was worth having for its own sake, from money to fame, through all the catalogue of what is attainable by humanity. And yet, Thomas Craik was an instance of a very successful man, who had some right to speak on the subject. Whether he had got his money by fair means or foul had nothing to do with the argument. He had it, and he could speak from experience about the pleasures of possession. There must be some truth in what he said. George himself had attained before the age of thirty what many men labour in vain to reach throughout a lifetime. The case was similar. Whether he had deserved the reputation he had so suddenly acquired or not, mattered little. Many critics said that he had no claim to it. Many

others said that he deserved more than he got. Whichever side was right, he had it, as Tom Craik had his
money. Did it give him any satisfaction? None whatever, beyond the material advantages it brought him,
and which only pleased him because they made him
independent of his father's help. When he thought of
what he had done, he found no savour of pride in the
reflection, nothing which really flattered his vanity,
nothing to send a thrill of happiness through him. He
was cold, indifferent to all he had done. It would not
have entered his mind to take up one of his own books
and glance over the pages. On the contrary, he felt a
strong repulsion for what he had written, the moment it
was finished. He admitted that he was foolish in this,
as in many other things, and that he would in all likelihood improve his work by going over it and polishing
it, even by entirely rewriting a great part of it. He
was not deterred from doing so by indolence, for his
rarely energetic temperament loved hard work and
sought it. It was rather a profound dissatisfaction with
all he did which prevented him from expending any
further time upon each performance when he had once
reached the last page. Nothing satisfied him, neither
what he did himself, nor what he saw done by others.

Thinking the matter over in his solitude the inevitable
conclusion seemed to be that he was one of those discontented beings who can never be pleased with anything,
nor lose themselves in an enthusiasm without picking
to pieces the object that has made him enthusiastic. But
this was not true either. There were plenty of great
works in the world for which he had no criticism, and
which never failed to excite his boundless admiration.
He smiled to himself as he thought that what would
really please him would be to be forced into the same
attitude of respect before one of his own books, into
which he naturally fell before the great masterpieces of
literature. He would have been hard to satisfy, he
thought, if that would not have satisfied him. Was

that, then, the vision which he was really pursuing? It was folly to suppose that he would be so mad, and yet, at that time, he felt that he desired nothing else and nothing less than that, and since that was absolutely unattainable, he was condemned to perpetual discontent, to be borne with the best patience he could find. Beyond this, he could find no explanation of his feelings about his own work.

The only other source of happiness of which he could conceive was love, and this brought him back to his kindly and grateful memories of Constance Fearing, and to the more disturbing recollection of his cousin. The latter, also, had played a part and had occupied a share in his life. He had watched her more closely than he had ever watched any one, and had studied her with an unconsciously unswerving attention which proved how little he had loved her and how much she had interested him. He was, indeed, never well aware that he was subjecting any one to a microscopic intellectual scrutiny, for he possessed in a high degree the faculty of unintentional memory. While it cost him a severe effort to commit to memory a dozen verses of any poet, old or modern, he could nevertheless recall with faultless accuracy both sights and conversations which he had seen and heard, even after an interval of many years, provided that his interest had been somewhat excited at the time. The half-active, half-indolent, wholly luxurious life at his cousin's house had in the end produced a strong impression upon him. It had been like an interval of lotus-eating upon an almost uninhabited island, varied only by such work as he chose to do at his own leisure and in his own way. During more than four months the struggles of the world had been hidden from him, and had temporarily ceased to play any part in his thoughts. The dreamy existence spent between flowers and woods and water, where every want had been anticipated almost before it was felt, served now as a background for the picture of the young girl who had been

so constantly with him, herself as natural as her surroundings, the incarnation of life and of life's charm, the
negation of intellectual activity and of the sufferings of
thought, a lovely creature who could only think, reason,
enjoy and suffer with her heart, and whose mind could
acquire but little, and was incapable of giving out. She
had been the central figure and had contributed much to
the general effect, so much, indeed, that under pressure
of circumstances he had been willing to believe that he
could love her enough to marry her. The scene had
changed, the hallucination had vanished and the delu-
sion was destroyed, but the memory of it all remained,
and now disturbed his recollection of more recent events.
There was a sensuous attraction in the pictures that
presented themselves, from which he could not escape,
but which he for some reason despised and tried to put
away from him, by thinking again of Constance, of the
cold purity of her face, of her over-studied conscien-
tiousness and of her complete subjection to her sincere
but mistaken self-criticism.

He wondered whether he should ever marry, and what
manner of woman his wife would turn out to be. Of
one thing he was sure. He would not now marry any
woman unless he loved her with all his heart, and he
would not ask her to marry him unless he were already
sure of her love. The third must be the decisive case,
from which he should never desire to withdraw and in
which there should be no disappointment. He thought
of Grace Fearing, and of her marriage and short-lived
happiness with its terribly sudden ending and the
immensity of sorrow that had followed its extinction.
It almost seemed to him as though it would be worth
while to suffer as she suffered if one could have what she
had found; for the love must have been great and deep
and sincere indeed, which could leave such scars where
it had rested. To love a woman so well able to love
would be happiness. She never doubted herself nor
what she felt; all her thoughts were clear, simple and

strong; she did not analyse herself to know the measure of her own sincerity, nor was she a woman to be carried away by a thoughtless passion. She loved and she hated frankly, sincerely, without a side thought of doubt on the one hand nor of malice on the other. She was morally strong without putting on any affectation of strength, she was clear-sighted without making any pretence to exceptional intelligence, she was passionate without folly, and wise without annoyance, she was good, not sanctimonious, she was dignified without vanity. In short, as George thought of her, he saw that the woman who had openly disliked him and opposed him in former days, was of all the three the one for whom he felt the most sincere admiration. He remembered now that at his first meeting with the two sisters he had liked Grace better than Constance, and would then have chosen her as the object of his attentions had she been free and had he foreseen that friendship was to follow upon intimacy and love on friendship. Unfortunately for George Wood, and for all who find themselves in a like situation, that concatenation of events is the one most rarely foreseen by anybody, and George was fain to content himself with speculating upon the nature of the happiness he would have enjoyed had he been loved by a woman who seemed now to be dead to the whole world of the affections. It was sufficient to compare her with her sister to understand that she was, of the two, the nobler character; it was enough to think of Mamie to see that in that direction no comparison was even possible.

"It would be strange if it should be my fate to love her, after all," George thought. "She would never love me."

He roused himself from his reverie and sat down to his table, by sheer force of habit. Paper and ink were before him, and his pen lay ready to his hand, where he had last thrown it down. Almost unconsciously he began to write, putting down notes of a situation that

had suddenly presented itself to his mind. The pen
moved along, sometimes running rapidly, sometimes
stopping with an impatient hesitation during which it
continued to move uneasily in the air. Characters
shaped themselves out of the chaos and names sounded
in the willing ear of the writer. The situation which
he had first thought of was all at once transformed into
a detail in a second and larger action, another possibility
started up out of darkness, in brilliant clearness, and
absorbed the matters already thought of into itself,
broadening and strengthening every moment. Whole
chapters now stood out as if already written, and in their
places. A detail here, another there, to be changed or
adapted, one glance at the whole, one or two names
spoken aloud to see how they sounded in the stillness,
a pause of a moment, a fresh sheet of paper, and George
Wood was launched upon the first chapter of a new
novel, forgetful of Grace, of Constance Fearing and even
of poor Mamie herself and of all that had happened only
two or three hours earlier.

He was writing, working with passionate and all-
absorbing interest at the expression of his fancies.
What he did was good, well thought, clearly expressed,
harmoniously composed. When it was given to the
public it was spoken of as the work of a man of heart,
full of human sympathy and understanding. At the
time when he was inventing the plot and writing down
the beginning of his story, a number of people intimately
connected with his life were all in one way or another
suffering acutely and he himself was the direct or indirect cause of all their sufferings. He was neither a cruel
man, nor thoughtless nor unkind, but he was for the
time utterly unconscious of the outer world, and if not
happy at least profoundly interested in what he was
doing.

During that hour, Sherrington Trimm, pale and nervous, was walking up and down his endless beat in the
little room at the club where George had left him, try-

ing to master his anger and disgust before going home to meet his wife and the inevitable explanation which must ensue. The servant came in and lit the gaslight and stirred the fire but Trimm never saw him nor varied the monotony of his walk.

At his own house, things were no better. Totty, completely broken down, by the failure of all her plans and the disclosure of her discreditable secret, had recovered enough from her hysterics to be put to bed by her faithful maid, who was surprised to find that, as all signs fail in fair weather, none of the usual remedies could extract a word of satisfaction or an expression of relief from her mistress. Down stairs, in the little boudoir where she had last seen the man she loved, Mamie was lying stretched upon the divan, dry eyed, with strained lips and blanched cheeks, knowing nothing save that her passion had dashed itself to pieces against a rock in the midst of its fairest voyage.

In another house, far distant, Grace Bond was leaning against a broad chimney-piece, a half-sorrowful, half-contemptuous smile upon her strong sad face, as she thought of all her sister's changes and vacillations and of the aimlessness of the fair young life. Above, in her own room, Constance Fearing was kneeling and praying with all her might, though she hardly knew for what, while the bright tears flowed down her thin cheeks in an unceasing stream.

"And yet, when he came to life, he called me first!" she cried, stretching out her hands and looking upward as though protesting against the injustice of Heaven.

And in yet another place, in a magnificent chamber, where the softened light played upon rich carvings and soft carpets, an old man lay dying of his last fit of anger.

All for the sake of George Wood who, conscious that many if not all were in deep trouble, anxiety or suffering, was driving his pen unceasingly from one side of a piece of paper to the other, with an expression of keen interest on his dark face, and a look of eager delight in

his eyes such as a man may show who is hunting an
animal of value and who is on the point of overtaking
his prey.

But for the accident of thought which had thrown a
new idea into the circulation of his brain, he would still
have been sitting in his shabby easy-chair, thoughtfully
pulling at his short pipe and thinking of all those persons whom he had seen that day, kindly of some, unkindly
of others, but not deaf to all memories and shut off from
all sympathy by something which had suddenly arisen
between himself and the waking, suffering world.

CHAPTER XXVIII.

The sun shines alike upon the just and the unjust, and
it would seem to follow that all men should be judged
by the same measure in the more important actions and
emotions of their lives. To apply the principle of a
double standard to mankind is to run the risk of producing some very curious results in morality. And yet,
there are undoubtedly cases in which a man has a claim
to special consideration and, as it were, to a trial by a
special jury. There have been many great statesmen
whose private practice in regard to financial transactions
has been more than shady, and there have been others
whose private lives have been spotless, but whose political doings have been unscrupulous in the extreme. There
are professions and careers in which it is sufficient to
act precisely as all others engaged in the same occupation would act, and in which the most important element
of success is a happy faculty of keeping the brain power
at the same unvarying pressure, neither high nor low,
but always ready to be used, and in such a state that it
may always be relied upon to perform the same amount
of work in a given time. There are other occupations

In which there are necessarily moments of enormous activity at uncertain intervals, followed by periods of total relaxation and rest. One might divide all careers roughly into two classes, and call the one the continuous class and the other the intermittent. The profession of the novelist falls within the latter division. Very few men or women who have written well have succeeded in reducing the exercise of their art to a necessary daily function of the body. Very few intellectual machines can be made to bear the strain of producing works of imagination in regular quantities throughout many years at an unvarying rate, day after day. Neither the brain nor the body will bear it, and if the attempt be made either the one or the other, or both, will ultimately suffer. Without being necessarily spasmodic, the story-teller's activity is almost unavoidably intermittent. There are men who can take up the pen and drive it during seven, eight and even nine hours a day for six weeks or two months and who, having finished their story, either fall into a condition of indolent apathy until the next book has to be written, or return at once to some favourite occupation which produces no apparent result, and of which the public has never heard. There are many varieties of the genus author. There is the sailor author, who only comes ashore to write his book and puts to sea again as soon as it is in the publisher's hands. There is the hunting author, who as in the case of Anthony Trollope, keeps his body in such condition that he can do a little good work every day of the year, a great and notable exception to the rule. There is the student author, whose laborious work of exegesis will never be heard of, but who interrupts it from time to time in order to produce a piece of brilliant fiction, returning to his Sanscrit each time with renewed interest and industry. There is the musical author, whose preference would have led him to be a professional musician, but who had not quite enough talent for it, or not quite enough technical facility or whose musical education began a little too late. There is the adventurous author, who shoots in Africa or has a habit of spending the winter in eastern Siberia. There is the artistic author, who may be found in out-of-the-way towns in Italy, patiently copying old pictures, as though his life depended upon his accuracy, or sketching ragged boys and girls in very ragged water-colour. There is the social author — and he is not always the least successful in his profession — who is a favourite everywhere, who can dance and sing and act, and who regards the occasional production of a novel as an episode in his life. There is the author who prepares himself many months beforehand for what he intends to do by frequenting the society, whether high or low, which he wishes to depict, who writes his book in one month of the year and spends the other eleven in observing the manners and customs of men and women. There is the author who lives in solitary places and evolves his characters out of his inner consciousness and who occasionally descends, manuscript in hand, from his inaccessible fastnesses and ravages all the coasts of Covent Garden, Henrietta Street and the Strand, until he has got his price and disappears as suddenly as he came, taking his gold with him, no man knows whither. There is the author whom no man can boast of having ever seen, who never answers a letter, nor gives an autograph, nor lets any one but his publisher know where he lives, but whose three volumes appear punctually twice a year and whose name is familiar in many mouths. Unless he is to be found described in an encyclopædia you will never know whether he is old or young, black or grey, goodlooking or ugly, straight or hunchbacked. He is to you a vague, imaginary personage, surrounded by a pillar of cloud. In reality he is perhaps a fat little man of fifty, who wears gold-rimmed spectacles and has discovered that he can only write if he lives in one particular Hungarian village with a name that baffles pronunciation, and whose chief interest in life lies in the study of socialism or the cholera microbe. Then again, there is the fighting author, grim, grey and tough as a Toledo blade, who has ridden through many a hard-fought field in many lands and has smelled more gunpowder in his time than most great generals, out of sheer love for the stuff. There is also the pacific author, who frequents peace congresses and makes speeches in favour of a general disarming of all nations. There are countless species and varieties of the genus. There is even the poet author, who writes thousands of execrable verses in secret and produces exquisite romances in prose only because he can do nothing else.

If we admit that novels, on the whole, are a good to society at large, as most people, excepting authors themselves, are generally ready to admit, we grant at the same time that they must be produced by individuals possessing the necessary talents and characteristics of intelligence. And if it is shown that a majority of these individuals do their work in a somewhat erratic fashion, and behave somewhat erratically while they are doing it, such defects must be condoned, at least, if not counted to them for positive righteousness. With many of them the appearance of a new idea within the field of their mental vision is equivalent to a command to write, which they are neither able nor anxious to resist; and, if they are men of talent, it is very hard for them to turn their attention to anything else until the idea is expressed on paper. Let them not be thought heartless or selfish if they sometimes seem to care nothing for what happens around them while they are subject to the imperious domination of the new idea. They are neither the one nor the other. They are simply unconscious, like a man in a cataleptic trance. The plainest language conveys no meaning to their abstracted comprehension, the most startling sights produce no impression upon their sense; they are in another world, living and talking with unseen creations of their own fancy and for the time being they are not to be considered as ordinary human beings, nor judged by the standard to which other men are subject.

It would not therefore be just to say that during the days which followed the breaking off of his engagement with Mamie Trimm, George Wood was cruel or unfeeling because he was wholly unconscious of her existence throughout the greater part of each twenty-four hours. By a coincidence which he would certainly not have invoked, a train of thought had begun its course in his brain within an hour or two of the catastrophe, and he was powerless to stop himself in the pursuit of it until he had reached the end. During nine whole days he never left the house, and scarcely went out of his room except to eat his meals, which he did in a summary fashion without wasting time in superfluous conversation. On the morning of the tenth day he knew that he was at the last chapter and he sat down at his table in that state of mind to which a very young author is brought by a week and a half of unceasing fatigue and excitement. The room swam with him, and he could see nothing distinctly except his paper, the point of his pen, and the moving panorama in his brain, of which it was essential to catch every detail before it had·passed into the outer darkness from which ideas cannot be brought back. His hand was icy cold, moist and unsteady and his face was pale, the eyelids dark and swollen, and the veins on the temples distended. He moved his feet nervously as he wrote, shrugged his left shoulder with impatience at the slightest hesitation about the use of a word, and his usually imperturbable features translated into expression every thought, as rapidly as he could put it into words with his pen. The house might have burned over his head, and he would have gone on writing until the paper under his hand was on fire. No ordinary noise would have reached his ears, conscious only of the scratching of the steel point upon the smooth sheet. He could have worked as well in the din of a public room in a hotel, or in the crowded hall of a great railway station, as in the silence and solitude of his own chamber. He had reached the point of abstraction at which nothing is of the slightest consequence to the writer provided that the ink will flow and the paper will not blot. Like a skilled swordsman, he was conscious only of his enemy's eye and of the state of the weapons. The weapons were pen, ink and paper, and the enemy was the idea to be pursued, overtaken, pierced and pinned down before it could assume another shape, or escape again into chaos. The sun rose above the little paved brick court below his window, and began to shine into the window itself. Then a storm came up and the sky turned suddenly black, while the wind whistled through the yard with that peculiarly unnatural sound which it makes in great cities, so different from its sighing and moaning and roaring amongst trees and rocks. The first snowflakes were whirled against the panes of glass and slid down to the frame in half-transparent patches. The wind sank again, and the snow fluttered silently down like the unwinding of an endless lace curtain from above. Then, the flakes were suddenly illuminated by a burst of sunshine and melted as they fell and turned to bright drops of water in the air, and then vanished again, and the small piece of sky above the great house on the other side of the yard was once more clear and blue, as a sapphire that has been dipped in pure water. It was afternoon, and George was unconscious of the many changes of the day, unconscious that he had not eaten nor drunk since morning, and that he had even forgotten to smoke. One after another the pages were numbered, filled and tossed aside, as he went on, never raising his head nor looking away from his work lest he should lose something of the play upon which all his faculties were inwardly concentrated, and of which it was his business to transcribe every word, and to note every passing attitude and gesture of the actors who were performing for his benefit.

Some one knocked at the door, gently at first and then

more loudly.   Then, receiving no answer, **the person's** footsteps could be heard retreating towards the landing The firing of a cannon in the room would hardly have made George turn his head at that moment, much less the rapping of a servant's knuckles upon a wooden panel. Several minutes elapsed, and then heavier footsteps were heard again, and the latch was turned and the door moved noiselessly on its hinges.   Jonah Wood's iron-grey head appeared in the opening.   George had heard nothing and during several seconds the old gentleman watched him curiously.   He had the greatest considera-tion for his son's privacy when at work, though he could not readily understand the terribly disturbing effect of an interruption upon a brain so much more sensitively organised than his own.   Now, however, the case was serious, and George must be interrupted, cost what it might.   He was evidently unconscious that any one was in the room, and his back was turned as he sat.   Jonah Wood resolved to be cautious.

"George!" he whispered, rather hoarsely.   But George did not hear.

There was nothing to be done but to cross the room and rouse him.   The old man stepped as softly as he could upon the uncarpeted wooden floor, and placed himself between the light and the writer.   George looked up and started violently, so that his pen flew into the air and fell upon the boards.   At the same time he uttered a short, sharp cry, neither an oath nor exclamation, but a sound such as a man might make who is unexpectedly and painfully wounded in battle.   Then he saw his father and laughed nervously.

"You frightened me.   I did not see you come in," he said quickly.

"I am sorry," said his father, not understanding at all how a man usually calm and courageous could be so easily startled.   "It is rather important, or I would not interrupt you.   Mr. Sherrington Trimm is down stairs."

"What does he want?" George asked vaguely and

looking as though he had forgotten who Sherrington Trimm was.

"He wants you, my boy. You must go down at once. It is very important. Tom Craik was buried yesterday."

"Buried!" exclaimed George. "I did not know he was dead."

"I understand that he died several days ago, in consequence of that fit of anger he had. You remember? What is the matter with you, George?"

"Cannot you see what is the matter?" George cried a little impatiently. "I am just finishing my book. What if the old fellow is dead? He has had plenty of leisure to change his will — in all this time. What does Sherry want?"

"He did not change his will, and Mr. Trimm wants to read it to you. George, you do not seem to realise that you are a very rich man, a very, very rich man," repeated Jonah Wood with weighty emphasis.

"It will do quite as well if he reads the confounded thing to you," said George, picking up his pen from the floor beside him, examining the point and then dipping it into the ink.

He was never quite sure how much of his indifference was assumed and how much of it was real, resulting from his extreme impatience to finish his work. But to Jonah Wood, it had all the appearance of being genuine.

"I am surprised, George," said the old gentleman, looking very grave. "Are you in your right mind? Are you feeling quite well? I am afraid this good news has upset you."

George rose from the table with a look of disgust, bent down and looked over the last lines he had written, and then stood up.

"If nothing else will satisfy anybody, I suppose I must go down," he said regretfully. "Why did not the old brute leave the money to you instead of to me? You do not imagine I am going to keep it, do you? Most of it is yours anyhow."

"I understand," answered Jonah Wood, pushing him gently towards the door, "that the estate is large enough to cover what I lost four or five times over, if not more. It is very important —— "

"Do you mean to say it is as much as that?" George asked in some surprise.

"That seems to be the impression," answered his father with an odd laugh, which George had not heard for many years. Jonah Wood was ashamed of showing too much satisfaction. It was his principle never to make any exhibition of his feelings, but his voice could not be altogether controlled, and there was an unusual light in his eyes. George, who by this time had collected his senses, and was able to think of something besides his story, saw the change in his father's face and understood it.

"It will be jolly to be rich again, won't it, father?" he said, familiarly and with more affection than he generally showed by manner or voice.

"Very pleasant, very pleasant indeed," answered Jonah Wood with the same odd laugh. "Mr. Trimm tells me he has left you the house as it stands with everything in it, and the horses — everything. I must say, George, the old man has made amends for all he did. It looks very like an act of conscience."

"Amends? Yes, with compound interest for a dozen years or more, if all this is true. Well, here goes the millionaire," he exclaimed as they left the room together.

It would be hard to imagine a position more completely disagreeable than that in which Sherrington Trimm was placed on that particular afternoon. It was bad enough to have to meet George at all after what had happened, but it was most unpleasant to appear as the executor of the very will which had caused so much trouble, to feel that he was bringing to the heir the very document which his wife had stolen out of his own office, and handing over to him the fortune which his wife had tried so hard to bring into his own daughter's hands. But Sherrington Trimm's reputation for honesty and his courageous self-possession had carried him through many difficult moments in life, and he would never have thought of deputing any one else to fulfil the repugnant task in his stead.

Jonah Wood left his son at the door of the sitting-room and discreetly disappeared. George went in and found the lawyer standing before the fire with a roll of papers in his hands. He was a little pale and careworn, but his appearance was as neat and dapper and brisk as ever.

"George," he said frankly as he took his hand, "poor Tom has left you everything, as he said he would. Now, I can quite imagine that the sight of me is not exactly pleasant to you. But business is business and this has got to be put through, so just consider that I am the lawyer and forget that I am Sherry Trimm."

"I shall never forget that you are Sherry Trimm," George answered. "You and I can avoid unpleasant subjects and be as good friends as ever."

"You are a good fellow, George. The best proof of it is that not a word has been breathed about this affair. We have simply announced that the engagement is broken off."

"Then Mamie has refused to change her mind," observed George, wondering how he could ever have been engaged to marry her, and how he could have forgotten that at his last meeting with Sherry Trimm he had still left the matter open, refusing to withdraw his promise. But between that day and this he had lived through many emotions and changing scenes in the playhouse of his brain, and his own immediate past seemed immensely distant from his present.

"Mamie would not change her mind, if I would let her," Trimm answered briefly. "Let us get to business. Here is the will. I opened it yesterday after the funeral in the presence of the family and the witnesses as usual in such cases."

"Excuse me," George said. "I am very glad that I was not present, but would it not have been proper to let me know?"

"It would have been, of course. But as there was no obligation in the matter, I did not. I supposed that you would hear of the death almost as soon as it was known. You and your father were known to be on bad terms with Tom and if you had been sent for it would have looked as though we had all known what was in the will. People would have supposed in that case that you must have known it also, and you would have been blamed for not treating the old gentleman with more consideration than you did. I have often heard you say sharp things about him at the club. This is a surprise to you. There is no reason for letting anybody suppose that it is not. A lot of small good reasons made one big good one between them."

"I see," said George. "Thank you. You were very wise."

He took the document from Trimm's hands and read it hastily. The touch of it was disagreeable to him as he remembered where he had last seen it.

"I had supposed that he would make another after what I said to him," George remarked. "You are quite sure he did not?"

"Positive. He never allowed it to be out of his sight after he found it. It was under his pillow when he died. The last words that anybody could understand were to the effect that you should have the money, whether you wanted it or not. It was a fixed idea with him. I suppose you know why. He felt that some of it belonged to your father by right. The transaction by which he got it was legal — but peculiar. There are peculiarities in my wife's family."

Sherry Trimm looked away and pulled his grizzled moustache nervously.

"There will be a good many formalities," he continued. "Tom owned property in several different States. I have brought you the schedule. You can have possession in New York immediately, of course. It will take some little time to manage the rest, proving the will half a dozen times over. If you care to move into the house to-morrow, there is no objection, because there is nobody to object."

"I have a proposition to make," said George. "My father is a far better man of business than I. Could you not tell me in round numbers about what I have to expect, and then go over these papers with him?"

"In round numbers," repeated Trimm thoughtfully. "The fact is, he managed a great deal of his property himself. I suppose I could tell you within a million or two."

"A million or two!" exclaimed George. Sherry Trimm smiled at the intonation.

"You are an enormously rich man," he said quietly. "The estate is worth anywhere from twelve to fifteen millions of dollars."

"All mine?"

"Look at the will. He never spent a third of his income, so far as I could find out."

George said nothing more, but began to walk up and down the room nervously. He detested everything connected with money, and had only a relative idea of its value, but he was staggered by the magnitude of the fortune thus suddenly thrown into his hands. He understood now the expression he had seen on his father's face.

"I had no conception of the amount," he said at last. "I thought it might be a million."

"A million!" laughed Trimm scornfully. "A man does not live, as he lived, on forty or fifty thousand a year. It needs more than that. A million is nothing nowadays. Every man who wears a good coat has a million. There is not a man living in Fifth Avenue who has less than a million."

"I wonder how it looks on paper," said George. "I will try and go through the schedule with you myself."

An hour later George was once more in his room. For a few moments he stood looking through the window at the old familiar brick wall and at the windows of the house beyond, but his reflections were very vague and shapeless. He could not realise his position nor his importance, as he drummed a tattoo on the glass with his nails. He was trying to think of the changes that were inevitable in the immediate future, of his life in another house, of the faces of his old acquaintances and of the expression some of them would wear. He wondered what Johnson would say. The name, passing through his mind, recalled his career, his work and the unfinished chapter that lay on the table behind him. In an instant his brain returned to the point at which he had been interrupted. Tom Craik, Sherry Trimm, the will and the millions vanished into darkness, and before he was fairly aware of it he was writing again.

The days were short and he was obliged to light the old kerosene lamp with the green shade which had served him through so many hours of labour and study. The action was purely mechanical and did not break his train of thought, nor did it suggest that in a few months he would think it strange that he should ever have been obliged to do such a thing for himself. He wrote steadily on to the end, and signed his name and dated the manuscript before he rose from his seat. Then he stretched himself, yawned and looked at his watch, returned to the table and laid the sheets neatly together in their order with the rest and put the whole into a drawer.

"That job is done," he said aloud, in a tone of profound satisfaction. "And now, I can think of something else."

Thereupon, without as much as thinking of resting himself after the terrible strain he had sustained during ten days, he proceeded to dress himself with a scrupulous care for the evening, and went down stairs to dinner. He found his father in his accustomed place before the fire, reading as usual, and holding his heavy book rigidly before his eyes in a way that would have made an ordinary man's hand ache.

"I have finished my book!" cried George as he entered the room.

"Ah, I am delighted to hear it. Do you mean to say that you have been writing all the afternoon since Mr. Trimm went away?"

"Until half an hour ago."

"Well, you have exceptionally strong nerves," said the old gentleman, mechanically raising his book again. Then as though he were willing to make a concession to circumstances for once in his life, he closed it with a solemn clapping sound and laid it down.

"George, my boy," he said impressively, "you are enormously wealthy. Do you realise the fact?"

"I am also enormously hungry," said George with a laugh. "Is there any cause or reason in the nature of the cook or of anything else why you and I should not be fed?"

"To tell the truth, I had a little surprise for you," answered his father. "I thought we ought to do something to commemorate the event, so I went out and got a brace of canvas-backs from Delmonico's and a bottle of good wine. Kate is roasting the ducks and the champagne is on the ice. It was a little late when I got back—sorry to keep you waiting, my boy."

"Sorry!" cried George. "The idea of being sorry for anything when there are canvas-backs and champagne in the house. You dear old man! I will pay you for this, though. You shall live on the fat of the land for the rest of your days!"

"Enough is as good as a feast," observed Jonah Wood with great gravity.

"What roaring feasts we will have — or what stupendously plentiful enoughs, if you like it better! Father, you are better already. I heard you laugh to-day as you used to laugh when I was a boy."

"A little prosperity will do us both good," said the old gentleman, who was rapidly warming into geniality.

"I say," suggested George. "I have finished my book, and you have nothing to do. Let us pack up our traps and go to Paris and paint the town a vivid scarlet."

"What?" asked Jonah Wood, to whom slang had always been a mystery.

"Paint the town red," repeated George. "In short, have a spree, a lark, a jollification, you and I."

"I would like to see Paris again, well enough, if that is what you mean. By the way, George, your heart does not seem to trouble you much, just at present."

"Why should it? I sometimes wish it would, in the right direction."

"You have your choice now, George, you have your choice, now, of the whole female population of the globe —— "

"Of all the girls beside the water, From Janeiro to Gibraltar, as the old song says," laughed George.

"Precisely so. You can have any of them for the asking. Money is a great power, my boy, a great power. You must be careful how you use it."

"I shall not use it. I shall give it all to you to spend because it will amuse you, and I will go on writing books because that is the only thing I can do approximately well. Do you know? I believe I shall be ridiculous in the character of the rich man."

CHAPTER XXIX.

Three years later George Wood was sitting alone on a winter's afternoon in the library where Thomas Craik had once given him his views on life in general and on ambition in particular. It was already almost dark, for the days were very short, and two lamps shed a soft light from above upon the broad polished table.

The man's face had changed during the years that had

passed since he had found himself free from his engagement to marry his cousin. The angular head had grown more massive, the shadows about the eyes and temples had deepened, the complexion was paler and less youthful, the expression more determined than ever, and yet more kind and less scornful. In those years he had seen much and had accomplished much, and he had learned to know at last what it meant to feel with the heart, instead of with the sensibilities, human or artistic. His money had not spoiled him. On the contrary, the absence of all preoccupations in the matter of his material welfare, had left the man himself free to think, to act and to feel according to his natural instincts.

At the present moment he was absorbed in thought. The familiar sheet of paper lay before him, and he held his pen in his hand, but the point had long been dry, and had long ceased to move over the smooth surface. There was a number at the top of the page, and a dozen lines had been written, continuing a conversation that had gone before. But the imaginary person had broken off in the middle of his saying, and in the theatre of the writer's fancy the stage of his own life had suddenly appeared, and his own self was among the players, acting the acts and speaking the speeches of long ago, while the owner of the old self watched and listened to the piece with fascinated interest, commenting critically upon what passed before his eyes, and upon the words that rang through the waking dream. The habit of expression was so strong that his own thoughts took shape as though he were writing them down.

"They have played the parts of the three fates in my life," he said to himself. "Constance was my Clotho, Mamie was my Lachesis — Grace is my Atropos. I was not so heartless in those first days, as I have sometimes fancied that I was. I loved my Clotho, after a young fashion. She took me out of darkness and chaos and made me an active, real being. When I see how wretchedly unhappy I used to be, and when I think how she first showed me that I was able to do something in the world, it does not seem strange that I should have worshipped her as a sort of goddess. If things had gone otherwise, if she had taken me instead of refusing me on that first of May, if I had married her, we might have been very happy together, for a time, perhaps for always. But we were unlike in the wrong way; our points of difference did not complement each other. She has married Dr. Drinkwater, the Reverend Doctor Drinkwater, a good man twenty years older than herself, and she seems perfectly contented. The test of fitness lies in reversing the order of events. If to-day her good husband were to die, could I take his place in her love or estimation? Certainly not. If Grace had married the clergyman, could Constance have been to me what Grace is, could I have loved her as I love this woman who will never love me? Assuredly not; the thing is impossible. I loved Constance with one half of myself, and as far as I went I was in earnest. Perhaps it was the higher, more intellectual part of me, for I did not love her because she was a woman, but because she was unlike all other women — in other words, a sort of angel. Angels may have loved women in the days of the giants, but no man can love an angel as a woman ought to be loved. As for me, my ears are wearied by too much angelic music, the harmonies are too thin and delicate, the notes lack character, the melodies all end in one close. I used to think that there was no such thing as friendship. I have changed my mind. Constance is a very good friend to me, and I to her, though neither of us can understand the other's life any longer, as we understood each other when she took up the distaff of my life and first set the spindle whirling.

"Was I heartless with poor Mamie? I suppose I was, because I made her believe for a while that I loved her. Let us be honest. I felt something, I made myself believe that I felt something which was like love. It was of the baser kind. It was the temptation of the eye, the fascination of a magnetic vitality, the flattery of my vanity in seeing myself so loved. I lived for months in an enchanted palace in an enchanted garden, where she was the enchantress. Everything contributed to awaken in me the joy of mere life, the belief that reality was better than romance, and that, in love, it was better to receive than to give. I was like a man in a badly conceived novel, with whom everything rests on a false basis, in which the scenery is false, the passion is false, and the belief in the future is most false of all. And how commonplace it all seems, as I look back upon it. I do not remember to have once felt a pain like a knife just under the heart, in all that time, though my blood ran fast enough sometimes. And it all went on so smoothly as Lachesis let the thread spin through her pretty fingers. Who would have believed that a man could be at once so fooled and so loved? I was sorry that I could not love her, even after we knew all that her mother had done. I remember that I began a book on that very day. Heartless of me, was it not? If she had been Grace I should never have written again. But she was only Lachesis; the thread turned under her hand, and spun on in spite of her, and in spite of itself — to its end.

"Grace is the end. There can be no loving after this. My father tells me that I am working too hard and that I am growing prematurely old. It is not the work that does it. It is something that wears out the life from the core. And yet I would not be without it. There is that thrust again, that says I am not deceiving myself. Grace holds the thread and will neither cut it, nor let it run on through her fingers. Heaven knows, I am not a sentimental man! But for the physical pain I feel when I think of losing her, I should laugh at myself and let her slip down to the middle distance of other memories, not quite out of sight, nor yet quite out of mind, but wholly out of my heart. I have tried it many a time, but the trouble grows instead of wearing out. I have tried wandering about the earth in most known and unknown directions. It never did me any good. I wonder whether she knows! After all it will be four years next summer since poor John Bond was drowned, and everybody says she has forgotten him. But she is not a woman who forgets, any more than she is one to waste her life in a perpetual mourning. To speak may be to cut the thread. That would be the end, indeed! I should see her after that, of course, but it would never be the same again. She would know my secret then and all would be over, the hours together, the talks, the touch of hands that means so much to me and so little to her. And yet, to know — to know at last the end of it all — and the great 'perhaps' the great 'if' — if she should! But there is no 'perhaps,' and there can be no 'if.' She is my fate, and it is my fate that there should be no end to this, but the end of life itself. Better so. Better to have loved ever so unhappily, than to have been married to any of the Constances or the Mamies of this world! Heigho — I suppose people think that there is nothing I cannot have for my money! Nothing? There is all that could make life worth living, and which millions cannot buy!"

The curtain fell before the little stage, and the eyes of the lonely man closed with an expression of intense pain, as he let his forehead rest in the palm of his hand.

www.ingramcontent.com/pod-product-compliance
Lightning Source LLC
Chambersburg PA
CBHW020832030726
47496CB00001B/197